The Offspring Trilogy
Book 1

THE
GENERAL'S
SON

CHARLOTTE GOODWIN

This is a work of fiction. Names, characters, places, and incidents either are the product of the author's imagination or are used fictitiously. Any resemblance to actual persons, living or dead, events, or locales is entirely coincidental.

Copyright © Charlotte Goodwin 2023

All rights reserved.

No part of this book may be reproduced or used in any manner without written permission of the copyright owner except for the use of quotations in a book review. For more information, address:
author@charlottegoodwin.co.uk

First paperback edition March 2023

Book cover design by Ryan Schwarz
Maps by Charlotte Goodwin

ISBN 979-8-3791-5292-5

www.charlottegoodwin.co.uk

For everyone who read this book before it was polished,

you helped me make it shine!

CONTENTS

Maps

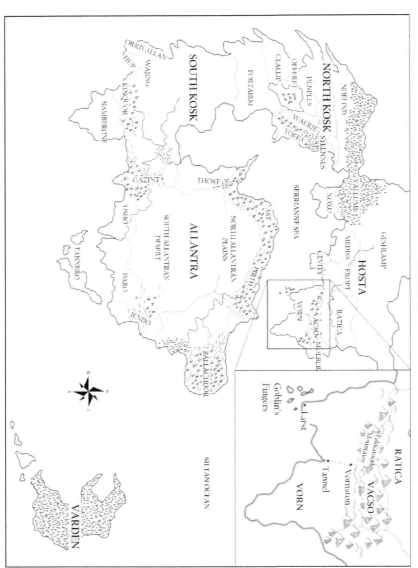

AUSTRALIA - AFTER NUCLEAR ATTACK IN 2030

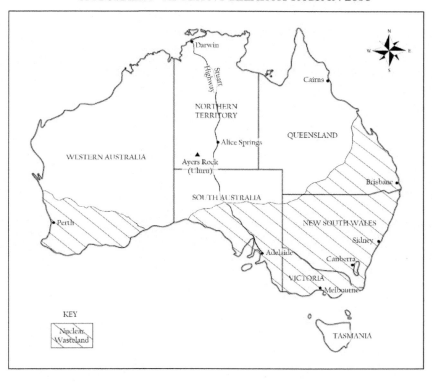

1. Awakening

Location: Central Kenya, Earth (Planet B13536)
Earth Year: 2034

The distant mountains shimmered through the misty haze, their snow-capped crowns floated above the expanse of the Kenyan savannah below. Aran found his gaze fixed in the distance; fixed but unfocussed. The tricks of the light weren't of interest to the exiled king. He was looking for something else: he was searching for magic.

It had happened at some point in the night, the ripple that shook him awake. A prickle of power had swept through his body, making his hairs stand on end, goose pimples swell, and a chill grasp his core. Magic, a wave of it. Just a little one, but he was tuned in to magic. He'd spent years searching for it, meditating, concentrating, tuning every fibre of his being into the smallest trace of mystical energy. He'd grown up with magic on his homeland of Gemini, where it was so abundant he'd never needed to search for it. But here, on Earth, the presence of magic was so faint it was barely perceptible.

So he'd come to this spot, where a tunnel once connected Earth to Gemini, where a miniscule amount of magic was still baked into the ground. He was hoping he'd find a change, a disturbance to show where the new source of power emerged from, but there was nothing. Nothing had changed here – nothing but the rock fig, which was now in bloom.

Here there was just a pile of rubble and his favourite rock; the smooth one with a flat top where he liked to sit. There were scattered trees and chirping birds. The water in the river rippled, the wind swished through the long grass. It was peaceful, beautiful, and boring.

He'd had enough. He closed his eyes and shook his head to clear the fuzz, then blinked them open until his normal vision returned. He hissed a long sigh through clenched teeth, slapped the rock, and forced

1

his numb behind to rise. He'd achieved nothing. If he was going to do nothing, he might as well do it in comfort. He turned on his heel and headed back along the track, back through his family's private game reserve towards the Wanjiku Safari Lodge, his home.

The lodge was quiet as usual. The numbers of guests had been steadily dropping for years. If Aran cared to be honest with himself, he would have admitted that the business had been failing since he'd taken over as manager after his uncle's death. But Aran was not prone to constructive self-reflection.

He meandered through reception, the grating chirp of the receptionist greeting him as he went. A sour-faced nod of acknowledgement was all he managed in reply as he continued towards the guest lounge. It was nice and empty, a bonus of business being bad. He collapsed into the cushions of the welcoming sofa.

His head slumped back, and he stared at the ceiling. A pencilled cross, which the receptionist had made at his request, was in the spot where the ceiling fan was supposed to sit – the one he'd not got round to installing. A droplet of sweat trickled down his chest, tickling his skin. He slapped his T-shirt to blot it away, harder than he'd planned, angry at the absent fan and resenting the air conditioning that dared to fail. It hadn't been serviced in a while, a pointless cost, he'd thought; things should just work!

There were only a handful of staff still working in the lodge. There were barely enough guests to cover their wages these days. He could sack the receptionist. His mother could cover that job, surely? Even at her age it would be manageable.

He shouted through to the receptionist to bring him a cold glass of cola and reached forward for the TV remote. He flicked it on. It was set to the news channel; there were so few live channels any more there was little else to watch. Everything seemed to be a subscription service – yet another waste of money he thought the lodge need not spend.

He was barely even focussing until his brain made sense of the images of destruction filling the screen. He'd not watched the news for a few days and hadn't spoken to many people other than to bark orders at them. He'd not been keeping track of what had been happening in Australia. He remembered hearing about a build-up of tension with China over some claim to an island or other in the South China Sea, but he hadn't paid much attention.

The images of flattened cities, scattered debris, broken trees, and human bodies amongst the ruins were hard to ignore. Huge swathes of land, of towns and cities where millions once lived, had been razed to the ground. He shuffled his bottom back into the sofa and turned up the volume.

"...these latest images have been brought to us by our own Channel Nine drones. This scene of devastation was once the city of Sydney. Little remains of this urban hub and there are few known survivors. We have drones over every major city in Australia, which show that not one has been left standing. The tiny northern city of Darwin remains the biggest settlement to have avoided China's devastating nuclear attack. Initial estimates suggest around seventy percent of Australia's population has been wiped out, and most of the country has been rendered an uninhabitable nuclear wasteland."

The receptionist arrived with Aran's drink. He glared at her as she passed it to him. Why had it taken so long? He couldn't be bothered to chastise her this time; he would sack her before long.

He continued to watch the news report. Images of the other destroyed cities flashed across the screen. He found himself in awe, glued to the images of devastation. The power unleashed by technology was immense. It dwarfed anything he could have done on Gemini, back when he had proper magical powers, and the strength to blast away a mountainside. Those abilities had been incredible by Geminian standards, but were nothing compared to the destructive power of nuclear weapons.

He found himself wondering what he could do with that amount of energy, if there was a way to access that kind of power himself. He smiled at the thought. It was nice to dream but not terribly realistic to think about getting his own nukes. A little more magic though? Surely that was achievable. He took another sip of cola, and a shudder shot up his spine – the cold drink perhaps? He took another sip. No, it wasn't. It was something else. It was like the tingle he'd felt in the night. Maybe the nukes somehow released more power. Maybe they'd tapped into something, and maybe if he tried to use some, he'd be pleasantly surprised.

'Aran!' His mother cackled as she stalked into the lounge. He almost jumped out of his skin; she always had an uncanny knack for sneaking up on him.

He let out a sharp breath through gritted teeth. 'Yes, Mother?'

'Why are you lazing around when there is work to do?'

He scowled, but she barely seemed to notice.

'Huts five and eight still have leaky roofs, and you know there's no money to pay for a repair. While it's quiet surely you could take the opportunity to fix them yourself?'

She genuinely expected him to do manual work? His grandfather had made him do that stuff. It had been humiliating, and now she dared to suggest he ought to return to such drudgery? His fists clenched.

'Or how about doing some more work on the website? Maybe we could get some more pictures, some better ones. We could run a special offer to get people back in…'

Her whining cut through him like a knife. She was nagging at him, again. It was all she ever did. His fingernails dug into his palms. His simmering blood boiled as the woman stood, hands on her hips, waiting for him to answer.

'Well?' she squawked.

'Oh, stop it, Mother!' he snapped. 'If you want to do work on the website, be my guest!' He shot to his feet. 'We can barely afford to pay the receptionist. You should think about doing something yourself instead of lording it up and trying to tell everyone else what to do.' His bony finger pointed at her; his words grew louder. 'You're not the queen anymore,' he yelled. 'I'm the manager here, and I'm in charge!'

He was almost trembling with rage – his fury had erupted surprisingly quickly this time, but it was hardly a surprise.

Someone sobbed.

He twisted towards the receptionist. She cupped her face in her hands, unashamedly weeping. The pathetic woman probably heard his outburst and realised she was for the chop. He rolled his eyes and let his gaze rest on the floor. If she knew now, he thought, at least it would save him a job later. He rotated back to glare at his mother; the woman was sympathetically gawping at the crying girl.

'Feeling sorry for the servants now, are you?' he hissed in disgust; he could barely believe his eyes. Sympathy was weakness, and his mother never used to be weak. 'You used to rule a continent,' he reminded her, 'you ruthlessly sacked whole cities, you blasted whole armies to pieces with your power! You didn't have much sympathy for ordinary people then, did you?' he scowled at her past his bushy brows. 'You're a shadow of your former self, coming to Earth has made you feeble.'

Lila's eyes narrowed to slits, her nostrils flared; she was getting riled at last. Good, that was the woman who'd raised him.

His scowl became a sneer, it seemed to make her worse. Her dark skin grew darker as blood rushed to her face; her fingers curled. 'You are only the manager because of me,' she replied quietly. Aran could almost hear her heart pounding. 'You would have had nowhere to go if it hadn't been for me.' Her voice was growing louder. 'If I hadn't come and got you from the police after you first arrived.' A wicked smile crept up on her face. 'The crazy man, they called you, the man who spoke no language anyone understood.' Her smile dropped. 'You'd have been left alone with no money, nowhere to stay, with nothing!' She was almost shouting.

The receptionist had ceased crying and seemed to be cowering.

'It was me who persuaded my father to let you stay after you were such a bad worker, after you skived time and time again, and were rude to the guests!' she yelled, Aran felt himself brace in the face of her onslaught. 'You'd have been out on your ear years ago if it weren't for me! If I hadn't covered for you, done your chores, made excuses, and spent hours patiently trying to teach you English when you were such a terrible student, do you think you'd be here? As manager?

'It's a tragic fact that my brother and his family sadly died,' she continued. 'But it worked out for you, didn't it? He'd never have tolerated you. When he was in charge, this place ran like clockwork. We were fully booked every week of the year. The profits flowed in, but now? You have run this place into the ground. I'm glad my father isn't alive to see what you have done to his legacy, destroying everything he worked hard to build. I know I'm not a queen anymore. Do you know you're not a king?'

The nerve was struck, the raw one. A red-hot poker on tender flesh. She'd reminded him of what could have been, what he was close to achieving before he was tricked by Mark, before he was foolish enough to believe the man who lied so well, who had managed to dupe Aran's magical senses. Aran had been a king – the most powerful man in Gemini – and now he was a manager of a failing safari lodge in Kenya.

His fingernails drew blood from his palms. With the anger came the magic, but this time it was different. This time it was stronger, he was sure of it. The adrenaline pumped the mystical energy through his veins.

5

He trembled. The urge to unleash the power became overwhelming. Red mist clouded his vision as the tingling spread down his arms.

He forced a sharp intake of breath; rational thought took over. He shouldn't waste his power, not like this, not on her. She was his mother after all, and he had other uses for his magic. Magic could breed magic; magic could help him find more.

Her narrowed eyes now showed their whites as she backed away with a tentative step. Sensing her fear felt good. It made the magic stronger.

He took a few deep breaths and turned from her; body tensed. He stormed towards the lodge entrance and out into the gardens.

He marched along the lodge driveway, ignoring the weeds which grew through the cracks in the paving. He ignored the bushes in desperate need of a prune. He didn't care about the rotten fence or the rust on the sign at the entrance. He didn't care about the lodge, he just cared about finding more magic.

He headed through the gates and back out into the bush. He stomped along the path towards the river. The long grass brushed against his legs, and the calls of a distant herd of wildebeest, thousands strong, swept across the plains. The sun beat down and shimmering waves of rising air blurred the distant mass of purple mountains. Such a tranquil place, a place of calm and peace, but Aran didn't care. Aran was blind to everything but his fury. He kept running through his mother's words in his head.

After a short walk, he arrived at his destination, back at his favourite rock by the river. The place he always visited to search for magic. Old habits die hard.

He sat on his rock and closed his eyes. He breathed deeply, concentrated on the magic, searching for every last tingle of energy coursing through his veins. He embraced his rage; he let it draw the power. He could feel it engaging with a magical field outside of himself. It was easier this time.

The wind swished through the leaves on the trees and the hot African sun beat down on his caramel skin as he sat meditating. His hands gripped his knees and his head flopped back as he strained with everything he had to feel the magic. He let his senses trace the magical flow, those fleeting wisps that were always so hard to grasp. His fury still raged. He let his mother's words run through his mind again, and he let his ire grow.

Round the wisps flew. His inner eye traced them. He watched them drift and he noticed something. They were travelling from left to right, meandering like a great a serpentine river gliding through the air. He stood, his eyes still closed, allowing himself to feel the flow. The tiny currents brushed against his flesh. He was facing south; the slight tingling came from his left. He turned to the east. The tingling moved to his front.

He let the miniscule prickles tickle his chest, then he opened his eyes. All he could see was the shimmering air, the rippling haze where the ground faded into the sky. There were no mountains to the east, just the savannah, towns and farms, and the sea. The Indian Ocean then Indonesia. South of that was Australia, if he was getting Earth's geography right.

Last night, Australia was nuked; today magic flowed from the east. He had no idea if there was a connection. But he knew he'd found more power and he was determined to find its source.

2. Shine At Your Peril

Location: Vorn Military Training Academy, Tannel, Gemini (Planet M69245)

The rain had been weeping from the sky all day like teardrops, crying on the sodden ground in a never-ending sob. A northerly wind brought a stinging chill. It came from the frozen wastelands of Geshlamp; it washed over the Takkatooth Mountains and dusted the peaks with snow. It danced towards the south and sang over the Serrianne Sea where the worst of its bite was softened by the warm watery mass.

On the military training grounds high above the shore, Recruit Garrad Bramston shivered. The sea-tamed breeze found its way through his oiled cloak, through his sodden jacket and his soggy shirt, through his woollen vest and his thin layer of fat. He was freezing, and desperate to fight.

The music of metal on metal chimed through the air as recruit danced with recruit. After weeks of marching, running, climbing obstacles, and horsemanship, they had finally been issued with swords. It was time to show the instructors what they could do. They were blunt training swords, but a sword was a sword, and even as Garrad's soaked hand chilled to ice in the freezing rain, he still gripped the hilt. It just felt good to hold it. He watched with failing interest as two other recruits were desperately attempting to show off their meagre skills with a blade.

The fight was going on too long. The pair were evenly matched and neither one was able to find their mark. Garrad watched with disdain. They were even, perhaps, but equally crap. One waved his sword and the other parried. One dodged to the side, the other missed. A feint, a swerve. To the untrained observer, it looked impressive. The other recruits watched with excitement and cheered on the two young men. Garrad was unimpressed.

It came to an end at last. Exhaustion eventually took one more than the other and the fitter of the two took his chance. A tap on the arm with his blunt blade signalled his win. He patted his opponent on the shoulder and retreated to the side-lines as the other recruits cheered.

'Bramston and Hendrill!' The instructor yelled out the names of the next two who were due to fight. At last, it was Garrad's turn. He took off his cloak and handed it to a fellow recruit – Mervin – for safekeeping.

'Don't worry, Mervin, you won't be holding it long,' Garrad said with a wink.

Mervin shook his head and smirked.

Garrad was not a short lad. He was already taller than his father, although at sixteen years old, he still had growing yet to do. Hendrill was even bigger, and broader. He was older, eighteen or nineteen. Many of the other young men would have been intimidated. Not Garrad. His father had been in the army and taught him to fight. Garrad was desperate to learn as soon as he realised a stick could be used as a pretend sword. He'd been given a wooden one when he was six and the training started then. By ten years old, he could sometimes outmanoeuvre his aging father, who was slowing down with his years. By fourteen, he almost always beat him.

His feet were barely in the sparring ring when Hendrill launched at him. He hadn't waited for the call to start, but it didn't matter to Garrad – he dodged with ease. His opponent stumbled out over the chalk line boundary.

The corporal instructor blew a whistle. 'Let's call that a false start, shall we? Back in the ring, boys. Hendrill, this time wait for my signal.'

'Yes, Corporal,' the bigger boy bellowed.

Garrad nodded and held his sword ready.

The whistle blew. Hendrill launched himself forward, but Garrad was as fast as lightning. He dodged, spun, and landed a tap on his opponent's behind. There was no whistle. Perhaps the instructor hadn't seen it. Regardless, he was ready to keep going. Hendrill whipped round; he swung his blade with enough power to break a limb. Garrad barely needed to clash his steel to deflect the blow, he manoeuvred himself with such skill that force was barely necessary. He made sure his sword was in the right place to slide his opponent's blade to where he wanted it. With a flick of his arm, he forced the sword to one side. Hendrill's own momentum unbalanced him, and he stumbled. His foot went outside the ring. Garrad slapped him again with the flat of his blade, this time against the back of his shoulder.

The whistle blew. Garrad had won.

Hendrill stormed towards the crowd of spectators, splashing muddy water over the cobbles as he went. A wide grin swept across Garrad's face as he strutted back towards Mervin.

'Show-off.' His friend landed a heavy slap on Garrad's back.

'Thanks!' Garrad replied, swiping his cloak from Mervin.

'You shouldn't have done that,' someone whispered from behind him. Garrad spun to see another of the young recruits, Wilf, a young man with the lanky, stunted form of a kid who was years his junior. He'd struggled in the early days, but Garrad helped him through, and he was now one of the few recruits Garrad could call a friend.

'Why?' he said, puzzled.

'Hendrill is Corporal Bremmer's cousin. They've been training together. Hendrill was supposed to win – you humiliated him.'

'So? I was the better swordsman.'

'Sure. Everyone knows that, but it won't win you any prizes. Not here, not in training.'

'What are you on about, Wilf? The best students get recommendations. They get rapid promotions. If we do well here, we can be lance corporals in a year. My father always taught me to do my best, he said to make sure everyone knows how good I am. He said...' He paused in the face of Wilf's rising eyebrows. 'What?'

'Your father was in the Army, right?'

'Yeah.'

'When?'

'I dunno, years ago. Before I was born.'

'And what rank did he make?'

'He left as a lance corporal. His own father needed him to help with the family business. He learned to be an awesome sword fighter though. Not so much when he was in the Army, but after. He led security on my grandfather's ships. He drilled the sailors every day in swordcraft, he was determined they'd not be victims to pirates and he—'

'Yep. As I thought,' Wilf cut him off.

'What are you on about?'

'I'm sure your father meant well, but it doesn't sound like he was a natural like you. Sounds like he trained hard to be good with a sword

10

and he wasn't the one who shone. He left as a lance corporal. If he was amazing, do you not think he'd have stayed longer?' Garrad was starting to get irritated at the apparent slight to his father. 'Look, if you shine around here without permission, someone will notice, and they won't like it. You see, only those who—'

'Bramston!' Corporal Bremmer bellowed across the training yard.

Garrad snapped to attention. 'Yes, Corporal?' he called back.

'Ring, now.'

'Yes, Corporal.'

The instructor stood in the ring, cloak off and sword in hand. It was clear what he had in mind. Garrad puffed out his chest and raised his head as he walked to meet him. Rain was dripping off his nose as he went, but he was suddenly oblivious to the cold.

The rest of the recruits cheered as he stepped into the ring.

Corporal Bremmer had his whistle in his mouth. He blew it, spat it out, and raised his sword above his head. Garrad planted his feet and stood ready.

Bremmer swung down, hard and fast. He was quick, faster than Garrad expected. He still managed to dodge in time. He ducked, spun, and whipped his sword round with both hands on the hilt. He used all the force and speed he could muster. He wasn't quick enough. The corporal caught his blow and pushed him back. Bremmer was shorter than Garrad but broader. He was in his twenties and had filled out. Years of sword practice had given him a strength Garrad couldn't hope to match.

Garrad had beaten his father as a boy, so he knew strength could be used to his advantage, but only when he was ready. But the power of Bremmer's parry was too much for the light stance Garrad had chosen. He was pushed back too fast and with too much force to steady himself. He stumbled, fell, arse splashing into a muddy puddle as Bremmer swung another blow. Instinct brought his blade to bear – with his back still on the ground, Garrad parried and rolled in one smooth motion. He flipped onto his feet, found his strength, and forced a pirouette, sword slicing in a graceful arc towards his foe.

The corporal took the power of the blow hard, his steel and brute force blocking with speed, but it was not without cost. His leg stumbled back to steady himself, foot spraying water as he went, failing to find the traction he'd hoped for, slipping, staggering. One hand slid from his sword as he tried to keep his balance, and terror flashed across his face

11

for a fleeting moment before he found his footing. With a steady stance, he lurched to grip his sword, quick, but not quick enough. Garrad's sword flew through the air, zipping past Bremmer's floundering blade. It slid round his opponent's attempt to block and found his arching chest as he desperately tried to avoid the unstoppable swing.

It thudded hard into his side as it found its mark. Bremmer called out in pain. The crowd of recruits cheered.

Garrad turned to face the crowd, arms raised high above his head, sword pointing at the weeping clouds, mouth stretching into a boyish grin, which widened as he heard Corporal Bremmer clamber to his feet behind him, growling and cursing as he rose.

'Bremmer!' came a deep, throaty roar across the training ground.

Everyone went quiet. Garrad spun on the spot to see his instructor behind him, desperately trying to sheath his sword. The crowd parted and Colour Sergeant Fornian stormed through the audience of recruits. The corporal grimaced as he lowered his sword and turned slowly.

'Corporal, my office, now,' the colour sergeant growled.

Bremmer snapped to attention. 'Yes, Colour.' He marched off, chest puffed out and stony-faced.

Colour Fornian watched the corporal leave. He wiped the rain from his face and turned to Garrad. 'What's your name, recruit?'

Garrad straightened at once. He rarely spoke to anyone more senior than a corporal. 'Bramston. Garrad Bramston, Colour,' he barked with nervous haste.

'You did well today, lad. I was watching you fight the corporal. He's not a bad swordsman, one of the best we have in fact, and you had him. How old are you?'

'Sixteen, Colour.'

'Did your father serve?'

'Yes, Colour. He taught me to fight.'

'He taught you well. Keep it up, lad. With skills like that, you'll go far.'

'Yes, Colour.'

Colour Sergeant Fornian did an about-turn and marched back the way he'd come, as if he couldn't help doing drill. 'Corporal Starn!' he yelled as he went.

'Yes, Colour?' someone answered from the crowd.

'Take over from Corporal Bremmer, if you please.'

12

'Yes, Colour.'

***

'It was good to finally get our hands on a sword, don't you think?' Garrad said to Mervin as he shoved the door to the barracks block open with a hard whack of his palm.

'Yeah, it was. Feels like we're actually proper soldiers now we have one of these on our hips,' Mervin patted the scabbard belted at his waist, 'even if it is just a training sword.'

'I do miss the sword my father gave me. It's not ornamental but it is bloody well balanced and it handles beautifully. This thing does the job for training, but it's not the same.'

'I'm sure you'll be allowed it once we pass out as soldiers. It's only a few more months to the summer, then we get to wield these things for real.'

They headed to their bed spaces in the long room, where bed after bed was set against each opposing wall. Their entire platoon lived in this block. They'd finished their evening meal and had been knocked off for the day. The recruits were filtering in, some limping or groaning in pain as they walked slowly.

towards their beds. One or two had taken a hit during sword practice today. No blood was drawn but there were plenty of large bruises.

Garrad unstrapped his sword and placed it carefully in the rack above his bed, taking a seat on the mattress.

'Mervin,' he began, 'you never told me why Corporal Bremmer was called away. Did I miss something?'

'Oh shit! Yeah, I forgot to say. Think he's gonna get it.'

'What for?'

'After you clobbered him and won the round, the arsehole got back to his feet as you faced the crowd. He swung his sword in the air and looked like he was about to whack you with it. Thing is, Colour Fornian was watching the whole time. He had a cloak on and was standing at the back somewhere, trying not to be noticed. Seeing how we all did, I guess. When Bremmer was about to hit you, he called time and told him to go to his office.'

'Shit! I guessed he was maybe just getting pulled for sparing with a recruit.'

'Not sure there's any rules against that one as such, but if he'd clobbered you from behind...' Mervin let the sentence trail.

'Fuck, good job Colour was there then, I guess!'

Garrad began his evening routine of cleaning and preparing his kit for the next day as the other recruits continued to file in from dinner. Hendrill stalked past the end of Garrad's bed. Garrad was expecting a comment, some insult or at least a scowl, but the man barely gave him a second glance.

Maybe he'd learnt his lesson. Maybe he'd figured out Garrad Bramston wasn't to be messed with. He grinned to himself.

Rumour had it Kyron Hendrill served time for a couple of years, which was why he'd joined late. Almost all the recruits were sixteen, even though you could still join up to your twentieth birthday. Garrad hadn't got along with the man since he'd started at the training school in the autumn. But he'd never clashed with him, until now.

It was almost time for lights out. Garrad made one last trip to the latrines before he bedded down for the night. The days were short at this time of year, and he could barely see as he felt his way along the muddy path. He'd done the route so many times before, he hadn't brought a torch; he could manage in the dark. He finished his business, pulled up his breeches, and closed the door behind him.

Someone grabbed him.

He tried to yell, but couldn't. A grubby hand was pressed against his straining mouth. He was hauled from his feet, carried away from the block and into the woods that ringed the barracks, far enough away that his screams wouldn't be heard.

He was thrown towards the soggy ground, hip cracking against a tree trunk as his legs flapped uselessly in the mud. He couldn't see who'd grabbed him. It was even darker in the forest, but the moon cast a little light. He could just about make out the three men who milled around him, their silhouettes black against the inky sky. The hawking rasp of gathering spit warned his ears too late, he could only grimace as it splattered on his face. His eyes screwed up to spider-like slits.

A heavy boot pushed on his chest as he desperately tried to scramble to his feet, gasping lungs fighting for breath, hands clawing at the leg that held him firm. The first punch was thrown. It collided with

14

his chin and his head snapped back, his skull hitting a root. A fist found his stomach. He coughed, winded, shamefully cowering as another boot found his thigh, then another punch struck his shoulder.

The pressure on his chest released. He wriggled to his side, cradling his head and lifting his knees to hide his chest. A hardened sole came crashing down. A rib cracked, and pain exploded across his chest. Something smashed into his nose. Salty iron dribbled down his throat — he coughed, he spluttered, he gasped for breath. He tried to rise but he couldn't. Someone held him down. He found his voice and yelled out. The hits kept coming. He heard footsteps: someone was running his way. The attack paused.

'Corporal Bremmer sends his regards,' a raspy voice muttered into his ear. A fist found his cheekbone. Everything went quiet.

3. Closer And Stronger

Location: Timor Sea, off the north coast of Australia, Earth (Planet B13536)

It was Aran's third day at sea, and he was sick of the incessant bobbing already. He had no idea how he'd tolerated weeks at sea when he was in Gemini, where the ships were driven by the fickle wind and some journeys could take months. There were certainly a lot of modern conveniences on Earth he'd taken a liking to – rapid travel was one of them.

There were no flights to Australia. The international airlines had stopped flying there after China's attack. The nukes came first, the smaller missiles followed, targeted to finish off what remained of the military and any remaining shreds of governance. After that the country descended into lawlessness. Without a government or even any senior military commanders left alive, the criminals took over and it became a land where the warlords and drugs barons ruled. Every self-respecting citizen who'd survived the attacks fled, most to New Zealand. Now the only way to get to Australia was by sea.

Aran managed to find a fisherman from East Timor to take him to Australia. It had taken years and he'd spent thousands on travel before he'd managed to get a clear idea of where the magical tingling was coming from. He'd confirmed it was from the east early on. He'd flown to Indonesia and from there the magic felt stronger to the south-east. He'd edged ever closer to Australia until he was satisfied that his suspicions had been correct. The nukes landed, the tingling surged, and he was now in no doubt that the bombs had triggered something. More magic had been released by the blast, he was sure of it, and now he sailed across the Timor Sea tracking the magical currents towards their source.

He'd become a master of tracing the magic. He'd spent hours in meditation, concentrating and focusing on the power. He had become so good at sensing even the tiniest field of magic that he could almost see it.

As the shore of the city of Darwin came into view, he'd never been more sure he was on the right track. He let the waves of energy flow into him, butterflies of tingling excitement fluttering though his body as he felt his power grow. The engine cut out and the boat bobbed to a halt.

'We at the end,' the captain of the boat called down to Aran from behind the wheel in broken English. 'We here, we at Darwin.'

Aran snapped. 'It's miles away! Why have you stopped? Take me to the shore!' he demanded.

'Too dangerous. Criminals. We stay here, you swim.'

'I can't swim that far! You have to take me or give me your small boat. I can sail it to the shore.' He pointed to the motorised dinghy resting on the stern.

'No, if you want boat, you pay extra. No way to get it back. Dinghy expensive.'

As Aran ground his teeth, he felt the creeping prickle of surging magic. 'I paid you to take me to Darwin,' he growled. 'Take me to shore or you will regret it,' his fingers curling into squeezing fists.

The fisherman's two crew members emerged from below decks and sauntered towards their captain's side. They had knives strapped to their belts and the strong physiques of men used to manual work. Aran was lean and unarmed.

'What you going to do?' The captain laughed. 'Throw us into the sea? You? Skinny man.' He continued to laugh, and the other crew members laughed with him.

Aran could feel the magic surge. He said nothing and let their laughter antagonise him as he reached for the flood of power. He let his rage fuel its strength; it rushed into his being and pulsed through his veins. He gripped it with his mind and let it pool in his chest.

Aran raised his hands and let his power flow. It shot along his arms like a bolt from a crossbow, flew from his fingers, and sped towards the men. He clung to the tendrils of power as they spun through the air. Whipping his hands to the sides, he forced a thrusting squall across the polished deck. Not quite as strong as he'd hoped, but good enough.

The crew were lifted from their feet and hurled sideways, taken by the sudden gust and shoved into the railings. The wind kept coming. The railings didn't hold them, the blast was too powerful, and the men were forced outwards, legs flipping as they pivoted over the railings. The three of them fell headfirst towards the sea.

17

The release of power swept through Aran's being with euphoric vigour. It felt incredible. He was panting, gasping through grinning teeth as he heard the splash, saw the spray, and rushed to see them bob to the surface. They yelled and they swam; the ladder was close. He didn't have much time. He rushed to the helm, turned the key in the ignition, and the engine roared to life. The water gurgled as the propeller spun and the boat began to move. The sailors screamed, but Aran smiled as their shouts were drowned out by the hum of the boat and the roar of the waves.

***

Darwin was the biggest Australian city that hadn't been destroyed by China. It had become its de facto capital. It was run by a drugs baron named Nickel. Darwin was a major trading hub for the export of narcotics and Nickel controlled the trade. No one got in or out of the seaport without the baron or his people knowing about it, and no one escaped the taxes.

Aran wasn't far from the port when two speedboats sped out to flank him. Each was crewed by four men and women, all of them armed. AK47s were aimed straight at Aran.

'Stop the boat!' The order was shouted through a megaphone.

Aran complied.

'How many on board?'

Aran left the helm and walked towards the railings, clutching the wire barrier and facing the boat bobbing at his starboard side. 'Just me. I'm alone.'

'What's your business in Darwin?'

'Trade. I have phones to sell.' Aran had brought several holdalls of the latest mobile phones with him; he knew he had to have a cover story to take him into Australia without suspicion.

'Phones? What types – iPhones? Samsung?'

'I have a mixture. The latest models. Satellite capable, no need for masts. Just what you need out here.'

The man with the megaphone grinned and whispered something frantically at the woman next to him, who still aimed at Aran. 'Throw a couple down and let's call it the down payment on your import duty. Got any iPhone 21s?' he called.

'I've got a few of those. Let me find some...' He turned to fetch the phones.

'Hang on there, mate, we're not gonna let you head off below decks,' the man in the boat interrupted. 'Someone's got to keep an eye on you. If you give us a couple of iPhones, we'll let you through, but first we need to do a boat inspection to make sure you're on your own as you say and everything's in order.'

His boat was searched by two armed guards. They found nothing of concern; the belongings of the missing crew were of no interest to them. After parting with a phone for every one of the eight guards, he was allowed to clumsily manoeuvre the small fishing boat into the harbour.

The docking fee was huge, far higher than he'd expected, but he didn't care. He let them take the boat. He wasn't going to need it again. He grabbed his phones and his luggage and ventured ashore.

Before the attack on Australia, Darwin's port was tiny. It had a marina and a small ferry port, but it had never been a trading hub. Now things were different, and The city had ballooned in size. It was a long way from the fallout zones of the east and west coasts and refugees had flooded into the city. It had also become the centre of the drugs trade. The manufacturing of crack cocaine, crystal meth and ecstasy were the main drivers of the local economy, and desperate refugees were employed in the factories. It had rapidly become the drugs capital of the world.

Aran wobbled down the floating jetty, past the luxurious super-yachts swarming with armed guards, dilapidated fishing boats with ragged crews, and speedboats with shifty men loading taped-up boxes. He edged towards the shore, arms aching under the strain of the holdalls, past dirty children who dangled makeshift fishing rods in the water and the characters who loitered by the sea wall, watching, keeping an eye on God knows what. A group of armed men strutted past, rifles slung on their backs, pistols at their hips. Almost everyone was armed here. Some more heavily than others.

His feet made solid ground at the edge of the harbour, which was a bustling sea of traders and stalls. Buyers and sellers of anything imaginable waited for boats to dock – a convenient market for his phones. He knew they made him a target, and he had no wish to hang on to them longer than he had to.

He was sauntering along the walkway scanning the stalls when a man came from nowhere and put an arm on his shoulder. 'I hear you have phones, the latest models. You got a buyer yet? If not, I'm more than happy to take them off your hands. How 'bout you step this way into my office?'

Aran scowled at the podgy fingers that dared to touch him then looked towards their owner's face. It was plump but smiling. Greasy hair dangled onto his creased clothes. But men were more than their looks alone, and this man was a genuine trader. His instincts – helped by a bit of magic – told him that.

The man led him into a rickety shack.

'Take a seat, please.' The podgy man gestured towards a plastic chair. Aran unslung his rucksack from his shoulders and dumped his holdalls on the floor.

'So how many you got? Both those holdalls filled with them, are they?'

Aran nodded.

'What makes you got? How 'bout you get 'em out so I can have a look?'

Aran was happy to comply. He wasn't bothered about getting a good price, he just wanted rid. After the sale of the lodge and the private game reserve, even after the debts were paid, he'd enough money to keep him going for some time. It wasn't his money, but he'd taken it anyway. It should have been split between his mother and his two surviving uncles, but they didn't deserve it. It was he who had seen the lodge out to its final days, he who had kept it going after he'd been forced into management. He was owed what money was left, so he took it and fled the country. No one would find him in Australia. Here, he could disappear and build a new life.

He took out a few samples from his holdall. 'I have the latest Samsungs, iPhones and Sonys. Just the three makes, but satellite ready and SIM card free. I've fifty each of the Samsungs and Sonys and forty-two of the iPhones – that's one hundred and forty-two in total. Shall we say one hundred and fifty thousand US dollars for the lot?'

It was a high opening price, but tech was expensive in the failed state. There was no functioning government. All imports were done via black market trade routes or individual entrepreneurs, people like Aran was pretending to be, who brought in goods from overseas hoping to make a quick buck.

They negotiated. Aran let his price fall until they had an agreement.

'Great doing business.' The podgy man shook his hand and checked through his merchandise. 'You heading off? Or do you plan to find some exports to take with you first?' The man raised an eyebrow. Drugs and anything salvaged from the nuclear wastelands on the east and west coasts were the only exports from Australia. 'If you do, I can put you in touch with some people. I have lots of contacts. Don't deal in that stuff myself, like. But for those with a head for it—'

'No, thank you.' Aran cut him off. 'I'm gonna stay here for a while. I'm going to head south. Do you know where I can get a car? A good one, a four-by-four maybe?'

'You're gonna stay? Through choice?' The podgy man looked baffled. 'No one comes to Australia from the outside to stay, unless they're running.' He tilted his head questioningly.

'I'm not running, I'm searching. There's something in the south I want to try to find.'

'How far south are you heading? It can be sketchy too far from Darwin. Out in the desert, the land is even more uncivilised than here. In the city, Nickel keeps things mostly quiet.'

'I don't know how far. I'm not sure yet.'

'You got a gun?'

'No.'

'You should get one. And sleep with one eye open.'

'I don't need a gun.'

The trader looked Aran up and down. His slight build was easily betrayed by his loose T-shirt and cotton trousers. He wasn't even especially tall. He was of medium height and looked like he'd never lifted anything heavier than the holdalls he'd carried ashore in his entire life.

'You good at kung fu? And know how to dodge bullets?'

'I can take care of myself.'

'Even those who have a gun and know how to use it don't travel too far south alone. If you want to live, I suggest you find someone to watch your back.'

Aran considered his words. The man might have a point. 'And where would I find someone I can trust?'

21

'Try Shenanigans. Irish pub. Every place has one, right? Even here. These days it's a hub for hired muscle. If you go in, ask at the bar for Sammy and tell him Ryan sent you.'

'Thanks for the tip. Any ideas on a where to get that car?'

'I'd find your muscle first. They may have a ride of their own, might save you a few dollars unless your heart's set on buying one.'

***

With the cash for the phones transferred safely into Aran's account, he ventured out of the harbour and into the city in search of the pub Ryan had mentioned.

He carried just his rucksack. He didn't have much with him. When he was royalty, he'd had servants who packed everything for him and transported it on his behalf whenever he travelled. Without such luxuries, he'd learnt to travel light. The less you carried, the less there was to worry about.

On the tropical coast of northern Australia, the air hung in a humid mist of enveloping haze. Aran was used to the heat but the humidity here was oppressive. Away from the sea breeze, the sweat was soon trickling down his back, his clothes sticking to his skin, and a raging thirst gripping his throat. He stopped to get a water bottle out of his pack. A young woman approached.

'Hey there, stranger, you looking for a good time?'

Aran glanced up from his rucksack. The woman was young, perhaps in her late teens, and she was wearing almost nothing. Some slivers of fabric covered the essential parts, and heavy makeup was plastered across her youthful face. Somehow, she looked neat and fresh despite the heat.

'No, thank you.'

Her breasts bulged around the fabric strips; her curvaceous but slender form drew Aran's eyes. He was tempted... No. He would not pay for sex. If he wanted it, he'd just take it. And this woman probably had a pimp nearby. He did not want to attract attention.

He slung his rucksack back on his shoulder and continued down the street. Trees lined the road, their branches trailing onto the pavement. Long grass dotted with litter grew round their trunks. Stinking black bags sat in piles in the shade of the leaves. A burnt-out car rusted in the sun; its bumper was still wrapped around the tree it had collided with.

Past the trees and towards the city, tall buildings with broken windows and graffiti-covered lower floors towered above. Thick steel gates guarded the doors of stone office buildings, and bars protected the windows. The few pedestrians looked broken or shifty. Gangs of youths loitered menacingly in the shade; the unmistakable aroma of cannabis drifting through the air.

Aran kept himself to himself as he continued down the street, trying not to attract attention. As he passed into the city centre, the shops became more numerous, but not a single one looked like it welcomed customers. Some had armed guards by the entrance, others heavy gates and an intercom system. And yet he'd been told this was one of the safer parts of Australia.

Shenanigans was not hard to find. It was straight down the high street; Ryan's directions were easy enough to follow. He was greeted by a large guard at the door, who grinned down at Aran, a cigar held in his teeth and a rifle in his hands.

'Any guns? Any blades?' he said, with a snigger. Aran knew he didn't look the type; he suspected he looked more akin to a lost tourist than the normal clientele of the bar.

'No.'

'Scan him,' the guard said to his colleague, who had emerged from the shadows, his rifle slung on his back and a metal detector in his hand.

'Drop the bag, mate, let's have a look,' the second guard said in a surprisingly friendly tone.

Aran did as instructed and the guard scanned it. The detector barely beeped, the bag contained mostly clothes. The only metal he could think of in there were the blades on his razor.

The detector scanned Aran too, before he was allowed to enter the gloomy bar. He pushed through the door into a wave of cool. The air conditioning was heavenly, but it did nothing for the smell of sweat mixed with spilt beer. Smoke from cigarettes choked his lungs and stung his eyes. The floor was hard stone, but his feet stuck to it as he walked. He headed towards the bar, weaving though the mass of large men and mean-looking women to try to get to the front.

A voluptuous barmaid with a low-cut top, big eyes, and cascading blonde hair beamed at him.

'What can I get ya?' Her white teeth sparkled as she spoke.

'A glass of Coke, please, and is Sammy here?'

Her brows lifted and her bemused face looked Aran up and down.

'A man like you might need someone like Sammy. He's here. How 'bout I get you that Coke and I'll let him know you're asking for him?' she said with a wink.

He sipped his drink and waited amongst the chorus of musical Australian accents, pulling his elbows in and propping them on the bar as he tried to make himself small to keep the crowds from nudging him. He was slowly getting irritated as the minutes ticked by.

There was barely any room to move, yet somehow the crowd seemed to part as a short, slim, clean-shaven man with waxed hair swaggered towards the bar. He found a stool and pulled it up next to Aran.

'You were asking for me?' the man said with a smile.

'You're Sammy?' he asked incredulously - somehow, he was expecting someone bigger.

'That's me,' he said with a nod. 'How can I help?'

'Um, Ryan sent me,' he began, hesitantly.

'You're not from around here, are you?' Sammy tilted his head to one side. 'Your accent is strange. It's a little African, but different somehow. Where are you from?'

The man was still smiling, and his friendly face was managing to cut through Aran's doubts. 'I'm from Kenya.'

'Kenya! And you've come all the way over here. I won't ask what brought you – people travel for all kinds of reasons, especially to places like this. But if you are in Shenanigans and asking for me, it is only for one reason. How many men do you need?'

By the end of the chat Aran found himself liking Sammy, despite himself. He was one of those infuriating people to whom everyone just warms, and even Aran was not immune to natural charm. Despite appearances, the man certainly seemed to know his business, and he said he knew just the man for the job, and he was in luck, that man happened to be at the other end of the bar.

Fred was everything Aran expected a hired thug to be. He was tall, built like a brick shithouse, and looked like he'd been in more than a few fights. His disjointed nose told of multiple breakages. The sag to his left eyebrow drew attention to the thick scar running above his eye socket.

The sleeves of his black T-shirt were tight on his bulging biceps and bloated belly. The man-made Aran feel tiny in comparison. He looked perfect.

Sammy had introduced them. Aran grilled him until he was content the man wouldn't kill him in his sleep, hack his phone, and steal his wealth. It didn't take much magic to check whether someone was telling the truth. Satisfied, he paid Sammy the broker's fee and took Fred into his employ.

***

Fred didn't have a car of his own, but he helped Aran buy one. They sorted it the next day, hit the road and headed south. They'd been driving for hours and barely a word passed between them; Fred wasn't much of a conversationalist, which suited Aran fine as he had nothing to say either. He sat and let his hired help drive the truck as he stared out of the window. He barely noticed as the farms became forests and the forests became a desert.

He did not see the trees or shrubs, the passing cars, or the bright blue sky. He stared at magic. After years of searching for it, scraping to grasp hold of every last wisp of the rare threads of energy, so faint they were almost undetectable, now he could see it. Like a blind person who learns to see using their hands, Aran could see magic with his eyes.

The faint lines wove through the air, spinning and swirling. They wrapped around all living things, they were drawn to the trees and birds. Even Fred was encircled by the faint wisps of light.

He'd never been able to see magic in Gemini. He had never needed to. But now he knew that should he return; the world would be lit up to him as clear as day, even on the darkest nights. The magic on Earth was nothing compared to the magic he knew existed on his home planet. As the truck rumbled down the never-ending road, Aran dreamed of home.

'We're gonna have to stop shortly, the truck's running low on gas,' Fred informed Aran, breaking the long silence and pulling Aran from his trance.

'Fine,' he snapped grumpily, 'do you know if there's a gas station nearby?'

'We're not far from Danston – there was a sign not far back. We can fuel up there.'

25

Danston was a small town in the midst of the desert that once survived on passing trade from the highway. Few travelled in and out of the desert these days; only the drug runners and anyone who wanted to live far from anyone else passed through these parts.

Piles of rubbish and burnt-out cars marked the outskirts of Danston. Windows were boarded in a futile attempt to protect homes from intruders, but their owners would never return to find their front doors prised open and everything of value gone. Dusty gardens with the skeletons of plants inside were graveyards to the homes they mourned. The desert slowly reclaimed its land.

Yet the gas station survived, a lonely monument to the town that was. People still travelled; cars still needed fuel. Electric cars would be useless here. Between power cuts and trashed infrastructure, any electric car would be out of power long before there was somewhere to charge it on the road that crossed a continent.

The place seemed quiet. The hum of a generator and an illuminated 'open' sign betrayed the life existing here. Fred pulled up at a pump and honked his horn. A woman of middling years with spare weight at her hips wobbled out of the shop and meandered towards the car.

'Fill up, is it?' she called as she approached.

'Yep,' Fred replied.

'It's five dollars twenty-three a litre,' the woman chirped, 'and payment's in advance. You taking just enough for your tank, or some containers besides?'

Aran baulked at the price; it was a couple of dollars cheaper in Darwin. Why hadn't Fred suggested they take some extra cans of fuel? He didn't say anything. He just sat and scowled and nodded.

Their truck was fuelled, and Fred went into the shop for a piss and to buy a few supplies, while Aran stayed with the vehicle. Fred advised it wasn't safe to leave it alone despite the apparent emptiness of the place – he'd said there were more folk than you might think lurking in the unloved buildings.

He was right. Aran was sitting alone trying not to fume at the fuel prices, trying to enjoy the sight of the magic once more, when two men and a woman emerged from somewhere. He saw the swirls of magic that rippled around them as they strolled into view. He saw it concentrate around their bodies, yet they both held something in their hands that looked inorganic. It barely attracted any power, but whatever it was, they

26

were pointing each of their objects right at him. He shook his head vigorously. He knew what it was. One man and one woman were pointing rifles at his face while another man knocked on his window.

Aran lowered it.

A man in his thirties with a missing tooth, a crooked nose, and close-cut hair grinned at him. 'Now matey, how 'bout you hand over the keys and there'll be no need for any trouble?'

Aran glared at him. The man's grin dropped.

'Come on, there's no need to be stubborn.'

Aran glanced at the shop, looking for Fred.

The man tracked his gaze. 'There's no point looking for your friend, he's having trouble getting out of the gents'. You're alone here, you, your truck, and the three of us. Get your skinny ass out of the truck, and we can all live to see another day.'

Aran still didn't answer. He fed his anger and concentrated on the magic, drawing the swirls to him. They drifted through the air, and he pulled them into his chest.

The magic was stronger here. Stronger than in Darwin, and it dwarfed the magic in Kenya. He concentrated, and let it build.

'Last chance, mate. Get out of the truck or I'll put a bullet in your head.' The man pulled out a pistol and pointed it straight at Aran.

Aran lifted his hands, appearing to surrender, but he had other plans. He let out a steady breath, let his power flow, and sent it streaming through his palms. It shot towards the pistol and the two rifles. They glowed hot with energy.

'Argh!' the man yelled, hands shaking furiously as his gun tumbled to the ground.

A wave of fatigue washed over Aran. The power he'd expended heating the guns had been more than he'd expected. He was growing weary already. When the angry car-jackers ran towards his truck, he had few options. He'd wanted to do something dramatic, to show them what he could do, but he didn't have the power. Not here, not on Earth. A simple spell would have to do.

He lifted his hands and let the magic he had left gush towards the three of them. It wrapped round their heads and sucked their conscious minds into resting slumber. Their eyes drooped, feet staggered, legs sagged, torsos collapsed into the dust. Their chests heaved with tiny gasps and whistling snores.

Aran sat in silence, drained and angry. Frustrated that he had done so little, that his foes still lived. He was considering getting his knife and slitting their throats when a rhythmic pounding caught his ear. It was coming from the shop. *Bang, bang, crash.* Something gave, collided with a shelving unit, and store goods clattered to the ground. Fred came running out of the shop.

He halted in his tracks, stared at the two men and one woman who lay on the ground, their weapons not far away.

'What the fuck happened here?'

4. Leaking Magic?

The Zargon observation vessel zoomed silently through space, fixed in permanent orbit, and invisible to any detection equipment developed by the primitive humans. From here, its occupants were able to watch the inhabitants of the planet, code named B13536, without interference.

As a highly advanced alien race, the curiosity of the Zargons led them to explore far and wide across the universe. Using synthetic wormhole technology, they could cover thousands of light years in an instant and had charted much of the universe.

A peaceful race, their interest in other planets was scientific. The Intergalactic Discovery Institute, or the IDI, was the governmental organisation whose role was to study and observe and remain unseen. For hundreds of cycles, the IDI had maintained a no interference policy and religiously stuck to this protocol. Until a female human inadvertently found her way from B13536 to an M-Class coded M69245, a planet with a magical field of energy, where she found she had extraordinary power.

She'd found a wormhole the Zargons hadn't known existed. She'd gone where she shouldn't have and put another world at risk. The Zargons intervened just this once. They'd set in motion the events that drew her home, back to B13536.

She'd been on the other planet a while; she'd become a Queen and had children and one of her offspring sought to continue her legacy of destruction. But he'd been tricked into following his mother to her home planet and after that the wormhole was destroyed.

Things were almost back to normal on the far away M-Class planet, but on B13536, things were not quite as they should be – magic was leaking onto the B-Class, and at least one specimen had noticed.

Garkan sat at the side of the control room, occupied with the monotonous endeavour of report-writing. The excited chirp of her first mate drew her from her trance.

'Captain, did you see that?' Cork exclaimed.

Garkan kicked the floor gently, jetting her chair in a hasty half-turn. She smiled at her young first mate. The mass of grey skin above the captain's large black eyes wrinkled to quizzical furrows. 'Cork, I've been buried in this log for storns, so I assume you speak rhetorically?'

'It's specimen H108 – he's at it again,' she blurted, bobbing in her seat as she spoke.

'At what again?' said Garkan, with a sigh.

'Magic, of course!'

'Are you sure?'

'Yes! Our new aurometers are detecting a reading. His observation drone measured a pulse of magnitude two point eight. I told you the burst of wind on that boat was magic, and now we have proof!'

Garkan's forehead remained creased as she rose to her feet, straightening the blue and green uniform of the Intergalactic Discovery Institute as she stalked across the room. She took a seat in her captain's chair next to Cork's and studied the holographic observation screens. Several of these hovered above the control panel; an island of buttons, knobs, and levers from which the majority of the ship's functions could be controlled.

The display on the largest screen was fixed on a truck rumbling south along a highway in sector seven. A smaller one focussed on three sleeping would-be car thieves lying on the ground in the desert sun. In a corner of the screen, the data Cork had mentioned was clear. Garkan stared at the figures. She shook her head.

'There can't be magic here. B13536 has no magic field. How is this possible?' she said.

'H108 is from M69245, an M-Class planet, if you recall. He was a very powerful sorcerer there – maybe he brought some magic with him?' Cork suggested.

'That's not how magic works!' Garkan exclaimed. 'Sorcerers can only manipulate magic in their environment. They can't take it anywhere. There has to be magic on Earth,' she scratched her small chin, 'but how?'

The door at the rear of the control room zipped upwards. Cork and Garkan turned in unison to see their third crew member enter. Both were trying their best to keep their faces neutral as she arrived.

'Greetings, *Captain*.' Lukin always spoke Garkan's rank as if she meant it with a degree of sarcasm.

'And greetings to you too, Lukin,' Garkan replied, without any attempt to hide the dryness in her voice. 'What brings you to the control room? Your shift doesn't start for hours.'

'Oh, did you not realise that when incidents of significance occur, all crew members are due to report to the control room? It's in section forty-three point two of the IDI's protocol manual.'

Garkan stared at Lukin blankly.

'It was such a long time ago when you were in training, Captain, I'm not surprised you have forgotten.'

'I hadn't forgotten. I also happened to remember the part of the policy stating that it is the captain's responsibility to call her crew members to the control room when such an incident occurs. It is for the captain, and the captain alone, to decide what constitutes an incident of significance,' she replied tartly.

'Oh, you are correct, Captain, but as the incident happened a number of tarns ago, and you hadn't informed me, I assumed you had not recalled the policy. I would have hated to have been left out of such an important incident.'

Garkan seethed quietly. Her newest crew member was a thorn in her side. Lukin had been appointed to their observation vessel with no prior field experience, just a career in government. Garkan was under no illusions about the real purpose of the posting of the Zargon to her ship.

Things were changing in government. The balance of power was shifting, and the Intergalactic Discovery Institute was slowly losing its independence. Individuals who actively opposed the no interference policy were now part of the senate. They no longer hid themselves, and they were content to speak openly about their aims to have a more 'active role' in species development, as they put it.

They were still in the minority, but they managed to convince the government the IDI should be better resourced. Having a two-shift system with a period each day covered by artificial intelligence was not sufficient, they had said, which was a valid point. But they had also managed to get their tendrils into the board that appointed the extra members of staff. Every one of them was hand-picked from within government. Garkan didn't trust any of them.

She let Lukin's thinly veiled insult go. She had no desire to give the Zargon any excuse to recommend she be retired early.

'Thank you, Lukin, for saving me the trouble of having to call you in from your bed,' Garkan said with all the insincerity she could muster. 'Cork has observed an incident of interest. I'm sure she'll be more than happy to fill you in on the details.'

Garkan left her first mate to talk to their colleague while she pretended to temporarily return to her report-writing. She was staring at the virtual noticeboard in front of her, unblinking, when the shrill voice of Lukin called over.

'Captain, have you filed a report yet?'

'What do you think I'm doing?' she lied.

'We will need to conduct a full investigation into the source of this magic. We will need to understand where it is coming from. As I recall, no volbirrium has ever been found on Earth. Perhaps there was a meteorite that deposited some. Have there been any of note during your tenure?'

'No,' she growled.

'I suggest we do a re-evaluation of the minerals on B13536 and a magic field survey. We will need to get some extra equipment ordered and—'

Garkan cut her off. 'Lukin, please kindly remember that I am the captain of this ship. Although I do not deny you make valid points, they are points I am equally capable of coming to on my own. I would therefore be grateful if you could keep your counsel to yourself, until I have finished my own assessment of the situation and am ready to make my own recommendations to IDI HQ.'

Garkan glanced from Lukin to Cork. Her first mate was desperately struggling to hide her smirk, while indignance gripped the face of her newest crew member. Garkan suddenly found herself biting her own cheeks to maintain a straight face.

'Yes, Captain,' Lukin replied. She stalked over to the lab area and appeared to study some samples.

***

Darkle was on shift alone, writing reports, again. She was the captain of the observation vessel monitoring the M-Class planet of M69245, a planet with a magic field and the only known magical planet with advanced species, so report-writing was an all-encompassing task. Her entire time on shift was filled with it these days. The IDI was getting ever more interested in her planet. They wanted more details about the Specimens of Interest, particularly the ones who originated from B13536 and their families.

The chime of an incoming call rang out. Darkle sighed. Yet another incoming request for data or returns from the IDI, she assumed. She spun in her chair to face the observation screens, and to her delight, the centre display was showing an image of Garkan. She recognised the captain of B13536's observation vessel immediately; they worked together often. Her mood immediately brightened.

'Ship, answer call,' she ordered the artificial intelligence system, before rising and heading to her captain's chair for a better view of her colleague.

'Darkle! Good to see you,' Garkan gave a cursory glance at Darkle's backdrop, 'and alone too, it appears.' Garkan grinned.

'Yes, you caught me alone. You do have a copy of our rota.' Darkle raised a corner of her tiny grey mouth.

'I know. But it's hard to be certain who I'll find when I call, with our spies on board...' Garkan leaned forward and studied the space behind Darkle again. 'Your spy *is* off shift, isn't she?'

'Yes, our third crew member is off shift,' Darkle replied. 'But you should stop calling them spies. You might get caught out doing that one day by someone who cares. Then early retirement might be coming your way sooner than you think.'

'But they're the Cooperative's stooges! You don't actually believe they were sent here to do anything other than keep tabs on us, do you? There's no way the IDI would have authorised such poorly qualified agents to work on our ships if the Cooperative didn't have some kind of other agenda.'

'I don't disagree,' Darkle replied quietly, eyes darting side to side as she spoke, 'but be that as it may, we have to assume they have the full backing of the IDI, and we should treat them with respect accordingly.'

Garkan looked at the floor guiltily.

'You've not been ruffling Lukin's feathers again, have you?' Darkle enquired, her large grey forehead wrinkling towards her bald scalp.

Garkan raised her head sheepishly. 'She deserved it; she was overstepping the mark – again! She's a bloody pain in the arse.'

'And she is one of Inkor's pets,' Darkle warned. 'Everything you say, every foot out of place, anything you do will go straight back to Inkor; a member of the senate! Lukin's not just any Cooperative stooge, she's one of their favourite little cronies.'

'I know, I know. Lucky escape for you, though, I hear she was desperate for your planet.'

'Everyone is. Luckily the chair of the IDI won the battle – our third crew member seems pretty competent, if a little boring. Zark hates her though. I think she feels threatened.'

'I suppose she is in competition to take over your mantle,' Garkan suggested.

'There is that, and Jink has experience at IDI HQ in her early career that will hold her in good stead when the time comes.'

'Do you suspect you are being reported on?' Garkan queried.

'Of course. I've never been under much doubt about the real reason government insisted we were supposed to have extra crew members, especially ones with back-office experience rather than field officers who cut their teeth on low-grade planets. But what can we do? I don't have anything to hide, so I'm not overly concerned.'

'Oh. Um…' Garkan hesitated. 'Do you tell Jink everything that happens on your planet?'

'Everything of consequence. Why?'

'What about stuff not on your planet?'

'What are you getting at, Garkan? Do you want to share something with me in confidence?' Darkle could tell Garkan did. She had known her fellow captain a long time. She'd been on her ship for more decades than she cared to count, but Garkan had been on hers for longer. They both monitored planets with humans; identical species on different planets were rare. The crews of the two ships had always needed to work together.

'Possibly, er – um, not really. Lukin already knows some of it, and most of what I have to say will be in the report anyway.'

'Most of what you say? What else is there to say? What don't you want government to know?' Darkle shook her head despairingly – there was no helping the wayward captain.

'Just the stuff that isn't in my report. The bits that are a hunch, rather than facts.'

'You know me well enough to know I'm very much a *need-to-know* kind of Zargon. If the IDI doesn't need to know... why tell them? Why should they care about your *hunches*, Garkan? They want to know about facts backed up by evidence. Do you have any evidence for your hunches?'

'Nothing solid.'

'Good. Come on, what's on your mind?'

'We've found magic on B13536.'

Darkle tilted her head to one side. 'Magic? Are you certain? I thought you said you had no solid evidence?'

'Oh, well we do for the magic, the magic will be in the report. It was Cork who suspected it. She put magic detection tech on one of our observation droids and it spotted some. It was generated by one of your old specimens, good old H108.'

'H108? That nasty piece of work? Thought he'd have disappeared into a spiral of depression at his lack of power by now.'

'No, he hasn't. He's found a bit of magic. Not much, mind – it's nothing compared to what he had on your planet but considering there ought not to be any magic at all on my planet, this is quite an issue.'

'Yeah,' Darkle said with a hefty sigh. 'Any idea where its coming from?'

'I have ordered some more equipment to do a full magical survey, to see if we can trace the source.'

'Sounds sensible.'

'Mm, but what if ...' Garkan stalled.

'Spit it out, Garkan, what's the bit that's not in your report?'

Garkan narrowed her eyes. 'What if it's filtering from your side? What if there's another wormhole?'

'Another one?' Darkle scratched her grey, hairless head. 'It's feasible – if the last one was a Gallantrian legacy, it's possible they could have left more.'

'Exactly. Isn't it the consensus that the other wormhole was a legacy of that extinct race of meddlers?' Garkan queried.

'That's the IDI's assumption. And if the Gallantrians made one wormhole, they could have made more, buried perhaps, like the first one was before the river eroded the way in. If there was another wormhole, even one that had recently been uncovered, why would magic track through it? There was no evidence it went through the last one.'

'No, but I've been reading up on it. Magic doesn't really cling to air, there's hardly any organic matter in it,' Garkan began, swinging from side to side on her swivel chair. 'And what there is, is too dispersed to allow it to track through. It's different in liquids like water though. Water masses on inhabited planets are riddled with parasites and bugs. There's plenty of organic matter to act as a reservoir – it's why we can see streams of power running through rivers.

'What if there was a watercourse running through another wormhole? If it flowed through and pooled somewhere, would it not act as a sink for magic? Every living thing coming through would have tiny particles of magic in their cells. Over time, it would surely collect and create a bank of power. What if this is the source of H108's magic?'

'It could be.' Darkle sucked her gums in thought. 'You said he'd used magic already – has he used it on any of your humans?'

'Several. There was an incident a few days back where we suspect he used it to blow three humans overboard on a boat, then there was the incident earlier where he put three other specimens to sleep.'

'Oh.' Darkle surprised herself at the concern she heard in her own voice.

'What do you mean, *oh?*'

'Um, the ones he put to sleep? They'll be triggered; they'll have the capacity to wield magic too, now.'

Garkan leaned forwards in her chair. 'You know more about magic than me, Darkle – are they likely to start using it?'

'Probably not, no. They wouldn't know they'd been triggered and certainly wouldn't know about magic. They'd need to be trained, like the humans native to my planet. Most of them have the capacity to wield it, but it takes years of training for them to even get a basic grasp. It would only be an issue if they came to my M-Class. In that case, they would have so much power it would most likely materialise on its own at some point.'

'The gene my humans have but yours don't really is quite a mystery, isn't it?' Garkan slumped back in her chair and stretched. 'Our planets have loads of parallel species. It's all but certain they migrated through Gallantrian-era wormholes from my planet to yours, but we haven't found any genetic diversions of that magnitude amongst any of the intermediate species. We've only found it in the humans.'

'There's still no solid evidence for the theory, Garkan, despite the insistence of the IDI that humans on my M-Class came from your B-Class. We both know it's impossible to tell for certain why the ability to wield magic is prevalent in your humans but not mine, and we can't rule out the possibility that it is a result of natural evolution.'

'In five thousand cycles, Darkle?' Garkan pulled her outstretched hands down and steepled them in her lap. 'Maybe it's another task for you, some detailed genetic profiling of your ancestral specimens, in case you've not enough to do already.' Garkan's rounded white teeth peeked out between the rims of her small mouth.

'Ha, ha.' Darkle said dryly. 'But I am starting to suspect I might be being bogged down with reports to keep me from looking into such things.'

'It's possible.' Garkan slipped her hands onto the arms of her chair. 'Anyway, getting back on topic, what if I'm right about there being another wormhole? What if there is a way through? H108 has been on the move – he's travelled from sector four to sector seven. He was the most powerful sorcerer on your planet before he left. He's been miserable ever since, without his power. Maybe he has travelled in search of magic, or he senses something. Maybe he's going to find another wormhole.'

'Your hypothesis is sound. Why the secrecy? Why do you not want to let Lukin know?'

'Do you not recall what happened last time government knew there was a wormhole connecting our two planets?'

'Of course I do. We risked our careers to destroy it!' Darkle exclaimed.

'Yep. And thankfully government decided it was the right thing to do… at the time. Government has changed since then. They might have other ideas.'

Darkle sighed. The reality of the creeping changes to their ruling class was a worrying development. 'What can we do? We can't interfere, we can't stop H108 from using magic, and we can't stop your investigation. Lukin will make sure of that. You might be right. There might be another wormhole, and maybe H108 will find it. There is nothing we can do about it.'

The reality of Darkle's words appeared to bore into Garkan. She stared back at her fellow captain, seemingly unsure what to say. At last, she shrugged. 'I guess not.'

'We have no power except knowledge, but knowledge can be power. I suggest we keep your hypothesis between us. Let's see if Lukin figures out what's going on. Let her take credit for whatever theory she comes up with, especially if you think it is wrong. We need to monitor this for now and see what happens.'

5. Dog Eat Dog

Location: Alice Springs, Australia, Earth (Planet B13536)

Sarah walked down the street like she owned the place. She was short and slim, but her biceps bulged; she liked to lift heavy things to keep herself strong. Her dirty-blonde hair cascaded down her back and her tanned skin was covered with beads of sweat. It was another hot day in the miserable stinking desert. Another day where more precious reserves of sun cream were used up. Her supplies were running low, and it was bloody expensive this far south. Like everything around here in the middle of nowhere.

She pulled her rifle sling out of her cleavage. A little air flowed between her breasts, a tiny bit of relief from the incessant heat. Of all the cars they could have stolen, why did they nick the one with broken air-con?

She'd just got a tip off, it had lifted her mood for all of five minutes, then she remembered the oven on wheels she'd have to get back into. It was a good lead, but it would mean more hours in the car if Vinnie agreed to follow it up, she thought, with a long, heavy sigh.

Stark and Jon were sitting in the shade near the car when she returned from asking questions. The two men were her partners. They watched her back, she watched theirs. They'd been working together since soon after the place got nuked. She'd met Stark when he'd tried to rape her. He'd underestimated her, as had Jon when he'd tried to rescue her. She hadn't needed his help. She didn't need anyone's help.

Sarah could survive on her own, like she had since she'd run away from home as a teenager. She'd got sick of her stepdad using her as his own personal whore and had chosen a life on the streets instead. She'd been living rough since before China attacked and all the normal folks were sent into a head spin. It had been easy to make a living after the place collapsed, it was easy to survive when the police were off your back and

39

the prey was vulnerable. It was at first, but these days things were getting harder.

The soft people left or got hard. The hard people got tougher, like she had. They'd had a good gig when they worked for Vinnie. Recruiting muscle was one of the straightest jobs she'd ever had. She didn't have to fuck anyone, she didn't have to kill anyone – not often – and it was more about coercion than threats. The threats came later.

But they'd had a dry spell. They'd found no one in weeks and they'd been given an ultimatum. Become the muscle or find a new employer. They didn't want to be the muscle. They'd all done their time on that one and they knew life expectancy tended to be short. It was why they'd got out. It was why they worked in recruiting: it was a far safer job.

They'd been served their notice in Danston, where Vinnie had left them and taken their Jeep. Arsehole. It wasn't a surprise though, and they'd been grateful to be left alive. It was another chance, another opportunity to find the muscle he needed. They had to find someone, soon, and the arsehole who'd burnt their hands and knocked them out was perfect. Vinnie would pay a lot to have him on his books.

They'd slept on the floor of the gas station forecourt for hours. No one could wake them, but someone had dragged them into the shade. When they did wake, they wasted no time in stealing their weapons back from the bitch in the shop who'd nicked them, then they stole another car. A crappy cross-over thing that just about had a four-wheel drive but rattled along like its wheels might fall off at any moment. It was a ride though, and it was enough.

They'd driven through the night, taking turns to keep moving and hoping to catch the man who'd floored them. The Stuart Highway ran from north to south, straight through Alice Springs, the last town of any size until the south coast, and most of that was nuked or blasted to shit. Anyone heading south would have to stop in the town, even if was just to get supplies. That was what they'd guessed, and they were right.

'I know where they went,' she announced as she got close enough for Stark and Jon to hear her.

'Great. Where?' Stark replied.

'They're heading south-west, towards Ayers Rock. They left not long back, an hour ago maybe?'

'So we go after him, alone?' Jon queried. 'He took the three of us down last time, what makes you think he won't manage it again?'

'Because this time we know what we're facing and we'll be ready,' Sarah replied, hands sliding onto her hips. 'And there'll be more of us.'

'You planning on magicking muscle out of your arse, are you?' Stark sniped.

Sarah cast Stark a sideways glance. 'When I explain what we're going after to Vinnie, I reckon I can persuade him to lend us some men.'

***

'You gonna tell me where we're going?' It had taken a while, but curiosity seemed to have finally got the better of Fred.

Aran's hackles went up. How dare his driver ask questions. He quietly seethed while he resisted the urge to react. On Earth Aran had learned you had to pretend to tolerate your servant's nonsense, to an extent. In Kenya, you could have cops on your back if you were too brutal with the staff. Here, Fred would walk if he pissed him off. And right now, he needed him.

He slowly turned to regard his driver. Fred's eyes were fixed ahead, on the road. 'South-west,' Aran snapped in reply.

'It was south when we set off, now it's south-west?' Fred appeared completely unfazed by Aran's tone.

'Does it matter?'

'I guess not, as long as I'm being paid.' The big man spoke calmly, as if he were used to people like Aran.

'I've paid you every day. I'll keep paying you every day until I don't need you anymore. I pay you to drive and watch my back. I don't pay you to ask questions.'

Fred raised an eyebrow. 'No problem. I won't charge for this one: What happened at the gas station? The one in Danston?'

Aran's irritation at Fred's questions was growing, but somehow, he found himself conflicted. Part of him admired the man's impertinence and he realised he had been getting bored of the silence.

'They tried to steal the truck. I decided to stop them.'

'You don't carry a gun, and I've seen more muscle on the arms of a ten-year-old girl. How'd you floor three thugs?'

'Magic.' Aran folded his arms, a smug smirk plastered across his stubbly face.

'Magic? You're kidding me.'

'Nope.'

'Fuck off.'

'You asked, I told you.'

'You're a mysterious man, Aran.' They drove in silence for a few more miles until Fred couldn't resist asking another question. 'If you can floor three thugs on your own, without a gun or a knife, what do you need me for?'

'I don't care to drive.'

'I'm an expensive driver. You can pay any old idiot just to drive.'

'I can't do magic in my sleep, I need someone to make sure my throat isn't slit in the night. And as it turns out, you have some experience that might be useful.'

'Really?' Fred said, a smirk threatening to break out across his lips.

'You used to work for a drugs baron, right?' Aran replied, ignoring Fred's growing grin.

'Yep. I'd like to say I was his right-hand man, but if I was, I'd be dead. Nickel killed his right-hand man. And his left-hand man and a few others besides.'

'You know about the drugs trade though?' Aran continued.

'I know a bit.'

'Seems like a good way to make a living.'

'It's a dangerous one,' Fred's grin had gone.

'I plan to settle here, in Australia. I need a trade' Aran said. His eyes were fixed forwards, but he could feel Fred's turning from the road to settle on the side of his face.

'Drugs is about the only one with any money in it anymore', Fred suggested. Aran saw him shrug out of the corner of his eye.

'Who is the biggest drugs baron in Australia? The one with the biggest empire? Does anyone lead them all?'

Fred chuckled. 'Are you serious about wanting to work in drugs?'

'Yes,' Aran said in a deadpan tone.

'People don't just walk into the drugs trade. It doesn't work like that.'

'Why not?'

'No one will trust you. You can't just join a new cartel; you have to do years of dirty work before anyone will even go near you. You have to... Fuck!' Fred exclaimed.

'What?'

A pickup truck sped past them, settled into the road ahead, and braked. It was slowing down. Another truck appeared to their left, bouncing along the desert as it flanked them. An old SUV was at their right, and another accelerated to their rear. They were surrounded. In unison, the vehicles slowed until Fred and Aran's car was forced to a halt.

'What's going on?' Aran asked, his panic betrayed by his voice.

'Looks like someone wants a word with us.' Fred looked to his left. A blonde woman climbed out of the SUV and knocked on Fred's window. He wound it down.

'Get out of the car, both of you,' she said.

Fred turned to Aran. 'I suggest we do as she says.'

Men with assault rifles emerged from their vehicles. Everyone pointed their weapons at Aran and Fred. There were nine of them. Aran was not confident he could disable them all, and just one bullet would do the trick if they took aim at him first. His anger prickled an angry flush on his skin as the magic coursed through his veins. He could feel there was more magic here than at the gas station, but it wasn't enough. He was still weaker than the most junior sorcerer he'd employed when he'd been king. He had less magic than a village healer would on his home planet. He found he could not disagree with Fred's assessment and grudgingly got out of the car.

The woman led them to a patch in the desert. The armed men surrounded them, their guns never leaving their targets. Aran regarded the woman, his dark brown eye slits beneath his heavy brows. She looked familiar. The men who surrounded him all looked similar. Most wore jeans with ragged boots, some wore vests, others T-shirts. Most had close-cropped hair of various shades of brown, and one had dark skin. One had a broken nose and a missing tooth. He recognised him. It was the man who'd tried to rob his truck. This wasn't going to end well.

He reached for his power. He had no choice. He would try to take them all and hope he had enough power. He let his mind find the fury. He closed his eyes, concentrated, and felt the power swell, build. He prepared to unleash it.

Something bit him in the back. Searing pain ripped through his body with an electrifying judder. His quivering body tipped helplessly towards the dust as the taser released fifty thousand volts. He smashed into the ground with a heavy thud, and everything went black.

6. Lust And Love

Location: Tannel, Gemini (Planet M69245)
Earth Year: 2036

G arrad lay naked, sheets long since hurled to the floor. His sweat was slowly drying, bringing a slight chill to his skin as the warmth from his earlier exertion faded away. Long, painted fingernails trailed across his chest, weaving through the small mass of hair adulthood had brought him. Her touch fuelled goosebumps and a ticklish tingle, making him squirm. He pulled out of her way and rolled onto his side. He reached over and wrapped a stray lock of her ebony hair round his fingers and let the silky strands slide through his hand.

'I'm going to have to go, Ellany. I have to get home,' he said softly, his voice tinged with regret. 'And I can't imagine Madame Orealle will tolerate me here much longer without charging me double anyway.' He smiled warmly – of the ladies in this house, she was his favourite.

She ran her tongue over her upper lip, her long eyelashes fluttering as her moist lips pursed into a smile. 'Sure I can't persuade you to stay a little longer?'

His body yearned for her at the suggestion. He was tempted, very tempted, but it was late enough as it was; he could almost claim he'd left the pub at this hour. If he was caught by his father as he sneaked home and into his bed, he could certainly try to peddle that lie. He suppressed his youthful lust and gave her one last peck on her rouged lips before forcing his legs off the bed. Twisting, he sat up and turned to her one last time.

She was as naked as he, her smooth young flesh on full display, pert round breasts thrust forwards. One last touch. It wouldn't hurt, surely. He reached a hand towards her silky skin. It was a mistake. His body possessed his mind, and he swung back onto the bed and took her in his arms.

***

He closed the door behind him at last and stepped softly down the stairs, hoping to leave unnoticed. He'd paid in advance, as was the way, but he'd certainly overstayed his allocated time. The sounds of the men and women enjoying each other's bodies faded as he tiptoed down the last few steps. It was quiet on the ground floor. It was late. The wine-fuelled receptions where the men chose their partners were long since over. The ladies who weren't still working had gone to sleep. But Madame Orealle didn't sleep, or so it seemed.

'Good evening, Mr Bramston.' She startled him, and he turned to see the brothel's mistress lurking in the doorway of a darkened room.

'Madame Orealle, good evening to you too.'

'I trust you were not trying to leave without paying for the extras.' Her long eyelashes fluttered. 'You know the rules if you stay longer than your allotted time.'

'No, of course not. Um, to tell the truth, I hadn't realised I'd overstayed.' He grinned his cheekiest grin. 'Time does fly when you're having fun.'

'Indeed, it does. But the rules are the rules.' She smiled back, twirling strands of hair through her fingers, with her chest thrust forwards and breasts well past their prime forced into mounds by her tight corset. The pose was second nature to a woman who'd spent her life making money from men's lust.

'Oh, I guess,' he conceded.

'I'll tell you what, as you are such a good customer, I won't charge you full price for your overstay. I can offer you a half-price discount for your extra time, if you are amenable?' She purred.

'Er, yes, thank you. How much do I owe?'

***

The streets of Tannel were quiet. The pubs had long since closed and the cabs retired for the evening. He'd be walking home tonight. He didn't mind the walk; he'd not had much to drink, and his head was pretty clear. It was late summer, the nights were warm, and the journey of a few miles was nothing to a fit soldier like him. He was conscious of the time – it was late. All chance of explaining away the reason for returning at such an hour had gone. If his parents or his brothers heard him come in, he'd be busted.

He slid the key in the door and turned it as gently as he could, but its soft clicking was like a racket in the silent early hours. The creaking as it swung on its hinges was like a screeching cat, the soft thud as it closed a hammer on stone. He pulled off his boots and stowed them out of sight, creeping up the stairs in his socks.

Everything was still silent – so far so good. Anther few steps, a creaky plank, a pause. No one stirred. Another step, and another. Something furry underfoot.

'*Screeawl!*' something yelled.

The cat. He stumbled, fell, and crashed onto the first-floor landing, where he collided with a dresser. The collection of ornaments on its shelves rattled. Silence. He lay still, panting. Noise. Someone stirred. Footsteps. A door opened, there was the glow of an oil lamp, and the face of his father glaring at him.

'Garrad!'

'Evening, Father,' he murmured through clenched teeth.

'What are you doing rattling around at this time of night?' Davod snapped, his sunken eyebrows shadowing his angry eyes in the shimmering flicker of the oil light. 'Are you drunk?'

'No, not really.'

Garrad was starting to rise when his father approached, inhaling deeply, checking for the tell-tale scent of liquor as his son slowly rose to his feet. Garrad knew he'd not had much, and what he had drunk had probably worn off by now anyway. But on this occasion that was a bad thing, his father would know he'd not been in the pub until this hour. His father glared at him, shaking his head.

'Go to bed, we'll talk in the morning.'

***

Someone was knocking. He'd heard it in his dream, but as consciousness found his mind, he realised it wasn't in his head – someone really was knocking.

'Garrad!' his younger brother, Elliah, called. 'Breakfast's ready.'

47

'Yeah,' he called back groggily. 'Thanks.' He was preparing to return to sleep when his door opened.

'Come on, get up! You can't stay in bed all day, it's your last day at home and you promised to spar with me this morning' the fourteen-year-old boy pleaded.

Garrad smiled. He'd only had a few hours' sleep, but he'd survived on less before. He groaned his way into a sitting position. 'Fine, I'm up. Breakfast better be good!'

'It's kippers and toast today – can you not smell it?'

Garrad sniffed. He was certainly partial to smoked fish for breakfast; his mother knew it was his favourite. She must have made it especially. Another reason to get his sorry ass out of bed.

He was still tucking his shirt into his breeches when he stumbled into the kitchen. His mother was serving breakfast as he arrived, and she greeted him with a warm smile.

'Morning, Mother.' He kissed her on the cheek. 'Father,' he said sheepishly, taking a seat by Elliah and avoiding his father's gaze.

'Late night, was it?' Andas smirked from across the table. Of his two brothers, Andas was the elder, but he was still a few years Aran's junior, and only just out of school. Perhaps he'd heard him come back and jumped to his own conclusions, or perhaps Garrad looked shattered. He certainly felt it.

'Yeah,' he said as he helped himself to some coffee.

'What did you get up to? Meet anyone nice?' He was so focussed on grinning at Garrad that he'd stopped eating.

Garrad's father shot his middle son a look, stern and firm. Andas's grin vanished; he continued eating in silence.

His mother placed her own plate down and took a seat by Garrad's other side and at last began to eat her herself.

'I can't believe it's your last day at home already!' she said between mouthfuls. 'It only seems like yesterday you were granted leave.'

'It's been two weeks!'

'I know, but it doesn't seem that long. Despite your base being just outside of town, we hardly get to see you! I thought with you being close, we'd get you at weekends at least.'

'He has other hobbies at the weekends,' Andas muttered under his breath. Garrad noticed another glare from his father, daggers shot from Davod's eyes in his last warning to the loose-tongued young man.

Lilian regarded her sons and husband, looking confused, but apparently deciding to ignore it. 'You go back as a lance corporal! I bet you're looking forward to that. Does it mean you get a room to yourself? Do you get to command your own squad?'

Garrad couldn't help but smile at his mother's naive view of the army. 'No, Mother, I get a smaller room, four or six of us together maybe. It depends on how it's allocated, and I won't be in charge yet. I'm only going to be the second in command of a section of eight men.'

'Oh, four is much better than twenty-odd to a room though, surely? And second in command, it sounds like a lot more responsibility.'

'It's the first step up the ladder. There's a lot more rungs to climb yet.'

'You don't have to climb the ladder,' Davod added. 'I left as a lance corporal, learned everything I needed to by then. The perfect groundwork for protecting my father's ships. Granted, I'd been in the rank for a few years when I left. I'd say it's certainly worth doing, but have you thought about coming out of the army and working in the family business? If we had you about, we could look at getting back into freight haulage and not just redistribution of other people's wares.'

Garrad chewed his bite of toast slowly as he tried to work out what to say; being a merchant sounded as exciting as watching paint dry. He'd always wanted to join the army. He loved wielding a sword, the marching, the exercises, the drills, and as a lance corporal he'd get his first taste of command. He had that to look forward to, also. There was not a cat in hell's chance he was about to jump ship before he'd even made corporal. He was born to be in the army – he was certain.

He ran a hand through his close-cropped hair as he met the hopeful gaze of his father, the man who'd raised him, who'd taught him to wield a sword and to ride a horse.

He swallowed. 'Maybe.' It was all he could think to say.

Davod nodded; a sad smile crept across his lips.

'Don't worry, Father.' Andas had been following their exchange closely. 'I'll always be there to help you, even if Garrad doesn't ever leave the Army. I can help you build the haulage side of things.'

'You could, lad, just as soon as you've worked out what that sword of yours is for. Freight needs security, not just brains.'

'I have skill with a blade, Father!' Elliah piped up. 'Garrad says I've come on loads since he came home and in a couple of years, when I finish school, I'll be nearly as good as him——'

'In your dreams!' Garrad chuckled.

Elliah frowned and folded his arms.

'Don't worry, short stuff, you ain't too bad. You can certainly hold your own, I'd say, and you'll definitely make a respectable swordsman when your reach matches your courage.'

'What have you got planned for your last day, Garrad?' Lilian asked, changing the subject.

'I promised Elliah I'd spend some time with him this morning, then after lunch I'll head back to camp. It'll be good to get back in time for dinner. I can catch up with the lads.'

'You'll be spending months with them! We won't see you again until the midwinter festival,' she protested.

He placed a hand on hers. 'We're all getting split up very soon – we'll be sent to different postings. Half of us could end up in Vornston or on the ships or some mission or other. I might only have a couple days left with some of them.'

She tilted her head and nodded with a small, forced smile.

'How about we ride back up to Tannel together, Garrad?' his father suggested. 'You take your mother's horse, and I can lead it home after. It will give us time to chat.'

'Sounds good.' Garrad swallowed a large mouthful of breakfast too quickly. He had a feeling his father might want a word.

***

They rode in silence for the first mile, Garrad nervously waiting for his father's talk. At last, the moment he'd been dreading arrived.

'You were late back last night – very late,' Davod began.

'I guess.'

'Where were you?'

'Just out.'

'Out where?'

'In the pub with some mates.'

'The pubs close at midnight. You were back close to dawn.'

50

'I took the long route home.' He kept his eyes fixed on the road ahead, trying to keep his face as neutral as possible as he attempted to lie his way out of his father's questions.

'Son, I know where you were. Stop trying to bullshit me. You're building a reputation, you know.'

Garrad's stomach sank into his gut. *Shit.* He had a reputation? And his father knew about it? He couldn't think of anything to say.

Davod sighed. 'We've all done it, pretty much every man in Vorn at a guess. Can't say I never visited the odd brothel before I met your mother, but it was only every now and again. I've been getting customers who have said they've seen you on Dilan Street, the street where there are loads of, um...'

'I know what's on Dilan Street, Father,' Garrad snapped, with too much confidence. He wasn't helping his case.

'Of course you do.' Davod was silent for a moment as he considered his next words. Garrad kept riding, staring forwards, praying for their journey to end. 'You see, there's nothing wrong with having fun, but the more you play the field, the more goals you're likely to score.'

Garrad turned to his father, dark eyebrows raised in question at his odd analogy.

Davod chuckled at Garrad's expression; he'd clearly realised how ridiculous he'd sounded. 'I'll give it to you straight. If you keep spending time with whores, sooner or later one will pop up with a sprog and try to claim it's yours. Especially if you start to do well for yourself. The higher your rank in the army, the greater the risk. The more money they think you have, the more they'll try to swindle out of you, and if you don't give them what they're after, they'll do their best to ruin you.

'That's one thing. The second is your mother. She doesn't know. I haven't told her, and the rumours haven't got to her yet. Andas seems to know though, or at least he suspects. It won't be long until someone says something. Do you think she'll want to hear that about her son? She fled her home country to escape gossip about herself. I doubt she'll want to start hearing it about her own blood. She's a respectable lady now. Do you want to hurt her by ruining it for her?'

Garrad blinked, clearing his vision, trying to clear his head. 'She fled her home country to escape gossip? What gossip?'

'Um, nothing – not really. Things that no longer matter. It's not important. What's important is that you don't drag the name of our family into the mud.'

'I thought she left Thost to marry you?' He held the reins in one hand as his other hand drifted to his scalp to attend an itch.

'She did.'

'Were there things said about a woman with Tribesfolk heritage marrying a man from Vorn?'

'Some things. It was mostly the dwarves who cared about that stuff. The humans in Darrudin are so mixed-up, none of them were too bothered, and in Vorn, folk just think she's exotic. But we're going off topic here. You know what I'm trying to say, and I'm saying it for your own good. Too much time with the ladies of the night will only get you into trouble. If you want a woman, find one you plan to marry and get a ring on her finger. You can bed her as much as you like after that, and no one will bat an eye.'

Garrad shuffled in his saddle, his shoulders squeezed into uncomfortable tension. 'The life of a soldier is no life for a wife,' he said dryly.

'So leave! Come and join the family business, settle down, find a nice woman. With your looks, they'll be queuing up.'

Garrad straightened his shirt and felt his skin warm at the compliment. 'Maybe one day. Just not yet.'

It was a lie, he knew it. He wondered if his father did too. *Give it a few years*, he thought. He'd wait until his brothers were settled into the business. His father wouldn't need him then; he wouldn't care that his eldest was still in the army, climbing the ranks, doing what he was born to do. Garrad was a soldier. It was all he'd ever wanted to be. He couldn't see himself being happy doing anything else.

He sucked in a long, deep breath and puffed it out between his flapping lips, staring into the distance, between the last few shacks on the outskirts of town, beyond the olive groves and laurels, into the sky. A bird, a black silhouette, was gliding high and free. He watched it swoop and glide, tracked it as it danced through the sky. It hovered, swooped, and vanished.

He thought on what his father had said about the whores. It pained him to admit it, even to himself, but the old man was right. He could whore his way to lance corporal; getting that far was a breeze. Before,

52

he'd been a private soldier, a nobody, not a penny left to his name after he'd frittered his wages away each month. He'd had lots of time and not much money. But he had a rank now, more money, less time, and the beginnings of a career. Maybe the ladies of Dilan Street had seen the last of him, he concluded. For now.

7. Boredom Breeds Mischief

Location: Vornston, Vorn, Gemini (Planet M69245)
Earth Year: 2040

Eliza sat at her dressing table, her chin leaning on her hands, elbows propped on the mahogany, gazing out of the window. She'd opened it to let in the breeze – what little of it there was. It was warm for the time of year, and still. Her room was high in the palace with lots of windows; it tended to get hot late in the day if the shutters were left open and the servants hadn't bothered to shut them. It was early in the year; she supposed it just hadn't occurred to them.

It would be dinner time in a few hours; another round of getting dressed up and going to sit with her parents and siblings and a load of boring nobles, probably. Her maid would be along soon to start preening her. She was bored of being preened like a porcelain doll and trying to feign interest in the arrogant lords. She was bored of the cocksure young men who were constantly trying to get into her good graces, normally after her older sister had rejected them.

She gazed past the soldiers who strolled along the top of the palace wall and out across the white rendered buildings of Vornston with their red terracotta roofs, and found herself staring at the birds that circled above the city.

Somewhere below, steel clashed with steel. Soldiers training, she presumed. She thought about sword-fighting and the last time she'd done it; she must have been eleven or twelve, but she hadn't kept at it. Her father was happy for her to continue, but the other noble girls teased her for it. They'd called her a tomboy; they'd said it was for the men to learn such skills. She'd stopped.

She thought about hunting. About riding out into the mountains with her brother and the sons of the nobles. About her skill with a bow, and how she had been able to hit a bird in flight at three hundred paces without magic. About the thrill of the chase when she joined the royal hunt and galloped across fields, through woodlands, and over streams in pursuit of a boar. She didn't do that anymore either. She'd been about thirteen the last time she'd done that, before she feigned interest in fashion, gossip, and the latest hairstyles in a vain attempt to fit in with the daughters of the other nobles.

Now she was eighteen, and the other girls were mostly betrothed. Some were married already. They talked of nothing but their weddings and their future castles or manor houses. How many children they'd have or how they planned to run their households. Tedium.

Eliza was lucky, in some ways. Her parents might be the queen and the prince consort of Vorn, and her marriage to the right person may have strategic benefits to the country, but despite pressure from their advisors and other nobles, her parents had been clear. Eliza could marry who and when she liked. And she had no plans to get married any time soon.

Someone knocked on the door.

'Come in,' Eliza called, turning lazily to see who it was.

The door creaked open. She was greeted by the smiling face of Alora, her cousin. Alora was the daughter of her mother's sister; they'd grown up together and she was closer to her than she was to her own sister, Hellenia. Unlike Eliza, Alora had shown little interest in swords or hunting. Indeed, Alora's fascination with all things girly was half the reason Eliza stopped doing that stuff. Recently, Alora seemed to have grown up and tired of the palace gossip and dreary conversations they endured every day. She had no desire to start sword-fighting, but she was certainly after excitement.

Eliza returned her cousin's smile. As always, she looked immaculate. Her long, simple day dress was trimmed with lace and was tailored beautifully to her womanly figure. Her black hair had been tamed into sleek curls and sat elegantly upon her head. Her naturally bronze complexion was set off beautifully by the hues of turquoise in her gown. Eliza shook her head slightly. Alora was certainly her mother's daughter.

Alora looked disapprovingly at her cousin. 'You're wearing breeches again, Eliza,' Alora said.

Eliza glanced down at her attire as if she didn't know what she was wearing. She looked at the cotton trousers and her loose linen shirt, turned to her cousin, and shrugged. 'So?'

'Those are men's clothes!'

'So?'

'What if someone sees you?'

'Like you?'

'You surely aren't going out anywhere like that, are you?'

Eliza sighed. 'No. I was seeing if they still fit. Doesn't seem like I've grown an awful lot since my early teens. If I wanted to go hunting again...'

Alora rolled her eyes. 'Really – you want to go hunting?'

'Why not? It's got to be more fun than hanging round here. Some of the lesser noble women do it, and even mother, on occasion.'

'Yes, and they do it wearing dresses! Riding dresses!'

'Sooo impractical.'

Alora smiled. 'You'll never be a lady, will you? Not in the heart.' She strolled over to Eliza's bed and took a seat on the mattress. Eliza shuffled her chair round to face her.

'Nope. I tried. I really did! It's not for me, I'm afraid.'

'Do you ever plan to marry?'

'Probably, eventually.'

'Do you think you'll find a man who will be happy for you to wear breeches? In public?' Alora's face was serious. Eliza couldn't help but laugh at the genuine concern in her voice.

'Oh Alora,' she chuckled, 'I have no idea. I don't think a man like Father – or even your father – will care one way or the other.' She paused, and her humour faded. 'But they aren't Geminian, are they? There's no one else like them in this place.'

'My father might tolerate it, but my mother would never permit it!'

'Your mother is Geminian.'

'So is yours.'

'Not really, she mostly grew up on Earth, remember? She has some very different ideas to your mother about what a young lady should be like.'

'Yes, and look how it's made you turn out.' Alora looked her cousin up and down again, her face still disapproving.

Eliza couldn't help but laugh again.

'Are you bored, Alora?' Eliza asked, after her attack of the giggles abated.

Alora looked puzzled. 'Right now? Your company isn't that tedious,' she said, with a half-smile.

'No, I don't mean right now. I mean in general. I mean with life. You're lucky, like me. No one is pushing you to get married—'

'I'm sure Mother would if Father let her. She is constantly trying to suggest suitors...' Alora interjected.

'Yes, I know your mother wants you to get married, but it's normally fathers who insist on it. They are the ones who do the bargaining and find the match to suit their business interests or to build family allegiances. Your father isn't about to do that though, is he?'

'No...'

'Exactly. Whatever your mother might *want* you to do, you're not about to be *made* to do anything, are you?'

'I guess not.'

'That gives us options. And options are difficult. If we knew our destiny was to marry whoever our parents told us to and make the best of it, that's what I'd do. I'd make the best of it. But it's not the case, is it? I'm allowed to do what I want, within reason. And it's hard!'

'Are you saying you want to be made to marry?' asked Alora, perplexed.

'No! Of course not. I'm just saying, because I can do what I want, it's too hard to decide. I find myself paralysed with indecision. And bored!'

'Oh. I understand. I'm bored too, I guess,' she conceded. 'I used to always think I wanted to be a healer, like my mother. She spends her days helping the poor and I'd go and help her, and it does feel nice to help people, but it's not terribly exciting, is it?'

'Exactly. Let's consider that you were the daughter of a healer, just a healer, and not the niece of the queen. You'd have grown up knowing you too would be a healer. You'd have known it would be your career since you were a girl, as long as your father didn't want to marry you off. Either way, your options would have been fixed from an early age. And you'd know what to expect in life.'

'I suppose...' Alora bit her lip and looked around the room in thought. 'You're a bad influence, Eliza,' she said at last.

'Me? Why?'

'Because you say things that make me think. I'm not sure I realised I was bored until you pointed it out, but you're right, I am. I don't want to be a healer, it's what my mother wants. I'd always been more interested in other kinds of magic – telekinesis or even portal magic. I could be a palace sorcerer if I trained more in those kinds of things. I could ask father…'

'Aha! You see what I mean? Options make you miserable. And bored.'

'I'm not sure I'm miserable.'

'Give it time.' Eliza grinned.

Alora returned the gesture and shook her head in mock despair.

'Our futures will take longer to work out than we have time for before dinner. How about we think of something to brighten up our evening? Play some kind of trick on Lord Bannavir's son over dinner? He's lecherous, he needs teaching a lesson,' Alora suggested.

'Mm, tempting. Certainly an option…' Eliza twisted back towards the window and rested her chin on her hand in thought. 'How about something more dramatic?'

'What have you got in mind?'

Eliza was sure she could detect a hint of excitement in her cousin's voice, and she turned back to face her with a mischievous grin. 'Have you ever been to a pub?'

'A pub?'

'Yes, a public house? A place serving beer and wine. Ordinary folk hang out there?'

'I know what a pub is!' Alora snapped. 'Why the heck would you want to go there?'

'We spend our lives surrounded by nobles,' Eliza slumped in her chair. 'The closest thing we get to ordinary folk are our servants, who are so institutionalised they don't count, and of course anyone we meet when we are on duty – for you when you're healing, for me when I'm doing visits. But that doesn't count, they know who we are, and they are so deferential and courteous it's not the same as *really* meeting them.'

'As soon as you step foot in a pub, they will see your clothes and know you are noble. They won't treat you as someone who is ordinary.'

Eliza tutted. 'We wouldn't go in our normal clothes. I'll get my maid to bring us some ordinary clothes and we can sneak out. We can both do cloaking magic – no one will have a clue.'

Alora sat in silence, apparently considering the idea. Eliza knew every fibre of her well-brought-up being would be telling her it was a terrible idea. She also knew her cousin had a mischievous side; she got it from her father. And she certainly knew what he would have done in her position.

'Fine. Let's do it,' Alora said at last.

Eliza smiled at her naughtily.

8. Power Source

Location: Australian desert, in the vicinity of Alice Springs, Earth (Planet B13536)

Piercing howls of agony filled the room. A somehow strangely satisfying noise to hear, a pleasant chorus to accompany the gratifying sight of another man's anguish. Aran leant against the wall and watched, with folded arms and crossed legs, and a thin smile gouging a widening line in his cheeks. Another fingernail detached, a shower of tiny drops of blood sprayed in a fine mist across the once pristinely white room. Sarah took this one quickly, she had speeded up, whether through pity or boredom, Aran wasn't sure, and he cared not. Short and sharp or slow and steady, the result was the same. Pain, lots of it. The simplest way to get answers, the best way to deliver a lesson.

Until he'd met Sarah, Aran had never realised that watching torture could be as exhilarating as doing it yourself. Especially when it was done by a woman, a woman whose every sadistic smile caused the hairs on his spine to stand on end. A woman as ruthless as he was, who shared his disdain for emotional weakness and his indifference to the suffering of others. Who would use whatever talents she had to survive and to thrive, from her heaving bosom and plump red lips to her own special talent for merciless cunning. She was a rare one – there was not another one like her on Gemini, probably not even on Earth.

His eyes followed her every curve. Her tanned skin was splattered with drops of blood, chest heaving and arms straining as she made ready to take another nail. He followed her rippling triceps to her delicate fingers. One hand firmly pinned down the victim's hand, the other was gripping the bloody pliers. The man she held barely struggled. He was tied down and there was no way for him to escape. He didn't whimper between pulls. He didn't beg, he didn't cry – he was taking it remarkably well.

The man strapped to the table in the basement of Aran's mansion was a drug runner named Kyle. He was young, in his early twenties. Despite his youth, until now he'd been a reliable type. He always delivered, and had a knack for passing through Darwin or Cairns without attracting too much attention. On this occasion, something had not gone to plan; he'd allowed himself to be mugged, or so he said. He'd returned without drugs or money, and had thrown himself on Aran's mercy. He had balls at least.

'That's the last one,' Sarah said as she took his thumbnail. A rasping gasp of breath hissed through her grinning teeth. 'Shall I start on his toes? Or how about his teeth? He can spare a few of those.'

The splatters of blood trickled into the enticing valley between her breasts. He tracked a droplet into the shadowy gap and grew hard. He licked his lips in aroused anticipation; some things were more fun than watching torture. He was in a good mood today. The ballsy idiot who had come crawling back would get a warning this time. Drug runners, like reliable staff, were hard to come by in these parts. It wouldn't do to scare every misfortunate idiot with an otherwise good record away. He'd let him earn back his losses. His fingernails would grow back, and Aran would leave it at that.

He considered her question, 'No. Let him go.'

'You sure?' Her musical Australian accent sang its soft tones in his ears.

'Yes,' he replied, his face saying everything else she needed to hear.

She unbuckled the straps. Aran grabbed the scruff of Kyle's neck and pulled his face close to his own.

'Just your nails, this time, Kyle. Next time I'll take your balls. Now fuck off.' He thrust the man back onto the bench. His head smacked into the solid wood, but he didn't cry out. He rolled swiftly to one side and fell onto his feet. He rubbed his bruised head with his bleeding hand as he staggered through the doorway.

Sarah shut the door and locked it. She looked at Aran hungrily, pouting her plump lips and flicking her trailing blonde locks with a sharp jolt of her head. She ran, jumped, and gripped him with her solid but slender thighs and set her plump lips to work, massaging his face with eager kisses, licking, sucking, and chewing until the blood flowed.

A stinging gash in his lip, a chilling tingle of pleasure. She'd made the first move; the game had started early this time. Aran thrust her down and slapped her face, hard. Her head snapped to the side as she toppled to the concrete floor. Her deft hands broke her fall. She spun back to face him with narrowed eyes as her roving tongue cleaned smeared blood from her teeth.

'Naughty girl,' he hissed through a wicked grin.

She flicked up her foot, sturdy boot landing a heavy thrust in his unsuspecting balls. He bent double. Pain shot through his groin, and he grew harder. Pain from Sarah was exciting.

She jumped to her feet with cat-like grace, grabbed his shoulders, and yanked him towards her. She half chewed, half kissed his neck. He reached a searching hand down her skin-tight leggings and squeezed until she squealed. She bit his neck hard. He pulled back at the pain, his neck throbbing, croaking out gasps as the warm blood trickled down his neck.

Sarah stared at him with wide blue eyes, arms folded beneath her breasts, thrusting them up. Aran snatched at her hands, yanked them apart, and grabbed at her T-shirt, tearing it from her chest and exposing her lacy bra. She reached behind her back and unclasped it, stepping forwards and pressing herself against him. He couldn't wait any longer. He wrapped his arms around her and grabbed her buttocks, lifted her slender form, and dropped her on the table. She shuffled back as he tugged away her leggings and lay still, naked, panting, her perfect body insatiably enticing. He yanked at his clothes with frenzied fervour and threw his naked self into her waiting arms. Skin on skin and sticky sweat on splattered blood, throbbing loins in frantic thrusts, moans of pleasure and carnal grunts.

***

They sat side by side at the edge of the windowless room, their backs against the wall, their naked bottoms on the cold concrete floor. They rested, panting. Aran was enjoying the moment. He was thinking about how far he'd come since the first day he'd met Sarah, the day she'd tried to steal his truck. He recalled the moment a few days later when she'd got the better of him.

She was a clever one; she knew there was something different about Aran. She had planned his capture, persuaded him to work for Vinnie, and helped him topple the drugs baron and take his place.

She knew he had magic. He'd told her and she'd believed him. He hadn't told many – he knew most others would think he talked bollocks. Most people didn't know how Aran had managed to get the better of Vinnie, how he'd used his power to manipulate and maim, to infiltrate and coerce, but they didn't care. They knew he was the man at the top of the tree, and it was all they gave a shit about.

And now that was where Aran found himself. De facto ruler of central Australia. Five years after he'd landed in Darwin, he commanded most of the county's interior. He owned the drugs factories and controlled the supply. He had authority over everyone on his patch. They paid him tribute, citizens and business owners alike, and he ensured a degree of protection and order remained.

He sold his drugs to the coastal exporters. He even managed to sell some on the streets under the noses of the barons who ruled the cities. He ran his cartel with an iron fist, with brutality, like he'd run his Kingdom in Gemini. That was why he was successful now, and why the lodge failed in Kenya. In Kenya, you couldn't treat people like that; there was the rule of law and the police. Some cops were for sale, but many weren't. And the guests had certain expectations too. Here, the law was what Aran decided it was, and he was the king of his own empire once again.

Sarah squeezed his thigh and gave him an unexpectedly gentle kiss on the cheek. 'Come on, we've got shit to do.' She tugged at his arm.

He smiled at her, pulled her towards him, and placed a tender kiss on her alluring lips. 'Once more? Gently this time?'

'We don't have time. I said I'd meet Stark at three – we're gonna chat about the men and...' she glanced at her watch. 'Shit, it's five to, and I've gotta get a shower.'

He let her go. She gathered her clothes off the floor and pulled on her leggings and bra. Her T-shirt was beyond repair, but he knew she wouldn't care – she had others. She was wearing enough to be decent.

Aran stayed on the ground as he watched her leave. She turned and blew a kiss at him before she pulled the door closed behind her. Aran smiled to himself, captivated by her beauty and her strength. He used to think his mother was strong; she wasn't. He'd discovered it was weakness that had made her leave Gemini. She'd seen some message from her parents and cried all the way home.

Sarah was different. She was a survivor, like him. She didn't squirm at doing what was needed. She didn't waste time and energy on compassion, she got on with things. She took what she wanted and did what she had to do. In this place, it was the only way to thrive.

***

After his aching desire faded, he realised he was actually glad Sarah was gone for the afternoon – he had something he wanted to do without her. He'd abandoned his quest to find the source of his magic since Sarah captured him five years ago. He hadn't been able to pursue it at first, as he'd been detained, then forced to work for Vinnie. After a while, he worked for him because he wanted to. He'd found a job he enjoyed. He'd found his forte and he had enough magic to do what needed to be done. Later, with Sarah's help, he'd killed Vinnie and taken his cartel. That was a couple of years ago. Now he'd made it secure, and he could afford to leave. He was ready to continue his search.

Sarah was his second in command, and would take up the mantle in his absence. He'd just let her know she had to take over for a bit – she would do it without even asking where he was going.

He stood, gathered his clothes, and went out into the shadowy corridor, up to the grand, open hallway, bare feet slapping up the polished oak staircase, and on towards his bedroom. He didn't care who saw him nude.

When he'd showered and changed, he found Fred, grabbed some supplies, and set off towards the south-west.

***

Fred had stayed loyal all these years. He'd been worth what he'd paid him and more. In the early days of working for Vinnie, a couple of words of advice from the big man here and there were invaluable. Aran avoided putting his foot wrong on a number of occasions because of Fred, and the man had saved Aran from being whacked himself more times than he could count.

Aran paid him well. He wanted to keep this one, and he was still his driver of choice. He knew how to drive a car, use a gun, and keep his mouth shut.

Fred and Aran drove in silence. The road took them south-west, then south, through the never-ending barren expanse of orange dust dotted with tufts of dying grass. Past the scattered trees with stunted tops, and distant mounds of rolling hills, tracking the magic. As they drove, Aran could feel it and see it flowing through the air in a weaving line of twisting energy. It pulled west as they drove south, but there was a turning, at last, and, back on track, they continued.

'It looks like you're taking us to Ayers Rock,' Fred said, the first word's he'd spoken since they had set off.

'Ayers Rock?'

'Yeah, that big lump of sandstone in the middle of Australia? Pretty famous.'

'I've heard of Ayers Rock!' Aran lied. He had no idea how he'd missed it.

'Either Ayers Rock or the west coast,' Fred continued. 'Not sure you want to go there though, most of it's a wasteland. South-west is nuked to fuck and the rest of it's been shelled by the Chinese or the warlords.'

'I don't think we'll be going that far. I have a feeling we're close.'

'Close to what?'

'To what I want to find!' Aran snapped. He'd worked with Fred long enough that the big man knew when it was time to shut up. They continued to bump along the road in silence.

It was early autumn, and the days were still long. Dusk had almost fallen when Aran started to feel the direction of the power flow shifting. He looked at his phone. He was tracking where Ayers Rock was on Google Maps and as their route took them past its northern edge, the magical stream veered to the south. The road ahead ran that way too — no need to go off-road and bump over the dirt and rocks just yet.

He read about Ayers Rock on Wikipedia as they drove. It was such an odd geological feature, strange, sticking up like it did in the middle of the otherwise featureless desert. It reminded him of the rock in which the last wormhole had been, except this one seemed an awful lot bigger.

He read that the place was sacred to the Aboriginals; they had a different name for it. Uluru, they called it, and it was special to them, or it used to be. It had been a tourist attraction too, apparently. He learnt that the strange folk of Earth liked to come and stare at big rocks in the middle of nowhere – the oddities of Earth culture never ceased to amaze him at times. There were no tourists in Australia anymore and the natives stayed away from what passed for civilisation these days.

According to the internet, the place was abandoned, and when they arrived, it looked like the internet was right. There were a few decaying relics of a time long gone, and signs for viewing areas; Aran read the words with a snigger. Why would anyone want to stop and view something they could see from their car window? There were signs for hotels, some for paths and infrastructure – a cultural centre. Whatever that was. But it was a building, and it was empty and would be a more comfortable place to spend the night than the truck. With darkness having well and truly fallen and a creeping weariness sucking out the last of his energy, he decided they would stop and rest. He could accomplish little without daylight anyway.

***

He woke up grumpy. He'd found a couch to sleep on in what looked like a staffroom, but it was short, with hard arms. He'd grown used to his large comfortable bed and slept terribly, curled up on the couch.

He flopped himself onto the floor and dragged his clothes onto his drowsy limbs, then sat and slumped back while his groggy brain ambled towards a state of alertness. He was gasping for his morning coffee but as his mind regained control of his thoughts, an eager sense of excitement gripped him. Magic. It swamped him like it never had before on this stinking planet. It swarmed and it flowed, out and away from the big rock he knew loomed in the desert not far away. The tingling prickle of magic shook his drowsy body awake; he pulled himself to his feet and stalked purposefully down the corridor towards the exit.

He edged out into the dazzling sun, pulling his sunglasses over his squinting eyes as he blinked to find focus. Dusty ground, scattered trees with tiny leaves – but beyond, towering high above the flat terrain, the orange mass of rock erupted into the air. Tall and very wide, red and smooth. Blackened streaks of shadowy grooves sliced down its flanks and vanished into the sea of trees dotted round its base like matchsticks. It looked strange, dark and shaded as the sun rose behind it. The streams of power swirled over it and through every surface, like streaky tendrils of slithering light. He watched the gentle ripples and elegant swirls in awe. He couldn't help himself – he felt drawn towards it, so he started to walk.

It was further than he thought, and grew bigger with every step along the road. He cut onto a path that followed the rock's southern edge, tracking the streams of magic as they flowed along the tall, smooth cliffs, swirling and swaying. They danced towards him, and he followed them upstream as they bent round the rock into a steep-sided gulley. As he rounded the water-carved gash in the monolithic rock, he was almost blinded by the magic. It intensified into a blazing extravaganza of glare. Every leaf growing on the trees shimmered with it; every rock on the ground was wrapped in it. It rippled down the stream and gushed through the air.

He kept walking. He was in the shade, but he hadn't noticed. His feet had found a metal grid; he hadn't noticed that either. He followed the power until he hit something – a barrier. He stopped and shook his head free of its focus on magic. His eyes saw daylight again.

Before him was a man-made fence. He was on a viewing platform, a place for tourists, he assumed. In front of him was a pool of water, but he didn't need to stare at the magic to feel its power. It was all-pervasive. A small stream filled the pool, and he sensed the energy swirling in its currents.

He vaulted the fence and splashed into the pond. Cool water drenched his legs and engulfed his feet. The power in the water prickled at his skin like static electricity, tingling and teasing. He closed his eyes and drew it towards him, sucking it in through his feet and into his chest. He gathered it there, and his thundering heart quivered with the swell of energy. He'd never felt so powerful, at least not on Earth. The sensation was incredible. He longed to release the force, to blast something, to show the world what he could do.

Footsteps. Aran spun on the spot, his eyes shot open as he scanned the gulley, his glare found Fred, he must have followed him. The big man was leaning on the barrier with a look of perplexed intrigue. Aran squeezed his fingers into white-knuckled fists and let the magic swell. A blurry haze suppressed his sight; the magic reappeared. He yearned to release it, to kill. He raised a hand, uncurled his fists, and stopped. He shook his head, cleared the fuzz – sense got there just in time.

Fred was useful and Aran didn't want to drive back himself. There was no need to show what he could do yet. He had found a reservoir of magic, and he could take it with him. He'd have to return with barrels and take them back to Alice Springs with him. Or better still, send someone else out to do it for him.

With the magic stored at his fingertips, he could do much more. Start to take the cities. Take his power with him and advance north and take Darwin, then Cairns. Stretch to the south and take what scraps of land were held by the Freedom Fighters. He could have it all. He could be king, not just of a city or a cartel, not even a country – he'd be the king of a continent.

9. A Sword Above The Rest

Location: Army training area, north of Tannel, Vorn, Gemini (Planet M69245)

The summers in Vorn were hot and dry, especially in the south, but Mark had grown used to the heat. Or perhaps it was a hell of a lot easier to handle when you could travel everywhere on horseback wearing a loose linen shirt. When you didn't have forty pounds of body armour and webbing plus your rifle and helmet as you plodded through the deserts of Afghanistan, you could almost enjoy being stupidly warm.

'What time does the assault start?' Alfor asked Mark.

'You're asking me? You're normally the master of timings.' Mark smiled. Lord Alfor Unwin was the Master of Sword; he was supposed to know this stuff.

'It's your visit. I just came for the ride. They asked for you, remember?' Mark was the commander of the queen's Armed Forces, so this kind of thing happened a lot.

'And when they ask for me, they get you by default. Everyone knows we come as a pair.'

Alfor spluttered out a laugh. 'Be that as it may, on this occasion, I can't recall the time they told us.'

'You're getting old, mate – showing your age! Shouldn't you be thinking about retirement soon?'

'I'm not sixty yet!' Alfor replied indignantly.

'We kick the soldiers out at forty-five.'

'That's you gone too then, by your logic. Long gone.'

'Enough with the *long*. I'm only fifty-four, still a spring chicken.'

Alfor twisted his head to the side, looking at him curiously. His old friend was used to Mark's odd use of language, and after a couple of decades of friendship, he still enjoyed perplexing Alfor with old sayings from Earth. Mark had an accent no one could place, and he was an enigma to Alfor. He had never told him where he was really from, and Alfor accepted the mystery eventually.

'It's the sergeant's cadre we're seeing today, right?' Alfor asked, changing the subject.

'Bloody hell, Alfor,' Mark shook his head in mock disgust, 'You aren't on the ball today, are you?'

'Told you, I'm along for the ride. This jaunt down to Tannel is your gig. They wrote to you to come visit, not me.'

Mark detected a hint of indignance in his tone. 'Aww, feeling left out this time, are you?'

'You'd think the course commander would write to the damn Master of Sword about an awesome swordsman, wouldn't you?' Alfor was ruffled this time. Mark's amusement was growing.

'Maybe Captain Tawbrid got confused, or maybe he thinks you're past it, mate.'

'Fuck off!'

Mark chuckled. 'Sorry,' he said. 'Uhm.' He cleared his throat and tried to regain a degree of professionalism. 'Yep, it's the sergeant's cadre. There's a corporal called Bramston that Tawbrid mentioned. To be honest, it was just a passing comment in a letter I asked him to write about how the cadre was going. With the courses having been up and running for a couple of years, I wanted to get the cadre commander's point of view of how the course was shaping up. I didn't tell him I was going to visit it. I didn't want the bells and whistles. I wanted a look at the exercise phase and thought I'd take the chance to get eyes on the corporal he mentioned while I'm here.'

'Ah, that answers why you have been secretive about this part of our visit to the training academy. I did wonder.'

'The best way to keep things low-key is to not tell anyone.'

'Not even me? I'm hurt,' Alfor said, somehow combining a frown with a grin.

'Yeah right – if I thought you'd give a damn, you know I'd have said.'

'Fair point. What are the princesses up to this morning? Was that the real reason for your secrecy? To keep them away?'

Mark sighed; his head flopped forwards. 'Is it that obvious I don't want them around?'

'To me it is. But I'm probably the only one who would openly question why the heck you'd want two young women in tow on a visit to our forces in Tannel anyway. Everyone else would be too scared to mention it.'

Mark turned his head, cocked it to one side and frowned. 'I'm not scary!' he protested.

'Not to me, or Alora, but to everyone else...'

'It's women, mate. Got a soft spot there. The wife and Alora; both of them have me wrapped around their little fingers and there's nothing I can do about it. I'm glad our army's a boys-only club. If there were women in it, I'd be screwed.'

Alfor laughed. 'Did Alora bully you into coming?' he teased.

'Yes,' Mark conceded. 'What can I say? I'm weak.'

They continued to ride along the rolling hills above the city of Tannel, a port city on the south coast of Vorn. The place was well located for the army training centre Mark had founded. With the navy also based here, it provided a perfect staging point to launch operations overseas, if necessary.

Mark swayed back and forth as he rode along the track, enjoying the pleasant sea breeze, which took the worst of the oppressive heat away. He let his mind wander, reflecting on all he'd achieved on Gemini in the two decades he'd lived here – on the faraway planet most on Earth didn't even know existed. The academy he'd built, the selection processes he'd put in place, training programmes he'd designed. He'd turned Vorn's rag-tag bunch of half-trained civilians into a professional fighting force.

Mark had ended up on Gemini almost by accident. He'd been an officer in the British Army when he lived on Earth, a company commander at the Infantry Training Centre in Catterick. But his old friend Tom appeared at the local courthouse, accused of being absent without leave for two years. He told him he'd been on another planet and said he was going back. Mark followed out of curiosity.

Twenty odd years later, he still had no idea how he, a good-for-nothing kid from the biggest sink estate in Manchester, ended up marrying a princess, having kids with titles, and being made a lord. He rubbed his clean-shaven chin in thought. It probably had something to do with being best mates with the husband of the queen. He'd never have guessed what the girlfriend of the idiot he'd dragged through officer training would turn out to be. He chuckled. He'd gone from nicking cars to—

Somewhere in the distance, swords clashed.

'Shit, we're late!' Mark announced. He jammed his heels into his horse's flanks and set off at a gallop. Alfor followed.

They stopped on a slope at the edge of a forest block, trying to look inconspicuous. They were wearing light and simple clothes today – the weather called for it – but they also didn't want the sergeants-in-training to get spooked by the presence of senior officers. Their usual bling would scream who they were from a mile away.

They weren't as late as they thought. The instructors had been doing a demonstration; the real fun was yet to begin.

***

'Who's that over there?' Corporal Draklin said to no one in particular, as he waited for the attack to begin.

'Who?' Corporal Bremmer pushed his way forward and looked at where Draklin was pointing. 'Ah, I see 'em – those two blokes on horses?'

'Yep, them.'

'Probably some bored officers out for some entertainment,' Bremmer suggested.

'They don't look like officers.'

'Oh, they're officers, alright. Look at their horses. Finer beasts than they give to the non-commissioned ranks, and see how they sit in their saddles? They are holding themselves like they're used to looking down on common folk like us.'

'Give over, you can't tell that from here,' Draklin jibed.

'I think he's right,' another corporal added. 'The one on the right, that's Lord Unwin – the Master of Sword?'

'I know who Lord fucking Unwin is, arsehole,' Bremmer replied crassly. 'How do you know the bastard so well to recognise him from here?'

'I had a posting at the palace in Vorn. He was coming and going all the time, and the other guy…' He squinted to try to get a clearer view. 'Yeah, I'm pretty sure the other one is Lord Harrison.'

'Commander of the queen's Armed Forces and the Master of Sword? Watching our little cadre?' Draklin said incredulously. 'Not a chance. You've been out in the sun too long.'

'How about them? Who are those two lovely ladies?' Another corporal pointed towards the distant figures of two young women cantering over to the men by the forest. 'You lot can argue all you like over whether those men are officers, but those women are definitely high-born. Look at their dresses. No ordinary girl wears that kind of garb to go for a ride.'

'Fuck me, it's the princesses,' the corporal from the palace insisted.

'Which princesses?' Bremmer asked.

'Princess Alora and Eliza. The pair of 'em are inseparable. Always together. I'd definitely not get those two mixed up anywhere. I spent far too many hours staring at those beauties.'

'If they are the princesses, you might be right about the men. Makes sense they'd pop out to see Alora's daddy. Can't see 'em visiting any commoners in a place like this.'

'Platoon, ready!' Bramston bellowed the order across his unit. He'd been appointed platoon commander for the final attack.

The corporals jumped into action. They straightened their lines, drew their swords, and made ready to march.

'Those lords are here to see Bramston, I'd put money on it,' Bremmer muttered to Draklin.

'Barmston? Isn't he the guy who made sure you marked time for years at the academy? After he humiliated you in front of the recruits and you went to whack him?'

Bremmer glared at Draklin. The bitter memory of the little shit who'd set his career back years was still an open wound. He'd learned to hide his animosity – if he hadn't, he would have been kicked out by now, and there weren't a huge number of career options for people like himself.

He worked hard to suppress the bitter memory and replied, 'The very same arsehole.'

'Is it time to get revenge? How 'bout you make the fucker look bad in front of his little audience?'

'Those days are behind me, and I'd never get away with it anyway.'

'You wouldn't, but I might. I owe you one, remember? Don't you think it's time I repaid the favour?' Draklin replied, with a nasty grin.

His grin was contagious. Bremmer couldn't help but return it.

***

Mark was staring at the soldiers and getting increasingly frustrated at the time it was taking for the instructors to get the exercise going.

'We've got company,' Alfor announced.

Mark turned and looked over his shoulder to see where Alfor was indicating. 'Fuck. That's our cover blown.'

Princesses Alora and Eliza were cantering towards them.

'Thought you said you didn't tell them where you were going today?' Alfor queried.

'No. But I probably should have done. I could have told them to stay away. You know they can track my location, right?'

'Ah, now you mention it, of course, but sometimes I forget they are sorcerers. I suppose it stops you from worrying about them gallivanting around the countryside on their own though.'

'You might think so, but don't underestimate their ability to get themselves into mischief.'

The thunder of hooves grew lounder as the young women approached.

'Hello, Father!' Alora greeted Mark as she pulled her horse to a halt in front of his. He was trying to hide his irritation at her unannounced presence. As she walked her horse to the side of his and kissed him on the cheek, his annoyance evaporated. He couldn't stay angry at his daughter.

'Good morning, Uncle, Lord Unwin.' Eliza arrived soon after. Her horse wasn't as swift as Alora's.

'Good morning to you both, Your Highnesses,' Alfor greeted them politely. 'What brings you out to the training area today? Fancy a show of a little fighting?'

'To be honest, we didn't know there was an exercise on. We were out for a ride when Alora noticed Uncle Mark nearby,' Eliza said to the Master of Sword, 'and we thought we'd come and say hello.'

'And you didn't notice the mass of soldiers near us and think we might be on business?' Mark growled. 'I said to stay away from our duties.'

'Oh, I, er...' Eliza's cheeks filled with pink as she bit her lip in embarrassment.

'Father,' Alora said playfully, 'don't be such a bore. We won't get in the way, but if you want us to leave, then say. We can make ourselves scarce easily enough.'

Mark sighed. Beaten by his daughter again. 'No, it's fine,' he replied grudgingly, 'stay if you want. Now you're here, it makes little difference anyway. We've come to watch a field exercise in the sergeant's cadre – there's a young corporal we want to look at. They're about to start and hopefully it should be a good show.'

At last, Mark heard the call of the platoon commander. Corporal Bramston had been put in command of the friendly forces. The cadre was split in half and the other group was playing the enemy. He was beginning to rally his troops.

Mark, Alfor and the two princesses sat in their saddles at the edge of a copse of trees. All of them now had their eyes glued on the milling mass of soldiers on the slopes below their vantage point.

'Do you think the enemy have spotted the flanking forces he's hidden in the dead ground?' Mark barely heard his old friend as he studied the tactics being played out ahead.

'Sorry mate,' he said after a brief pause, 'um, flanking forces, where?' Mark stood up in his stirrups for a better look. 'Oh, nope, don't think so, looking at how they are organising their own formation. Clever lad,' he said with a grin.

The attack was soon under way. The enemy charged, while the friendly forces held their ground, shield wall at the ready. At the last minute, Bramston's platoon retreated.

'He's drawing them up the hill – he's stopped on the slope.' Alfor announced excitedly.

'Is it better to fight on a slope, Lord Unwin? Does it not make it more difficult to balance?' Eliza wondered.

'If you are fighting downhill, it puts gravity on your side. Look at how they are using their shield wall to push them back. There are less of them because of the men he hid in that ditch over there, but he still has the strength to force them back because of the position he's taken.'

It was starting to look like Corporal Garrad Bramston had the enemy where he wanted them: at the bottom of the slope, with a rise to their rear. He gave the nod, and a soldier at the back waved a flag on a long pole. The hidden forces attacked.

The enemy were sandwiched at the bottom of a ditch. Mark smiled to himself as he watched the trap being sprung.

Soldier after soldier was pulled from the battle as the instructors told them they were 'dead'. Any man who was hit in the right place with a convincing strike was taken from the fight. The enemy were dropping like flies.

The appointed platoon commander threw himself into the fray along with his fellow corporals. His skill with a sword was good enough that Captain Tawbrid had seen fit to write to the Lord Commander about it. Mark assumed it would hardly be a secret to the rest of the cadre. Now it looked like everyone wanted a chance to defeat him and to get the kudos of being the one who took down Corporal Bramston.

The corporal was single-handedly keeping three different attackers at bay. Dodging and swiping, no blade could touch him. He caught one soldier on the arm. His victim tried to pretend it hadn't happened, but an instructor spotted it and pulled him out. Corporal Bramston continued to fight another two with ease.

He was about to land a blow on the hip of a second opponent when something made him reel. His leg buckled; he lost his balance. One of his attackers took the advantage and lunged. Corporal Bramston swerved as he fell but didn't have time to pull his arm from his shield grip and catch his fall.

Mark realised he was still standing in his stirrup and lowered himself into his saddle as Barmston vanished amongst the crowd.

'That's the cadre commander's shining star down,' Alfor noted.

'Aye, and he was doing well. He almost had those other two and he seemed to drop,' Mark observed. 'Something's not right there.'

'An old injury? Maybe something jarred.'

'Maybe, or someone took him down. Someone who doesn't want him to shine.'

'Why would anyone do that, Father?' Alora asked.

'Some men don't like it when someone else looks good. They think it makes them look bad.'

'That's a terrible way to behave!' She looked mortified. 'Surely they should celebrate the success of their fellow soldiers.'

'You might think so, but if we've been recognised, and there is anyone down there who doesn't want to see Bramston shine, it would be all the more reason to take down the top dog. Can't have the likes of us being impressed.'

'Gosh, surely you saw he did well regardless, and you should reward him accordingly anyway? You can't let the saboteurs win, can you?'

'Actually, you can. You see, there are a few things here. First, we can't prove there was anything amiss. Maybe he had an injury, in which case, do we want to be trying to raise him up? A crippled soldier is one with a short career. Maybe he lost his balance? If he did, he's not as good a swordsman as we thought. Or maybe someone did trip him. If that's the case, the lad has some issues with his mates – he has problems building loyalty. Either way, when he went down, his chance went with him.'

***

Garrad managed to pull his shield off his arm, using all his willpower not to scream out in pain. His arm flopped onto the grass, bent in an unnatural direction. Excruciating pain radiated in jagged throbs; every thud of his heart brought a new pulse of agony. He was lying on the ground, face contorted, when he noticed the clash of swords had stopped and half the men were cheering. He dared to unscrew his eyes, and lifting his head, he looked around: the men who were cheering were his men. The enemy had been 'killed', his platoon had won.

The senior instructor spotted him on the ground. 'You alright, Bramston?'

'Sir.' Garrad winced.

'Your arm doesn't look too healthy. Think we'll need to get you to a healer – can you stand?'

'I think so.' He started to struggle to his feet. The sergeant major went behind him and hauled him up. 'Argh,' he yelled. Pain shot up his leg. He suddenly remembered the wound in his calf muscle; his throbbing arm had taken his mind off that. His legs buckled and he began to tumble but the instructor caught him.

'Got a nasty gash on your leg there. You should sit while we get that bandaged up.' He lowered him to the ground. 'Colour!' he yelled to another instructor.

'Yessir.'

'Send a runner back to camp and get a healer out here, would you? Bramston needs help.'

'Yessir.' The colour sergeant turned on his heels and went to find a suitable volunteer.

'You did a good job out there today, Bramston,' the sergeant major told him. 'Good use of ground and a solid use of tactics. You had it nailed until you dropped. Thankfully, Bremmer was able to step in and finish off the attack. I'm sure you realised your side still won.'

'Bremmer,' Garrad growled through gritted teeth. He looked at the pool of blood under the gash on his calf. 'Fucking arsehole,' he muttered.

'What was that, Bramston?'

Garrad looked at the sergeant major, not sure what to say. The sound of beating hooves broke the tension. He turned to see the mysterious riders who had been watching by the forest approaching. Two men followed by two women. He'd spotted them earlier but paid them no heed, he had been distracted with preparing for the battle.

The sergeant major's face dropped into an expression of abject fear; he recognised the approaching riders. As they drew closer, he seemed to catch himself and snapped to attention.

'Sirs!' he barked as he threw up a salute. 'I wasn't expecting a visit, but you are most welcome. We have just finished our exercise.'

Garrad was baffled; he had no idea who these riders were. The men were dressed in ordinary clothes with the finely dressed women in tow. He was desperately trying to work it out. The senior instructor was clearly nervous of them – they had to be senior officers to get him so ruffled. The men seemed to have the bearing of officers. One had dark hair and olive skin, the typical complexion of someone native to Vorn. The other had green eyes and a decent tan, but looked like he was from somewhere further north.

'Sergeant Major, at ease, please,' the olive-skinned man said softly.

'Thank you, sir.' The sergeant major dropped his arm and clasped his hands behind his back.

A salute, and he called him sir? Definitely an officer, Garrad thought.

'We were watching the attack – a very well executed endeavour, I must say. You have trained your men well.'

'Thank you, sir,' the sergeant major replied.

The green-eyed man looked towards Garrad, who was desperately trying to struggle to his feet; it wouldn't do to be on his arse in the presence of officers.

'You alright, Corporal?' the officer said in bemusement. Garrad was in so much pain he barely noticed.

'Father!' One of the women jumped off her horse and rushed towards him. 'Can't you see he's injured?'

'Yes, but…' The man was grinning, until the young woman cast him a look that wiped the grin swiftly from his face.

The other young lady had dismounted and joined her companion. 'Can you heal him?' she asked, concern rippling through her voice.

'I can.' The other woman proceeded to move to his side, and gently put her hands on his shoulders and encouraged him to lie down.

The sergeant major looked at the officers questioningly.

'Don't worry, Sergeant Major, she's a very good healer. She'll have him back on his feet in no time.'

'Of course, sir – the Princess Alora, I presume?'

'Yes, that's my daughter, and Princess Eliza too.'

Eliza was at the other side of Garrad, fussing over him and trying to make him comfortable as Alora got to work.

They were princesses? And the man was Princess Alora's father? *Shit!* He suddenly realised one of the men was Lord Harrison, the man in charge of the Army, and he had fallen on his arse in front of him. A wave of nausea washed through his gut. He took a deep breath – the air was filled with the scent of the princess's perfume, and his head swam in a dizzy haze as he battled for his brain to focus.

As his vision blurred, his hearing sharpened, and a wave of muttering erupted from the nearby soldiers. They must have overheard who the visitors were.

'Get back, the lot of you!' the sergeant major yelled. 'Colour!' he bellowed to another instructor.

'Yessir?'

'Get the men formed up and begin the march back. We will do the debrief in the barracks.'

'Yessir.'

Garrad wondered if he'd died and gone to heaven. Two of the most beautiful young women he'd ever seen were leaning over him. They wore fine dresses and delicate jewels. One had skin like cinnamon with delicate black ringlets falling from the sculptured hairstyle atop her head. The other's piercing blue eyes looked at him from between the flowing tawny locks of her un-braided hair, her twinkling stare cutting through to his core.

'What's your name?' she asked. Her soft voice seemed to purr.

Garrad suddenly forgot who he was. 'Er...'

'Er?' Eliza smiled. 'That's a funny name.' She seemed oblivious to the effect she was having on him.

'Don't tease him, Eliza,' the other princess jibed at her companion. 'My name's Alora,' she said to Garrad. 'I'm a healer and I've just used my magic to scan for injuries. I'm sorry to say your arm is broken and you have a nasty cut on your leg.' She bit her lip and forced a smile. 'You are otherwise OK. Oh, except for a bruise on your hip, it might hurt tomorrow. Would you like me to fix that too?'

'Er...' Garrad's eyes were lost in Alora's. She had dark brown eyes and a perfect complexion, and he couldn't work out which of the women was more beautiful. His mouth had gone dry. He'd lost his ability to talk; he couldn't think of the right words.

A horse snorted, and he heard a man chuckle. He turned his head to look at Lord Harrison; seeing the commander of the queen's Armed Forces didn't do anything to help his nerves.

'His name is Corporal Garrad Bramston,' the lord commander called over. 'Come on, Alora, get him patched up so we can let him get back to his duties.'

Alora twisted her graceful neck to meet her father's eye. 'Yes, Father,' she said tartly, before turning back and smiling the most beautiful smile Garrad had ever seen.

'I'm going to have to put you to sleep while I fix your arm,' she said softly, her gentle hands delicately touching his tender skin.

He nodded, his voice still lost, his head rattling with thoughts. *She's a princess, an actual princess, a gorgeous princess. I'm going to be healed by the most beautiful woman in Vorn. I'm...*

The black sheen of slumber found him.

10.   Route To Revenge

Aran had grown to love the technology of Earth. Electricity, mobile phones, the internet, decent plumbing. But he was growing increasingly frustrated at the limitations of the pneumatic drill.

His men had been at it for weeks and they were only a few hundred meters in. They'd been hacking at the soft sandstone in shifts, directed by Aran, following the course of the waves of magic whose source Aran was obsessively trying to find.

He'd taken the magic-infused water from the pool in the gulley — barrels of it. It worked as he'd hoped for a time. It gave him a boost to his strength and it stopped him getting drained quickly, but once he'd taken it, it didn't come back. The resource was drained. It turned out the water had a shelf life too; the longer his magical water was in storage, the more the power seeped away on its own. Ayers Rock was hours from Alice Springs, and it was a long way to come to keep getting fresh supplies of the water.

His appetite for more power was insatiable. The extra magic from the water was not enough; he wanted to find the source. The pool was filled from a spring emerging from the rock. The streams of energy trickled out from somewhere inside, and Aran wanted to find out where. He would drill it out. He planned to trace the course of the spring back into the sandstone. He had his men on the task, chipping away with breakers, making a tunnel big enough to walk through.

It had taken a while to get the kit he needed. Breakers were unsurprisingly rare in Australia, but he'd got some eventually. He'd set up camp in the visitor's centre, brought a generator, bribed his men to work the drills with the promise of extra pay. They hated the work, but money could make men do anything, especially in Australia.

***

The never-ending rattle of the drills had stopped. He was sitting on his own in the shade, lost in his thoughts, when Fred came to find him.

'Smithy's found something,' the big man announced.

'What?'

'It's a cave, a natural one by the looks of it. Stream's reappeared at the bottom of it but it's not quite on our line. We wanted you to come and look to see if you want to follow the cave or if you want us to carry on digging in a straight line.'

Aran glared at him – he glared at most people. He nodded and rose to his feet, setting off down the gulley towards the tunnel entrance, clambering over the piles of debris and into the pool at the tunnel mouth. He paused to strap a head torch on before he ventured into the gloom.

He stood staring into the darkness as he tuned himself in to the magical waves. They rippled towards him, like an invisible river flowing through the air. He took a few deep breaths and waded from the pool into the stream running along the tunnel floor, its tingling waters washing waves of power up his legs like pulsing charges of electricity. A little way in, the natural course of the stream veered to the side. Aran had told his men to keep digging in a straight line when they got to this point. The water carried the magic. The stream twisted and turned; he felt the source straight ahead. It made no sense to follow a meandering stream when a straight line would do.

The dry tunnel stretched on, and he kept walking, his inner sight tracking the flow of magic. The tunnel changed; he stopped. Chiselled walls became the smooth sides of a cave, and the faint sound of trickling water caught his ear. He looked down. A stream coursed along the ground ahead and disappeared into the darkness to one side. He'd come to a T-junction. His tunnel had intercepted a natural cave, albeit at a sharp angle.

He pointed his torch up the stream, its beams of light shimmering from the silky-smooth sides, mesmerised by the eerie beauty of the rippled walls carved into smooth undulations over the millennia. Wavy surfaces swayed down the passage, winding left and right and away into the darkness.

'There's a rockfall downstream,' Fred announced from behind him.

Aran almost jumped; he'd forgotten the man had followed him. He could walk surprisingly quietly for someone as big as he was. He slowly turned to face him.

'Looks pretty recent,' Fred continued. 'Water backs up, but it seeps under the rock and vanishes. It could join the spring that emerges down the tunnel. There's no way to know for sure.'

Aran nodded. 'Has anyone ventured upstream yet?'

'No, told 'em not to. Thought you might want to have a look yourself first.'

'Good. Wait here. If I'm not back in an hour, by all means try to find me.'

'No probs, boss,' Fred replied, backing into a dry stretch of tunnel before leaning against the wall and slumping to the ground. 'I'll make sure no one gets curious and heads your way before you get back.'

Aran gave a nod of acknowledgement before twisting to gaze back up the cave.

He let himself see the magic again. The river of power had become a torrent; it flooded down the cave towards him. He walked upstream and was soon heading ever deeper into the sandstone and closer to the magic.

He thought about the rockfall Fred mentioned. Had the nukes caused a tremor? Had the stream been diverted? Perhaps that was what caused the sudden release of power. He kept plodding on, but his thoughts were soon interrupted when he was almost blinded.

A wall of glaring illuminance was before him – it filled the cave, consumed it. The magic was so bright he had to snap back to seeing with his eyes. He edged forwards, the brightness gone, now only seeing the gloomy cave lit by the light from his head torch. He stretched out his hand, hoping to feel where he'd seen the wall of magic. He concentrated, used the skill he'd only learned since arriving on Earth: the ability to feel the magic.

A couple more steps, then his fingertips found something, a prickling in the air. A couple more steps and it immersed him. Every part of his body tingled; he was engulfed in a tickling blanket of power that hugged him, was all-encompassing. It danced and quivered and stroked his skin. It took the slightest effort to pull the power into his core. He drew it in – so much came so quickly, unexpectedly that he was overwhelmed. He let some go and held the rest inside.

He was energised, invigorated. He suddenly felt like he'd been nothing but a zombie before, the walking dead searching for its life force. He held out a hand, let the power flow. He made a fireball, let it grow and grow, and almost singed his own eyebrows. He pushed it forwards and basked in the heat. He closed his eyes, breathed deeply, and grinned.

The feeling of so much magic was like warmth rippling through his veins, like a shot of whiskey on a cold night or a snort of coke after a tough day. He revelled in the feeling until he'd had his fill, letting the power charge him, fill him, make him feel like the man he'd long since left behind on another world. At last, he opened his eyes and took a few steps back down the cave, just to see. He passed through the wall, and he juddered – his fireball vanished.

He glanced at his watch. Time was getting on. He wanted to explore further, and he didn't want Fred to come looking for him. He went back through the wall and made a fireball again. He turned off his head torch and continued to splash upstream.

Aran forced himself to stop feeling the power; the tingling was becoming distracting. He tried to desensitise back to the state he'd always known before he came to Earth. On Gemini, magic was just there, all around him. He'd never even noticed it unless he summoned it. When he first arrived in Kenya, he was so oblivious to it he hadn't even realised it had gone. But on Earth it was sparse, barely there. He'd learned to find what little there was, and he'd become in tune to the power. He was alive to its every flicker, wave, and ripple.

The cave rose steadily uphill; the stream bed was smooth. He kept walking but it was not much further before he saw the first shadows cast by a distant light. He waved his hand, his fireball vanished, and he edged onwards.

The cave mouth found him sooner than he'd expected; the light from the sun outside was weak. The landscape of the Australian outback that he'd left behind was dry, a sea of orange dust and reddened rocks, weedy trees and wilting grass. Quiet, dead, lifeless. Not here. Here, the roaring chorus of a thousand lives sung a thousand tunes. Chirping birds and humming bees, marching ants and howling monkeys. As he edged towards the opening the humid blast of forest air slapped him in the face.

From cool cave to stuffy heat, and air so thick it was clotted as though it could be cut with a knife.

Aran ventured out into the shady world of crowded life. Leaves and vines and towering trees, sprawling shrubs and heaving grasses. Flopping foliage drooped through every void, green on green with tall brown trunks and flashes of flowering colour.

There were buzzing flies and fluttering moths – he swatted at his sweaty cheek. He twisted and looked around. Not a splash of sky to be seen, the voluptuous canopy blocked all view of it. He couldn't tell if it was early here, late, or even midday. He closed his eyes and let his magical senses feel for the presence of the sun. Its flaming ball of energy was easy enough to find. It was low and sinking, so it was definitely dusk, yet it was noon in the land he'd left behind. He'd entered another world. And with this much magic it could only be Gemini. He was home after twenty years away – it was the only explanation.

But where in Gemini? He still had no idea. He'd never been to a place like this. There were no tropical forests in his homeland of Vorn, or even his home continent of Hosta. He recalled there were slithers of trees in the east of Thost; he'd seen them on a map. But the dwarven realm wasn't this hot and humid. He was somewhere else, and he had to find out where.

He looked for a spot to sit and concentrate, to study the world, to get his bearings, but there was nowhere clear enough to park his backside. The stream from the cave wound away through the forest, its rocky banks engulfed in greenery, and the spaces to the sides were a congested mass of plants.

Behind him was the craggy rock structure housing the cave, grey-brown rock, not red sandstone like the mass he'd left behind. He was definitely on another world. He scowled at the sheer cliff face as he edged towards its fissures, found the smoothest spot he could, and propped his bony backside in place. He closed his eyes and drew on his power.

A long, deep breath flooded through his nostrils as he filled his lungs with air and his core with power. The breath was expelled, long and slow. He began to search. At first, he wasn't sure what for – he let his senses scan the land. He found clusters of power that scuttled and scurried; small signatures that could only be animals. He searched further. More creatures, thousands of them. He ignored them and tried to find humans. He found none. He searched ever further afield. Still no humans – and then the landscape changed.

The power was below ground level in a great heaving mass of tiny lifeforms. It was the ocean; it was all around him. He realised he was on an uninhabited island. He drove his senses across the seascape, on and on, until he found a great land mass and, at last, he found somewhere he recognised: Ballachdor. He could identify the signature of the reclusive elven realm easily; he'd searched for it many times before. The mountainous region was protected by a great cloaking screen, making it almost impenetrable to those from the outside. The signature of the barrier was unmistakable.

To the east of the island was nothing but open sea. Far to the northwest was Ballachdor, and the great continent of Allantra stretched away beyond. Curiosity drew him north towards his long-lost kingdom of Vorn. He scanned across the Serrianne Sea to the continent of Hosta, and let his magic filter through the thousands of faint magical signals of ordinary humans. He was no longer interested in them. He was looking for more power, he was looking for sorcerers, one he recognised. Those who were unable to wield magic of any significance flashed past his searching in the blink of an eye – from on-shore sailors to house maids, from shopkeepers to pub punters. He zoned in on a healer, an apothecarist, and a couple more boring sorcerers besides, but dismissed them soon enough.

A little north of the southern city of Tannel, he found something much stronger than a pathetic native of his home planet like a village sorcerer; he found an Earthling. With such a blazing blast of magical power oozing from their aura, he was under no doubt about that.

He scanned, focussed, zoomed in on the source. A creeping grin stretched over his sweaty cheeks. He'd found someone he knew. His old adversary: the man who tricked him into going to Earth, and left him trapped there. The bastard had got back to Gemini as he'd always suspected. He still lived, and he was in Vorn, radiating magic like a pulsing star.

The creeping fury of the treachery pulsed through his veins in a rabid rash of heat. His fists clenched as his pulse raged through his rigid form. His magic swelled, grew, and tingled down his arms. A rattling thought cracked through his ire. *Not yet.* A long deep breath. There was a saying on Earth — 'revenge is a dish best served cold'. He could not disagree.

He funnelled his surging power into a new focus, cast his senses to the periphery of the blaze of power. He felt the lifeforce of the horse Mark rode and of the non-magical human who rode beside him. Behind him were two others. They were sorcerers too, but he did not recognise them. They were powerful, and they were mounted like the others. Their physical signatures were small – females, he presumed.

It took little effort to recall how to possess the mind of a man. There was just one human amongst them who wouldn't detect him, so he forced himself into his head.

***

Aran looked through the eyes of his host. He was riding a bay-coloured horse along a dusty track on a hillside. Far in the distance, he could see the port city of Tannel and the Serrianne Sea beyond. He knew these lands; he had been here before. Mark was right next to him, within touching distance. A sword was sheathed at the hip of the man he'd possessed. He just needed to take it – one quick swipe and Mark would be dead. He trembled with excitement at the thought.

Doubt, sense, and rational thought pushed back. What if he missed? What if Mark parried him? He'd use his magic and know at once that Aran was back. Revenge would become much harder then. He must be patient; he would bide his time.

Aran sensed that Mark had a full grasp of his magic. When he'd last seen him, his adversary barely knew he had the potential, and was certainly unable to wield it at will. Now the man was a master sorcerer, and the tamed power was pulsing through him.

He looked behind him at the two other sorcerers. They were young women as he'd thought. One had a likeness of his sister.

He suddenly realised Mark was talking to him.

'Alfor?' he asked.

Aran stared back at him blankly.

'Alfor, are you alright?'

'Yes, I'm fine,' Aran said in the voice of his host.

'Father, look!' one of the women called out to Mark. 'Look at that stag, its antlers are huge!'

A deer was emerging from the forest in the distance.

'It's a beauty, certainly.' Mark turned to Aran. 'Think you can get that bow strung in time, Alfor?'

It was time for Aran to leave.

From the eyes of his host his suspicions had been confirmed. It was Mark. Older, certainly, but fit and well and with a young woman who'd called him father? A woman who looked like sister? Had the treacherous bitch married his enemy and spawned a brat? A sorcerer? It would make sense, if she was their daughter, she'd have two sorcerers as parents and these things tended to follow the family line.

Who was the other woman? She was a sorcerer too, but not as powerful. Could she be Thomas's spawn? Possibly. That didn't really matter.

He concentrated on Mark's signature again, and got a fix on the two young sorcerers behind him. He secured their unique form in his mind so he could find them again.

Daylight was fading and time was passing. He didn't want Fred to come and find him. He didn't want his men to find a route to his homeland. Yet more humans from Earth on Gemini could lead to no end of trouble. For now, it was his secret. He had much to think on, much to plan. He ventured back into the darkness of the cave and headed back to Earth.

***

Mark cocked his head, 'Alfor? Alfor, are you OK mate?'

The Master of Sword shook his head. 'Yeah, I'm good thanks. That was odd.'

'You looked like you'd lost your mind for a moment, like your head had gone somewhere else.'

'It felt like that, too! It was like I was here but not in control, a passive observer inside my own body.'

Mark laughed. 'You really are getting old, mate. Sure it's not time you handed in your sword?'

'Not before you, arsehole. Not a chance I'm letting you run Vorn's Armed Forces without my supervision.'

Mark couldn't help laughing some more at his old friend's jibe.

'Lord Unwin!' Alora snapped. 'Do you think such language is appropriate?'

Alfor turned to the princess behind him, looking sheepish. Eliza had a big smirk on her face. 'Please forgive me, princess, I did not mean to offend you.'

Mark continued to grin.

'And Father,' she continued, 'you should not encourage him.'

He wiped the smirk from his face. 'Yes, dear,' he replied, before turning back to face the road and trying his hardest to keep a straight face. His daughter was so like her mother at times.

Alfor cast Mark a sideways glance and they shared a look of understanding.

'Uncle Mark?' Eliza asked, breaking the momentary silence.

'Yes, Eliza?'

'The young corporal Alora healed, will he be OK? Will he still be promoted? Falling like that won't go against him, will it?'

'No, he'll still promote. The corporals on that cadre aren't far from the end of the course. Most that weren't gonna make it have already dropped out.'

'Or they've been kicked out,' Lord Unwin added.

'Or kicked out,' Mark agreed. 'At this stage, unless they do something dramatic, they are all gonna become sergeants.'

'Didn't you say something about being there to look at him in particular?' Eliza asked. 'If he had done well and not fallen, would he have got something else? A higher rank?'

'We could maybe have put him on accelerated promotion. Alfor could have him tagged for greatness and put him in some special role or other,' her uncle replied.

'I will still probably ensure he gets a good posting. The lad certainly showed promise,' Alfor added.

'Yeah, as he says,' Mark agreed, 'it might have an impact, but if he's good, he'll still do well.'

'I'm glad to hear that. The wound on his leg was clearly from someone who was out to get him. It came from behind – it had to have been from one of his own.' A frown spread across Eliza's face.

'I can't disagree. Soldiers can be...' Mark was struggling for a good word, conscious that he was likely to get told off again if he swore.

'Not the most pleasant of characters?' Eliza suggested.

'Yeah, let's go with that. Not terribly pleasant. It puts a question mark over how he inspires loyalty though, if his own go after him. We'll need to spend more time looking at him.'

'The lad certainly shows promise though,' Alfor added, 'I'll certainly keep an eye on that one.'

11.   A New Can Of Worms

Location: Zargon observation ship, 400 km above Gemini (Planet M69425)

It was the beginning of another shift for the Captain of Planet
M69245's observation vessel. She smiled in anticipation of another
spell of exploratory excitement as the door to the control room
zipped up into the ceiling.

Her first mate was sitting at the control panel, and spun in her chair
as Darkle strolled into the control room, 'Captain, I'm glad you're here!'
The words exploded from Zark.

'Why, – what is it?' Darkle was used to her first mate's outbursts.
She was young, and she tended to get excited by things.

'H108.'

'Zark, you just blurted a specimen number at me. Please forgive
me for not having an encyclopaedic memory of every specimen of interest
we have ever monitored, but I really have no idea who H108 is.'

'Sorry, Captain. H108 was the specimen who left M69245 some
twenty cycles ago. He got stuck on B13536 when the wormhole was
destroyed.'

'You mean when you destroyed the wormhole.'

'Semantics, surely, Captain?' Zark grinned.

Darkle shook her grey head in despair as the chirp of a barely
suppressed chuckle escaped from her small mouth. 'Perhaps. Anyway,
what about H108? If he's the one who got stuck on B13536, as you say,
wasn't he also a powerful sorcerer and the king of the colony they call
Vorn for a while?'

'He was indeed, Captain.'

'Why bring him up now?'

'He's back. Or he was, for a short while.'

'Are you sure?'

91

'Yes, Captain, certain. He was spotted during a routine scan. There was a magical signature in sector six. The place is uninhabited, naturally it attracted attention. He was under the canopy of trees, so it was hard to get a satellite to see him. I sent a drone down. I got visuals and confirmation he was there and was using magic. He was back up to his old tricks... I also got a call from Captain Garkan.'

Darkle's large black eyes widened, trying to take in what Zark had told her. 'OK...' She walked to her captain's chair, plonked her bony behind down, and tried to think. 'Right, a specimen from B13536 has appeared back on our planet... How?'

'I'm not sure. It must be another wormhole. It's the only explanation I can think of.' Zark was gripping the arms of her chair with her long grey fingers, waiting for her captain to reply.

'Gosh,' Darkle replied.

'When Captain Garkan called,' Zark blurted, 'she asked if we'd spotted him. Seems she'd lost one of her Specimens of Interest.'

'And we found him?'

'Yes, Captain.'

'How long ago?'

'Not long. I would have pulled you on shift, but I wanted to keep it quiet. I wasn't sure if you wanted to involve our third crew member. Garkan was certainly keen to keep hers out of the loop.'

'Heck. Let me sit down.'

'You are sitting, Captain.'

'Oh, er. Um. Heck, Zark, do you know what this means?'

'Another wormhole, Captain.'

'Obviously, but... shit.' She slumped in her chair, her arms sagging over the sides.

'What is it? Are you OK?'

The captain took a deep breath and exhaled slowly. She regarded her first mate. 'I assume you remember what happened last time there was a known link between the planets?'

Zark furrowed the part of her head where eyebrows would have been, if Zargons had them. 'Of course, Captain.'

'And with government being as it is, if things kick off again... we're screwed.'

'Really?'

'Yes!' She sat up in her chair. 'H108 is back on our planet. The specimen who was very close to bringing a host of other specimens from B13536 to M69245. The specimen who nearly gained sufficient power to destroy the culture of every other advanced species on the surface. The specimen who almost ensured those interfering agents in government got their way and started using our planet as a lab for their hideous experiments!' Darkle felt herself getting flustered, a very rare thing for her to do.

'Oh.'

'Oh? Is that all you have to say?' She squeezed the arms of her chair even harder.

'Now you put it like that, it could be an issue.'

'You think?'

'It's possible, Captain, but he just turned up, did a bit of magic, and left not long after. He arrived on an uninhabited island. It's not even certain he knew where he was.'

'You think the most powerful sorcerer our planet has ever seen wouldn't have worked out where he was? Why do you think he was doing magic?'

Zark scratched her hairless scalp. 'I hadn't considered that. He could have used it to work that out, I suppose.'

'Assume he did, Zark.' Darkle sighed. She took a few deep breaths, trying to calm her nerves while Zark sat silently in her chair, waiting for her captain to speak. 'There's another wormhole, Zark.'

'Yes, Captain.'

'How do you think it got there?'

'I-I'm really not sure.'

'Do you not recall the theory about the last one, the one you destroyed?'

Zark scratched her head again, and her eyes suddenly widened. 'Ah, yes! We assumed it was a legacy of the Gallantrians. We had a theory that the humans on M69245 were descendants of humans on planet B13536 — we traced the genetics back to common ancestors five thousand cycles ago.'

'Exactly. It was investigated by the IDI, and it was assumed they had indeed migrated, but they couldn't prove it for certain. Now there's a second wormhole... Is Garkan still on shift?'

'She said she had just come on shift when she called.'

'Ship, call the crew of B13536's observation vessel.'

'Calling B13536's observation vessel,' the artificial intelligence system replied.

The main observation screen turned black briefly before the captain of Earth's observation vessel appeared, smiling. 'Darkle! Good to see you. I assume Zark has given you the news?'

'Yes, of course. What the heck are we going to do?'

'Do we need to do anything?' Garkan asked quizzically.

'What is wrong with the pair of you! Why are you relaxed about this?'

'What is there to get excited about?'

Darkle sighed. 'Have you and Zark been chatting about how best to downplay the biggest threat to my planet in twenty cycles?'

'Erm, not quite. I wasn't sure if it was a significant issue just yet. H108 has made a life for himself on our planet. I'm not sure he'd want to go back to yours even if he had worked out where he was, and how to get off the place.'

'You know he can teleport, right?'

'Oh, I'd forgotten,' Garkan confessed. 'Anyway, on our planet, he has built up an empire for himself. He rules an area of sector seven far bigger than the colony he used to rule on your planet, and he seems content with his lot here. He has a mate, lots of minions, and has adapted well to his new environment.'

Darkle took a moment to think. 'Maybe H108 doesn't pose the threat I thought he might,' she conceded. 'What if this wormhole brings the Gallantrian construct theory back into the limelight? We managed to bury it after it was decided it was irrelevant because of the independent cultures that had evolved. What if government decide to reopen the investigation? To do more digging?

'Even if they do, the argument about the culture preservation still stands,' Garkan said.

'You really think there's nothing to worry about?'

'I wouldn't go that far.'

'Heavens help me,' Darkle muttered to herself. 'Come on, Garkan, talk to me, please? I haven't tracked this specimen since he left M69245. And since then, government has become ever more pro-interference. We have additional crew members on our ship of

94

questionable backgrounds to prove it! If there is another wormhole, surely it opens a whole new can of worms – excusing the pun.'

'That's a saying form our planet, of the English dialect, if I recall correctly. What has got into you, Darkle?'

'After spending decades watching specimens from your planet, I've started to pick up their lingo. That's not important. We both know what this could mean. Why are you relaxed about it?'

Garkan smiled. 'I'm getting old, Darkle. Older and wiser. We've had this hot air from government about interference for over two decades. We have our extra crew members; they spy and report, but nothing has come of it. And as for the Gallantrian issue? We suspected the last one was Gallantrian, and IDI HQ agreed, but they couldn't prove it. What makes you think they'd be able to prove this one has anything to do with them? Unless H108 suddenly decides to give up everything he has on B13536 and embark on a campaign to take over Gemini again, I don't think we have much to worry about.'

'What if he does?'

'Unlikely. We did a personality profile on him not long back as part of our monitoring schedule. He's far more settled than he used to be. He seems to have found his niche as a narcotics baron and appears content. I don't think he would give it all up – he seems happy where he is.'

'That's reassuring.' Darkle wasn't even sure if she was being sarcastic or not. 'Fine, I get it, no need to panic yet,' she said, with the conviction of a guilty criminal pleading innocence. 'What about our third crew members? What do we tell them?'

'You give us the full details of any current developments, of course.' Garkan jumped – Lukin had crept into the control room without Garkan noticing and stood behind her captain, grinning.

'Lukin, how nice to see you,' Darkle lied as she smiled at the Zargon though the screen. 'Are you due on shift already?'

'No, not for a while yet, but I was awake, and I thought my captain might like some assistance.'

Garkan rolled her eyes.

Darkle caught herself as the corners of her mouth rose in a smirk. 'I'm sure Garkan appreciates your support.'

***

Lukin was on shift alone. Garkan's shift had ended earlier, and the second mate was taking the opportunity to review the ship's log. She tried to re-run the conversation between Garkan and Darkle.

'Access denied,' the ship informed her.

Lukin tutted. It was the prerogative of the captain to keep her conversations confidential; it wasn't exactly a reportable offense.

She looked through the log from the previous shift. There was nothing of note: logs of specimen activity, some results of DNA profiling, a report on a technological advancement in sector three. Nothing to get excited about. But there was something going on. Her captain was keeping something from her, and she knew it involved Planet M69245. She'd overheard bits of conversation between the captains of the two ships before. She'd already worked out they were more than colleagues – they were friends. They shared more than was professional to do so. And with M69245 being the unique planet it was, if there was anything they knew that they were keeping from her, that was a punishable offence. Captains were obliged to share details of their planet with crew members. It was IDI protocol.

She methodically searched through the logs of every Specimen of Interest from her planet of B13536. She started with those with connections to M69245. There were only two of them; H095 and H108. H095 had nothing in her log. She had stayed in her residence and its vicinity for the last few weeks, as was usual for her. She had done little of interest since she returned from the M-Class planet to her homeland. But H108? Something was odd there. He was a far more interesting specimen; his movements were normally closely logged but there was a gap in his record. A period of just over an hour where there was nothing to report. Recorded observations were normally logged every few minutes. She checked the last detail before the gap. He'd entered a tunnel into a large rock feature. Then nothing until he exited.

What had he been doing inside? Why was there nothing to report? This was strange; this needed reporting to government. She had been instructed to bypass the IDI with observations such as this. There were those in authority with a special interest in M69245, who were particularly interested in any anomaly, no matter how small.

12. Mischief Breeds Mayhem

Location: Tannel, Vorn, Gemini (Planet M69245)

Eliza marched into the dining room of Lord Hamin's house in a fit of fury. She was so riled up and ready to snap at someone that she was thoroughly disappointed to find no one there but the servants. The footmen stood rigidly tall and impeccably dressed. They bent at the waist in such faultless bows there was no way she could bring herself to snap at the poor men who were simply doing their job. She made do with a scowl and huffed as one of them pulled out her chair and offered her tea. A simple nod would suffice – it was better than a curse.

It was late. Her maid hadn't woken her. When she summoned the girl to her chamber, she'd said she'd been told not to – her uncle had said she'd needed her rest.

The tea arrived. She was starting to sip from her cup when her cousin meandered into the dining room.

'You've been left behind too?' Eliza mumbled to Alora as she took a seat next to her.

'Um, left behind?' Alora seemed baffled.

'Yes! I assume you know how late it is? Uncle and Lord Unwin must have left hours ago!'

'I suppose.'

Eliza turned to study her cousin. Her glazed eyes seemed to focus on nothing. 'Are you alright, Alora?'

'Oh.' Alora blinked. 'Yes, I'm fine.'

'Did you sleep OK?'

'Er, I think so.'

'What?' Eliza's eyebrows furrowed. 'You either did, or you didn't. It's not normally a difficult thing to work out.'

'I think I slept well. I nodded off fairly quickly and woke up late, but it was just my dream – it was so vivid, so real. When I woke, I felt groggy, like I'd woken from a deep slumber but not fully rested, like I'd actually been doing the things I'd seen in my dream.'

'You're not making much sense, Alora. What the heck did you dream about?'

'I was in a jungle – a tropical forest. There were hanging vines and huge leaves, wild and exotic animals – parrots, leopards, monkeys. There was something else. A horse with cloven hooves and a donkey's tail. It was brilliant white, and its mane was silver...' Her voice trailed off.

'Sounds like you saw some kind of messed-up dream animal to me,' Eliza suggested.

'No,' she snapped back into focus, 'there was something else too. It had a long, twisted ivory horn sprouting from its head, between its ears. It was a unicorn.'

'You dreamed about a unicorn. It sounds lovely. How would it stop you resting properly?'

'It was so real. Like the unicorn was enchanting me somehow.'

'You're being ridiculous. You do know unicorns are extinct, right?'

'What if they still survive somewhere? Somewhere where there's a tropical forest?'

Eliza sighed. She plonked her chin on her hands and regarded her cousin with a wide smile. 'Yes, Alora, unicorns survive, and they are enchanting your dreams. It sounds very lovely. Can you snap back into reality and join me in my outrage at being left behind?'

Alora bit her lip and a grin of her own spread across her face. 'Yes, I am equally outraged,' she said, without much conviction.

'Oh, I can tell!' Eliza sat back and folded her arms.

A servant arrived and delivered their breakfast. He returned to his position of duty in the corner of the room, a goodly distance from where they sat in the large and very grand dining room.

'Do you get the feeling your father and Lord Unwin don't want us here?' Eliza whispered, before taking a bite of her bread with cheese. Crumbs sprayed everywhere as she tore off a chunk with her teeth.

'It occurred to me,' Alora replied, pulling a face at Eliza's poor table manners. 'Do you have to eat so messily?'

'I'm irritated! And there is no one here who cares, anyway.'

'I care!'

Eliza took another bite of her bread, a small, polite nibble this time. 'Better?' she asked after she'd swallowed.

Alora shook her head in despair and ate her own breakfast with the impeccable manners Eliza knew she was incapable of disregarding. They continued to eat in silence for a short while. Eliza soon finished, took a long sip of her tea, and turned to her cousin.

'It's not really a surprise, is it?' Eliza continued her earlier thread. 'Why would they want us along? Two princesses who know nothing about soldiering, tagging along to visit Vorn's military units? I bet Uncle is still annoyed about how we blew his cover the other day. Perhaps he is getting his own back?'

'You're probably right about them not wanting us here,' Alora agreed, finally appearing to have snapped out of the clouds filled with unicorns. 'I had to beg Father to let us accompany him. But even after the incident at the cadre, he shouldn't have left us like this, telling our maids not to wake us, scheming to keep us away from today's visits. He should have been honest!' She pouted.

'You're thinking of something, Alora – are you plotting?'

Alora leant back in her chair, a manicured fingernail tapping her rouged lips as they spread into a wicked smile. 'If Father is keen on leaving us behind, keeping our lives as dull and boring as they were up in Vornston, perhaps we should make our own fun.'

'What have you got in mind?' Eliza queried, a wave of excitement suddenly rippling through her.

'How about today we go into Tannel, take a few guards and our maids, make it look proper. Maybe do a little shopping in the market?'

'Oh, Alora, that sounds like a day filled with fun!' Eliza exclaimed sarcastically. 'Shopping! How lovely. Just my idea of a perfect day out.'

'I can't deny I wouldn't enjoy it, even though your strange aversion to such things suggests you may not, but that's not why I want to go. I want to go and have a look round Tannel, get our bearings, work out where things are in preparation for what I have in mind later.'

Ah, this was sounding more promising. She could tolerate shopping if it was a cover for something else. 'Go on, Alora,' Eliza smiled mischievously, 'what are you thinking?'

Alora spotted the servant who still stood attentively in the corner. She shuffled her chair closer to her cousin's and spoke quietly. 'Remember the night we went out in Vorn, dressed as peasant women?'

'How could I forget?' Eliza said with a grin. 'Those young men we were chatting to – the wood cutter and the blacksmith? Their tales of ordinary life were fascinating. Such a change from the boring drivel the young lords spout.'

'Exactly. How about we do that again, here, in Tannel?'

Eliza thought for a moment. It was risky, but the thrill of the idea pushed her to the edge of her seat. 'Can't say I'm not tempted,' she whispered back. Trepidation tempered her intrigue. 'Wouldn't we be missed? We are expected for dinner with Lord Hamin every night here – if we didn't go, it would look rude.'

'We go to dinner. We say we are exhausted after such a hard day of shopping. We leave early, then we sneak out. I took the liberty bringing our dresses from last time. Our maids need not even know a thing. We let them put us to bed and we go out and use magic to hide our identities like last time. This time, we'll find a soldiers' bar. After seeing them fighting at the cadre – oh...' She paused. 'They seem exciting.'

'Alora, can you hear yourself?' Eliza leaned in closer to her cousin. 'First the pub in Vornston and now a plot to visit one in Tannel? You are starting to sound like me. It's normally me who comes up with these hare-brained schemes.'

'You must be corrupting me.'

Eliza laughed so loudly she caught the attention of the servant. She swiftly regained her composure and continued her quiet plotting. 'I like your plan – we just need to work out where to go.'

'That's the brilliance of what I have in mind. While we are out and about, we'll talk to our guards. Lord Hamin's men will know the bars where the soldiers go. We'll chat to them and drop it into conversation.'

'Perfect. Sounds like a plan.'

A mischievous smile spread across Alora's young face. Eliza grinned back – the day had suddenly got a whole lot better.

***

'Come on mate, you should be cheerier than this. We found out we all passed the cadre, we're as good as promoted,' Mervin said to Garrad as they strolled through the streets of Tannel. Garrad glared at him. 'If you carry on like this, you will start to try the patience of even me. We did well to get through – there are a good number who didn't. What were you expecting from it? A double promotion? To come out as a colour sergeant? Fuck me, if that's the case, you might as well sod off. I'm not sure I want to spend the evening with someone with such ridiculous delusions of grandeur.'

'Sorry, Mervin.' Garrad made a conscious effort to look cheerier. 'It's not that. I never expected to end up double promoted as you put it. I keep thinking about how Lords Harrison and Unwin rocked up. What were they doing there? Why were they watching our cadre? It was a routine sergeant's cadre. They run loads every year and I've not heard of them watching any other one.'

'Delusions of grandeur again, Garrad? You think they were there for you?' He raised an eyebrow. 'Gods, mate, they were probably visiting as part of a trip down south. Just having a look at lots of courses and cadres. I heard they inspected the recruits today. Think they were looking for anyone special there?'

Garrad looked idly at shopfronts, their doors barred for the night, and loud-mouthed groups of merry soldiers who had already had one drink too many. His eyes were drawn to a pile of horse dung in the middle of the cobbled street. At last, he replied, 'Yeah, you're right. I'm being an arrogant arsehole.'

'That's the spirit!' Mervin jovially slapped him on the back.

'I'm just pissed that someone swiped my calf, took me down, and let Bremmer steal my victory in front of the two most senior men in our army.'

'Anyone would be pissed about that, but these things happen. Could have easily been a slip that brought you down. Hell, could have been an accident, a stray spear at a bad angle.'

'Pushing it slightly, mate, but possible.'

'Get your arse out of the dumps – cheer up and let's have a good night. We're gonna get new and hopefully interesting postings in a few days, and we only have a couple more nights before we get separated. Let's enjoy ourselves while we can.' Mervin put an arm on Garrad's shoulders.

Garrad at last found a smile. He had a quiet word with himself and resolved to enjoy the evening.

They continued down the cobbled alley, away from the shops and into the quarter of Tannel known for its bars. They were heading to the Black Horse, a pub usually frequented by soldiers. As they strolled along, they started reminiscing about the cadre, the highs and lows, the challenges, the banter. Garrad had almost forgotten about feeling sorry for himself when someone brushed a hand across his behind. He spun. Two large breasts were practically thrust in his face, the nipples only just covered by the tight corset poking out from the skin-tight dress.

'Fancy a good time, handsome?' The breasts were attached to a face, apparently. The woman was young, but not too young. Her face was fresh – no signs of pockmarks. Her hair was clean and well-groomed, and her scent was intoxicating. He was almost tempted.

'Er, no, not just yet, thanks.'

Mervin tugged at his arm. 'Come on, nob rot, we have drinking to do.' Mervin yanked Garrad away, and his focus returned.

'Yeah, course.' He staggered on, looking behind him, his eyes fixed on the bulging breasts.

'Look where you're going!' Mervin yanked him out of the way of an approaching rider. 'That cock of yours is going to get you in trouble one of these days.'

'Hey! I've barely touched a woman since I was promoted to lance corporal. Not had the time – too busy schooling your sorry arse to keep you on the same promotion track as me. I need at least one person to watch my back.'

'Give over! Without me helping you practise, you'd never have been good enough to make sure your loose jaw was overlooked for your skill with a blade. Not to mention the number of times I've talked you out of trouble. You wouldn't have even made corporal without me.'

'Ha! You're admitting I've knuckled down and stayed away from the ladies.'

'I wouldn't go that far. I don't watch you every minute of every day. You still have a reputation, you know.'

'You're jealous 'cos the women flock to me.'

'Could your head grow any bigger? Those biceps and your chiselled jawline might draw the whores, but it means fuck all when it comes to finding a decent woman. The good ones aren't drawn by looks; they're more interested on what's on the inside.'

'Keep telling yourself that, mate.' Garrad grinned mockingly at his friend.

Mervin lightly elbowed him in the ribs. Garrad couldn't help but laugh at the indignance plastered across his friend's face.

'This way, arsehole, we're here.' Mervin pulled him towards the pub door.

***

The atmosphere in the Black Horse was as expected – rowdy and jolly. A man with a ukulele was performing in one corner, singing as he played, and men danced to his tune. Garrad and Mervin headed to the bar and ordered their drinks.

The place was busy. There were no tables free, so they stood by the bar and sipped their beer and chatted. They'd not been there long when Mervin's attention was drawn towards the doorway.

'Didn't think they let the whores in,' Mervin commented as two women entered.

Garrad's interest was pricked. The two young women were wearing cloaks with their hoods up, but their womanly shapes could not be easily disguised as they walked. Something about their gait was unusual. They glided rather than walked, and their heads were held high, like they were used to being respected. Peasant women were always hunched somehow, as if they were trying to be inconspicuous.

They dropped their hoods as they approached the bar. Their hair was clean and smooth. It shone in the light of the oil lamps, styled and very well groomed, and their skin was perfect, their makeup neat. He knew straight away these were no ordinary women.

'Don't think they're whores, mate. They are showing far too little flesh to be attracting any trade tonight,' he replied bluntly, keeping his other observations to himself.

'If they ain't whores, what are they doing in here? Respectable women know better than to come to this place.'

'Maybe they're lost.'

'Yeah, right!' Mervin's rough cheeks dimpled as he sniggered. 'They are probably just after soldier company.' He managed to straighten his face. 'They're certainly a pretty pair of ladies. How 'bout you have a go at actually chatting to a woman for once? I can show you how it's done.'

'Not tonight, mate. Not in the mood.'

'Not in the mood? You looked eager enough earlier.'

'You don't have to talk to whores.'

103

'I don't fancy it without a wing man.' The bartender delivered another round of drinks. 'Thanks,' Garrad said to the bartender before turning back to Mervin. 'Spotted a table yet?'

'Nope.'

'Fair enough. We're still good here, for now.' Mervin pulled up a bar stool and made himself comfortable.

'That didn't take long.' Garrad was looking at the two women again.

Mervin followed his gaze. 'Didn't think it would.'

A group of men had descended on the women, approaching like a pack of wolves toward a pair of lambs. Through the gloom of the smoky pub, Garrad strained to get a good look at one of the men. His eyes widened.

'Fuck me, mate, that's Bremmer.'

'Shit, yeah.' Mervin sighed. 'Come on, let's go over there.' He indicated to the far side of the pub. 'I don't want any trouble tonight, and I imagine you don't either.'

'I'm not moving for him, why should I? Let's ignore him and enjoy our drinks.'

'Fine,' Mervin conceded, proceeding to down half the contents of his beer mug.

They chatted jovially about the last four weeks in the cadre while they minded their own business and went unnoticed by Bremmer. He seemed far more interested in the two women and hadn't cast Garrad a single glance. Every now and then, Garrad turned to check on them. The women seemed to be enjoying the male attention. He found himself drawn to them. He thought he recognised them, but every time he tried to place their faces, his mind became a blur. It was odd. Like he knew and couldn't grab the memory.

He forced his attention back to his friend and was continuing to revisit the highlights of their cadre when the raised voice of a woman caught his ear.

'I said, don't touch me!' the woman said firmly. Garrad's head shot round – he tuned in to the conversation. Bremmer had his arm around one of the women.

'Darling, surely you didn't come to a place like this if you didn't want attention. How 'bout you come back to my place? We can get to know each other properly there.'

'We'd better leave,' the other woman said to her companion.

Bremmer tightened his grip on the first woman. 'That's not how things work round here.' He pulled her in and forced a kiss onto her lips.

'Get your hands off her!' Garrad yelled. The bar went silent. 'The lady said she wasn't interested, now let her go!'

Bremmer's head spun towards Garrad; he still hadn't let go of the woman.

'You!' He puffed out his broad chest and squeezed the woman until she winced. 'Corporal Bramston. Sticking your oar into someone else's business. What a surprise.'

'The lady told you not to touch her – let her go!' Garrad took a few steps forwards.

'Fuck off,' Bremmer spat. He turned back to the woman and tried to kiss her again, but he didn't get chance.

A pulse of energy forced him back; he was hurled through the air and smashed into a table. Garrad's mind cleared for a few seconds as Bremmer fell. He looked back towards the woman. His jaw dropped, and his eyes widened as his mind found the memories that had been clouded, out of focus. His gaze met hers. The blurriness returned, and she fled, pulling the other young woman by the arm as she went.

Bremmer climbed to his feet, wobbling. He staggered and found his balance. Someone passed him a beer mug; he took a big gulp and a step towards Garrad.

'Corporal Bramston.' His words were slurred, while his eyes brimmed with fury. 'The fuckwit who set my career back by years.' He took another step towards Garrad. 'Made me mark time, you did, you little shit. Now you stand there, bold as brass, and scare my date away.'

Drops of his putrid spit landed on Garrad's cheek; he almost choked on the vile smell of rotten teeth and stale beer that emanated from Bremmer's jaws.

'She wasn't interested, Bremmer,' Garrad replied, pulling his head away in disgust at the smell.

One of Bremmer's friends stepped to his side and put an arm round him. 'Leave it, mate, he's not worth it.'

'I've left this arsehole alone long enough. It's about time he got what's coming to him.' Bremmer slammed his beer mug on the bar, its contents splashing down its sides.

'Don't do it – I've seen him fight!' his friend warned.

'No fucker can fight against eight men. There are just two of them.'

***

Mervin was by his friend's side, his arms folded high on his solid chest, brow-shadowed eyes glaring. His blood rose: he'd had just one beer, but it was enough to loosen him up, to take away that little bit of control that usually kept him out of trouble.

He remembered the night he'd found his friend bloodied and beaten after Garrad kicked Bremmer's arse earlier that day in the training ring when he was a recruit. He remembered how, when Bremmer was their instructor, he'd bullied everyone, and how much better things got when he was kicked off their course. He thought about the cadre. Bremmer had been OK at first. Mervin thought he'd changed, chilled the fuck out, but he'd seen how he'd sucked up to the instructors, how he'd been lazy but jumped into action whenever anyone was looking, how he'd happily trip someone up or meddle with their kit to make them look bad.

He'd watched when Bremmer stole Garrad's glory in the final exercise. He'd given him no credit, boasted about how he'd won to everyone who cared to listen. Bremmer had to be behind Garrad's fall. Garrad could be an arrogant dick at times, but he didn't deserve the shit he got from this arsehole. His blood simmered to bubbling froth; Mervin lost it.

His fist took control and threw itself at Bremmer. It swept through the air, bang on target, but his target moved. Bremmer was quicker than Mervin, despite his alcohol-raddled head. He jolted to the side, the fist skimmed his ear, and he stumbled. A hard, heavy fist jabbed at Mervin's stomach, bending him double. He coughed, staggered, then someone yanked him back. Flailing arms and blurry eyes. He hadn't seen it coming, despite Garrad's attempt to pull him from harm's way. The fist found his jaw with a heavy thud. His teeth snapped shut, his head snapped back, and his knees turned to mush. A sudden stab of dizzy pain. Light turned dark, his body sagged, and he tumbled to the floor.

***

'Shit,' Garrad muttered as Mervin slipped heavily from his grasping hands. No point trying to hold on. The guy was out for the count.

'One against eight? I don't like your chances, Bramston,' Bremmer taunted as he smacked his knuckles into a palm.

Garrad glared. Bremmer's men sneered. There were five behind him that he could see but he hadn't spotted the other two, the ones that moved without warning to his sides, grabbing his arms, holding him fast. He twisted, he pulled with all his strength. Years of sword practice and extra training besides had made him strong, and he had always been good in a fight. But the other men were soldiers too. Their grips were firm; he couldn't wriggle out of this one easily.

'You've had this coming to you for a while, you jumped-up little shit.' Bremmer leered, swaying slightly. 'You never figured it out, did you? It takes more to make it in this army than just being good with a sword. If you'd any sense, you'd have let me win all those years back. What the fuck did you hope to prove by beating your instructor? That kind of crap will only get you so far before you make one too many enemies.'

The fingers held him tight. Bremmer was close. Garrad's lips edged apart, as if to reply, but he didn't. With a flick of his tongue, he gathered his spit and shot it straight into Bremmer's face. His old enemy's face exploded into a fit of fury, and he launched himself at Garrad, but Garrad was ready.

He lifted his feet and shoved them at Bremmer with everything he had. His boots slammed into the corporal's chest. He tumbled back into two of his mates who stood behind him, while the sudden jolt of Garrad's thrust was enough to loosen the grip of the men who held him. He twisted, he yanked. He was free.

A clenched fist was aimed at Garrad's jaw. He ducked. He found his balance, swung his knuckles upwards and found a chin. His hand jarred, but his fighting fury had taken control and he barely noticed. A knee brushed against the back of his thigh, clumsy and now the man behind had given away his position. Big mistake. Garrad shot his elbow backwards, and it found something soft.

'Ughhh,' someone wheezed, winded.

The pile of men in front of him began to find their feet — it was time to stop that happening. He hooked a foot round Bremmer's leg and shoved, causing him to tumble back into two other men, taking them down with him. A dark body caught the corner of Garrad's eye, movement, a lunge, and he dodged in time. The body whipped past him and collided with the man opposite.

A lumbering punch met his shoulder. It spun him and he staggered. He found his feet and looked up in time to see an arm swinging towards him. He jolted sideways; the attacker's momentum kept him coming. Garrad launched an upper cut and found the man's stomach.

'Corporal Bramston!' someone yelled from the side.

Garrad straightened up, twisted, searching for the sound of the voice. He attacked with his fist, colliding with a cheekbone through the smoky haze. Garrad caught sight of the man's face in the shadowy glare of an oil lamp, and the world slowed in painful horror. His eyes widened as the shock of recognition cut him like a blade. He'd hit him and he couldn't take it back. Colour Sergeant Fornian fell, arching over staggering legs and crumpling. Someone caught him just in time to stop him from smashing into the hard stone floor.

It was already too late to save Garrad.

'Oh shit.'

13. No Good Deed Goes Unpunished

Garrad hadn't slept much. He'd spent most of the night bulling his boots, ironing his uniform, and polishing his buttons till they gleamed. His interview without the pleasantries of coffee was first thing. The other Colour Sergeant – the one he didn't know – had told him it would be. A mate of Colour Fornian, he presumed; a colour who called himself Hamville.

It should have been his day off today; it should have been the cadre commander's too. Captain Tawbrid would not be happy to be on duty this morning, which would only make things worse.

Garrad stood outside the captain's office. He stood to attention, as rigidly as he could, trying to look his best in case the commander appeared without warning.

The training centre office building was hot. He stood in the corridor, alone; no one was working this morning. The doors were shut. There was no breeze to soften the blow of the blazing sunshine as it beat down on him through the windows. Sweat trickled down his back; beads collected on his forehead and stuck his hat to his head. The dense woollen dress jacket was not designed for summer. Whoever had come up with the style had either only ever expected soldiers to wear it in winter, or they'd been a sadist.

By the time the door at the end of the corridor opened and slammed shut, Garrad was soaked with sweat. Bootsteps stomped along the stone floor, growing louder, echoing Garrad's pulse in his ears.

Captain Tawbrid's sturdy yet surprisingly short form crossed Garrad's vision. Garrad shot up a salute.

'Sir!' he greeted the commander. He looked over the top of the captain's head, staring out of the window as the captain lazily returned the salute and regarded the corporal, giving him a good look up and down and betraying just a hint of approval of his appearance.

'Come in, Corporal Bramston,' Tawbrid said with a sigh as he unlocked his office door. It swung open with a creak, the captain strolled to the chair behind the desk and plonked his arse on the wooden seat. Garrad marched in and came to a halt.

'At ease, Corporal.'

Garrad carried out the drill instruction, his right leg lifted and shot down half a pace from his left, his hands snapped to the small of his back where he gripped his right with his left, his thumbnail punishing his palm as he stood.

'It really is a shame, Corporal,' Captain Tawbrid began. 'I can't deny I'm sad to see you in my office, I'm not quite as sad as I am about missing the hunt this morning to deal with the misdemeanours of my cadre students, but sad none the less. I'd have expected better from you.'

Garrad stared at the wall behind the captain. He stood rigid, teeth clenched, his face as stern and blank as he could hope to hold it. He wanted to receive his punishment and get it over with. Ten lashes? Sounded about right. Maybe marking time as a sergeant for a bit. A year maybe? They'd all passed the cadre. He was a sergeant now, not a corporal; all he needed was his sergeant's stripes to make it official. They wouldn't take that away from him, he told himself. He was the best student – the army needed men like him, and brawls happened all the time. He'd never known anyone to get bumped a rank because of a brawl before, even when they hit a senior rank.

'It's most unfortunate, Corporal, that you chose to get into trouble when you did.' The captain paused, leant forwards on his desk, rested his elbows, and clasped his hands. 'You see, with Lords Harrison and Unwin in town, it makes it difficult to do anything but the maximum punishment. I was late this morning as I had to speak to the commander of the Training Centre regarding your punishment. Yours, and that of the others in the bar.'

Garrad raised an eyebrow.

'Yes, they will be punished too,' the captain replied, answering the unasked question. 'Corporals Bremmer and Drund, as well as the others you engaged in the brawl with – they will get appropriate reprimands too. But they did not hit a colour sergeant, a man who by all accounts was trying to break things up. A man with a fractured cheekbone who, despite his injury, still tried his best to talk you out of trouble.

'Unfortunately, the commander doesn't agree with Colour Fornian. He thinks you deserve the maximum penalty we can give. It seems our visitors have been talking with him about discipline recently, making noises about how it should be maintained and praising the high standards of the men as they've observed training. Which doesn't bode well for you, I'm afraid.'

Garrad swallowed hard, an invisible lump sinking to his queasy stomach.

Captain Tawbrid sighed. 'The commander is of the view you should not be allowed to graduate from the cadre. You are to remain a corporal for another five years before you are allowed to re-attend.'

Garrad's jaw dropped as he tried to take in what he was being told.

'And you should also receive ten lashes, to be administered after the promotion ceremony tomorrow, which you shall attend. Of course, you will not be receiving your sergeant's stripes.'

Garrad stared in disbelief. He was to mark time for five years as a corporal and be publicly humiliated while his course mates got promoted on the square? He was struggling for words. His mouth was dry — he suddenly realised he was desperate for a drink. He stuttered.

'The others?' was all he managed to spit out.

'They will be promoted tomorrow, but they will receive ten lashes too. The commander was keen that brawlers would be made a public example of.'

Five fucking years as a corporal, while the others got a hiding. He hadn't hit Colour Fornian on purpose. He'd been fighting eight men, for fuck's sake, in a dark and smoky bar. How the hell was he supposed to have recognised him when he was fighting for his life? His mouth opened in disbelief as the red mist descended. His blood boiled, burning rage flooded his seething core. It took control of his faculties. It started to move his tongue.

'That arsehole Bremmer gets virtually fuck all while my career is ruined?' Garrad was only in his early twenties and five years seemed like a lifetime.

'Corporal Bramston, I'd suggest you check your language in the presence of an officer,' the captain warned.

'Fuck my language and fuck you!' Garrad bellowed. A part of Garrad was horrified at his own words, but they exploded out of his mouth, driven by anger. He was like a passenger in his own mind as his

111

mouth kept talking. 'This is disproportionate. No one even bothered to ask my side of it. Bremmer started on me; I was trying to protect a girl he was hassling. There were eight of them for fuck's sake! Why would I start on eight other men? I was with Corporal Drund – there were only two of us! This makes no sense, and you know it!' At some point, the rage gripped his hand and made it point at the captain. He swung an accusing finger to animate his point.

Tawbrid remained seated, his face giving little away. He squeezed his clenched hands together until his knuckles turned white.

Garrad was silent as the captain took a few long breaths while his own heaving chest forced noisy puffs from his flaring nostrils. His trembling hands were hidden behind his back, thumbnails clawing his skin, scraping gouges. His mind was consumed by flaming ire as he bit his lip and waited.

At last, the captain sighed, relaxed his hands, and placed them palms-down on his desk. 'Corporal Bramston, I understand your frustration at the severity of this punishment, so I am willing to overlook your outburst. There are no witnesses here. Let us forget it happened, shall we?'

'No!' Garrad snapped. 'I'm not going to take this. I've already been made to look shit in front of the lords by someone, probably Bremmer. Did you hear about how I fell and broke my arm on the field exercise?'

'Yes.' The captain slowly shook his head in despair.

'I fell because someone sliced my leg! The princess healed it for me, along with my arm, but everyone saw the wound. Bremmer's had it in for me since I was a recruit – he was my instructor and he tried to beat me in the ring. He didn't, and he's hated me ever since. He's behind this, now you're giving him what he wants. You're doing his dirty work; you're taking me down!'

The captain rolled his eyes. 'Corporal Bramston, I suggest you cease talking and take your punishment or I will be forced to take you down another rank and give you additional lashes. Your otherwise good record is currently the only thing stopping me from busting you right here!' He slapped the table; the temper of the normally patient captain apparently starting to fray.

'With all due respect, sir, fuck off. If you're not interested in hearing the whole truth, if you're—'

112

Captain Tawbrid shot to his feet. 'Corporal!' he screamed. 'Lance corporal it is, then!'

'Two ranks down? You'll knock the best swordsman on the cadre down two ranks because of a good-for-nothing fuckwit who likes to stir stuff up?'

'I can make it three! Do you want to leave this office a private?'

'No, I'll leave a sergeant. It's the rank I earned, and the rank I'll keep. You can fuck your demotions. I quit!'

'You signed up for ten years!' The captain's face turned a deep shade of crimson. He leant forward, both hands pressed on the table. 'You have four more to serve, *Private* Bramston.'

Private? He'd called him private. Garrad had smashed his way through the ranks. He'd worked hard, he'd practiced and trained when others drank, he'd even given up whoring for his bloody career. He'd made his way up as quickly as he could. He'd given everything to being a soldier. Now Bremmer and this jumped-up captain wanted to rip it away. What control he had left evaporated. His fist took over. It lurched at the cadre commander and took him squarely in the jaw. The surprise at what he'd just done matched that of the captain's as the pain surged into his knuckles. He pulled the punch, but it was too late, the damage was done.

***

After the first ten lashes, his back stung like hell. The strokes began to overlap, agitating the already weeping welts. Why did they pause so long between hits? Why couldn't they get it over with? Garrad clenched his teeth and braced himself for forty more. It could have been ten. If he'd kept his mouth shut, his punishment would be over, this part of it at least. The five years as corporal? It would have been shit, but at least he'd still have a job, he'd still be a soldier. Now he was nothing. Soon, he'd have no skin on his back and a year's hard labour to look forward to. Then no job. Nothing. He'd have go crawling home to his parents, his tail between his legs – dishonourably discharged and a convict besides – and hope his father was still as keen for him to come into the family business as he had been before Garrad had left home to join the Army.

By the thirtieth lash, the pain was becoming unbearable. Blood trickled down his back in crimson rivers of gore, pooling on his breeches, soaking through the cotton hem. He was sure there was no skin left. His back felt like every inch of flesh had been ripped away. The lashes kept coming.

By the time the final five came, the pain was so all-encompassing he barely noticed the extra strikes. A raw back being penetrated by a thousand boiling needles was just normal now. He had forgotten what a back without pain felt like. He stopped fighting his legs' cries to sag. His knees buckled, he drooped, and let himself hang by the ropes holding his hands above his head. He barely noticed the bonds cutting into his wrists. His head was spinning. Blood flowed freely, and he sagged as his consciousness started to drift away.

***

'He's taken it well, I have to say. He lasted longer than I'd have expected,' Lord Alfor Unwin said with a degree of respect. He was sitting with Mark on a makeshift platform that had been built for them. The Training Centre commander insisted on putting them in pride of place for the promotion ceremony. The new sergeants had been given their stripes; the two lords had inspected them and now they were enduring watching the lashings. Discipline was part of army training. They couldn't leave for this bit – it would look bad. But Mark made the princesses leave. He wasn't having them watch the ten men get the skin torn from their backs, especially not the last one. Fifty lashes was a hell of a lot for anyone to endure.

'It's bloody barbaric, don't you think? He'll have some right welts when he's healed,' Mark observed. He'd found himself cringing with every hit.

'Easiest way to discipline 'em though. It's certainly something the men understand, a few lashes,' Alfor said.

'He's down for hard labour, too, isn't he?'

'I believe so. The Training Centre commander was very pleased to tell me so. I must say…' Alfor glanced to his side to check if anyone was within earshot. He spotted the commander, who was engrossed by the lashings. The gasps of the crowd with every lash muffled Alfor's words anyway. 'It seems disproportionate. The kid's getting kicked out, his career's in tatters. The year in the quarry is probably going too far.'

'Should we intervene?' Mark replied quietly.

Alfor thought for a bit. 'I've a suspicion the lad's getting it bad because of us.'

'How do you mean?'

'The Commander's being hard on them because we're here. He's trying to show off how tough he is on discipline.'

'If you were in his shoes, what would you have given for hitting an officer?' Mark queried.

'Mm...' Alfor rubbed his chin. 'I was the Commander of the Training centre myself, years ago.'

'I know, it's why I asked.'

'I'd probably give him thirty lashes and bust him to private.'

'That's that, then.'

'What's what?'

'I'm having a word. I'm not letting him go to the quarry. He just can get the hell out of here and try to find a new path. I hope his family have something for him.'

'I heard his father was a merchant,' Alfor noted.

'He should be fine then; I imagine he can get in on that trade. I'll ask Alora to pay him a visit too. He'll hardly be able to walk with a back like that.'

The two men watched as Garrad was cut down, his unconscious form flopping into the waiting arms of the two newly promoted sergeants who dragged him away from the square.

***

Garrad ambled over the cobbles of Tannel with his pack slung over his shoulder. He stared at the ground as he walked, not caring if he bumped into anyone. Fuck them. They could move out of his way. It was late in the day, and the light was starting to fade. The streets were quiet anyway.

He didn't need to look where he was going; he knew the way. He'd been raised in the city. His father had to be close to the harbour to ply his trade. The Military Training Academy being in the city too was a bonus. He'd been able to make a few trips home on his days off whenever he'd had courses there. He knew he'd always be well fed when he went home to see his parents – his mother was brilliant cook and she loved to feed her sons. Army rations could get very boring very quickly.

Normally, he'd march through the streets at pace. He couldn't abide people who dawdled; he'd always thought it such a waste of time to travel slowly when you could get there swiftly. But not today. Today he was in no rush to see his parents.

He'd been kicked out of the army, dishonourably discharged. He'd brought shame on the family. He'd had to tell them; they'd have come to the promotion ceremony otherwise. Having them turn up to see him lashed was more than he could bear. He hadn't told them about that. He'd said he was just being sent down; they didn't need to know about the lashes. He would keep his shirt on, hide the scars. The princess had healed him. He was as good as new now, except for the scars.

He thought back to the moment he'd woken after the lashing. He recalled the gentle burning sensation as the skin was drawn back together. He'd recognised it as soon as he'd come round; it was the feeling he'd had when his leg was healed. He'd felt the strange tingling as the princess had pulled the skin back together, fused the muscle and flesh, accelerating the body's own healing powers to unimaginable speeds. When she'd healed his back, it had felt the same – with every wound she'd fixed, a little more pain vanished. One less welt, one less searing gash in his skin.

As the last welt was finally turned from oozing wound to scar, he'd heard her soft footsteps as she left. He'd rolled over, desperate to see who'd healed him, to be sure it was the princess as he'd hoped. Before she left the barracks block, she'd turned. He'd caught those mahogany eyes that pierced his soul. He recognised them. The same eyes he'd seen when he'd broken his arm, but he'd seen them somewhere else.

He shook his head to clear the daydream and stopped in his tracks. Something clicked in his mind. He knew where he'd seen her – the memory flashed into his head. It was in the bar. The woman Bremmer had been bothering, the woman who blasted him away with magic, or so he'd assumed. How else could she have done it?

He recalled his mind being blurry when he looked at her in the pub; he'd assumed it was the beer at the time. Seeing her again at last allowed him to make the connection. It was the princess in the bar. She'd been using magic to stop her being recognised. When she blasted Bremmer, the veil slipped.

It all made sense. Sorcerers were rare, most were old, and he couldn't imagine any would be stupid enough to come into a soldier's bar. But the princess was young and naïve, probably bored.

116

Had she had a word with her father about the incident? Was that why he'd escaped hard labour and she'd come to heal him? He could think of no other explanation.

The thought of the princess's gratitude put a smile on his face. He lifted his head and upped his pace. He'd been kicked out of the Army, but he'd helped out a beautiful princess and she'd shown her gratitude. No one else knew, but he did. And the knowledge was almost enough to make it all worth it.

14. Bad To Worse

It started to rain. A few tiny drops at first, then bigger ones. Big fat ones plopping on the ground and making a little splashing sound, soaking the dusty ground, which had been crying out for moisture. It was autumn, it hadn't rained in months, and the streets were starting to stink. Cat piss, dog piss, and horse piss; the streets reeked of it. Sewers had been built years ago, but the animals didn't care. They went where they liked, like the men who'd had a few too many to drink.

A summer of piss drying on piss without rain to wash it away had left a strong aroma; it lined the nostrils with putrid stench, drawing a nauseous retch from all who got too close to the smell. It was too late for Garrad. The autumn rains landed on his bare arse and dirty clothes. He lay on his belly, his face in a pool of vomit. It might have been the stench of urine that had done it, it might have been the beer. But he didn't give a shit. He felt like shit.

The rain drenched him, and he shivered. His head pounded like a banging drum. He managed to roll over, using what little strength he had to keep his head out of yesterday's dinner. He grabbed his breeches and wriggled them up, buttoning them at the crotch, hiding his shame.

'One, two, three...'

He jolted himself up and sat on the ground. The sudden movement was a mistake; a surge of pulsing pain exploded in his head. Big blobs of water landed on his matted hair; he gripped his scalp with his grubby hands. The pounding pain was almost unbearable. Somewhere not far away, horseshoes clattered down a street. Someone was calling out, 'Get yer pies! Freshly baked, come and get 'em!'

He turned his head, slow and steady, doing everything he could to stop the headache from getting worse. He was in an alley; the main road was ahead. A prim-looking woman walked past at the junction, with a servant who carried a rain shelter for her. She stopped and glared at him, turned up her nose, and continued on her way.

'Snotty bitch,' Garrad muttered.

He sucked a few deep breaths – a mistake. He retched a dry and raspy retch, spitting blobs of greenish gunk onto the stinking ground.

The market was open. He was late for work already; his father would scold him, again.

'Fuck,' he hissed.

He rocked forwards onto his hands and knees, managed to kneel, forced his legs to work and found his feet. The world span, and he nearly fell. He grabbed the wall for support, rested his head on the bricks, and sucked in deep breaths of air, pleasant air this time – a few extra feet of distance from the ground made all the difference.

A few more breaths. 'Walk,' he told himself.

He managed it. He got to the end of the alley and looked around, figuring out where he was. Not far from his favourite bar. He'd not covered much ground since closing time and was still further from home than he'd have liked.

He patted his pockets, hoping desperately he still had some money left for a cab. Nothing. He turned them inside out. Still nothing.

'Fucking whore,' he spat. He vaguely remembered the woman. She'd led him down the alley and he'd pulled his pants down; the rest was a blur. She'd taken his cash, probably when he'd blacked out. He had no idea if he'd even got his money's worth out of her.

He started staggering down the street. He'd have to walk, there was no other option.

By the time he left the slums behind, his headache had turned from feeling like he was being clubbed with a mace to being whacked by a hammer. He made it as far as the fountain in the middle of the city square, which was fed by a spring and had water clean enough to drink. He rushed over, practically dunked his head into the rippling pool, and drank and drank until his stomach could take no more. Then he vomited.

A well-dressed man on a horse trotted by. His tut was so loud that it sniped straight to Garrad's ears despite the clatter of iron-shod hooves on the cobbles.

'Mind your own business, you nonce!' Garrad bellowed. He rinsed out his mouth and filled his stomach once more. It stayed down this time, thankfully.

He continued into the east of the city, where the modest houses of the merchants, bankers, and shop keepers were. Small, but detached and well-kept. They had their own gardens and privies with proper plumbing. It normally smelt of roses and lavender here; somehow the smell of piss didn't linger. But it had been raining for a while now, and everything just smelled wet.

Home wasn't far. Another turn, another, then the wooden gate and the picket fence. He tried to straighten as he walked down the garden path, doing his best not to look as destroyed as he felt. He opened the door and dripped into the hallway.

Footsteps pattered over the ceramic-tile floor.

'Garrad!' His mother ran to him and put her arms around him, oblivious to how dirty he was or how wet he was making her. She let him go and raised up on her tiptoes to kiss his cheek. He was still too high up; he obligingly bent down to let her kiss him.

'Hello, Mother,' he mumbled.

She stepped back and slapped him hard and fast across the face. The ringing blast sent a throbbing wave of agony through his pounding head. He'd seen it coming; had known it would hurt like fuck, but he took it.

'Where the hell have you been? I've been worried sick!' she snapped.

'Just out, that's all.'

'Out – what do you mean, *out?*' She inhaled deeply. 'You stink.' The pungent aroma of vomit was unmistakable. 'You've been sick, have you been drinking again, Garrad?' She sighed. 'You can't keep doing this. You promised me, you promised your father. He'll be furious when you get to work!' Her high-pitched tone was making his headache worse – he wanted to get away, to lie down. But he couldn't. He had to go to work.

'I need a bath,' was all he said, brushing a tender hand over his mother's tensed shoulders as he ambled past to plod up the stairs.

'You can draw the water and heat it yourself!' she yelled after him. 'I'm not having Tilly do it!'

Garrad ignored her. He had no intention of asking the servant for help. The woman despised him, and he was planning on having a cold bath anyway – he didn't deserve anything better.

***

Davod stormed about his warehouse, his mood souring with every passing minute. He glanced at his watch again. It was almost noon. Where was

120

his bloody useless son? He'd been trying his best to focus on his work, to check the latest batch of wine barrels which had just arrived, but as the hours ticked by, he was finding it harder and harder to concentrate.

He'd tolerated his eldest son's tardiness for months. At first it was a couple of times a week; he'd arrive hung-over and maybe an hour late. Even so, he had to give it to the lad, once he got going, he was a grafter. The challenge was getting him to work in the first place.

The couple of times a week turned into several times a week, then it was every day and the mornings had been getting later and later. That Garrad wasn't here on time today wasn't a surprise. He wasn't in his bed when Davod left this morning. He left for work with just his second son, Andas, secretly glad he wouldn't have to look at the shell of a man who would eventually stagger in.

Davod gripped a barrel of wine. The waves of seething fury were rippling so potently he was struggling to function. As he forced himself to breathe, the sound of heavy footsteps echoed into the warehouse. His head jolted towards the doorway.

'Where the bloody hell have you been?' Davod roared at his son, tearing his hands from the barrel and slapping them on his hips.

Garrad screwed up his eyes, recoiling from his bellowing voice. 'Hello, Father,' he murmured.

'Do you know what time it is?' Davod barked.

Garrad stared at the space where his watch should have been. It wasn't there. 'No, about midday at a guess?' he said, in a despondent tone.

Davod sucked a few deep breaths through his gritted teeth; he tucked a stray strand of his long hair behind his ear and regarded the sorry figure in front of him. He was clean, but his sunken eyes were lined with shadowy pits. His sleeves were loose where they were once filled with muscle. His belly swelled from too much beer; his shoulders sagged with a desolate hunch. His hair was now long and unkempt, and he'd grown a straggly beard which he had never sported before. He held himself like a broken man. Somehow, the sorry form standing before him quelled his anger. Garrad looked like shit.

Davod shook his head in dark despair, the tears pricking the backs of his eyes. He wrenched his gaze from his son and found himself studying the wine barrel in front of him, tracking the grains in the wood while his heart broke into shattered shards.

'Father?' His son's soft, questioning tone was tinged with worry. It cut, it burnt, it made the sorrow worse.

Normally, Davod shouted, he yelled and chastised, then he ordered his son to work. Today things were different. After weeks of building sorrow and fury, something in Davod had cracked. Sadness beat the flaming ire at last. Today the fire was extinguished, and the smouldering ashes of sad acceptance were all that remained.

'D-did the delivery you were expecting turn up?' Garrad stammered. 'Do you want me to get on with sorting through it and getting it ready for our customers?'

'Andas has already done it,' Davod said softly. 'We had to get it out by midmorning.' Brimming tears blurred his vision.

'How about the next wine order? Do you want me to head to the docks to get some prices for next season's vintage?'

'That's where Andas is,' Davod muttered.

'Oh.' Garrad paused, running a hand through his scraggly hair. 'What about those dud swords at the back of the warehouse? Do you want me to have a go at seeing if I can find a blacksmith to tidy 'em up? If we can get the balance on them sorted, they could be used as training weapons.'

'Go home, Garrad. You look like you need some rest.' He knew Garrad wanted to do nothing more, but he also knew the lad's grit wouldn't let him. Despite his growing dependence on drink, his honour still remained. He'd work his hours, go straight to the pub, get drunk, go whoring again, probably, then it would start again.

'Father, I'm late. Surely there's work to catch up on? I'll stay into the evening tonight and make up for the time I've missed.'

Davod walked over to him slowly. He placed his hands on Garrad's arms and looked up into his son's eyes. Garrad was taller than Davod, and broader. Davod peered at the young man's face, tilted his head, and caught a glimpse of the bright young man he had known until three months ago. He was still there, buried. Maybe there was another way to bring him back.

Davod sniffed a short, sharp sniff, turned, and wiped away a tear, hoping his son hadn't seen. His heart pounded as his mind comprehended what he was about to do. It was the only thing he could think of, the only thing that might save him. If he lost his son's love, but the man survived, it would be enough.

'Come with me, son.' He gently slapped one of Garrad's arms and headed towards his office space in the corner.

Garrad obediently followed. Davod took a seat at his desk and waited while Garrad made himself comfortable on the wooden chair opposite.

'What are you doing to yourself, Garrad?' Davod said calmly as the lump in his throat choked him. He cleared his throat, and waited while his son fidgeted his restless hands in his lap in pitiful silence. 'You're going to kill yourself if you keep going like this. If it's not the drink that takes you, it will be some cut-throat in the shithole end of town you insist on drinking in.'

'The beer's cheap there,' Garrad muttered defensively.

'Cheap, and it tastes like horse piss.'

Garrad shrugged, feet tapping.

'Is that what you want? To die? If you do, there are more honourable ways. You could get a job as security on a trading ship. They are always looking for men who are good with a sword. At least if you died doing that—'

'I don't deserve honour.' Garrad's feet stopped tapping. His hands lay still, and he tracked the cracks on the floor with apparent interest.

'You do!' Davod tried his best to sound sincere. Somehow, he knew that his voice lacked conviction. 'You messed up – it was once and you did it for the right reasons, from what you said. The bit in the bar maybe. I'm not sure about punching your captain.'

'Everyone called me a liar. They laughed at me. I'm a joke, the whole town knows it. The idiot who got kicked out of the army, the fool who claims to have helped a princess. Everyone knows who I am.'

'Everyone's forgotten. No one cares anymore.'

'I care. I'm a useless idiot.'

Davod closed his eyes and screwed them up as he battled more tears. He opened them to see his son still staring at the floor. Garrad couldn't have noticed his torment. Good. His son had never seen him cry and he planned to keep it that way.

'You plan to drink yourself to death? Is that it?' he said at last.

'Why not?' Garrad sighed.

'Because I didn't raise you all these years to see you throw everything away! You're the greatest swordsman this town has ever seen – you make me look like an amateur, and I was considered good in my day. You were born for great things. Maybe not in my business – I don't think you'll ever make much of a trader – but you have many skills. You could achieve so much.' Exasperation seeped into his words.

'I was supposed to be in the Army. It's what I was born for. But not now. There's nothing for me.' Garrad's sorry state of forlorn hopelessness was threatening to rip the blanket of sorrow from Davod's quelled fire of fury, but he worked to put it back; shouting wouldn't help. There was only one more thing, and the time had come. He took a few more deep breaths and quelled his smouldering rage. He built the courage to say what needed to be said.

'I knew a great man once,' he began.

'Good for you,' Garrad sniped, folding his arms.

'Don't you interrupt me!' Davod bellowed. A shred of anger had escaped. This was hard enough as it was – Garrad's impudence wasn't helping.

Garrad glared back, looking smug. Perhaps he wanted Davod to shout? Not today. Davod was determined not to yell, not this time.

'A man with your namesake, a man called Garrad.'

Garrad narrowed his eyes with a growing insolent pout, but Davod ignored it. He'd started, so he would finish.

'That man was the son of the Master of Sword – he was born for great things. He had a skill with a sword to rival yours when he was just a boy. His father was killed, and Queen Lila cast his mother out of the palace.'

'Unfortunate,' Garrad said dryly.

'Later, his mother died of a fever, and he was left an orphan. With no family, he was adopted by the new Master of Sword, a man who'd been a great friend of his father.'

'Things worked out for him then,' Garrad said sullenly.

'No!' Davod banged the table with his fist, his anger leaking to the surface again. 'Queen Lila took a dislike to his adoptive father too, and the pair of them were forced to leave Vorn. They went to Walrie and started all over again. His adoptive father joined the Walrian army and rose quickly through the ranks. From nothing, he became Master of Sword again, this time for the king of Walrie, and Garrad did well too – he progressed quickly and became a general.'

'Good for them.'

'A man who was Master of Sword had to start again as a private soldier in another country! And you are whining about being dropped from corporal.'

'Sergeant! I earned that rank,' Garrad snapped.

'Maybe you did, but you didn't keep your temper in check long enough to have it made official, did you? If you'd walked away from the brawl...' Heat surged in Davod's face – trying to stay calm was becoming a lost cause.

'Shouldn't have lost my temper, eh?' Garrad rose to his feet and slapped the desk. 'Where do you think I get that from? You do the same at every opportunity – you lose your rag. I know you got into brawls yourself as a young man, I've heard the stories. The men on the docks talk.'

'I do lose my temper; I can't deny it. But you losing it has nothing to do with me!'

'You're my father!'

Davod shot to his feet. 'No, I'm not!'

Garrad gasped, his eyes bulging. He looked vacant, confused.

Cutting, stabbing, shooting daggers of pain went through Davod's already shattered heart. His knees trembled; he slapped his hands to the desk to keep his balance and let his behind sag down into the waiting chair. He stared at the man he'd raised as his own, the man whose jaw still hung open, the man whose limp body collapsed back down into the chair opposite.

'You're not my father?' Garrad said at last, so quietly that it was barely above a whisper.

Davod swallowed what saliva was left in his dry mouth and inhaled deeply. 'Son, I'll always be your father. I've been there since you were a babe. I promised your mother I'd raise you as my own, and I have. I hope you never think I favoured Andas or Elliah over you. You are all my sons.'

'But you're not my *real* father?'

'I'm sorry son, no.'

'You're Andas and Elliah's real father.'

He nodded.

Moisture flooded Garrad's eyes, and he turned his head and wiped them, as keen to hide his tears from the man who'd raised him as Davod was to hide his own feelings. Garrad sniffed, turned back, and took a deep breath. 'Who *is* my father?' he rasped, voice quivering.

'Your father's name was Garrad. Garrad Gragor.'

'The man you said you admired? You married his lover?' Garrad's face was aghast.

'Your father died before I met your mother. He died in Darrudin, trying to protect Queen Emma during Queen Lila's attack on the city. He was protecting the queen and your mother at the time, and your mother's parents. He had the noblest of deaths.'

'Was he married to Mother?'

Davod shook his head slowly.

'So I'm a bastard?'

'No one ever need know; you are my son. You are Garrad Bramston.'

'I'm not though, am I? I'm Garrad Gragor, the bastard.'

'He would have married your mother if he'd have lived.'

'But he didn't live. He was happy to fuck my mother and get her knocked up without bothering to make a decent woman of her.'

'Don't you dare speak about your mother that way!' Davod growled.

'Why not? It's true, isn't it? For all your talk about how honourable he was, he was nothing but a prick who couldn't keep it in his pants.'

Davod's heart pounded; this was not how he'd imagined Garrad would take the news. Somehow it had backfired, and he was under attack. His instincts told him to defend himself. He was using every ounce of self-control he could muster not to scream back at his son, not to strike him, to punish him for the awful words he'd said about his mother and natural father, a man admired by all who knew him. He squeezed one hand with the other and clenched his teeth.

'I suggest you leave and come back when you've had the chance to calm down,' he said at last, slowly and deliberately.

Garrad jolted to his feet, 'Fine,' he barked, and turned on his heel and left.

15. Last Resort

Location: Vornston, Vorn, Gemini (Planet M69245)

L ilian sat on top of a short stone wall and stared at the view which stretched away into the distance before her. The wall lined the road to the palace, and she was waiting as close to the gates as she dared. Waiting, hoping and trying her best to enjoy the scenery.

She couldn't deny that the vista was incredible. Whoever had chosen this location to build the home of the rulers of Vorn certainly had an eye for a great spot. The massive palace complex was set on a plateau on top of a gently rolling hill. The city of Vornston cascaded gently down the slopes, a sea of whitewashed polygons with terracotta rooves. Winding viaducts snaked through the place in elegant curves and graceful arches, the statues stood tall between the audience of buildings, and the magnificent temples towered above all, their intricately carved masonry projecting high above the sea of shops and inns and homes.

Whitewashed shapes with splashes of green. The autumn rains had long since quenched the summer drought and brought the browning leaves of spindly trees into emerald vigour. A massive wall stood beyond the whites and greens and terracotta orange. The sturdy city wall, in hues of grey rock, jutted high above the homes it protected. Tall and turreted, absorbing the solid footsteps of patrolling soldiers, the outer rim of the capital city of Vorn was impenetrable.

Beyond the walls, a patchwork landscape of mismatched fields billowed out towards sprawling forests of towering trees. The leafy giants crawled far up onto the slopes of distant hills before fading into withered specks, one of which drew Lilian's gaze. She stared at the green-grey blob mindlessly, until at last, her eyes blurred and she blinked away the fuzz.

She found herself drawn to the matchstick form of a marching soldier who patrolled along the wall, his steel armour glinting in the sun, his spear pointing skywards from his shoulder. He was too far away to see much detail; she could almost pretend she was looking at her son. He walked tall and proud, like Garrad once had – her first-born son, born of lust, love, and a longing for a man who would never know his child.

A sad smile played across her lips while a tear welled in her eye. She tried not to think of how she'd failed her son, how she had let it come to this. How it was that she found herself hundreds of miles from home, sitting on a cold stone wall outside the palace of the Queen of Vorn, clutching at the smallest of straws in her plight to save him.

A firm hand reached around her back and pulled her to one side. She turned to see the smiling face of the most amazing man she knew. The man who'd fallen for an unwed young mother and raised her son as his own. Her sad smile widened, and she flicked the tears away.

'It can't be much longer,' Davod began, as if reading her thoughts. 'I refuse to believe they don't come out most days, one of them at least. You knew the prince consort and Princess Kia as well as the Queen, right?'

Lilian sniffed a gentle sniff to clear her nostrils. She nodded. 'I knew Queen Emma the best – we were together for weeks in the mountains as we fled Queen Lila – but I met Prince Tom and Princess Kia too. They came to the village of my mother's people when we were hiding from Lila, but I didn't get to know them well.'

'And they met Garrad too?'

'No, not then. I still did not know I was with child. The queen and the prince came back to the village later. It was then they met Garrad as a baby. I told Emma I wanted him to serve her. When he joined the army, I thought he was fulfilling that promise, but...'

Her head sagged into her waiting palms as the tears flowed. Davod reached around her and pulled her into his firm embrace.

'I'm so sorry, Lilian.' Davod placed a soft kiss on his wife's head. 'This is all my fault – if I hadn't opened my big mouth...'

She pulled away from him, sniffed away the tears, and wiped her eyes with her sleeve. 'No, Davod, don't ever say that. This is not your fault. You did what you thought was right, like you always have. Without you, I'd still be in Thost, an old maid with my parents. Garrad would be a nobody. I'd have never been able to keep my promise to Emma.' She fought to keep the tears at bay.

His hands slipped from her sides, and he took her hands in his. 'There's no way you'd still be alone if I hadn't found you. Someone else would have snapped you up – you're far too special for it to have gone any other way.'

Her teeth edged into her lower lip as she returned a squeeze to his hands. She leant slowly forwards and kissed him softly on the cheek, then shuffled closer and rested her head on his shoulder.

'My bottom's starting to go numb,' she muttered after a while, with a soft giggle.

'Aye, mine too. It's our second day of waiting and we never recovered from yesterday.'

'Are you sure she'll see us? I'm starting to think this is hopeless, even if they do come out. It's been so long since I last saw her, and she never replied to my letters.'

'We discussed this, Lilian. Do you think I'd have come all the way to Vornston with you if I didn't think this plan would work? I don't believe for one moment the queen reads her own letters. One of her aids will have got it, laughed at it, and thrown it in the bin. She'd never have even read it.'

'The guards wouldn't even pass on a message for us!' She scowled at the soldiers who loitered by the palace gates – it was the fourth time today she'd exchanged her vilest of looks with the stubborn sentries. They had tried to gain entry yesterday; they'd tried everything to persuade them to pass on a simple message, but they refused. All they could do was sit outside the palace and hope someone Lilian knew would come out, hope she'd be recognised, and hope they'd hear what she had to say. There were a lot of hopes to line up, but there was nothing else she could think of to save her son.

Davod's warm eyes were sparkling. A surge of warmth flooded his kindly face.

'Thank you, Davod,' she said, in barely more than a whisper. 'Thank you for coming with me and thank you for loving Garrad like he was your own.'

'Lilian,' he began, squeezing her hand with renewed vigour, 'Garrad may not have my blood, but he will always be my son and I will do everything I can to save him. Hell, half the reason he is drinking himself to death is because it was me who blurted out who his real father was. But we have to make the most of things – we can turn my mistake into an advantage. Now he knows the truth, we can ask for help; the queen has the power to get him back in the Army. If we can sort it, he'll be saved.

He's got too much of his real father in him to ever be a merchant. If we want to save him, we have to get him serving. And if we can get him sober enough for us to talk to him, I'll try my darndest to talk some sense into the idiot and try to get him to control that bloody temper of his!'

Lilian couldn't help but smile at his last words. She leaned towards him and kissed him on the cheek. 'I don't know how. But he gets his temper from you.'

'That's what he said!' Davod shook his head.

'Not all traits our children develop come from the blood,' Lilian said with a smile.

***

'Emma, are you sure you can't find time for the hunt? You've not had a day or even a morning off in weeks!' Tom called across to his wife, who was sitting at her dressing table in her nightgown, going through some paperwork.

'I said I'd see. I've looked through this lot and it's no use, I simply can't afford the time. There are so many needing my signature and I can't sign them without reading them. That would be a slippery slope.'

Tom tutted at his wife's resolute tone; there was no use arguing further, so he resumed his attempt to get dressed. 'Why do they make these so tight! Bloody archaic clothing.' Tom was battling with his breeches.

Emma turned away from her papers and regarded him curiously. 'Two things,' she said with a smirk. 'One, you've had clothes made for you that need a manservant to help you get into.'

'I don't need a bloody manservant!'

'Two,' she continued, 'you've put on a few pounds.'

Tom was mortified at her smirking face. He glanced down at his belly and grabbed a handful of flesh. 'Just skin, Emma. I haven't changed since the day I came to Gemini.'

'Yeah, right!' She laughed. 'When was the last time you went for a run?'

'It's not befitting for princes to go running,' he replied indignantly.

'Like that used to stop you!'

'I'm older and wiser. I understand Gemini better.'

'Bollocks,' she said, her words barely disguised by a cough.

'It's certainly not befitting for a queen to use that language!' Tom was hopping and pulling as he spoke.

'No, I agree, but only in public. Around you, I can say what I want.'

'No respect!' he said, with feigned disgruntlement.

There was a knock on the door.

'Come in!' Emma called, gently.

A woman of middling years in a simple but impeccably neat dress entered and curtsied to the queen, keeping her eyes away from Tom and his battle with his clothes. She was used to seeing the man half-dressed, and she always did her best to ignore him.

'Are you ready to be dressed, Your Majesty?'

'Of course, Silanne.' Emma dropped her papers and rose to her feet. 'Go without me, Tom, I'll see you at lunchtime.'

'OK.' He had a breakthrough with his breaches; his second leg popped in and he just about managed to fasten the button at the waistline. Quietly satisfied with his efforts, he walked over to his wife and kissed her on the lips. 'On one condition.'

'What?'

'You spend some time today checking with your secretary about when you can be released for some time off!'

'Fine, deal.'

***

It was going to be a quiet affair this morning. Just Tom and Mark and their sons, Olli and Monty. Eliza had kept talking about coming too, but she kept coming up with excuses as to why she had to miss out at the last minute. Tom couldn't work her out. But she was a teenage girl, and they were a strange breed. Emma seemed to think she was self-conscious and was probably waiting for her mother to go out with them too, so she wasn't the only woman. She was probably right. Even more reason for his wife to come with them.

Tom ambled across the stable yard to where Mark and their sons waited for him, already mounted and ready to go.

'Don't worry mate, you take all the time you need. You are the prince; you take it easy.' Mark mocked his old friend with a toothy grin.

'Sod off, Harrison,' Tom snapped, fighting to mask his own smirk. 'You know I'm married to the queen, right? We share a bedroom and everything. She held me up. Every morning she spends a good hour asking me how best to run the country and...' He stopped talking when Mark, Olli, and Monty all laughed in unison. 'Oi!'

'Tell us another one, Father!' Olli chuckled.

'If you want to make up stories, try to make them believable,' Mark mocked.

Tom scowled at them and vaulted into his saddle. It looked graceful, he proudly conceded. He regretted it at once. As he swung his leg over the rump of his horse and slapped his arse down, his upper thigh creaked and groaned. His face contorted.

Mark tutted and shook his head. 'You can try and look like you're still in your thirties, mate, but that won't make it so. You're getting old and out of shape.'

'You sound like bloody Emma!'

'Maybe we have a point!' Mark replied.

The boys sniggered at Mark's casual mockery of the prince of Vorn. Tom glared at his son and nephew; they stretched their faces into forced seriousness.

Tom took his reigns in hand, straightened, and regained his composure. 'Right, are we ready?'

The clatter of horseshoes on cobbles rattled through the courtyard as the four of them trotted out of the inner keep, along the tree-lined avenue of the vast gardens that surrounded the inner keep, and towards the main gatehouse. They approached the outer wall, and the guards began to open the massive gates. They were soon out of the confines of the palace grounds, with far-reaching views of the city and the fields and forests beyond.

It was a chilly day in early winter, but it was sunny and dry. Tom was itching to get moving, to warm himself as he moved with his horse. He wasn't looking at the road in front of him, and when a flash of movement caught the corner of his eye it was too late to react.

'Lilian!' someone called.

Tom's mare reared. At least his horse was looking where she was going. His hunter was not a warhorse; she was not trained to mow people down.

Tom felt his balance go; he was tumbling headfirst to the ground. He managed to get his feet out of his stirrups and engage his magic in time to soften his fall.

Boots thudded down the road, chain mail jingled, swords rattled. The gate guards had surrounded the woman who'd startled his horse before Tom could get back on his feet. One of them rushed to Tom to help him up, while Mark and the boys watched with amusement.

A soldier brushed Tom down. 'I'm terribly sorry, Your Highness, if we'd known she was going to do that...'

'Tom!' The woman was calling his name as she was carried off.

'Let her go!' a man called out.

Tom? Tom thought. *Who calls me Tom except my family?* He stepped round his horse to watch the woman being dragged towards the gates; a man was also being restrained.

'Tom!' she called again.

'Halt!' Tom bellowed at the guards. 'Let me see the woman.'

They executed his command at once, and they parted. The woman was being held firmly by two of the guards. He could see her in her entirety now. Tom looked her up and down; he knew her, he was sure of it. Her dark, tightly curled hair, her caramel complexion, the large innocent eyes of the young woman who had doted so much on his long-dead friend. A young woman who was much older, but her eyes had stayed the same.

'Lilian!' He rushed over to her and wrapped his arms around her in an embrace. The confounded guards released her, not sure what to do with themselves.

'Tom, oh Tom, it's good to see you.' She squeezed him back tightly.

'You will refer to His Majesty as Your Highness!' barked the senior guard.

Tom relaxed his embrace. 'If this lady wishes to call me Tom, I have no objections. Do you, Sergeant?'

'I, er – of course not, Your Highness.'

'Good.' Tom turned to Mark. 'You remember Lilian, right, Mark? Didn't you meet her in Allantra?'

'No, I don't think I did.' He scratched his head. 'I've heard you talk about her though.'

Tom pursed his lips for a moment. 'Mark, how about you take the boys and go for that hunt? Lilian and I might have some catching up to do.'

Mark's brows squeezed into a furrowed ridge. He looked from Tom to Lilian to the other man, who stood protectively by Lilian's side, and shrugged. 'Fair enough, see you later.' He dug in his heels and his horse clattered away, the young princes following.

***

Tom led Lilian and Davod inside the palace walls, keeping conversation to a minimum, not wanting the guards to overhear anything they discussed. He recalled that Lilian was his friend's lover. He remembered meeting her son months after his death, and he had just been introduced to her husband. He had no idea why they were suddenly here, but he sensed the topic could be sensitive. He sent a servant to notify his wife of their arrival, took them into the main palace building, and found a quiet room where they could chat out of earshot of guards or servants.

'Take a seat, please.' Tom indicated towards a fine red-velvet couch and took a seat in an armchair opposite. 'You can relax, Lilian.' He sensed her discomfort; she stood rigidly, scanning the lavish surroundings of the palace interior. He smiled warmly at her, trying to put her at ease. Her husband took her arm and pulled her softly to the couch.

Lilian smiled back as she took a seat and sat as rigidly as she'd stood, back straight, her hands gripping her knees tightly. 'Your Highness, I'm grateful you agreed to see us,' she said.

'Please, call me Tom. I've never been too keen on royal titles.'

'If you're sure?'

'Of course! When I knew you, I was Tom, and I'm still Tom. When you see Emma, she will be happy to be called Emma too.'

'The queen is content for my wife to address her as such?' Davod asked in astonishment.

'We are far more relaxed about such things than you might think, around friends.'

'Of course, Your Highness. But please do not expect me to call you anything else. I could not bring myself to use any name but your titles.'

'Whatever makes you comfortable,' Tom said reassuringly to Davod. 'Lilian,' he began, his attention switching to the man's wife. 'I can't deny it is good to see you looking so well after all these years. I...'

A servant entered the room carrying a tray of fine porcelain cups on saucers and a pot of tea. They waited patiently for the tea to be poured and the drinks to be served.

'Thank you, Hopkins,' Tom said to the servant, and tracked the man out of the room as he sipped his tea. 'Sorry about that, where was I? Ah, I wanted to ask...' He glanced cautiously towards Davod. 'Erm...'

Lilian sensed his trepidation. 'About Garrad's son?' she guessed.

'Yes.' Tom let out a small sigh of relief. 'Garrad Junior, is he well?'

Lilian's face dropped and her eyes sank to the floor. Davod took her hand in his.

'Oh, I'm sorry, he's not – er...'

Lilian cut him off. 'He's alive, if that's what you're wondering. But I'd be lying if I said he was well.' She swallowed hard. 'He – he needs your help. That's why we're here.' Davod nodded for her to continue and squeezed her hand supportively. 'He...'

'Of course, Lilian, how can I help?' Tom leaned forwards in his chair.

'He—'

'Lilian!'

Emma appeared in the doorway and rushed towards her old friend. Lilian appeared to panic at the sight of the approaching queen in her fine gown and jingling jewels. She and Davod leapt to their feet.

Emma engulfed Lilian in a hug. 'It's so good to see you!' She squeezed the woman tightly. Lilian returned the embrace. Emma relaxed and beamed at her. Her eyes flicked to Davod and back to Lilian, her face questioning.

'Sorry, Your M-Majesty...' Lilian stuttered.

'Please, call me Emma while we are alone.'

'I did tell her that,' Tom added.

'Sorry... Emma. I – um, I'd like you to meet my husband, Davod Bramston.'

'Mr Bramston, it's lovely to meet you,' Emma said warmly.

'And you too, Your Majesty.'

'Please relax, the pair of you. Sit down, please.' Emma took a seat in another armchair next to Tom.

135

'They're hoping for help with Garrad's son.' Tom told his wife.

'Oh.' Emma's face flooded with concern. 'Is he well?'

'Not quite. I'm sorry to bother you with such trivial matters as the welfare of my son, Emma, but we didn't know where else to turn. We...'

'Please do not apologise,' Emma interrupted. 'Garrad served me bravely. I have known no other man to show such loyalty, such honour.'

Tom turned to his wife, looking hurt.

'Except you,' she said, slapping him gently on the thigh. 'Garrad was a great man. I owe my life to him, but sadly I can never repay the debt to the man himself, so if there is anything I can do to help his son, you need only ask.'

Lilian nodded, glanced quickly at her husband, who looked back supportively, then turned back to the queen and began her tale.

By the end of her story, Lilian was in tears; the poor woman was sobbing inconsolably. Emma had moved to the couch and was sitting next to Lilian. She took her hand in her own, squeezing it gently.

'We knew Eliza and Alora had been to a pub in Tannel,' Emma began. 'My brother-in-law, the lord commander, caught them sneaking back. We had no idea there'd been an incident while they were there. The girls left that detail out.' Her voice was stern as she finished: 'And Garrad was there, you say, he was involved? He got into a fight because of them and that's what led him to hit the colour sergeant?'

Lilian nodded – more tears streamed. Emma pulled her into her arms and held her head against her shoulder.

'Yes. Definitely,' Davod replied on behalf of his wife. 'He hadn't realised who it was at first. He thought maybe they were using magic to hide who they were, but somehow, he figured it out. He went round telling everyone he'd been kicked out because he'd saved a princess. No one believed him. He was just about managing before then. He'd settled into working in my business; he drank but not so much it stopped him doing his work. As more and more people heard his tale and told him he was nuts, he stopped believing his own story. He concluded he'd been thrown out for nothing.

'When he'd thought it was because he'd saved a princess, he could deal with that. Once he'd convinced himself it was some whore or other that he'd saved, his downward spiral began. He drank more and more, became more depressed, started whoring again, or at least doing it without giving a damn who knew about it.'

Lilian pulled her face away from Emma and cast Davod a sharp look.

'What?' he exclaimed. 'He was, we can't deny that.'

Lilian let out a breath as more tears flooded down her face.

'We need to have a chat with the girls,' Emma suggested.

***

Tom went for the princesses. He found them seated in a private sitting room, gossiping with some of the other ladies while they did some embroidery. Eliza looked incredibly relived to be liberated as Tom pulled her and her cousin away to meet Lilian.

'What's this all about, Father?' Eliza asked as they walked through the palace.

'I'll let your mother explain.'

'Ah, there you are, please take a seat.' Emma's voice was stern. Tom recognised that tone; he knew the girls did too. He watched, bemused, as the two young ladies sheepishly sat down, casting curious glances at the unfamiliar commoners as they did.

'The pub you ventured into in Tannel a few months back – did anything of interest happen while you were there?' Tom asked.

Eliza's eyes were wide, her mouth open. Alora mimicked her look of terror. *Guilty as charged*, Tom thought. He summoned his magic to cast a simple spell, one that would let him know at once if they lied.

'Um...' Eliza seemed to be desperately trying to think of a way to talk her way out of this. 'Um...'

'Eliza? Alora? Do either of you care to answer?' Emma asked again, firmly.

'It was nothing, a brawl. Nothing to do with us!' Eliza blurted.

Tom's magical senses were rattled. 'You're lying, Eliza,' Tom said sternly. 'Try again.'

'Maybe the brawl had something to do with us, but we didn't really see it,' she corrected herself.

'Better. How about you give us the details? Did you see anyone you recognised while you were there? Any of the soldiers you'd come across while you were out visiting the sergeant's cadres with the lord commander and Master of Sword?'

Out of nowhere, Alora erupted into tears. 'I'm sorry, it's my fault!'

Eliza reached for Alora's shoulder, holding her, perhaps to comfort herself as well as her sobbing cousin.

'Alora, what wasn't your fault?' Emma asked softly.

'It's my fault Corporal Bramston got the lashes. A soldier was hassling me, and the corporal tried to defend my honour. I didn't need his help, of course – I used magic to push the letch away and we fled. After I did it, I recognised the corporal from the training exercise.' She sniffed. 'He was the one who'd had a broken arm and I fixed it. The next thing I knew, Father asked me to heal his back. It was horrific. I'd never seen anything like it. He barely had any skin left!' She could no longer control her sobs and buried her face in Eliza's shoulder.

'You never told me it was him you were sent to heal!' Eliza whispered.

'Garrad was telling the truth!' Davod exclaimed. 'He did save a princess, or try to?'

'You doubted him?' Lilian chastised her husband.

'I, er—'

'It doesn't matter, does it? Not now,' Emma concluded. 'The important thing is the brawl that got Garrad into the cadre commander's office started because of the girls. And the bad news that he gave Garrad made him react badly and punch him. You should be aware, Alora – punching an officer is why he got fifty lashes and not ten.'

'But I started it!' She began to wail some more.

'We both did, Alora. I'm as much to blame as you.' Eliza was doing a far better job at keeping herself composed.

'What a right old mess this is,' Tom concluded. 'But I think we've got to the bottom of things. Now we need to work out what the heck are we going to do to save young Garrad.'

138

16. Second Chance

Location: Tannel, Vorn, Gemini (Planet M69245)

He'd forgotten how good anonymity felt; it had been a while. Tom ambled down the cobbled street. Here and there the polished face of a rounded stone smiled up at him from between the veins of shit and filth. Horse dung mixed with good old-fashioned dirt and rotting slops had been compacted onto the street over decades. Here, no one cleaned the streets.

Tom had been in Gemini for over twenty years. Before he came to the planet, he was an officer in the British Army. He'd been in the Corps of the Royal Engineers. He'd always liked building. The lack of proper sewers in his adopted land of Vorn was one he'd been keen to sort out. No society could be healthy without sewers. The Romans had them, but they'd been left abandoned for fourteen centuries in England before the Victorians got round to building some more. That was after the Industrial Revolution was under way, when society had gunpowder, rifles, cannons, and a load of other shit Tom couldn't remember. Before that, they still didn't have proper sewers.

Tom wasn't going to let Vorn wait that long – in his first few years as prince consort, he'd sorted sewers in all the major cities. But in this part of town it seemed the folk didn't know what they were for.

It stank. Piss and shit and human filth. Every grubby peasant he walked past was a fresh source of vile fragrance. Humans who hadn't washed in months, possibly years. People so grimy he wondered how they were still alive, how they had not been poisoned by the bacteria that infested their hovels as much as it encased their being.

Tom could do much, build much – or at least he could get the country's engineers and builders to build things. Emma was more than happy to let him take the lead on such things. But he couldn't change a society. It was out of his skill set. He was no sociologist, he was a Sapper. An engineer and a sorcerer.

Like all Earthlings on Gemini, he had the capacity to wield magic with a power much greater than any native sorcerer. Their own abilities were trivial in comparison to his. To cast a spell to make himself anonymous was easy, but it was rarely necessary.

Dressed in ordinary clothes, what a peasant might wear before it became tattered and worn and filthy, he strolled down the street, the only remarkable thing about him being that he was clean. That attracted few stares. Most of the miserable people here were too absorbed in their own troubles to care if one of their own bothered to wash. Thankfully, most of Tannel wasn't like this part of the city. Most of it was clean and well-kept.

He walked past the slums. Rough wooden doors were braced with fat bars of steel. Timber-framed houses were patched up with wattle and daub. There were no windows, just heavy shutters where the light might be allowed to enter during the day, when those who existed inside were satisfied they could protect what little they had from those who wanted to take it.

It was late afternoon. The days were short at this time of year. The sun hadn't set yet, but it teased the horizon. From what Garrad's parents had told Tom, the lad would already be on his way to being hammered, and Tom didn't want to find him when he was too pissed.

He left the slums and came to the nice part of the crap part of town. Businesses operated here; the shop keepers and pub landlords knew nicer streets meant more trade, so they did a bit to keep it looking decent.

There were pubs aplenty; the peasants needed somewhere to drown their sorrows. Tom had his destination fixed in his head. He'd used his magic to get a fix on the lad. It was hard. He'd only met the son of his old friend once, when he was just a baby. He'd bear no resemblance to his infant self now. But the image of Garrad's father was still fixed in his mind. It had never left. The man who'd died to save his wife would never be forgotten, the memory of the father was enough to let him find his son.

He knew he was nearly there; the presence was inside the building to his right. The sign showed the shape of a crown, faded and dirty, a kind of mucky yellow with some orange and brown blobs. There was no writing as most of the peasants couldn't read. Tom's attempts at setting up schools hadn't been as successful as his sewer building.

The door was ajar. A pub with a closed door was a pub where you could barely breathe. The smoke from the chimney, which probably hadn't been swept in years, had to escape somehow. He took a final breath of fresh air and strolled into the gloomy pub. Winters in Vorn were chilly at times, but inside, the fire raged.

Oil lamps gave the murky interior a boost. The sun was starting to hide for the night, the open windows and doors were good for letting the smoke out but not so much the sun's rays in. As Tom's eyes adjusted, he let his magic home in on his target. Amongst the battered tables, where groups of men hunched over their drinks – the only reprieve of their miserable existence they could afford – a figure sat alone on a stool. His elbows were on the table, forehead in his hands, staring at the clay mug of beer beneath his sagging head. The man reached for a jug and refilled his mug. He barely looked at what he was doing. The well-practiced ritual of keeping the beer ever ready to drink needed little attention.

'There's a table at the back, over there, sir.'

The well-endowed serving wench caught Tom unawares. He suddenly realised he had been standing in the middle of the pub looking lost. *Sir*, she'd called him. He looked himself up and down and realised how posh being clean made you round here.

'That's OK, I'm meeting a friend.' He smiled at her and started walking to where Garrad sat. 'Oh,' he turned back, 'can I get another jug and a mug, please?' It was beer or beer in this place. No need to specify.

'Of course, sir, I'll bring it over.'

He pulled up a stool and sat opposite Garrad. The young man ignored him.

'Mind if I join you?'

Garrad didn't lift his head. 'Looks like you already have.'

'I guess. Are you happy to share your table? It's getting busy.'

'Suit yourself.'

Tom waited for his beer in silence. The wench brought his jug over quickly; she perhaps sensed he had more cash than most in this place. Tom placed a silver coin in her hand. 'Keep the change,' he said with a wink.

She looked at the silver. 'Thank you, sir, you are most generous.' She sauntered off, leaving them alone.

'No one does that round here,' Garrad muttered.

141

'Does what?'

'Tips the bar staff.'

'I'm not from round here.'

'That's plain to see.'

'How do you know? You've not taken your eyes off your mug since I sat down.'

Garrad laughed. 'You're not a soldier, are you?'

Tom felt a little offended by the comment. It had been a couple of decades, but he certainly was a soldier once. *No*, he corrected himself, he'd been an officer, not a soldier.

'You're saying soldiers see stuff others don't?' said Tom.

'Bingo.'

'If you're a soldier, what are you doing here, clutching a mug of ale alone? Shouldn't you be training? It's not a leave day today – the others are in the barracks or on exercise.'

'How the fuck do you know that?' Garrad looked up. Tom felt his every feature being scrutinised – the young man was clearly getting the measure of him. Garrad narrowed his eyes. 'You're more than you seem, aren't you?'

Tom feigned ignorance. 'Why do you say that?'

'Most would think you a jumped-up shop keeper. Trying to show off that he can afford to have a bath. But you ain't a shop keeper. You're built like you've trained with a sword at some point. Perhaps not so much recently, now you carry a bit of flab where muscle used to be.'

Tom was hurt, but he tried his best not to show it.

'Your face is clean-shaven, proper neat. Like you can afford a decent mirror to do it, or even someone to do it for you. Your hair has been trimmed by someone who knows how to do it, like a barber. No one round here pays for barbers. Your face – you've seen some action. Your nose has been broken and you have a few scars. Old ones, but they're there. And your hands... Fuck me, what the hell happened to your hand?'

'You still think I'm not a soldier?'

'No, you ain't. You're something else.'

'Mm.' Tom leaned back, clasping his arms across his chest, impressed at Garrad's observations. He studied his left hand and grimaced at the memories of his torture. He'd been captured by Prince Aran and been at his mercy for weeks. Every finger had been broken; his knuckles smashed. He'd been healed by his wife's sister afterwards. There was no better healer in the land. The hand worked fine now, and only ached occasionally, when it was really cold. Thankfully, Vorn was warm most of the time and princes weren't expected to hang around outside when it was chilly.

Tom held his mutilated hand in front of him and opened and closed his fist. 'Some dick shit smashed it to bits,' he said.

Garrad grinned. 'Must have really hurt. I hope you killed the fucker after.'

Tom couldn't help but laugh. 'No. I didn't. A friend of mine got rid of him though. He got trapped somewhere he can never return from. I hope he rots there.'

'Sounds risky to me. Live enemies have a way of finding their way back to you.'

'Trust me, he's stuck.'

'Are you sure?'

'As sure as I can be.'

Garrad took a long sip of his beer. Tom did likewise. It tasted like piss. Fermented piss, with hops and barley thrown in, and certainly more than a hint of alcohol. It wasn't exactly the fine ale he was used to. It reminded him of the crap his soldiers used to drink back when he was an officer on Earth. He still remembered the barbeques with the lads where there was nothing else to drink. But he hadn't turned his nose up at it; he had never wanted to look aloof.

'Why are you here?' Garrad asked. 'A mysterious man who knows about the Army's days off and had his hand smashed to bits, at this end of Tannel. And at my table to boot. What do you want?'

The kid was sharp, Tom thought. The lad swayed slightly; he'd had a few already. This was probably his second jug, but he could still think in spite of it. There was no point beating around the bush. 'I'm here to talk to you.'

'Thought as much. Why? Did my mother send you? She is about the only one who knows where to find me.'

He hadn't wanted to get to the point this quickly. But fuck it. 'Yes. She sent me – she and your father. They're worried about you.'

'He's not my father. I don't have a father. My father's dead.'

143

'He is the man who raised you and he loves you like a father. That should be enough. You should give the man credit; he seems like a decent chap.'

'Seems? Did you only just meet him?'

'Yes, a week or so ago. He and your mother came to see me.'

'Why the fuck did they think you could help me? Who the hell are you anyway?' Garrad seemed to be losing patience; he clearly wanted to drink his ale in peace.

'I was a friend of your father's. Your real father.'

'Oh. That fucking arsehole.'

'Garrad Gragor was one of the best men I have ever known,' Tom said sternly.

'Maybe you need some more friends. The man was a dick.'

'Look, you little shit.' The atmosphere changed in an instant, and the friendliness in Tom's tone vanished. 'Garrad was great man. He was strong and brave. He was an excellent tactician. He knew how to lead, to make men follow him. He was loyal and put duty above all else. He died for that duty, he died to protect our queen.'

'I've heard.' The dryness in Garrad's tone was infuriating.

Tom took a few deep breaths and restored his composure. 'And you do not think this makes him a good man? You do not think saving our queen is a noble feat?'

Garrad shrugged.

'He also died to save you, and your mother and her parents.'

Garrad said nothing. He tilted his head to the side, his face questioning. Tom let the silence stand.

'Who the fuck are you?'

'My name is Prince Thomas of Vorn.' Tom said quietly, so as not be overheard.

Garrad laughed.

'Don't believe me if you want, that's up to you. Here's the thing. You might be wrong. I might be who I say I am. You have to agree there's a chance.'

'More chance I'll start shitting gold coins, I reckon.'

'I'd say there's a chance of that – check your pants.' A smirk spread across Tom's face.

Garrad reached down into his breeches and pulled out a shiny gold coin. 'What the fuck?'

'I assume you know Prince Thomas is a sorcerer? Getting one of my coins into your pants is not a difficult trick.'

Garrad gawped at him.

'Why are you here, Garrad?'

'To have a drink, why do you think?'

'And why were you here yesterday?'

'I wasn't. I was in The Mason's Arms.'

'You know what I mean.' Tom brushed off his petulance. 'Why are you drinking your life away? Why the fuck have you let being kicked out of the Army destroy you like this? Your father was a great man, not just because he was a great solder and a leader, not just because he gave his own life for those he cared about, but because when the world fucked him over, he picked himself up and tried again. He wouldn't have given up; he wouldn't have thrown everything away like this.'

'I don't give a shit what Garrad Gragor would have done. The arsehole knocked my mother up and couldn't even be bothered to wed her. He might have died to save the queen and my mother, but when he did, he cursed me to become nothing but some dead dickhead's bastard. In the last few months, I've not only lost my career, the job I was born to do, the only thing that ever made sense. I've lost my father, my family, and my fucking legitimacy. I'm nothing now. I'm a nobody. That's why I drink. The booze dulls the pain and eventually it will kill me. One less bastard for the world to give a shit about.'

Tom sighed. 'Do you know who else is a bastard, Garrad?'

Garrad raised an eyebrow.

'Lord Harrison,' Tom answered his own question, the Commander of the queen's Armed Forces, was born to an unwed mother, a woman who raised him alone. He had a father he barely saw. The most senior man in Vorn's army is nothing but a worthless bastard.'

'Fuck off.'

'How about you ask him yourself?'

Garrad forced a laugh.

'Garrad, if the two worst things in your life are being kicked out of the Army and being a bastard, don't you think Prince Thomas would have the power to fix those? I can't turn back time, but I can certainly put you in touch with Lord Harrison. You two can have a long chat about what it means to be a bastard. He will tell you it means fuck all. And I can certainly sort out your career problems.

'It's up to you – stay in this shithole, drink yourself to death, and give up, or get yourself home, have a good night's sleep, and head to the Training Academy in the morning. Lord Harrison is there. He travelled down to Tannel with me, and we arrived yesterday. Think about it.'

Tom stood and headed towards the pub entrance.

***

Garrad watched Tom go; his head was all over the place. He was still staring at the door when he felt something in his breeches. He reached down and found three more gold coins in his pants.

'Fuck,' he muttered, pocketing them quickly before anyone saw.

17. There Is Hope

Eliza sauntered down the corridor towards the dining room, pulling her shawl tightly around her shoulders to defend against the morning chill. Another dawn of another day in the palace. Breakfast with her cousins and siblings, probably, parents, aunt and uncle absent, most likely. They were always busy. Half the time, they had breakfast earlier than their children – the other half, they had breakfast with nobles or dignitaries. They worked from morning till night, but Eliza was spared from most breakfast formalities. She was normally only drawn into attending official events at mealtimes during lunch and dinner.

On this occasion, she was glad for the likely absence of her parents, aunt and uncle. She was still irritated with her uncle for how she and Alora had been left out of things on her trip down to Tannel. Their visit to the pub had gone wrong; she blamed her uncle for that too. If he hadn't left them out of things, they wouldn't have decided to go to the pub, and the brawl would never have happened.

Her uncle hadn't shown a shred of sympathy when he'd caught them sneaking back into Lord Hamin's house, or when he'd used his magic to make them tell the truth about where they'd been. After, he'd made a portal on the spot and sent them home to Eliza's father, who was none too pleased to be woken and told about his daughter and niece's misdemeanour. They'd been grounded for a couple of months. She'd already served her time as far as she was concerned, and now, after her parents found out what happened after they'd left, they were grounded again.

It wasn't fair. Because the stupid corporal got carried away, she was being punished for the same crime a second time. She and Alora were stuck inside the palace walls for god knows how long, no end date given. Her dreary existence had been made a whole lot duller.

She ambled into the dining room. Her sister was there — Hellenia the goody-goody. She couldn't recall the last time her older sister had got into trouble, put one foot out of place, done a single thing to earn a cross word from her parents.

'Good morning, Sister,' Hellenia greeted her, a nauseating smile plastered across her face.

'Good morning, Hellenia.'

'Did you sleep well?' Hellenia asked, with feigned sincerity.

'Yes, of course,' Eliza lied as she took a seat as far from her sister as the place settings would allow.

Alcohol never led to a good night's sleep. She'd had one too many glasses of wine with dinner last night, emptying her glass far quicker than was ladylike to do so. It was the only way to get through a night of hosting when she was sulking so much, and completely not in the mood to do her duty. She forced a smile, determined not to let her sister know how she was feeling. She'd seen her disapproving looks as she'd finished another glass. She couldn't bear the thought of Hellenia's smug satisfaction if she knew Eliza was feeling the worse for wear.

She inwardly grimaced and made use of a lifetime of being trained to be the perfect lady. 'Do you have much planned for today?' she asked, attempting to show interest in Hellenia's day. She braced herself for the reply, fake smile already fixed on her face.

'Oh, yes, busy as always. First, I'm going to visit the city orphanage. I've been there a lot recently. The poor children always seem glad to see me when I go, and I do love to lift their spirits.'

Flipping do-gooder, Eliza thought while she nodded politely.

'And then I'm due to meet the mayor for a tour of the city. He is keen to show me the improvements he has been making to the roads recently, and I have been invited to lunch after.'

Her tone is sickly. I want to throw up, or punch her in the face. If only it was ladylike to do such a thing. I'm sick of being a lady. Do I really care if I look ladylike?

The princess droned on while Eliza dutifully listened, smiling and nodding at the right intervals, picturing Hellenia's face if she actually got up and whacked her. Alora arrived and saved her from her misery.

'You're here early!' Alora exclaimed, oblivious to the conversation she was interrupting. Eliza noticed her sister's huff and indignance at being interrupted and ignored, but pretended she hadn't as she turned to smile at her cousin.

'Morning,' she said to her cousin, 'I woke early today.'

'That's not like you!'

'I had an early night,' Eliza replied. Eliza had left dinner early, but only because if she hadn't, she might not have left the dining room walking in a straight line. That and her sister discreetly, but sanctimoniously, suggested she left before she made a fool of herself.

Alora took a seat by her cousin and waited patiently while a servant rushed over to pour her a cup of tea, and another arrived with Hellenia's breakfast. 'Are you ready to order, Your Highnesses?' he said to the two other princesses.

They ordered their food and continued to chat and ignore Hellenia, who finished her breakfast in silence. She never ate very much, so it didn't take her long.

As Hellenia was leaving, their brothers arrived, walking in together, dressed for riding. The pair were as inseparable as Eliza and Alora.

'Good morning, Sister, Cousin,' Monty greeted them cheerfully. They replied in kind. 'What are you two up to today? Olli and I are going for a ride. We reckon we can get into the mountains and back in a day. I'd have asked you to join us, but you're still grounded, aren't you?' he teased with a grin.

Alora glared at her brother. 'You know we are.'

'Tut, tut, tut. That will teach you for sneaking off to pubs and causing brawls. When Olli and I drink, we do it in the palace. It's far more sensible, much less chance of being caught. I'd always thought you were cleverer than that, Sister.'

Olli was sniggering at his cousin's jibe. The two princesses scowled at the boys.

'It wasn't about the drink! We wanted to meet ordinary people, as equals, not as princesses!' Alora protested.

'That's the most ridiculous thing I've ever heard.'

'The most ridiculous? You need to get out more,' she sneered.

'Oh, didn't I say? We are doing! What will you be up to? More embroidery perhaps? Enjoy!' He chuckled.

Olli joined him as they took a seat further down the table. Alora scowled at her brother and turned to Eliza, ignoring him.

'He's such an idiot,' she whispered.

'That's boys for you!' Eliza replied quietly. 'You never know, they might grow up eventually.'

'I hope so.'

'I'm sick of being grounded though, Alora. I know it's only been a few days, but Father didn't even give us an end date this time!'

'I know, and he said we'd have to wait until my father got back before we'd be told how long we'd be stuck inside. Father never said how long he planned to stay in Tannel – it could be weeks before he's back!' Alora sighed and collapsed back into her seat, slumped, back arched – a rare slip of her normally perfect posture.

Eliza twisted to study her cousin's face. It looked drawn and pale. 'Are you OK, Alora? Did you sleep OK?'

Alora cast a glance towards the boys; they were seated apart from them and were engaged in their own chatter. 'No. I mean yes, I'm fine. I didn't sleep too well. I had that dream again.'

'The one with the unicorn?'

'Yes, it was so real, so perfect,' she said quietly. 'Every time I have the dream, I feel my mind drawn to it, like I'm being led to where I'll find it. I'm close to knowing where. It's drawing me to its home, I'm sure of it.'

'We've talked about this. It can't be real, unicorns are extinct.'

'I've been reading up on it. It turns out that it's only assumed they're extinct because no one has seen any in Hosta and Allantra for over a century, and they've been gone for even longer than that in north or south Kosk. But how do you prove an elusive creature is extinct, anyway? What if they're just hiding to stop themselves being hunted, what if they survive the there are no humans to find them? The place where the unicorn is drawing me to is an island far to the south-east, out in the Siltan Ocean. I've checked on a map. I'm not sure the island is even charted.'

'Oh, it's possible there's an uncharted island over there. I'm not sure that part of the world has ever been properly explored. And if there is an island with no humans, it's possible unicorns survived there I suppose.' Eliza found herself suddenly wanting to believe – anything to offer light relief from her boring existence stuck in the palace.

'I want to find it, Eliza. I need to learn to portal. I've found a book; I took it from Mother's library. I'm going to learn.'

Eliza took a sharp intake of breath. What had happened to her cousin? First trips to pubs, now plans to learn magic they'd been forbidden from mastering by their parents? Alora had always been sweet and innocent, such a perfect young lady, so much like her mother. Now she was turning into her father, and Eliza liked it. A sly grin crept across her face.

'If we could portal, we wouldn't be trapped in the palace, would we?' said Eliza. 'We would never be grounded again. Even if your dream isn't real, imagine the places we could go.' She trembled with the excitement and the possibilities.

Alora smiled. She nodded and sat up; her decorum having returned.

***

Garrad was stone-cold sober. He couldn't remember the last time he had been. Normally the beer from the night before saw him through until lunchtime, and he'd have a shot of whiskey or two every so often to tide him over until he went to the pub.

He'd left the pub early last night. After the strange man who'd said he was Prince Thomas had left, Garrad hadn't drunk another drop. He'd gone home, to the astonishment of his mother, who hadn't even gone to bed herself by the time he arrived. He wasn't in the mood to talk though; he'd gone straight to bed and slept longer and deeper than he had done in ages.

When he woke, his head was clear. Not even a bit of a hangover. Just a yearning for a drink. But he hadn't reached for his whiskey flask — he'd resisted. He'd gone down and had breakfast with his mother, adoptive father, and brothers. He barely talked to them but his parents' pleasure at seeing him up and sober was evident.

He'd put on his best clothes and left without saying where he was going. He had taken the horse of the man who raised him without asking and set off towards the Military Training Academy. It was a little way out of town. To walk there would take too long and he'd arrive sweaty from the climb up the hill. He wanted to stay looking his best.

He had an unusual emotion – hope. It was a feeling he'd not had in a while. Doubt still riddled him. Something kept telling him he was an idiot for believing a fraud's tales. That the man who'd claimed to be a prince was some no-good backstreet sorcerer with some kind of hidden agenda. Hope told him otherwise. There was a possibility he could get his life back. Hope dangled too big a prize in front of him to ignore. Doubt would have to fuck off. He was going to see if there was a chance. There was very little doubt could do to persuade him it wasn't worth checking.

He glanced at his watch. It was still early, before first parade. He'd made good time. He trotted up to the guardhouse and swung off his horse, nervously leading the gelding towards the private soldiers who had been put on duty today.

'Good morning, Private.' Garrad greeted the man who'd edged forward to challenge him, outwardly oozing confidence, inwardly trembling like a leaf. 'I'm wondering if you received news I might be visiting today.'

'What's your name, sir?'

'It's Bramston, Garrad Bramston.'

The private's face hinted that this meant something, but he hid it quickly. 'One moment, I'll check.'

As the private went into the guardhouse, Garrad's heart pounded. Doubt was cheering on his terror, the terror of being laughed at – that the private would come back and tell him he knew who he was, he was the idiot claiming to have saved a princess and no one was expecting him here, that he'd been spun a lie by a fraud.

But he was here now. Too late to turn back. He squeezed his horse's reins and tried to peer through the guardhouse's cheap glass panels with their cloudy finish. He thought he saw someone put their face up against the window, but it disappeared quickly.

A familiar face emerged from the building. He wore full dress uniform, crisply pressed and starched to perfection. The silver sheath of his sword was so polished it gleamed. Officers only wore that attire when they had some kind of formal duty, or when there was royalty visiting. Hope gave doubt a punch in the face.

'Garrad Bramston,' the officer said with a grin. 'It's good to see you again.'

'Sir!' Garrad couldn't help but salute, even though he wasn't in uniform or even in the Army. He recognised Captain Tawbrid, his cadre commander, the man he'd punched in the face, and he actually looked genuinely pleased to see him.

'Don't salute, Bramston – you aren't in the Army...yet.' Tawbrid raised the corner of his mouth towards his twinkling eyes. 'It seems you have friends in high places, so high that a captain has been sent to meet you, should you turn up this morning. Colonel Instarg insisted it be me. He wanted an officer to meet the young man who was summoned by the prince, yet he was sure you wouldn't come. I didn't doubt it though. Despite your quick temper, I knew you weren't so stupid as to pass up a chance like this.'

Garrad struggled to take in the words; the thudding of his heartbeat in his ears didn't help. He really had met the prince; the captain just confirmed it. *Shit.* Doubt almost had him – doubt told him it had all been bollocks. Hope was grinning smugly from ear to ear.

'Sir, do you have any idea what the prince has in mind?'

'Me? God, no. I'm just a captain. Senior enough to be given escort duties, but certainly not important enough to be included in any conversations about the plans of the prince for wayward ex-corporals.' Captain Tawbrid looked at his watch. 'We should go. The earlier you are, the better it will look.'

One of the privates from the guardhouse took Garrad's horse and they strode across the dusty training yard towards the office block.

Garrad suddenly felt an urge to get something off his chest. 'Sir, I wanted to say I'm sorry. I'm sorry I punched you.'

The captain stopped and regarded Garrad for a moment. He looked him up and down and placed a hand on Garrad's shoulder. 'You know what, I'm sorry too.'

'Sorry for what, sir?' Garrad was baffled.

'For not fighting the commander when he gave you such a harsh punishment. It was way over the top, and I knew it. You lost your temper in my office that day, but so did I. Seeing you have the skin ripped from your back and kicked out, the best student on the course, the man I'd eyed up for great things and even written about in a letter to Lord Harrison...' He studied the ground before returning his gaze to Garrad. 'You should have got your stripes; I shouldn't have let him take them. I'm sorry it came to that.'

'You wrote to the lord commander about me?'

'Not exactly. But I mentioned you in a letter about the cadre. I've never seen anyone as good as you. It's a shame you fell on that exercise while they watched.'

'I was taken down; someone sliced my leg, Bremmer had to be behind it.'

The captain tilted his head. 'Probably. But you can't prove it, and neither can I. We are where we are and that shit's in the past. Right now, for whatever reason, the prince of Vorn wants to see you. And this time there's coffee with the interview. And tea, I imagine, if you prefer.'

***

Captain Tawbrid led Garrad to Lieutenant Colonel Instarg's office. He knocked on the door. The colonel answered it. Surprise flashed across his face at the sight of Garrad, but he hid it quickly.

'Garrad Bramston, please come in.'

'Sir!' Garrad braced up smartly, resisting the urge to salute.

'Thank you, Captain, that will be all.'

Captain Tawbrid saluted and did an about-turn before marching off.

Garrad's heart was pounding again as he edged into the fine office, body tensed as he fought the urge to tremble. The Training Centre commander had a plush place to work, oak-panelled, with fine paintings and teak furniture. It was the kind of place you'd bring a prince. The colonel indicated to the right. The man from the pub stood, smiling. He was dressed in his finery this time. A smart jacket, silk waistcoat, quality cotton shirt. Gold braiding, polished buttons – and possibly the grandest sword he had ever seen strapped to his hip.

He was not alone; he was with someone else. Garrad recognised him too. It took him a minute to place him. Despite Lord Harrison's change of attire since the last time they met, Garrad still recalled his face. He was wearing military uniform, that of a general, but with more decoration, and his sword was as fine as the prince's.

Garrad felt like a peasant in their presence. He breathed deeply, stood rigidly, and had a feeling he looked terrified, despite his best attempt to hide it.

'Good morning, Garrad, I'm glad you found your way to see me.' Prince Thomas began.

'Sir!' Garrad barked, not even sure how to address a prince.

'You should address the prince as Your Highness, Bramston!' the commander snapped.

'It's fine, Colonel. Please, could you leave us?' said the prince.

Lieutenant Colonel Instarg barely managed to hide his indignance at being sent away, but to argue was unthinkable. 'As you wish, Your Highness.' He saluted and left in short order.

'Take a seat, Garrad, please.'

Garrad did as he was told. He pulled a chair from under the carved wooden table and edged his behind onto the leather cushion.

'Can I get you a drink? Tea, coffee?' the prince asked.

Garrad flapped his jaw like a goldfish. The prince was actually offering to make him a drink. Ex-Corporal Bramston. Dishonourably discharged, drunk, son of a merchant of no consequence. He checked his own thoughts. No, he wasn't, he was the son of a great general, a man who'd saved the life of the queen. That was why he was here. His mouth still flapped.

'I'll make us all a cup of tea, Tom,' Lord Harrison answered for him. 'Do you take milk, Bramston?'

His jaw flapped some more. The commander of the queen's Armed Forces was brewing up for him.

'I'll do it white then,' he said with a grin.

'Cheers, Mark,' the prince said as he took a seat opposite Garrad. 'How's the head?'

'It's fine, si… Your Highness.'

'Call me sir if you like, there's no one in this room who cares one way or the other.'

Garrad nodded.

'Did you stay long after I left you?'

'No, I went straight home, as you said.'

'Good,' Prince Thomas said with a smile. 'There's hope for you yet.'

Lord Harrison finished pouring the tea and placed a cup in front of Garrad. His stomach churned; the last thing he wanted was to drink it, but to leave it would be rude. He sipped it while his arm trembled. Memories of the times he'd sworn at the prince last night rattled through his head.

The lord commander took a seat next to the prince and waited for him to lead the conversation.

'Last night, I said I could fix your career. I lied. I can't,' said the prince.

Garrad's heart sank, and he nearly dropped his tea. Then a hint of a smirk crept across the prince's face.

'But Lord Harrison can, and I've known the man a while. He's amenable.'

Prince Thomas looked at Lord Harrison, corners of his mouth raised, his teeth showing, appearing to be taking a sadistic pleasure in the way he had taunted him.

'Aye, lad. That I can,' Lord Harrison said to Garrad. 'I've read your reports and I've talked to your cadre commander. I've also talked to my daughter.'

'Your daughter, sir?' The words fell out of Garrad's mouth before he even knew what he was going to say.

'Yep, Princess Alora. The young woman who fixed your arm that day we met on the field exercise, the lady I sent to fix your back after your lashing, and the silly woman who decided to venture out into The Black Horse the night you got yourself into a scrap.'

Garrad stared at Lord Harrison in disbelief.

'You see, Bramston, back when we first met, I didn't know who your father really was and when you were lashed, I didn't know the details of your misdemeanour. I'd been told you'd been caught brawling and punched a colour sergeant... then your cadre commander. The latter offence possibly did warrant you getting kicked out but not the year of hard labour. I put a stop to it.'

'You did that, sir?'

'Yep.'

'Thank you.'

'Don't mention it. The thing is, if I'd known back then this whole debacle started as a result of you trying to protect my daughter's honour, I'd have stopped you getting any punishment at all. Maybe a few lashes for hitting the captain, but that's about it. If you are content, I am happy to say, effective immediately, your position in the Army is reinstated, with the rank of sergeant.'

Garrad's chin sank to his chest. 'Sir, I don't know what to say.'

'Yes, sir will do nicely.'

'Yes, sir. Of course, sir. Thank you, sir.' Garrad was close to tears but refused to let his emotions show. He swallowed hard and tried desperately to contain his shock at his sudden fortune.

'That's cleared up. Thanks, Mark.' The prince turned back to Garrad. 'The second thing we chatted about was your father, Lord Garrad Gragor. You didn't seem to have a very high opinion of him. I told you mine. I still maintain the man was honourable. If he'd have known your mother was pregnant, he'd have married her before you were born.'

'He didn't know when he died?'

'No. He didn't.'

'You didn't tell me.'

'You didn't ask. Your mother would have told you, if you'd asked her.'

'I've never discussed him with her.'

'Maybe you should. I'll leave you to do that in your own time. The point is, Garrad Gragor was a friend, a great friend. I mourned him for years when he died. I still think about him, about what he could have become, how he could have been the Master of Sword in Vorn, helped me defeat Prince Aran. But he's gone, and you're here, his legacy, and yet you still reject his memory.' Prince Thomas took a sip of his tea. 'I know it's hard to find out something you have always believed is a lie. You'd always thought Davod Bramston was your father. We know he's not, but you were bloody lucky to have him raise you. You should be proud to have such a man wedded to your mother, a man who came to see the queen to beg for help to save you, a man who still wants the best for you despite you not being his blood.'

'I am proud to have him, sir, I know he's a good man.'

'Good, you should be. You can still love your adoptive father while embracing your bloodline and your heritage. Your father wanted to do nothing more than serve the queen... I met you as a baby, you know.'

'You, you did?' Garrad stuttered.

'Yes, out on the North Allantran Plains. You were not even one year old, and your mother said something about you to my wife. She said she wanted you to serve the queen of Vorn,' the prince replied.

'She never said.'

'Of course she didn't. Things changed, she got married. She didn't tell you who you were to protect you, to stop you being labelled as a bastard, the title that grates on you so much.'

'I am a bastard, and anyone who finds out who my real father is will know.' Garrad said dryly.

'Don't tell them.' Prince Thomas turned to Lord Harrison. 'How many people in this kingdom know you are a bastard? The father of the queen's niece and nephew, the husband of her sister. A bastard. How many people know?'

'Er...' Lord Harrison counted on his fingers. 'Four, excluding myself. The queen, my wife, Prince Tom, and now you.'

'And how many care?'

'None of them.'

'Are you angry with your father?'

'Yep, but only because he was an arsehole and a waste of space. He was a womaniser and a petty thug. The dick was nothing like Lord Gragor. Jesus, if I'd had a dad like that? God, I dreamed of a dad like that.'

'If my own brother-in-law can be a bastard and marry a princess, what's to stop you being a bastard and serving the queen, Garrad?' the prince said.

'Nothing,' Garrad replied.

'Good, because I have a posting in mind for you, lad. A legacy of your father's perhaps, and your mother's wishes for you, but it's not serving the queen, more the queen's family. What do you say?'

18. It's Complicated

Location: Takkatooth Mountains, Vorn, Gemini (Planet M69245)

Garrad blinked his heavy lids hard to clear the fuzzy glare. His eyes scrunched to stretched-out spiders as he tried to clear his thoughts. The grogginess still lingered, a pressing weight on his aching head, while feeling flowed back to his body with a prickling sensation, and the paralysis faded away. He shivered; it was cold, bitterly cold. Why the hell the princesses wanted to come riding up into the mountains on a day like this, he had no idea. Slushy snow covered the ground, dreary clouds blanketed the sky, and a bitter northerly wind pierced him like a needle.

The princesses... He looked around him – trees, shrubs, rocks, and snow. Nothing else.

'Fuck!'

He turned his horse and scanned the ground. One set of hoof prints, his own. How long had he been out this time? *Royal bitches*. He took a deep breath and thought. He had to find them; he was desperate to know what they were up to. Every other time he'd failed – he couldn't fight their magic. He was just a soldier. He hadn't even mastered fire-starting with the shreds of magic he supposedly had. It was the one part of basic training he'd actually been bad at.

They'd find him when they were ready, experience had taught him that. He was scared for his job; they were scared of their fathers, neither wanted to return alone. If he wasn't able to find them this time, he was starting the think that perhaps he should come clean, he should tell Lord Harrison that his daughter and Princess Eliza kept sneaking away from him to get up to gods knows what. It might cost him his posting; it might cost him more. But he was getting to the point where he'd had enough.

Being assigned to guard the princesses sounded like an amazing job at first. He could still remember when he first met them; when he had a broken arm and Princess Alora healed him. He remembered thinking they were the most beautiful women he'd ever seen, and he still thought that. But they were a royal pain in the ass. They didn't want a chaperone; they'd made it clear from the start. They'd been rude, difficult, and recently they'd started disappearing.

He sat up in his saddle, hissed a long breath through his chattering teeth. He'd not let a pair of over-privileged girls get the better of him. He'd find them this time. He'd tell them this was their last chance, that he'd had enough.

He retraced his steps through the snow, back down the mountain and below the snow line. It was a mile or so back the way he'd come where he found their tracks. They'd been careless this time, they'd left him where the ground was soft enough to leave hoof prints. Garrad wasn't exactly an expert tracker, but it wouldn't need an expert to track them this time.

The spot the princesses had broken track was the last place he remembered before the magical fuzz had taken him, where they'd enchanted him to keep him riding in a daze while they turned downhill and left him to saunter away. He always snapped out of their spells eventually, normally with a clear head, but this time he felt like he had a magical hangover. It wasn't the first time his head had felt like this, but it was the first time it had kicked in just after the princesses messed with his head.

He didn't like these weird sensations, and this latest one was the weirdest yet. His resolve was hardening. He was starting to think he should tell on them regardless, whether they agreed that they wouldn't do it again or not.

The hoof prints continued down the slope and into some woods. The ground was drier here, but tracking was still pretty easy. They really had chosen a stupid place to run off to this time.

He pushed his horse from a trot into a canter. The woods weren't dense; the footing was good. He wanted to gain on them – he wanted to find out what they were up to.

His horse's hooves thudded on the forest floor; branches whipped across his face. He kept his eyes forward. The tracks were still fresh, and easy to follow. Something flashed up ahead, bright and light. It was quick, but the flare exploded out through the bushes in an unmistakable burst of radiance.

He reined in his horse. He swung a leg over his mount's rump and vaulted to the ground, landing with a soft thud. He tied the beast to a branch and crept forwards, his footsteps careful, avoiding twigs and piles of dead leaves as he edged silently through the woods.

The unmistakable chirping of female voices filtered through the branches; he kept sneaking. The sounds grew louder as he went, and before long he could make out the words.

'Come on, Eliza, we should go through!' It was the distinctive voice of Princess Alora. Garrad continued to creep.

'I'm not sure, not yet. I think we need more time to practice, to make sure we're getting it right, and anyway, it's getting late,' Princess Eliza replied. 'We still need to find our babysitter and get back to the palace before it gets dark.'

Babysitter? Was that what they thought of him? Garrad was getting increasingly irritated. He edged forwards through the trees, towards the glow and the voices. He could see the outlines of the women, silhouetted against something bright and swirling. He'd have been mesmerised if he wasn't pissed off.

'How long do you think he will keep letting us get away with this?'

Alora's words made something in him snap. Garrad's self-control evaporated. The red mist descended.

'Not another day!' He bellowed his answer to the princess's question as he launched himself through the leaves and into the clearing where they stood.

Alora waved her hand; the swirling glow vanished in an instant.

'Sergeant Bramston!' The surprise on Alora's face gave Garrad satisfaction, but not as much as the horror on Princess Eliza's.

'Your Highnesses,' he replied sternly.

'Oh, it's such a shame we got separated again, isn't it?' Alora blurted, her voice tinged with desperation.

'Really?' Garrad folded his arms. 'You tried that the first time. I didn't believe you. You even spouted the same nonsense the second time. By the third and the fourth time, I even told you I knew you were using magic on me, and yet you still spout the same bullshit?' He inhaled quickly. Had he actually just sworn at the princesses?

Alora looked mortified; Eliza smirked.

'We... Sorry, Sergeant, we needed time alone,' Eliza spluttered.

'Eliza!' Alora exclaimed.

161

'What? You can't think he's so stupid he actually thought we *got separated*.'

'I'm not stupid at all, Your Highnesses. I know you're taking the piss here,' said Garrad, and Alora's face was a picture again, 'and I don't care if you don't like my language, you've pushed me, and pushed me, and I've had enough! My job is to keep an eye on you two, to make sure you don't go into any bloody pubs filled with squaddies again, or get tangled up with people you shouldn't, or wander off to places you'd best not go. You are princesses, for heaven's sake! You can't do as you please all the time. When you do stupid stuff, it has consequences.' His voice grew louder. 'I have fifty scars on my back because of you two! This has gone far enough; I won't keep your secrets any longer!'

Once Garrad had started, he'd been unable to stop. His tongue had run away with him. He'd never given the women these home truths before – he'd always been the epitome of the dutiful sergeant. But the anger had taken control. His temper, which was the real reason he'd ended up with fifty scars, had risen to the surface.

The women were speechless. No one spoke to them like this. Alora looked at Eliza. Eliza shrugged, apparently unmoved by Garrad's outburst, but Alora looked to be flooded with guilt.

'I'm sorry, Sergeant.' She stepped towards him, sorry-looking, regarding him through her long, fluttering eyelashes. She reached out and took one of his hands in hers. 'Can you forgive us?' she said softly.

He felt her delicate skin on his rough soldier's hands. She was close to him, so close he could hear her breathing, smell her perfume, the intoxicating fragrance filling his lungs. Her eyes were filled with welling tears; she looked genuinely devastated. Garrad's temper evaporated like a cup of water on a raging fire. His heart softened to kneaded putty; his knees struggled to hold his weight.

'Of – of course.' His stupefied mind had been cleared of rational thought by a pretty face and a tender touch.

'And you won't tell on us this time, either, will you?' Alora gently squeezed his hand.

'Of course not,' he stuttered, hard resolve seeping away, like blood from an open wound.

Alora wiped her eyes before any tears could fall. Something changed in her face. Sorrow turned to innocence. Garrad was powerless; he was under her spell.

'Because if you did, you might not get to look after us anymore, and you wouldn't want that, would you?' she said.

All he wanted to do was stay with Alora for ever, to grab her, to pull her towards him, to feel her lips on his and her body tight against him. He was dreaming, he had to be. She came towards him, pressed her lips on his – soft, full, so warm and carefully placed every woman he had ever known before seemed like nothing in comparison.

He wanted the moment to last forever, but it didn't – it was over in seconds. She pulled away, dropped down to the ground from her tiptoes, and let go of his hand. He felt empty, alone, desperate to pull her back. He didn't. She was a princess, and something was telling him he was being played like a violin. The same part of him that told him not to lie with whores, but he'd ignored that voice often enough.

Princess Eliza was looking thoroughly perplexed. He narrowed his eyes. The hint of a smile was edging onto Alora's pretty face. He closed his eyes, shook his head. These women would be the end of him.

'Shall we go back?' Alora asked. 'It's getting awfully late.'

***

Aran jolted back into Varden, back into his own mind. He was repulsed; had he kissed his sister? It certainly felt like it. Alora looked so much like her mother. But no, his sister had darker skin and she must be older by now, she'd be in her forties. He had last seen her twenty years back, when she was not much older than Alora was at present.

He didn't need to stay in Bramston's head anymore anyway. He'd seen enough for the day. He could head back through the tunnel and get some rest. It was dark in Varden, the middle of the night, but dawn was breaking back in Australia. His spells on Gemini were messing with his sleep. He was losing track of what time it was. It was worth it. Today had been a good day. The young sergeant who provided such a convenient host had showed him what he'd hoped for. The princesses had managed to make a transport portal. They'd be here soon.

It was time to get some rest. He'd need to be back before long to make sure his niece had that dream again. It wouldn't do for her to lose her focus.

***

'Fucking hell, Mervin, what a day.' The words exploded out of Garrad as soon as the two of them were out of earshot of the palace.

'Princesses driving you nuts again?' his friend enquired.

'You could say that. It seemed like such a good job when the prince first mentioned it, telling me I'd be guarding the second in line to the throne and Lord Harrison's daughter – two of the most gorgeous women in Vorn – but now? I wish I had your posting, more than anything. Guard section commander sounds fucking awesome in comparison.'

'Trust me, mate, you don't want my job. It's boring. Hanging around at the palace gates all day? Dealing with snotty nobles and ignorant peasants? It's not great, in fact it's a bit shit. But it's a job at the palace and it looks good on my career profile.'

'It sounds simple, and heavenly.' Garrad sighed deeply.

'What have they done this time? Have they left you again?'

'Yeah. But this time I found 'em.'

'Surely that's a good thing.'

'You might think so! Thing is, I was resolved to grass 'em up this time. I wasn't going to let them get away with it again, but...' Garrad's voice faded away.

'What?'

'Princess Alora, she got emotional, and she – she...'

'She what?'

'She kissed me.'

'She kissed you?' Mervin stopped in his tracks.

'Yeah.' Garrad spun and met the gaze of his incredulous friend.

Mervin tilted his head and took a step towards him. He placed a hand on Garrad's shoulder. 'You sure?'

'Course I'm fucking sure! It's not my first time.'

Mervin sniggered. 'Half the whores of Tannel can vouch for that.'

'Oi!'

Mervin light-heartedly punched his friend in the ribs. 'What you gonna do? Still gonna grass 'em up?'

'Fuck knows. I want to... I want to quit.' He paused. 'No I don't.' He dropped his head and sighed. 'Yes, I do.'

'Make your goddammed mind up!'

'I had made my mind up. I was going to tell on 'em, and—'

'The woman got into your head. She's playing you, mate.'

'I know. Fucking bitch.'

'There's not a cat in hell's chance a princess is interested in you, so if you thought that for even a second, throw the thought in the midden where it belongs. She knows she'll be in the shit if you tell on her – she's trying to manipulate you.'

'Do you think I don't know all that!'

'Your brain might, but have you told your dick?'

Garrad couldn't help but laugh.

It had been a couple of months since Garrad was dragged from the gutter by Prince Thomas. As they continued down the hill towards the centre of Vornston, Garrad reflected on his troubles. They weren't half as bad as they had been not so long back. He swept a hand over his close-cropped hair then ran it down his jawline. Clean-shaven face and groomed mop. It felt good to look respectable again. He glanced down at his clean, pressed clothes and his biceps swelling in his sleeves like they had when he'd been kicked out of the Army. He was in shape again and looked every part the off-duty sergeant he was. The sword swinging at his hip confirmed it.

He'd hardly drunk since the day he met the prince in the pub. Just the odd one when it was polite. Mervin had been trying to get him out for weeks, but Garrad turned him down. Mervin didn't have a clue what happened to him after he was kicked out. Only the regulars in the shittest pubs in Tannel, his family, and the prince and lord commander knew, and he planned to keep it that way.

Today, he needed a drink.

Garrad didn't know the pubs in Vornston, so Mervin led the way to The King's Chariot. Not a pub exclusively frequented by soldiers, but it certainly had a few regular visitors. They strolled inside. The place was clean and cosy looking and seemed far classier than the places he'd frequented in his dark days in Tannel.

'It's one jug for me tonight, mate, I'm working tomorrow,' Mervin announced on entry.

'I know, you said, but don't forget I am too.'

'Working is a strong word. Following princesses around doesn't seem like proper work to me.'

'Your usual, is it?' the serving girl enquired as they settled at a table.

'Yes, please, Hanily,' Mervin replied with a smile.

165

She thrust her ample bosom in Garrad's direction before turning and heading back to the bar.

'There's a woman who's more in your league.' Mervin nodded towards the serving girl. 'You've got a chance with her. You could do with a steady girl in your life.'

'She's not my type.'

'What is your type, princesses?' he jibed. Garrad glared at him. 'You could do worse than a serving girl – didn't you tell me your mother was once a barmaid?'

'She was. It was a long time ago.'

'You know, I've asked but you never gave me a proper answer...'

Garrad cocked his head.

'How the fuck is it that Garrad Bramston, the fuckwit who punched a captain and got kicked out, managed to blag his way back in and be appointed babysitter to two princesses?'

'Enough with the *babysitter*!'

'Sorry, bodyguard? What is your actual job title, anyway?'

'Protector of the royal houschold,' Garrad said proudly.

Mervin raised an eyebrow; the corner of his mouth went with it. 'Really?'

'Yeah, what's wrong with that?' Garrad folded his arms.

'You follow princesses around; you don't protect the entire fucking family.'

'I protect some of it.'

Mervin sniggered as Hanily arrived with a jug of beer and two clay mugs.

'Thank you,' Garrad said with a smile while his friend continued to chuckle. He poured them both a mugful then stared sternly at Mervin, while he waited for his laughing to end.

'Anyway,' Mervin cleared his throat, 'you still haven't told me how you got back in, or how you landed that gig.'

'Ah, yeah.' Garrad took a long sip of his drink.

'Well?'

Garrad sat back on his stool and regarded his friend. He'd known the man since basic training. He trusted him with his life and his unshared secrets were boring at him from the inside. 'This goes no further; I don't want half the army gossiping about me.'

'Sound's bloody mysterious.'

'You gonna keep this to yourself?'

'Course.' Mervin scowled indignantly.

'Fine. My father sorted it – getting me back in the Army, and the job.'

'Your father? A nobody merchant from Tannel? What the fuck?'

'He's not my father.'

'What are you on about?'

Garrad took a deep breath and placed both palms on the table. 'I'm a bastard.' He paused and took a sip of his beer while Mervin stared at him incredulously. He set his mug down and continued, 'Turns out Davod Bramston wanted to make an honest woman out of my mother and raise me as his own. Fair play to the chap, there's not many who'd do that.'

'Hang on, you're a bastard? And this somehow gives you some special job in the palace? Who the bloody hell is your father?'

'Was. He's dead,' Garrad said dryly.

'Shit, he's dead?'

'Yeah, like before I was born.'

'Did he know your Mother was knocked up?'

'What's that got to do with anything! You sound like the bloody prince.'

'You've been taking to the prince?' Mervin asked incredulously.

'I guard his fucking daughter, course I've spoken to the prince.'

'So you guard princesses and chat to the prince.' Mervin shook his head slowly then took a sip of his beer before slamming his mug on the table 'Out with it then, who the fuck was your father?'

'Some arsehole named Garrad Gragor,' Garrad replied with a sigh.

Mervin leant forwards.

'Careful!' Garrad swiped Mervin's beer mug away before it got nudged onto the floor by Mervin's chest.

'Lord Gragor was your father,' said Mervin.

'So I'm told.'

'Noooo.'

'Yep,' Garrad said with a sigh.

'No.'

'Yes.' Garrad took another long sip of his beer.

Mervin stared at him.

'Whenever you're ready, mate.' Garrad was getting perplexed by Mervin's reaction. Garrad hadn't expected his father to be famous; he'd never heard of the chap until he was told his name.

'The son of King Harthur's Master of Sword? You're the grandson of a Master of Sword?' said Mervin.

'Apparently.'

'The son of the man who left Vorn and managed to become a general in the Walrian Army from nothing?'

'That's the guy.' Garrad glugged some more of his ale.

'The guy who was loyal to the queen before anyone else, the man who was at her side when Darrudin was attacked, who single-handedly saw off thirty dwarves to save her life? That Garrad Gragor?'

Garrad sighed. 'You seem to know more about the man than me.' He leant forwards, plonked his chin on his palm and his elbow on the table, not sure what to make of his friend's surprised reverence for the man whose blood he carried.

'The guy's a fucking legend. How do you not know all this?'

Garrad shrugged. 'I'd never heard of him until a few months back.'

'You been on another planet all your life?'

'Maybe someone told me at some point. It just didn't fix in my mind.'

'Gods, mate, how the hell did your mother, a barmaid, pull a guy like that?'

'Dunno, I never asked.'

'You sure she was a barmaid?'

Garrad jolted upright on his stool. 'What are you trying to say?' Garrad snapped.

'Sorry, mate.' Mervin backtracked quickly. 'Nothing. She is a looker though, she probably caught his eye.'

'That's my mother you're talking about!' Garrad had lifted his beer mug, but he plonked it back on the table, contents sloshing over the sides. The hint of a smile gripped his face as he lifted the mug back towards his lips. 'You're probably right though.' Garrad sighed. 'She caught his eye, got knocked up, then he died. No wedding, no nothing. Man can't be that great, going round getting women up the duff.'

'Oh, sorry, I forgot about your morals. Garrad Bramston has never shagged anyone without getting hitched first. You could have bastards of your own all over Tannel that you don't know about.'

'I don't.'

'How do you know?'

'I just do.'

'Whatever. I don't get it, mate – how are you not shouting about this? Being Garrad Gragor's bastard has more kudos than being the legitimate son of a merchant.'

'No, it doesn't.'

'Yes, it does.'

'If you say so.'

'You could jump straight to officer with that kind of bloodline. How are you still a sergeant?' Mervin asked, shaking his head in disbelief.

'I want to earn my commission, not be handed it on a plate like some jumped-up fucking noble.'

'You know officers are selected these days, right?'

'Yeah, from a choice of thousands,' Garrad chided sarcastically.

'Its hundreds, at least. They might only be selected from those with the right blood, but at least they're selected. The idiots don't get to be in charge anymore, no matter how much cash or status their father has.'

'Yeah, so what? I told Prince Thomas I wanted to keep who I was a secret. I don't want to be anyone's bastard. It doesn't matter who my father really was.'

'You met the prince?'

Garrad rolled his eyes. 'I told you that earlier! Anyway, who the fuck do you think got me back in? That's not something that's pulled off easily.'

'Gods, mate, you have gone up in the world. Don't forget me when you are the next Master of Sword. I always fancied a commission of my own one day. Want another jug?'

'You said you were only having the one,' Garrad replied with a smirk.

'Yeah, but fuck me, after what you've just told me I definitely need another.'

19. The Trap

'Shit!' Garrad sat bolt upright. *Thud, thud, thud.* 'Alright!' he yelled. He ripped his blanket away, then launched himself out of bed. He ran to the door and yanked it open.

Mervin's sunken eyes, pale skin, and sagging shoulders greeted him. He looked as bad as Garrad felt. 'Do you know what time it is?' Mervin said.

'Of course I do!'

'Well why the hell are you still here?'

'You just woke me.'

'That's bloody obvious. You need to get your shit together and get on your horse like an hour ago. The princesses blagged their way past my guards without you. Can't believe the fuckwits let them through but I—'

Garrad cut him off. 'They've gone out? Without me?'

'That's what I said!'

'Shit. Can you do me a favour and get my horse ready?'

'I've already got a man on it.'

'You're awesome, mate.' Garrad was already hopping about his room as he pulled on his clothes.

'I'd say the same about you, but you got me pissed last night. My head feels like it's been trampled by a bull.'

'*I* got you pissed?'

'It's usually your fault.'

'We've not been out drinking in ages!'

'Yeah. But before that, it was definitely always you who led me astray. I'm going off experience.'

Garrad couldn't help but grin as he recalled the good nights they'd had together; he conceded it probably was his fault. 'I'd had a tough day, I needed it.'

'Today's about to get a whole lot tougher if you don't find those princesses. You better hope no one spots you heading out on your own. I won't tell but if anyone else—'

'Yeah, I get it. I'll wear a cloak.' Garrad fastened the last button on his jacket and strapped on his sword. 'Right, which way did they go?'

***

Garrad's horse's hooves thundered down the forest track. His head pounded. He'd overslept, and he never overslept! Except when he drank too much. Having his own room was a privilege and a curse. No fucker to wake you, no one to notice when you slept in.

Garrad reported directly to the commander of palace security, who was usually far too busy to pay too much attention to Garrad or to check if he was on duty on time. It was assumed the princesses would report him for stuff like that.

His horse was tiring, but it wasn't far. He knew where the princesses were; he hadn't a clue how he knew, he just did. The numb tingling was in his head again. What games were the princesses playing? He assumed it was their magic messing with him, and they were guiding him towards their location. Maybe they felt guilty about running off. After yesterday, they'd seemed apologetic and promised not to do it again. *Lying bitches.*

He wanted to report them, but he couldn't. He'd slept in, he'd let them go out without him, and they could report *him*. He'd be the one in the shit today. They had him. Had they made him sleep in? Was it their magic that stopped him waking? Either that or the five jugs of beer he'd drunk. It didn't matter, he had to find them.

He'd been riding uphill into the mountains since he'd left Vornston, and his mount was on its last legs. The stallion's breathing was laboured, and his pace had begun to slow, but he kept going. A little further and he'd let the horse rest. Garrad leaned forward and patted his neck. 'Come on, boy, not much further.'

The horse faltered. His head jolted up and his ears went back. There was a flash up ahead. Garrad nearly lost his balance. He pulled the horse to a halt. Garrad urged him into a walk, heading towards the shimmering beams of light flickering through the leaves.

'You go first!' It was Alora – her high-pitched chirp ripped through the trees.

'No, you go. This was your crazy idea,' he heard Eliza reply.

Garrad kept his horse walking towards their voices.

'How about we go together?'

'Fine.'

'Shit.' Garrad jumped off his horse and careered though the bushes. He entered the clearing in time to see the women vanishing into the swirling vortex of light. Garrad sprinted. He jumped, and arms-first, he dived into the magical eddy.

He tingled from head to foot as he flew through the light of the portal. It engulfed his body like a blanket of warmth. It was a frosty morning in the mountains, but whatever was on the other side of the weird, simmering magical disc, it was certainly hot. It was like diving into an oven.

His vision cleared; the ground approached. His palms found the dirt and they skidded. The rest of his body followed. His left knee found a tree root. 'Ouch.'

'Bramston!' Eliza exclaimed.

'Bramston?' Alora repeated. 'How the heck...'

'I thought you said he wouldn't be able to get through!' Eliza was staring at Garrad. He rolled onto his side and started to rise.

'That's what the book said, but where did he come from?' Alora said. 'We were on our own in the forest before we left.'

'Good morning, Your Highnesses.' He was on his feet now. 'Care to tell me where the fuck we are?'

'Bramston!' Alora exclaimed. 'You need to watch your language, we are royalty. I don't want to have to tell you again, otherwise I'll have to tell Father!'

Garrad spun on the spot, consumed by quizzical awe as he studied the large drooping leaves, the hanging vines, the monstrously wide tree trunks and tall grasses. 'My language ought to be the least of your concerns; I can tell you for nothing, it sure as hell isn't a concern of mine.' He was sweating already. The air was close, hot, and humid. He removed his cloak.

'Erm,' Eliza began sheepishly. 'I suppose we don't need to be too worried about your language right now.' Her mouth stayed open, as if she thought she ought to be speaking but wasn't sure what to say.

'I galloped for miles from the palace straight to where you were. I have no idea how I knew where to go, I just knew. I arrived to see you passing through some weird magical portal and dived through after you, and I arrived, bang on cue to see your little display of magic. The timing was too much of a coincidence for me. Someone's playing with my head, and you are the only sorcerers I know of who would have even the remotest interest in messing with me.'

'We weren't in your head! We don't even know how to do that. It's not the kind of magic we've been taught,' Eliza insisted.

'I believe you…' he said sarcastically. The strange numbness in his skull exploded. He screwed up his eyes. Something ripped through his head. He opened his eyes, tried to speak, but he couldn't. Then he did. 'I believe you,' he said again, this time with conviction. *What the fuck?* He said the words in his mind. His mouth wouldn't cooperate.

'Good. Thank you, Sergeant,' Eliza said aloofly.

Silence followed. The women appeared to be expecting him to speak but he couldn't. Try as he might, he was paralysed, his face fixed in a compliant smile.

'Anyway. You're here so you get to investigate this special place with us.' Eliza said.

Something made Garrad's head nod. It wasn't him; he'd been relegated to a passive observer in his own body.

'Right.' Eliza tilted her head to one side. 'Are you OK?'

'I'm fine,' Garrad heard himself say.

'Um, great.' She turned to Alora. 'Now we're here, what's your plan?'

'The place looks as it did in my dreams. The unicorn came almost every night – it was her who drew us here. We can wait for her, or… Do you think we should try to find her?'

'We could go for a walk, certainly. Let's look round, see what we can find.' Eliza looked up through the trees. The sky was obscured by the dense canopy above. 'It might be getting late here though. I don't think we have long before it gets dark.'

'How do you know? It could be dawn, maybe the canopy is making it gloomy,' Alora suggested.

'Who cares? We can leave whenever we want anyway.'

'Do you think we'll find the unicorn if you scanned for her? Would we recognise her signature?'

'I'm not sure,' Eliza replied. 'It might be worth doing anyway, to see if there's anyone around.'

They both closed their eyes and began to use their magic to search the forest around them. It didn't take long before Eliza opened hers. 'I see something.'

'So do I,' Alora said.

'Is it a large animal with a powerful signature? That has to be the unicorn.'

'No, it's a human – someone with a magical signature too. A powerful one.'

'A sorcerer?'

'I guess.'

'Wait – the creature is coming this way... Shh.'

Garrad wanted to scream at them. Why were they being stupid? They'd come here to find a unicorn and spotted a sorcerer? It had to be a trap. These girls were idiots! He was still paralysed, unable to speak or control his own body. Fixed there, with that inane smile.

'I hear it,' Eliza whispered.

A twig snapped ahead, leaves rustled, the songbirds went quiet, and through the sea of green, a brilliant white creature emerged. Garrad stared in awe. The women stared too as the mysterious animal approached.

The creature was a horse with a long, flowing mane threaded with strands of silver. It had a tail like a donkey's, with more of the fine silver hairs at its tip. Its hooves were cloven, like a goat's, but the most incredible thing of all was the long, spiralling horn sprouting from between its ears. Fine ivory, with shimmering veins of pearl. There was no doubt in his mind – this was a unicorn. How? They were extinct; no one had seen one in centuries.

'She's beautiful!' Alora gasped. The unicorn kept coming forwards. Alora held out a hand; the creature came close enough to be touched. She ran her hand down its neck. 'Its hair is like velvet,' she whispered.

Eliza came close. She laid a hand on the unicorn too, and softly stroked its flanks. 'She's incredible.'

The unicorn pulled away and began to retreat into the leaves.

'Where are you going?' Alora asked. The unicorn stopped, turned its head back towards the princesses, and flicked its nose forward, as if beckoning them to follow. 'She wants us to go with her.'

They walked after her, as if in a trance, and completely oblivious to Garrad, who was still rooted to the spot.

'Where are you going!' he yelled at them from within the bubble of his head. *'It's a trap, it has to be!'* His legs began to move; whoever controlled his body was moving him after them. Eliza looked back to see if he was coming, and smiled at him. Garrad smiled back. *'The stupid bitch thinks I'm OK with all this!'* He tried to think, but there was nothing he could do. He was powerless to do anything other than watch as his charges were led through an unfamiliar forest by a magical horse.

Alora turned to Eliza, who walked behind her. 'She's taking us towards the sorcerer.'

'Do you think it's safe? Who knows who they are?'

'Of course it's not safe!' Garrad screamed the words in his head.

'Why would a unicorn lead us to danger?' Alora asked. 'Unicorns are peaceful creatures; they've never harmed anyone.'

'I suppose,' Eliza conceded.

'Maybe the sorcerer can give us some explanation? Maybe the unicorn is taking us there so they can tell us why we were drawn to this place.'

'Oh, I suppose that makes sense.'

'Idiots, idiots, idiots! Naive royal bitches!'

They hadn't walked much further when they arrived at a small clearing by a stream and a sheer rockface. There was a cave entrance. The stream flowed into it and by its side, leaning casually against the rock, stood a man – a slim man of middling years, with caramel skin and dark curly hair, wearing the strangest clothes Garrad had ever seen.

'Welcome, princesses,' he greeted them, and stepped forwards. He placed a hand on the unicorn's nose and stroked it gently.

'Who are you?' Alora asked.

'My name is Oberon.'

'Do you live here? Was it you who drew us to this place?' Eliza wondered.

'Yes, I do live here, and I did draw you here, but only because Sallantria asked me to.'

'Sallantria?'

'Yes, the unicorn is called Sallantria.'

The unicorn whinnied at the sound of her name.

'Why did you want us to come?' Eliza said to the creature, then turned to Oberon. 'Can you talk to her?'

'Yes. So can you. She understands us.' The mysterious man was still petting the unicorn. 'To hear what she has to say takes practice.'

'Why us?' Alora asked.

He twisted his thin neck, a sickly smile on his face as he regarded Alora. 'Why you, do you not mean? Was it not you who had the dreams, Princess Alora?'

'How do you know who I am?'

'Sallantria told me. She wanted to meet you – she has a particular affinity to princesses, especially beautiful ones like yourself. She is pleased you came, and with a friend too. Sallantria extends her welcome to you, Princess Eliza. Unicorns are magical – they can sense magic in all its forms. You are the most powerful princess in Gemini, Alora. That is why she was drawn to you.'

'She's beautiful!' Alora was gently stroking the unicorn's neck.

'Sallantria wants to show you something – it's in this cave.'

'She does?' Alora asked Oberon, before turning to Sallantria. 'Sorry, you do?' The unicorn appeared to nod. 'What do you want to show us?'

'It's a surprise,' Oberon said. 'It's amazing though, she's sure you'll like it.'

'Oh, well lead on,' said Alora.

'She wants you to go first. The tunnel is narrow, and she is worried her body might block your view of what she wants to show you.'

'Alright.' There was a hint of trepidation in Alora's voice. Eliza looked equally unsure.

'It's fine to go in there,' Garrad said. 'This man seems trustworthy to me – my soldier's sense isn't picking up on anything that makes me concerned.'

'Nooo! Don't go in there!'

'If Bramston thinks it's OK...' Eliza said hesitantly.

'You will not be disappointed, princesses. The secrets of this cave are incredible. Your view of the world will be changed forever once you see them,' Oberon reassured them.

The unicorn nudged Alora from behind with its nose. She turned to look it in the eye. Garrad recognised the look on Alora's face; it was one he recognised in himself every time he was faced with a gorgeous woman, probably the same one he'd had the day Alora kissed him. He knew how powerful the feeling that matched that look could be. This time he was a bystander. He watched in horror as the princess edged towards the cave, Eliza following, his own body being moved along behind them.

Oberon made a fireball to light the way and followed them into the tunnel. He held it above his head. It provided more than enough light to see as they tried to pick their way down the passage without getting their feet wet. They tried for a while, but it was no use — before long the stream spread across the whole of the cave floor. Alora and Eliza lifted their dresses and tiptoed through the water in their riding boots. All signs of natural light soon vanished from behind them; only gloom was ahead.

Garrad was panicking. Every fibre of his consciousness sensed danger. The princesses were in trouble. It was his job to keep them safe and he was powerless to do a thing. He kept trying to scream, to yell, to take control of his body. Then something happened. He stopped. His body wasn't being controlled anymore. He tried to raise a hand, and it twitched. He could move his own head.

'Princesses, get out of here!' he bellowed.

Something went *bang*. The sound pounded his eardrums and shook the cave around him. Something stung his leg with the blazing pain of a red-hot poker. It went limp. He couldn't control it. The leg collapsed, and he fell. *Splash*, he was in the water. He touched the spot where he'd been stung; there was a hole. Pain. Searing pain. It shot up his leg and he gave a jagged rasp of agony.

'Arghh!' he yelled.

The princesses turned. Oberon was facing them; the unicorn was nowhere to be seen. Garrad fought to control his screaming as he clasped at his bloodied leg. The sorcerer held something in his hand — it was black and metal. It had a tube on the top, and another section attached at right angles, which Oberon held.

Eliza gawped at Garrad and Oberon. 'What have you done?' she screamed.

Alora raised her hands, as if trying to use her magic on Oberon, and Eliza did the same, but nothing happened.

Oberon stood behind them, blocking their route out of the tunnel, grinning at them. The fireball hovered above his head; the metal object was still in his right hand. He reached into a pocket with his other hand and brought out a strange object. He flicked it with his thumb and light cascaded out of it. He strapped it to his head and advanced forwards a few steps. The fireball vanished. He walked past Garrad, and the women backed off, deeper into the cave.

'Your magic doesn't work here, ladies – to get past me you will need to use force, but I don't recommend it.' A wicked smile slithered up his face. 'This here is a gun,' he tapped the metal thing with the tube that he held in one hand with his other, 'or a pistol if you like. It's not magical. It uses technology to work. It fires bits of metal very quickly. Quickly enough to pierce flesh, to kill. It's far faster than an arrow. Try to get past me and I'll pull the trigger and one of those bits of metal will find you, like one found young Sergeant Bramston.'

Garrad stopped crying out in pain. He clutched his leg, one hand on each side of his thigh. The metal had passed right through; blood was sending a crimson trickle through the shadowy stream. 'Come on, arsehole, who are you really? What do you want with the princesses?' he managed to hiss through gritted teeth.

'Oh, I'm very glad you asked. Let me introduce myself, properly this time. The first time, as you might have guessed, was a lie.' His tone was sickly. 'My name is Aran. King Aran of Vorn. I'm Alora's uncle and the true ruler of the kingdom stolen from me by Eliza's mother.'

'My mother is the rightful queen!' Eliza protested.

'She's a usurper. Princess Emana died as a girl. But that's of little consequence now. I have no desire to return to Vorn and rule that stinking backwater. I have a new kingdom, a better one, with electricity and flushing lavatories. That usurper can keep Vorn. That's not to say my interest in your homeland has vanished entirely. It still provides sanctuary to your parents, in particular your father, Alora. How is Mark?'

'My father will find you and kill you for this!' said Alora.

'Oh, I hope he tries. I am hoping he will come to find his precious missing daughter, and I hope Thomas comes too. It would be nice to meet him again after all these years. I never did get chance to work on his other hand, and I hate to leave a job half done.'

'Our fathers won't come. They don't know where we are. They will never find us, they will never find you, and your plan will fail!' Eliza blurted.

'Oh dear, Eliza,' said Aran. 'Such little knowledge you have. I know you are a sorcerer, but were you not schooled in the art of searching for loved ones?'

'We have no magic here. It requires magic to be able to find someone.'

'You make a valid point, which is where young Sergeant Bramston comes in. He will bring them to me.' Aran sneered, his gaze switching to Garrad, lying injured in the stream. 'You will crawl out of this cave, Sergeant. You look like a strong lad, you'll manage it. Go back to the jungle and wait. The young ladies' fathers will find you; I have no doubt. When they do, you can tell them where their daughters are. You can tell them Aran has them on Earth. Here.'

Aran put a white rolled-up piece of cloth into Garrad's hand.

'It's a bandage. I can't have you bleeding to death before they arrive. Lead the way, princesses,' Aran said to the women, nudging his gun towards them as he spoke. 'There's a lovely surprise for you at the end of this tunnel.'

20. Spying And Secrets

Location: Zargon observation ship, 400 km above Earth (Planet B13536)

Lukin was on shift alone. It was the best part of her day. The other pesky crew members were off duty, sleeping, doing their own thing; she didn't care as long as they stayed out of her control room. She sat in her chair in front of the control panel, keeping one eye on the screens while she perused the logs of the previous shifts, looking for any more anomalies, especially in the log of H108. He was an interesting specimen indeed. Something was going on with him. She still recalled the first blacked-out period from half a cycle ago, she suspected there'd been more. The logs looked like they might have been tampered with to cover the gaps in the drone's video record somehow, but she couldn't be certain.

The suspicious episodes always happened when she was off-shift, at roughly the same time of the day on their planet usually. But it was not regularly enough for her to be able to predict it or to be in the control room at the right time.

She'd read everything she wanted to. She slumped in her chair and ordered a cup of carrowcel, then sat watching the Specimens of Interest go about their business. One was in the middle of a long car journey – how dull. Another was engaged in an act of reproduction with a female. More interesting, but routine. One was in a meeting, another sat at a desk, and H108 was walking towards a geological anomaly; a large sandstone feature in the middle of sector seven.

He'd visited the place a lot recently, she'd seen that in the log. It tended to be at the same time as when she spotted her presumed cover-ups. This time he was doing it when she was watching. She'd know if he did vanish.

She leant forward in her chair and watched with interest; she enlarged the screen. She watched him leave his car and walk up a gulley and into a tunnel. The drone stayed with him. She tracked him underground and the drone followed for a while longer before he vanished. The screen went black, the signal lost, the drone suddenly unreachable.

'Ship, report on location of H108's drone.'

'No signal detected,' the ship replied.

'Ship, check recent drone report for signs of faults.'

'No faults detected.'

'Ship, has the loss of signal on this drone been reported before?'

'Invalid question.'

Lukin scowled. 'What do you mean *invalid question?*' she muttered. 'Ship, check log of H108's drone for previous gaps in the reporting record.'

'Invalid question.'

Lukin huffed and prodded at buttons on the control panel in an attempt to find the answer manually. She spent a while searching, scouring the logs, trying to find some hint of evidence to reveal a cover-up, but she had no luck; the information didn't seem to be there. She glared at the black screen as if staring at it would make it come back to life and give her the answers she sought. It didn't change. She shuffled in her chair, folded her arms. She had an idea; she checked the rota for M69245's crew. As she suspected, Jink was on shift on the other ship too. It was odd how their shifts were altered to miss the assumed gaps in H108's record. She narrowed her eyes in thought and tapped a thin, grey finger against her rounded white teeth. Or, perhaps it was not really odd at all.

'Ship, call crew of M69245's ship.'

'Calling M69245's ship.' A musical chime sounded; the blackened screen suddenly erupted in light as the image of Jink appeared in the centre of the largest monitor.

'Jink! It's good to see you.'

'And you too, Lukin,' Jink said hastily, her eyes not on her own camera, clearly focussed elsewhere.

'Have I interrupted?'

Jink didn't answer, engrossed in something else.

'Jink?'

'Oh, sorry, Lukin, what were you saying?'

'Is something going on there?' Lukin asked curiously.

'Yeah, um, Lukin?' Jink turned to face Lukin for the first time since she'd called.

'Yes, Jink?'

'Have you lost a specimen?'

'You've found H108?' Lukin guessed.

'One second...' Jink tapped away at the control panel in front of her. 'Yep, just double checking. We have the drone. It's H108 alright.'

'My specimen's on your planet?'

'Yep,' Jink replied.

A wave of excitement washed over Lukin. 'There's another wormhole, there has to be!' she exclaimed.

'I guess.' Jink said flatly, her focus looked to be elsewhere.

'Jink!' Lukin's frustration at Jink's inattention was starting to show. 'What's going on over there?'

'A bit of activity – sorry, can I call you back?'

'Sure.'

The screen went black again and Lukin collapsed into her chair, miffed at being cut off. She ordered some more carrowcel and sat impatiently, waiting for Jink to reappear. She knew something was going on. Something was happening with her specimen, and she was being left out of it. She drained the last drops of her drink and tapped the arm of her chair as she stared at the blackened screen, too ruffled to think about doing anything else constructive.

At last, the chime of an incoming call sounded. She answered, then let out a sigh of relief as the beaming face of Jink re-materialised.

'Sorry, I had to do a bit of urgent work at my end,' said Jink. 'I was trying to make sure the ship's AI didn't call Darkle on shift.'

'What is going on over there?' Lukin demanded.

'Um, you're about to get your specimen back. Plus a couple of mine.' A wide grin exploded onto Jink's face.

'What?' Lukin lurched forwards and gripped the arms of her chair.

'I think there's another hidden wormhole, another legacy – it has to be!'

'A Gallantrian legacy?'

'Yes!' Jink exclaimed.

'Wow. After the last one was destroyed, I'd never considered there could be another,' Lukin sagged back in her chair, 'but so what? Everyone more or less agreed your planet was a Gallantrian experiment cycles ago. It didn't change anything; the government still decided the culture was worthy of preservation.'

'Yes, but government has changed since then. They are more sympathetic to our cause these days. If a new wave of destabilisation happens as a result of a Gallantrian legacy wormhole, it might be what we need to push our cause.'

Lukin's large black eyes disappeared behind a long blink as the penny finally dropped. 'Of course! This could be what we need to get things going again, especially if we are able to give it a little help. That cultural destruction that nearly happened last time could finally take off this time!'

'You're jumping ahead, Lukin. We've found a new link, and the traffic has been from my planet to yours, not the other way round. That's not exactly going to cause the destabilisation on mine that we are after. We'd need your humans to come my M-Class.'

'I suppose, but with the new wormhole in place, there's a chance. There was none at all before.' Lukin pursed the rims of her lipless mouth. 'Do you think our shipmates know about the wormhole?'

'I'd put money on it.'

'And they are keeping it from us?'

'Probably.'

'Why would they do that?'

'They want to keep things as they are,' said Jink. 'They don't want any interference; they want to keep their precious planets unchanged. Their Luddite minds are closed to the possibilities controlled interference could bring.'

'Do we tell them we know?'

'No, I think not. If they've been hiding what they know from us, let's return the favour. We might be able to use this to our advantage, in time. Let's keep pleading ignorance, play the game, and bide our time. See how things play out before we do anything...' Jink's voice faded away.

Lukin was distracted. 'I have him!' Lukin exclaimed. 'My screen's come alive again. The signal's back. And as you suggested, he has two human females with him.'

'Good, that's him gone from my side. Zark's due on shift soon,' said Jink. 'I'm going to have to do some work to cover this up before she gets here. I'm not sure I want her to know I know about the wormhole yet. I'll let them tell me when they're forced to, and I can act surprised when they do.'

'Likewise. I'll pretend we didn't have this conversation. As far as Garkan and Cork are concerned, H108 vanished and appeared with two unknown specimens. I'll let them work out any further details themselves.'

'Playing dumb and subservient has its advantages,' Jink advised.

'Yeah, I'm starting to figure that one out!'

21. Out Of The Frying Pan...

Location: Ayers Rock, Australia, Earth (Planet B13536)

The light streamed in from the end of the tunnel in blinding rays of dazzling light. Eliza staggered to a halt and shaded her squinting eyes. Something hard jabbed her back.

'Ouch!'

'Move.'

Eliza spun and glared with furious scorn at Aran. Her fingers curled into a clenching fist as she fought the urge to thrust it into his stupid nose. The pistol prodded her again, hard, in the ribs. She recoiled with gritted teeth, but kept her jaw clenched shut. She'd not give him the satisfaction a second time; she'd keep her pain to herself. She forced her feet to walk, splashing as she went.

Alora was ahead, skirts bunched in her fists as she edged her way through the shallow rim of a pool, trembling and taking tentative steps through the crystal-clear waters in this strange new land. They'd emerged into a gulley, with a pool sandwiched between its steep walls. A pool that turned into a stream, snaking away down the crooked gorge, twisting and turning and vanishing behind an outcrop. Wiry trees and wilted grasses tried to grow here, thirsty and sucking from the tiny stream, with the cliffs giving shelter from the relentless sun.

Eliza picked her way through the water and scrambled through the grasses, past a strange platform built from a metal grid with painted metal rails. Everything was so smooth, perfect, strangely neat. As she moved round the rails, the raspy breaths of her captor tickled her hair and his gun kept tapping her back, hurrying her on – her skirts were being snagged on thorny plants. She huffed as she upped her pace, then struggled onto the weed-strewn path of dusty orange with shades of red, the colour was everywhere. On the ground, the cliffs, between the trees; everywhere was dusty, dry. So different from the world she'd left behind.

She kept walking down the gulley and into the unknown, through the shadows and out into the illuminated expanse of a vast, empty world. More reds, more oranges, but mixed with sandy browns and pastel greens. Scattered trees with tiny leaves and dying tufts of withered grass were strewn upon the barren earth. A flat, featureless land stretched as far as she could see, except for something very strange parked amongst the dotted trees. It was the most bizarre carriage she'd ever seen, with no shaft or traces at the front to tie a horse. It was shiny, silver in colour but dusty, and it looked to be made of metal. Its spokeless wheels were impossibly thick and dull with grooves round the edge. Smooth panes of glass, clear and large, adorned the carriage's top half.

Eliza almost stopped again, then she remembered the gun thing Aran kept prodding her with, the thing that ripped a hole into Sergeant Bramston's leg with nothing more than a bang. Such a strange device. She knew it to be deadly.

She knew where she was. She was on Earth, she was on her father's home planet. He'd met her mother there. Her mother was abducted by aliens as a girl and sent to Earth for her safety, then returned to Gemini as an adult to take back her throne – from Aran, her uncle, the man who held them captive.

She could see a bit of her cousin, Monty, in Aran. Monty was Aran's nephew, his mother, Kia, was Aran's sister; there was definitely family resemblance there. She was under no doubt who this man was, and under no illusions as to how dangerous he could be. She'd been taught about the history of her country. She knew about her mother's stepmother, Queen Lila, the woman who tried to exterminate every elf, dwarf, and goblin in Gemini. Her parents had managed to defeat her; they'd crushed her power and managed to persuade her to return home, to Earth.

Eliza knew about King Aran, the man who claimed the throne of Vorn after his older brother suddenly died. The man who was defeated by her father in the elven realm of Ballachdor, and again in Vorn by her mother, father, and Uncle Mark.

Uncle Mark tricked Aran into travelling to Earth. He'd knocked him out and had run back to Gemini, and the tunnel connecting the two worlds was destroyed. No one on Gemini had known there was another route, another tunnel, connecting the two worlds – until now.

Eliza's father would search for her, and her Uncle Mark would search for Alora. They'd find Garrad, and they'd come after them. They'd risk their lives to save them. They could end up dead in this strange land and it was all her and Alora's fault. She'd been stupid, naive. Her veneer cracked. She could already hear Alora weeping, but no, she would not cry. She'd be strong. They'd find a way out of this. They had to.

'Get in.' Eliza turned to Aran, scared and questioning. They both had no idea how to. Aran rolled his eyes. 'Fred, open the door for them,' he barked in English. Eliza's parents had made her learn it. For what purpose, she hadn't had a clue. They'd said it was about knowing her heritage; she'd thought it ridiculous. But learn it she did, and now she was certainly glad she had.

A clunk and a click. A panel hinged open, and a huge man stepped out. He looked Eliza and Alora up and down and raised an eyebrow. Eliza glared at the man. He looked mean, a scar on his face, framed by stubble, and was wearing a shirt with short sleeves and no buttons and long blue trousers to the floor. No one wore long trousers; they stopped at the boot rim or the top of the stockings. But he wasn't wearing stockings, or boots. He wore some kind of slippers with laces.

He put his hand onto a handle in a panel in the strange-looking carriage and pulled. *Clunk, click* – it hinged open like the one the big man had emerged from. He grinned. A smile that would have been perfect except for the big chip in one tooth. He bowed and gestured for them to get in. He was mocking them.

As Alora staggered ahead, she turned and looked at Eliza, tears streaming down her face. Aran raised the gun at her. She gathered her skirts and climbed in. Eliza followed. *Clunk.* The big man shut the door. *Click.* The locks were closed, but it was for nothing; they didn't know how to open the doors from within any more than they'd known how to do so from outside.

Wheeze, rumble, growl. Movement. The strange carriage glided forwards. Smoothly, like they were on a ship. Gentle bounces, a vibration, but fluid – if Eliza hadn't been terrified, she'd have been in awe. The scenery whizzed past, as if she were at full gallop, possibly faster. She gripped her seat in fear. It didn't last long. Deceleration, and they stopped. The growling ceased, the door clunked, and the big man got out and opened their door.

She tripped over her skirts as she clambered out. She stumbled. The big man grabbed her. He was surprisingly gentle for one so big, but she scowled at him regardless – how dare he touch her? She'd rather have fallen.

'Inside, go!' Aran ordered, his gun pointed at them again.

The big man led. He walked towards a building part cladded in wood, part rendered. Strange paintings decorated it in places; its doors were large and glazed. Such big, clear panels set into such smooth wooden frames.

The man herded them down a corridor where aging paper curling at the edges hung from the walls, stamped with rusty metal objects at the corners.

Dusty footprints preceded the group. They followed them forwards, then left, right. A door swung open. A slender woman appeared and stepped back to let them in.

'You got them?' she asked.

Eliza found herself fascinated by the oddly attired woman. She was almost naked, wearing short tight bloomers and some kind of cropped petticoat, with as much of her breasts visible as Eliza would have expected from a woman who sold herself. Her belly was on show; her legs were visible. She had a gun at one hip, a knife at the other. Her hair was tied on top of her head, and streaks of blonde tumbled past her face. She showed so much flesh yet seemed to have no shame.

She paced around them, hands behind her back, looking at them in captivated awe. Perhaps they looked as strange to her as she did to them. She licked her lips slowly. Eliza's heart pounded with raging thuds in her heaving chest.

'Yes, lovely, aren't they?' Aran purred.

'Young and innocent, and terrified.' She moved closer to Alora and gently flicked a tear away from her cheek. 'Do they know what we're saying?'

A tear trickled from Alora's eyes; Eliza was fighting back her own urge to sob with every bit of strength she could muster.

'I doubt it,' said Aran. 'Almost no one speaks our language where they're from.'

'But you can talk to them?'

'Of course.'

188

The woman placed a hand on her hip. 'Mm. Ask them which wants to go first.'

'Sarah, this one is my kin.' He pointed to Alora. 'I'm not going to play with her – not like that, anyway.'

'Oh, shame. Can I play with her?' A wicked grin spread across Sarah's face. She danced towards Eliza, Sarah's arm brushing against hers as she circled her like a shark round a drifting boat. The feeling as the woman's smooth skin met her own sent shivers down Eliza's spine.

'Maybe later,' said Aran. 'But the other one, she's fair game. She is nothing but the spawn of the usurper.'

Eliza couldn't help herself: 'That's not true, and you know it!'

'She speaks! She has such an exotic accent,' Sarah observed.

'You do speak English! Is that what Mummy and Daddy spoke at home?' Aran teased. 'How about you?' He put a soft hand on Alora's chin. 'Do you understand us too?'

She spat at him. His hand formed a fist and shot towards her face, colliding with a heavy thud, snapping her head back. She stumbled over her skirts and fell, bottom and elbows banging on the hard tiled floor.

'Now, now, I will not accept any rudeness,' said Aran. 'I've killed men for less... and women. Behave yourselves, and remember, it is not essential I keep you alive. Your daddies will be as eager to take your corpses as your living flesh.'

'She doesn't speak English! Leave her alone!' Eliza yelled.

'Oooh, you're feisty, aren't you? I'll enjoy breaking your spirit.' Aran sneered.

Panic gripped Eliza. Her heart thudded so loudly her pulse pounded in her ears. Sarah was licking her finger, her eyes on the two of them like they were pieces of meat. Aran's eyebrows were lowered, regarding them through his thick eyelashes with sadistic hunger. Alora was sobbing openly, curled up on the floor. Terrified and unable to move or think, Eliza felt powerless, paralysed with terror.

'Shall I tie the other one up?' Sarah said softly as she flicked her head towards Alora. 'Let's make her watch.'

Aran nodded. Sarah pulled some kind of tie from a pouch on her belt and fixed Alora's hands together. She yanked her to her feet and used another tie to fix her to some pipework jutting out from the wall.

Eliza was frozen in terror. It was gloomy, the lights were off, and the blind was down. The light spilling in around the sides was all that illuminated the hellish hole she found herself in.

She made herself breathe deeply, steady her heart, and take control of her head. Thoughts at last returned. *Escape.* The word burst into her consciousness. There had to be a way out, a way to get free. But the door was locked; she'd seen Sarah do it. Where had she put the key? She tried desperately to recall if she'd even watched. How could she had not have seen that bit?

Sarah stood at the edge of the room. Her lips were parted, her head tilted back. Eliza didn't know of that expression, but it drove fear into her regardless. Sarah's arms were folded. She leant against the wall and those eyes pierced Eliza, made her feel naked, exposed. She pulled her gaze away.

Aran was in front of her, kicking off his laced slippers; he was unbuttoning his trousers. Slowly, deliberately, enjoying her terror.

Escape, she told herself again. How? She was trapped, she had no magic, and there was no way out. *Escape.* The tears trickled out as hope faded. Alora continued to cry, tied up, forced to stand, her gaze fixed on the floor. Aran was grinning a nasty grin.

Eliza's rigid form began to shake, and a wave of nausea engulfed her as Aran kicked off his trousers. He approached. Her frozen body thawed enough for her to take a step back, then another. The wall stopped her in her tracks. He dropped his undergarments – she gasped. Her terror at the sight of his manhood flooded through her with a deadly chill, cold sweat seeping through her hairs and making them stand on end.

Alora's sobbing grew louder. Eliza's eyes flicked to her cousin, a fleeting moment of hope, of strength, keeping her from screaming out, from begging for him to stop, to leave her be. She kept silent. He could do what he might, but she'd not give him the satisfaction of the audible manifestation of her despair. He'd tortured her father. He was about to torture her; if he could survive it, so could she.

Aran grabbed Eliza's quivering shoulder and yanked her from the wall. He hooked a leg behind hers and shoved her. She collapsed onto the hard floor, her bottom, elbows, then her head making contact, thudding hard, bruising. The pain was jarring but still she stayed quiet. She would not scream – that tiny promise she made to herself as she bit her cheeks to hold her mouth closed.

She was frozen and shaking, dizzy mind growing numb, emptying of thoughts of escape. She had a dry mouth and a racing heart as her uncle dropped to his knees and began to pull up her skirts. There was nothing left to do. No way out, no chance of escape. Alone with Alora on another world. No magic, no power, no means to halt the nightmare. She prayed for it to end.

A rhythmic thud in the distance, *Duh, duh, duh, duh, duh.* The sweaty hands slipped away from her thighs. *Duh, duh, duh,* the sound was growing louder, nearer. Aran tensed; his naked legs were pulled from hers. She dared to peep through a crack in her eyelids. A growing growl, several growls perhaps, like the sound the strange carriage made, then that sound again: d*uh, duh, duh, duh.* Aran's blurry shape shot to his feet.

'Shit!' he snapped.

Eliza let herself believe. She blinked her eyes open and filled her lungs, then let out a long, quivering breath. An interruption at the nick of time. *Escape*, a distant echo found its way into her chaotic mind.

Sarah rushed to the window and pulled back the blind. 'Shit!' she reiterated. 'It's the bloody FFA.'

'You sure?' Aran grabbed his jeans and hopped across the room, pulling them on as he went to look for himself. 'Shit.'

The flow of a gentle breeze from an open window swept over Eliza's exposed legs, giving her a slight chill as the air met cold sweat. She grabbed at her skirts and thrust them down, mind beginning to clear.

Aran was by the window with Sarah. Eliza struggled to her feet. She staggered towards Alora and tried to still her shaking hands enough to find a way to free her ties.

Duh, duh, duh. It was like the sound the gun Aran had shot Garrad with, but there were so many thuds, so close together. The sound was so loud now, it made the building rattle.

The sounds of growling and wheels rattling over the desert grew louder. Men were shouting, and the thud of the guns continued. She continued to tremble as she fingered Alora's ties, failing miserably to work out how to loosen them.

'There are loads of them, and they've got drones!' Aran exclaimed. 'We can't hold against that many, we gotta go.'

Eliza glanced over to him. He slipped on his laced slippers, not even bothering to tie the strings, then grabbed Eliza by the wrist, yanking her away from her cousin. Sarah drew her knife and freed Alora from the pipe, but her wrists remained bound. Sarah grabbed her by the hand and dragged her along behind her.

Duh, duh, duh, duh. The guns continued to rage outside. They rushed down the corridor towards the door at the back. The big man from the strange horse-less carriage was on his belly on the ground next to the machine he'd driven. He was firing his own gun, his body jolting with every bang. Other carriages were approaching, men firing even bigger guns from their tails – shafts of dust exploded from the dry ground with every round that missed its mark.

A stray bullet cracked above their heads; the glass in the door behind them smashed. Aran dived to the ground, pulling Eliza with him.

Eliza's wrist was sweaty. Aran's hand was smooth. He dived, trying to pull her down with him, but his grip slipped. She twisted and yanked. She was free.

Aran's pistol had fallen from its holster; it was in the dirt. She grabbed it, threw herself backwards, landed on her bum, and faced him.

'You don't know how to use that!' Aran sneered.

Eliza had both hands on the grip; her finger found the trigger. She didn't know how to use it, but she guessed. She pulled the trigger – it fired.

Sarah screamed. Blood oozed from her shoulder. Aran turned in horror.

Alora scrambled on hands and knees away from her captor. Sarah had let her go. Eliza fired again, trying to aim this time. Aran jolted back as the bullet hit; he yelled.

Eliza hurried to her feet – her cousin was scrambling to her own. Their eyes met, and they ran. They sprinted across the desert. To their right, Aran's men sheltered behind their carriages, firing with endless thuds.

The FFA sped towards Aran's men, their guns rattling a relentless chorus of snapping bangs. Stray rounds were peppered around the women's feet. Clouds of scattered dust exploded from the ground but still they ran. Cracks and thuds and screaming men, rumbling vehicles and screeching wheels, pounding feet and whirring drones – the battle raged but on they went. Only one thing was on their mind, escape.

The coursing prickle of adrenaline-fuelled blood flooded their body as they held their skirts high. Eliza compelled her legs to move, to keep going, to drag them from the battle until the cracks of weapons became faint, her lungs ran out of air, and they began to falter.

22. No Plan Survives Contact

'What the hell are those women doing?' Lieutenant Joe exclaimed. He stared incredulously from his truck as two females careered like creatures possessed across his line of fire. His men and women would be unlikely to shoot them on purpose, but he couldn't be certain they wouldn't hit them by mistake.

'Sir, I have fifteen heat signatures ahead, ten are currently static, five are pulling back into the cover of the building.' The ever-calm voice of Sergeant Butterworth came into Joe's earpiece, pulling his attention away from the mad women.

'Roger that, Sergeant,' he replied.

Fifteen. Joe let the number rattle through his head. Fifteen with no fire support wouldn't be difficult to defeat. He was confident his platoon could take them easily enough, but to do so one-on-one would result in casualties. It was pointless to throw life away when it wasn't needed.

'Pull back. I say again, pull back to ERV four.'

'Roger, sir,' his platoon sergeant acknowledged through Joe's earpiece, before relaying his command to the sections.

'Shit!' Joe ducked on instinct – far too late to avoid the round that came through his windshield; had it been on target, it would have hit his head. He was back up in an instant. It wouldn't do for the platoon commander to hide while his driver kept his own head up, his hands on the wheel, manoeuvring the truck in an impressive hair pin to take them back the way they came.

He spun to check what had been hit. There was a brand-new hole in the rear windshield near the top. The gunner on the tail looked uninjured; they'd been lucky, again. The truck shook. The gunner was returning fire, and the machine guns rattled the whole vehicle. *Duh, duh, duh, duh.* Joe hadn't expected there to be anyone at the visitor centre, but someone had given the FFA a tip-off that Aran was there, and it was worth a look.

The Freedom Fighters of Australia, or the FFA for short, were a group of ex-soldiers and soldier wannabes who wanted to take their country back from the scum who'd stolen it. Joe commanded a platoon in the small but growing fighting force. He'd been sent down with his guys and gals to check out the tip-off, and it turned out it had been accurate. He'd found Aran with a few men but no backup; no drones, no heavy guns. The man clearly wasn't expecting company. What Joe found most interesting was that someone in his crew had ratted on him. Whoever the rat was, Joe hoped he wasn't about to kill them.

The drugs baron had become a thorn in the side of the Freedom Fighters. They'd made good progress in the south and the west since Colonel Marie York scraped together what was left of the Australian Army five years ago, and they'd slowly but surely grown. Their numbers swelled as despairing Australians with nothing left to live for flocked to the Colonel's cause. She trained them, she armed them, and she'd led them to begin to take their country back from the drug barons and warlords.

The man they knew only as Aran proved difficult to budge. He held the centre, north and east – as far as, but not quite including Darwin and Cairns. He'd been spreading his tendrils; the coastal towns would soon be his too if he was left unchecked. Colonel York wasn't about to let that happen.

Joe was just a platoon commander, a junior officer near the bottom of the tree, but he was as determined to take back his country as his leader, and he planned to make his mission a success.

Joe's truck screeched to a halt at the emergency rendezvous point, wheels skidding in the dust as his driver spun it round to give the platoon commander a view of the enemy. They were out of range of the gunfire; his platoon was safe for the moment. It was time to up the ante.

'All sections, deploy drones. Corporal Ainsworth, get some rockets on that building. We need to keep 'em out in the open.'

His junior commanders acknowledged his orders through his earpiece. The whir of drones buzzing into the air replaced the thud of the machine guns, and a rocket whizzed overhead. *Boom.* The first missile found its mark – the blast of the shattering cultural centre erupted into the air. A Jeep began to move, speeding into the cloud of dust, and vanished into the opaque plume of falling debris.

'Sergeant, get a fix on that car – the one heading due east.'

195

Another rocket zoomed overhead; another truck went *boom*. Aran's men were sprinting for cover, but the FFA's kill drones rained down their deadly showers of bullets as they ran. The fleeing men dropped like defenceless flies. One or two made it into the remnants of an outbuilding, before it too was ripped apart by another explosion.

'Sit-rep on the car, Sergeant,' said Joe.

'It's accelerating, losing ground on us rapidly. The drones are staying with it, but we've had no hits so far.'

'No hits? How many drones you got on it?'

'Three, sir, but none can get anywhere near it, they keep getting repelled.'

'Try another drone.'

'Yes, sir, I'll re-task some of the others... Crap!'

'What is it, Sergeant?'

'Two of them collided.'

Joe was baffled. War drones never collided; they'd need to have a major software malfunction for that. 'You sure?'

'I have the footage from another drone.'

'Can you get a fix on the car? Let's get a rocket fired.'

'Yes, sir.'

Woosh. Seconds later, the guided missile was launched. Joe grabbed his monitor screen and watched. An observation drone had line of sight on the car, which was still speeding away through the dust. It wouldn't take long for the missile to find its mark.

Boom. The missile exploded in mid-air. It hadn't found its target.

'What the fuck?' Joe muttered to himself.

Is this why we keep missing the arsehole? He'd heard about how hard Aran was to hit. The FFA had been trying for years. Cut off the head of the snake and the rest normally crumbles. But they'd never managed to get Aran; he was as slippery as a fish. He must have some kind of tech that was helping him, stuff the FFA didn't. He was probably being helped by the fucking Chinese.

'Shall I fire another, sir?' Sergeant Butterworth asked.

Joe looked at his monitor and the cloud of dust speeding into the distance. 'No, let's save our rounds. What's the situation on the ground, Sergeant?'

'Wait out, sir.'

Joe sat in his seat and stared at the smoking ruin of the building, what was left of the visitor centre. He'd always wanted to visit Ayers Rock as a kid, but his folks weren't into that kind of stuff, and now? Tourism wasn't a thing anymore. At least not in Australia.

Another wasted building. There'd been more than he could count. He'd lost track of how many he'd flattened, and there weren't even many left in this fucked-up country. The Chinese took most of them out six years back. First the nukes, then the missiles, wiping out most of what was left of the Army. That would teach Australia to stand up to them, they'd said – not quite in those words. And it sure as hell did. It taught everyone. No one would dare challenge China.

'Sir, we have one casualty, a cat three, a bullet wound to the arm. All enemies on position have been neutralised. We have a drone still tracking the car, but at a distance. Vehicle damage is minimal, trucks still roadworthy. Ammo state good. Shall we clear through the position?'

'Thanks, Sergeant, yes, I'll lead.' Joe instructed his driver to move off, and the other three trucks followed. As they approached the smoking ruin, he suddenly remembered the crazy women. 'Sergeant, I want a scan of the perimeter. Get a drone in the air to check for anyone who's fled the scene.'

***

The truck rumbled over the rocky desert, weaving through the few hardy trees and plants that were managing to survive in this stinking wasteland. Joe grew up in Melbourne where it actually rained and even got cold sometimes. He hated this arid shithole.

The drone found two heat signatures. It was the women, he suspected. They couldn't get visuals on them easily; they seemed to have hidden under a bush.

'Here will do, Private Kerr,' he said to his driver, and they both jumped out of the truck. The men and women from the back jumped down too. All armed with rifles. The security of the area was already being checked. Despite the drone picking up little of concern, there was no point in taking chances.

Joe drew his pistol, flanked by his driver, who held his rifle at the ready. Joe edged towards the bush he knew the mysterious women were hiding under.

He got down on a knee, then on his stomach, and could just about see a flash of colour though the leaves. Dusty red and emerald green; he remembered the colours of the women's dresses as they ran. *Who wears long dresses like that in the middle of a desert?* he'd thought as he'd watched their skirts billow behind them.

'Hi there.' He tried to make his voice sound as friendly as possible. 'You can come out; we won't hurt you.'

He heard whispering and shuffling. One woman then the other wriggled out from under the bush.

They climbed to their feet and stood facing him with rigid postures and stern faces; defiance radiated from them both. He ignored their scowls – instead he found himself smiling as he looked them up and down. They looked like they'd escaped from a costume drama. Long, elegant dresses and fine jewels, hair that had been intricately styled at some point, although now dishevelled. Covered in dust and drenched in sweat. He didn't know what to make of them.

'Care to drop the pistol, miss?' he said.

One had black hair, dark eyes and olive skin, the other had light brown hair with blue eyes and a milky complexion. The fairer of the two glanced down at the weapon, like she hadn't realised she was still holding it. She looked up and regarded Joe and his driver.

Joe put a hand on Private Kerr's rifle, gently pushing it down, and he replaced his own pistol in its holster. Something told him these women were not a threat. And his instincts were normally right.

She opened her hand and let go. The weapon dropped with a thud.

'Would you mind telling me your names?' Joe asked.

The defiant aura faded from the dark-haired woman. Her red-rimmed eyes betrayed fear, yet the other young woman, although trembling, stood with clenched fists and piercing eyes. She studied him with interest. Joe was in uniform. A military desert-pattern camouflage shirt and trousers. Sand-coloured boots, pistol holster at his hip, and a lieutenant's rank slide on his chest.

She eventually spoke. 'My name's Eliza and this is Alora.' She spoke softly, with such a strange twang, as she gestured to her companion.

Joe straightened his beret. 'Pleased to meet you, Eliza. My name's Joe, or Lieutenant Morris, if you prefer.' He pulled his cheeks into a smile; he knew his boyish grin had a disarming affect. 'That's an interesting accent you have there – care to tell me where you're from?'

'I – er...' She glanced at Alora, who was still shaking like a leaf. 'I'm not sure I can tell you.'

'OK...' Joe was flummoxed. He looked towards Private Kerr, who shrugged. 'How about you tell me what you are doing out here in the desert? I saw you running from the firefight – were you two held captive there?'

'We were. Aran had us, we escaped.' She spoke in quiet, quivering tones, red-rimmed eyes not weeping, but they clearly had been. She held her shoulders back and raised her trembling chin defiantly.

He nodded, one hand slowly rubbing his clean-shaven cheeks. 'Aran, you say?' *That answers that one.* They'd checked the bodies at the building; they hadn't found Aran. 'Did he get away in the Jeep?' he asked.

'Jeep?'

'Erm, the car. The one that sped away.'

Eliza still looked confused. 'I don't know, I wasn't looking. I didn't see him again after we ran.'

'What did he want with you two, anyway?'

The other woman whispered to the one he was talking to. She whispered back. Joe tried to listen in, but the words were unintelligible. Not a language he recognised.

'He wanted to use us...' Her mouth stayed open, and she looked to be considering her next words carefully. She slowly dropped her gaze to the floor. '...for his pleasure,' she finished at last.

'Oh.' Joe bit his lower lip. 'I – I'm sorry to hear that. Did he—'

'No!' Eliza cut him off. 'We escaped before he did anything to us.'

'Good, I'm glad to hear it,' he said, surprised at how relieved he was to get that answer. 'Ladies, I'd love to offer you two a ride somewhere and let you get on your way, but something tells me there's more to your story than you're letting on here, and the colonel will want a chat with you. I'm going to have to ask you to come with me, I'm afraid.'

'We need to go,' she gasped, 'we have to get home.' The young woman looked suddenly panicked.

'And where did you say home was again? Maybe I could drop you there after the colonel has had a chat with you.'

'Er...'

'Thought so. How 'bout you take a seat in the truck?'

***

Aran sat in silence, seething and in pain. As the Jeep rumbled on towards Alice Springs, he kept reliving the moment he was shot by a woman who was barely more than a child. A bloody Geminian, for fuck's sake, someone who had no business knowing how to fire a pistol. She was a sharp one, he conceded. But she was Thomas's daughter, and he'd underestimated her father before.

Twelve men dead, or so he presumed. Three trucks destroyed or worse, in the hands of the FFA. Twelve rifles, ammo for twelve weapons – all in the hands of his enemy.

He'd kept hold of all his land, so far. He'd been too dismissive of the rag-tag bunch of military wannabes in the FFA, though. They'd taken the south, what was left of New South Wales, and South Australia. They had Western Australia too, but the good bits had been trashed by nukes. Only the Northern Territory and Queensland were worth having, and those were his, except for Darwin and Cairns; the last two cities of note on the continent still left in good nick. They had formidable warlords in command of them, and Aran wasn't ready to take them on yet.

But the south and the west? Before the FFA took them they'd been controlled by a bunch of halfwit drugs runners and try-hard warlords. Easy pickings for anyone. Aran would have taken them himself eventually, but he was happy to let the FFA make his job easier, it was a simpler task to defeat one enemy than many.

This time they'd got him. He'd had no idea they were so close. How could he have missed that? He kept regular overwatch with drones, so he knew the land was secure for a hundred miles or more. Fifteen men was more than enough to see off any mavericks or freelancers. But it wasn't enough to defend against rockets and war drones. He hadn't even realised they had that kind of kit – someone had to be backing them, New Zealand probably. The only county who bothered to openly condemn China. New Zealand was the country that mopped up most of the weak Australians who couldn't hack the new way the country was run. He guessed that maybe the place was now so overrun with refugees they'd started to wear the government down, nag it into action, make it defy the international community and pick a side.

200

If the FFA were getting state assistance, he might start to struggle. He'd have to up his game if he was to survive.

The Jeep rolled into the poppy fields outside of Alice Springs. Normally the sight of the drugs crop cheered him up. Field upon field of the raw ingredient of heroin, the drug of the west, the drug that made him rich. It was amazing what you could grow in a desert with a bit of water and fertilizer. When he'd first taken over around here, it was one of the first things he got up and running. Meth labs were great – they were a steady earner, as was the coca grown in the forests in the northwest to make cocaine – but diversity was the key to any successful business, and the heroin proved a huge success. The profits poured in.

As the green of the fields vanished and the dreary sight of the once thriving town of Alice Springs came into view, Aran's mind wandered back to the princesses and their escape, how they slipped from his grasp and ran into the desert. The FFA probably had them now. Not much chance of getting them back, not easily.

He was working hard to rationalise it. It didn't matter that they'd got away, he managed to conclude. It would have been great to see the looks on the faces of Mark and Thomas when he reunited them with the beaten, raped, and ragged excuses for women. Breaking the bodies of young lithe females would have made a welcome change from the hardened men he was used to playing with. He'd have relished the chance to watch them being used by his men right before their fathers' eyes, but that was not his main aim.

Mark and Thomas were his target; they were the ones he really wanted. When he got them, he'd keep them alive for weeks, possibly months, as he slowly tortured them to death. He could tell them he'd raped and murdered their daughters; he could tell them he'd done everything he'd imagined, which would be some consolation.

They'd be along soon. He didn't need to be there to capture them. He'd set up a trap. They'd be held nice and secure until his men could get them and bring them to him. Two men with swords and no magic were no match for twenty of his best men.

The gates of his compound swung open as his Jeep approached. He ignored the salutes of his guards; he was in no mood for niceties. Fred drove on through the immaculately maintained and irrigated gardens towards a large white mansion. His predecessor had taken this house, the nicest in the town, but it was Aran's now. His home, his office, his base of operations.

A short, squat man ran down the steps and pulled the door open for Aran. 'Boss, you alright?'

'Do I look alright?' Aran barked.

'Sorry, boss. I've got the doc here, waiting for you. She's got the med kit set up and ready in the treatment room.'

'Just the one doc? You only got one?' he snapped.

The short man's face drained of colour as Sarah emerged from the back seat, a bloody bandage wrapped around her shoulder.

'I'll get another at once,' he said. 'I, er – Doc Evans might be in town still. I'll find out...'

Sarah glared at him. 'You better get me a doctor within thirty minutes, or you might soon find you need one yourself!' The threat rolled off her tongue like acid.

'I'll get right on it.' He gulped and scurried off, phone in hand, dialling as he ran.

'Jenkins!' Aran barked; the man stopped so quickly he nearly stumbled.

'Yes, boss?'

'Find Sniper. Send him to me.'

'Yes, boss.'

Aran marched through the grand entrance. The wave of air-conditioned coolness hit him like a blast of heaven. The air-con unit on the Jeep needed re-gassing and they hadn't been able to get any new refrigerant. Scarcity of goods was another thing making life less than perfect in this desert-like hellhole. But here Aran was king, and he had magic and technology, all the drugs he wanted, and a woman who was a rare match for his unique preferences. He'd survive without air-con in the Jeep for as long as he had to. After all, there was no air-con in Gemini.

The room at the back corner of the house was usually where he took massages. It doubled up nicely as a medical room. He ambled in and glared at the doctor. The fat, ugly bitch wasn't much to look at, but she was good at her trade and knew how to keep her gob shut.

He lay down on the treatment bench. 'Get on with it then!'

'Of course,' she replied calmly as she began to unwrap his bandaged arm. 'Any other injuries you know of, or just this one?'

'Just the one,' he growled.

'Good.'

She soon got to work. Aran gritted his teeth at the pain. He refused morphine; he needed to keep his head sharp. Local anaesthetic should be fine, but it hadn't fully kicked in. He'd been lying there for a good few minutes, getting increasingly agitated at Sniper's tardiness, when the sound of heavy boots on the marble floor announced his arrival. The door thudded open.

'You send for me, boss?'

'Ah, Sniper.' Aran's face contorted as the doc began to clean his wound.

'You alright?'

'Fine,' he snapped as he forced himself to ignore the pain. 'FFA — give me an update.'

'They've bugged out.'

'What do you mean *bugged out?*'

'As you asked, I got a drone over there sharpish to see what was what. I got eyes on them. They mopped up the two women you mentioned then headed south and back out of our territory.'

'What were they doing on our land? Why would they attack us like that?'

'Thought you said our guys opened up on them?'

'Oh, I don't bloody know! The witnesses are dead or were as good as when I left. Our men probably did open up on them, but what would you expect them to do when four trucks worth of fucking Freedom Fighters creep up on them?'

'Erm...' Sniper looked to be thinking, careful not say the wrong thing.

'If they hadn't fired, they'd have been captured anyway. That's worse than them being dead. They'd have spouted all kinds of crap to the FFA that we don't want them knowing.' The pain was abating; the aesthetic was starting to kick in. 'How's it looking, doc?' He turned to the rotund woman.

'It's mostly a flesh wound. The bullet ricocheted off the side of your humerus. I'll check for any fragments of bone that might have chipped off. With a bit of hanztropine you should be fully healed in a few days.'

'What the hell is hanztropine?' he growled.

'Healing enhancer. New drug, developed in the US a couple years back. How have you not heard of it?'

'Because I don't make a habit of getting shot!'

'OK, fair enough. I've been using it on your guys though – did you not notice they got better quickly?'

'You think I give that much of a shit?' He turned back to Sniper. 'The FFA is clear of our patch, you sure about that?'

'As sure as I can be.'

'Good. I need you to take a squad and get back to Ayers Rock.'

'Yes, boss,' Sniper scratched his head, 'but what for?'

'Remember the trap we set up?'

'Yeah.'

'We might find it will be triggered very soon.'

23. The Trap

*E*ek, eek, eek. 'Fucking creatures,' Garrad muttered. The sound never ended. It was insects of some sort, he assumed; their squeaky chirp was relentless. His arse was numb. He wanted to move, but the blood had just about stopped oozing, and he didn't want risk his wound re-opening. Weakness infested him and he didn't like it. He was low on blood. He had to keep what he had left in his body, to live, to save those bloody princesses. His numb arse could just be numb.

Dawn was breaking. He was desperate to sleep, but he couldn't. The pain in his leg wouldn't let him. It throbbed, it pounded. With each beat of his heart, a new gush of blood rushed from the wound, squished and squeezed around the puncture in his flesh. Every pulse agitated the nerves, reminding him of how much of an idiot he was.

This was his fault, and he knew it. He should have reported the princesses weeks ago, after the first time they vanished. He hadn't. He'd let them get away to be on their own, to practice portal magic. Magic that brought them here, that got him shot, and them captured.

This was the beginning of his downfall. Lord Harrison would kill him. They'd find him and when they did... *Shit.* He couldn't even lie his way out of this one. The man was a fucking sorcerer, he could detect lies.

The chirping kept going. A bird squawked, and in the distance something howled. The stream babbled. He tried to focus on its sound. He didn't mind the stream so much; it was relaxing. He concentrated on the bubbling, and his eyelids drooped. He slumped forwards. Sleep found him.

***

'Is he dead?' The words filtered into Garrad's dream.

A hand shook his shoulder. His head whipped back – *whack*. He hit it on the cliff face behind him. 'Ouch!' He checked for blood – nope, a bruise. More pain. At least the ache in his leg had subsided.

'Bramston! Where are the girls?'

Garrad looked up in a panic. Prince Thomas and Lord Harrison loomed above him.

'I... er... I...'

'Spit it out!' Lord Harrison yelled.

'They're gone, Prince Aran took them!' Garrad blurted.

'What the fuck?' Tom spluttered.

'What do you mean, Prince Aran took them?' Lord Harrison boomed.

'He tricked them,' said Garrad. 'He enticed them here with magic. He had a unicorn – he was using magic on that too, I think. And on me! He got into my head, and I couldn't do anything to stop him or even warn the princesses. He took them into the tunnel.' He pointed towards the opening to his side. 'He said he wanted you to go after them.'

'There's another wormhole, there's got to be!' Prince Thomas exclaimed, his voice quivering. Garrad had never heard the prince speak like that. His face had gone white.

'Oh, good god.' Lord Harrison took a sharp intake of breath and staggered, hands landing on the cliff as his head dropped between his arms. He thumped the rock with his fist. 'He's got them, the evil torturous bastard has our little girls!'

'I'm sorry, sirs,' said Garrad. 'I tried to stop them, I warned them not to...'

'You knew about this? You knew where they were going?' Lord Harrison grabbed a handful of Garrad's shirt, tugging him sideways. He nearly toppled, his hand shooting out to steady himself, and his leg twisted.

'No!' he protested, pain shooting from his wound. He suddenly felt the need to be on his feet. He tried to rise; he grimaced in agony.

'Sit the fuck down, dickshit.' Lord Harrison let go of his shirt and shoved him back down onto his numb arse. 'If you manage to get to my eye level, I'm not sure I'll be able to control my fist. What the hell happened to your leg, anyway?'

'Prince Aran did it. He said it was a gun he used; I've never seen anything like it.'

'He shot you?' Mark examined Garrad's leg. 'Good, you deserve it.'

'Mark!' The prince edged forward, a degree of concern on his face. He dropped to his knee to take a closer look. 'Did it go all the way through?'

Prince Thomas started to prod the wound gently through Garrad's blood-soaked bandages and breeches. 'Arghh!' Garrad cried out.

'It's missed the bone, which is bloody lucky,' said the prince. 'I'm not sure even Kia could do a perfect fix on a shattered femur.'

'I don't give a shit about his injury; we need to find the girls. Let's get our arses in that tunnel,' Lord Harrison screamed.

'You're gonna have to calm down, Mark – rushing in isn't going to help. If that tunnel does lead to Earth, we can't charge through with our swords. We'll need gold, we'll need to buy some kit, some guns, a car maybe? Some phones so we can get maps? Who knows where we'll be when we get through?'

Lord Harrison was barely listening. His crimson face was a picture of worry and fury. He was beathing deeply, trying to get himself under control.

'Gold, right.' The lights suddenly appeared to come on in his head. 'You know this is a trap, right? Aran took our girls to get us. Do you not think he'll be waiting for us on the other side? He'll be right outside the exit with ten other thugs armed with shotguns. We'll have no magic, just swords. What the fuck do we do? Get bows and try to get them with arrows?'

'Jesus, mate, I don't know. But what choice do we have? Aran won't want to kill us; he'll want to torture us, I imagine. He'll keep us alive, like he'll keep the girls alive. He'll want us to see them suffer. This gives us time. He'll probably catch us, beat the shit out of us, but we have both escaped him before – we can do it again.'

'You're right,' Lord Harrison growled. 'He's got us, Tom, the arsehole's fucking got us. We have no choice. We're gonna have to bite the bullet.' His head shook, a white sliver of his clenched teeth peeping through his lips. 'Shall we go home? Get some supplies and come back?'

'I guess. What about him?' Prince Thomas was staring at Garrad.

'Fuck the little shit. Let's leave him here to die.'

'Mark!' Prince Thomas said, with a degree of reprimand in his tone.

'Fine, we take him back. Kia can heal him. He can stay in the dungeon until we get back.'

'He's not got any magic. How can he go through a portal?'

'How did he get here?'

'I went through the portal, sir' Garrad dared to reply. 'I saw the princesses disappear through, I dived in after them, and ended up here.'

Prince Thomas turned to Lord Harrison. 'He shouldn't be able to do that.'

'Maybe he's got some special fucking gene. He went one way, so he can go back.'

***

Prince Thomas raised a hand and made a circle in the air, muttering to himself as he did. A spiral of light appeared out of nowhere. It grew larger and larger until it was taller than a man. Garrad was transfixed.

The two men grabbed one of Garrad's arms each and hauled him to his feet. He grimaced in pain but managed to keep himself from yelling out as he took his weight on his one good leg. He made the mistake of trying to move his injured one.

'Ow!' he spluttered. Fresh blood oozed down his thigh.

The Lord Commander and Prince of Vorn hauled him from the ground. Garrad found himself hopping forward, his other leg dragging along the forest floor – the pain was excruciating.

'I'm not gonna lie, lad, there's no easy way to do this,' the prince said. 'We're going to have to jump you through. Can't get the portals any lower, I'm afraid. They have to be clear of the ground. Ready?'

Garrad nodded.

'On three,' Prince Thomas began. 'One, two, three!'

Lord Harrison and Prince Thomas leapt forward with Garrad held between them. Garrad used his good leg to jump as best he could. He was lifted into the air. His face approached the swirl, then *thunk!* He hit something. The prince and the Lord Commander vanished. Garrad bounced backwards and collapsed onto the ground, screaming in agony as his injured leg crumpled under him.

He was lying on the ground, staring up at the canopy above, trying not to let the tears escape. He gritted his teeth and forced his damaged leg out straight, sucking hissing gasps of air.

The portal still spun, Tom leapt back through it from the other side, only just avoiding landing on Garrad. He stumbled but caught himself then stood staring at him, baffled.

'Any idea why you didn't get through?' Prince Thomas said with a shrug.

'Sorry, no, your Highness.'

'No idea how you got through last time?'

'I can guess Aran had something to do with it. He got into my head, maybe he got me through the portal somehow.'

'Possible. Fuck me if I have any idea how to do whatever he might have done.' Garrad's pain made it difficult to focus. Through the fuzz and the swirls, he detected a hint of sympathy in the prince's face.

Prince Thomas sighed. 'I'm going to have to bring Kia here. We can work out what to do with you after your brain isn't fuddled with pain. Hang in there, lad.'

Thomas jumped back through the portal; it vanished behind him.

***

At some point, the daylight faded to black. Garrad lost consciousness. But when his eyes flickered open, he felt strange – the pain had gone. He pulled himself onto his elbows; he looked around. He could see the prince rooting in a rucksack and he could see Lord Harrison standing close to a slender woman with thick black hair and a fine dress. She leant forwards and kissed him. She must have heard Garrad shuffle, and he turned to look at him.

'Oh, you're awake. Good,' she said softly, with a smile so much like her daughter's'.

Garrad recognised Lord Harrison's wife. 'Thank you, Your Highness.' The pain in his leg was gone; he struggled to his feet through his stiffness. 'I am most grateful for your help.'

Everyone knew she was the best healer in Vorn. He was lucky yet again to be able to get such a service from another talented sorcerer.

'It's fine.' Her smile vanished. Her eyes were red, her face forlorn. Her daughter had been taken; a bobbing lump swelled in his throat. She turned back to her husband. 'Are you sure you have everything you need?'

'As sure as I can be,' Lord Harrison said.

209

'What are you going to do with him?' She glanced towards Garrad.

'Take him with us. This island's uninhabited. There are no boats for thousands of miles and maybe the little shit can try and help us. He's good in a fight, he might be some use.'

'Don't blame him, Mark,' she said softly. 'He'd have stopped them if he could.' She placed a hand on her husband's shoulder. 'Don't underestimate Aran. He can be more ruthless and underhand than you give him credit for.'

'I fucked over the arsehole last time, didn't I?'

'Mark!' she exclaimed, in objection to his language.

'Not you as well. I get enough of that from Alora.'

'Well watch your language! You shouldn't swear around ladies.'

'Yes, sweetness.' He leaned forward and kissed her on the cheek.

'I'm going now – please bring my daughter back safely.'

'I'll do everything I can.'

Tears flowed down her cheeks. 'I know you will. Bye, Tom, and good luck, Sergeant.'

In seconds, she'd formed a portal and vanished through it. Garrad was alone with the second most senior royal in Vorn and the commander of the queen's Armed Forces. He looked at the fathers of the women he'd lost in terror. He fully expected Lord Harrison to hang him when he got back for this. He would do everything he could to give him a reason not to.

'Right, Sergeant,' Prince Thomas began, 'do you have any idea where we are going?'

'Er…'

'Thought so. Time to share a few secrets – listen carefully and listen well. I'm going to give you a bit of a download of information, and you need to pay attention. It might sound insane but trust me, very soon you will realise everything I'm going to say is true.'

Garrad nodded.

'OK, the tunnel, we're pretty sure it leads to another planet, a place called Earth. It's where Mark and I are from. People from Earth have a lot more magical ability than those from Gemini. Every sorcerer with extreme power on our world has some Earth blood in them, including Princess Kia, me, Mark, and our children. On Earth, no one can use magic – our power is useless there.'

Garrad stared. *The Prince of Vorn is from another planet? He's a gods-damned extra-terrestrial? Is that why he's such an awesome sorcerer and so bloody strange? It would sure as hell explain a lot.*

'You know Vorn's history,' the prince continued, 'so I won't bore you, but Prince Aran, as you have probably worked out, didn't die when Queen Emma took Vornston from him. He was left on Earth, alive. Which is why we are pretty certain this tunnel leads to our home planet.'

Garrad nodded slowly.

'When you get to Earth, you need to know you won't be able to talk to anyone. No one on Earth speaks the common tongue, except Aran and his mother. I'm not sure we'll meet her. She has to be getting on by now.'

'He's talking about Queen Lila.' He cocked his head. *'She's still alive? On Earth?'*

'Depending on where this tunnel takes us, Mark and I should be able to do the talking, or at least bluff our way through until we find some translation software. Don't start gobbing off. Just make out like you don't speak much. We don't want to attract attention. When we arrive, we will look ridiculous to the locals. No one dresses like this on Earth, we'll look like we're in fancy dress.'

Garrad's brows furrowed. *What the hell is he on about?*

'Oh, fancy dress is where you dress like something unusual,' Tom answered the unasked question, 'like another character. Like if you wanted to dress like a pirate.'

'Why would I want to do that?'

'You wouldn't. You're not from Earth and not on a stag do.'

'What?' *This is getting weirder by the minute.*

'Never mind. Anyway, the point is, be aware you'll look ridiculous to everyone. If Aran doesn't grab us straight away or we manage to escape, getting some new clothes will be a priority. And we might have to ditch the swords.'

'My father gave it to me!'

'We'll try to keep hold of them if we can. On Earth, people use guns, not swords. Metal tubes that fire out metal at a rate of knots. You've already met one of those, but from what you said, it was probably one of the least deadly kinds. If you see a long one that needs two hands to fire, you should know their range is much further and they can fire

211

multiple bullets very quickly. You can be shot dead by one of those bad boys at six hundred paces or more, if the guy is a good shot.'

'Six hundred paces?' Garrad gasped, incredulous. *I'm going to die. This is where it ends, on some mental mission to another planet, killed by some guy too far away to see.* 'Shit.' *Could be worse, could be pissed-up in a gutter.*

'Yep. Right, Mark, you got the kit sorted?'

Mark had been busy sorting weapons, tools, first-aid kits, and gold into packs for them. 'Pretty much.'

'Great, grab a pack and let's go,' the prince instructed.

'Of course, Your Highness.' An order, nice and simple – he could handle that. Pick up a pack, walk through a tunnel, panic like fuck later.

'Oh, one more thing. From the moment we enter the tunnel to the moment we get back here, my name's Tom and he's Mark. We'll call you Garrad. If we use our titles on Earth, people will think we're barking. No one will understand you, but it will feel nuts if you start calling us that there. On Earth, we're nobodies.'

Prince Thomas led the way down the tunnel, a flaming ball of magical fire lighting the way. Mark went next and Garrad followed nervously at the rear. A stream ran along the tunnel floor, but he paid it no heed as they splashed their way deep underground.

Then, a couple of hundred paces in, the fireball went out.

'That's us on Earth then, I guess,' the Prince said in the darkness.

Lord Harrison took a few steps back and bumped into Garrad. He grunted but didn't apologise as he magicked a fireball of his own into the air.

'Recon I'm still on Gemini then,' he observed.

'I guess. Might as well use magic to light the torch though before we go any further.' Tom took a few paces towards Mark and held a torch into the magical fire.

They resumed their progress down the tunnel, the Lord Commander's fireball vanished after just a few more steps. The smoky torch was now the only source of light as they continued deeper into the unknown.

Clunk, thud. They spun on the spot in unison. 'Damn!' Tom exclaimed as iron bars shot across the passage behind them.

A steel door was in front, iron bars behind. They were trapped. The prince and the lord commander were sorcerers; this was surely not a challenge? Garrad couldn't bring himself to believe their magic

212

wouldn't work here. It had to be a joke, a lie. Despite what he'd seen earlier when Aran took the princesses, there had to be some other explanation. Magic didn't run out, it was everywhere — it always has been. He'd known it all his life.

Boom. Lord Mark rammed his shoulder into the steel door barring their path.

'Ow!' He rubbed his bruised bones. He'd used brute force; he'd not even tried to use his power. Garrad squeezed his torch even harder as he tried to grasp the reality that the two most powerful sorcerers in Gemini were now nothing but ordinary men past their prime.

'We're trapped!' Tom blurted.

'Well done for stating the bloody obvious,' Mark sniped.

'We've tripped a sensor. Aran must have set up some monitoring systems — can you see any cameras?'

Cameras? What were they? Garrad's eyes darted about the small space as he tried to figure it out.

'There!' Lord Mark pointed.

Garrad looked up towards the corner. A small circle of glass twinkled, mirroring the flames from the torch.

Mark walked over and grabbed hold of it and yanked. Its fixing came free from the crumbly sandstone; the wall plug still held the screw. 'So tiny!'

'Tech's moved on in the twenty years since we were here, remember,' said Tom.

'Yeah, if I wasn't fucking furious right now, I'd be curious.' Mark dropped the camera and stamped on it.

'Can you see anything else?'

Garrad spotted a small black dome above the door. 'What's that?'

'Good spot.' Mark walked towards it and tried to rip it down too. It was stuck. 'This one's fixed a bit better. Don't think it's a camera, though, looks more like a sensor to me.'

'It's probably what triggered those bars,' Tom suggested.

'Probably.' Mark drew his sword and used the hilt to bash the sensor. It quickly splintered into shards of plastic and mangled wires. 'That's that dead, now what?'

'We wait for Aran to find us?' Tom said, tongue-in-cheek.

'Ha! We need to bust our way out before he comes. Come closer with the torch, boy.' Mark glowered at Garrad. Garrad held the flame as

213

Mark crouched and studied the lock on the steel door blocking their exit.
'You got that Leatherman, Tom?'

'Yep! Once a Sapper, always a Sapper.'

Leatherman? Sapper? These guys are making up words.

'Can't believe you've kept that thing since we left Earth,' Mark sniped.

'It's bloody useful.'

'For a prince? What do you do with it, use it to pick caviar out of your teeth?'

Garrad couldn't help but smirk at the Lord Commander's mockery. The prince was smiling too. There was no disguising the fact that these two liked to take the piss, like he and Mervin did with each other; the two most senior men in Vorn bantering away like ordinary folk.

'Whatever. Here.' Tom handed Mark the small, folded metal tool. Mark unfolded it to find a tiny flat-blade screwdriver. 'Think you can pick it?'

'I'm gonna give it a go.'

And the lord commander knows how to pick a lock? Where the hell does a bloody noble learn that?

The torch was burning low when Mark eventually gave up. 'Fuck!' He launched the Leatherman at Tom's feet.

'Careful, mate,' Tom chastised his friend as he collected the tool. 'What now?'

'Brute force?'

'We're not going to break through that door.'

Garrad looked at the solid sheet of steel. Heavy and sturdy. Not a chance it was going to give with a kick. It was fixed to the rock, and the rock didn't look nearly as solid.

The two older men stared at the door in silence.

'Should we not at least try?' Garrad at last found the courage to speak. 'The thing you pulled out of the wall came down easily – maybe the door's not fastened to the tunnel sides well either.'

Butterflies fluttered in his stomach as the prince looked silently from him to the lord commander. He suddenly regretted talking. It was not his place to contradict royalty; he was a bloody sergeant. What was he thinking!

'Go on, be my guest.' The prince broke the silence at last.

There was nothing else for it. Garrad passed the torch to Mark and started to kick.

Garrad smacked the door with the sole of his boot. He hit it again, and again. Dust trickled down the walls. The gentle flow of tiny particles of rock made him keep going. Another kick, then another. Harder and harder with every strike.

'I think it's moving,' Tom observed. 'Keep it up, lad.'

He continued to pound the door until he was sweating despite the coolness of the tunnel. He kicked until the torch had almost burnt out, until his face was red and he was ready to drop.

'That's enough for now.' The prince dropped a hand on his shoulder.

Garrad was convinced they were enjoying watching him sweat, busting a gut to near exhaustion while they stood and watched. But he'd lost their daughters, and he was lucky to not have been hanged.

'You've definitely shifted it,' Tom conceded. 'Let me have a go.'

The prince began to pummel the door. He managed more force than Garrad expected for a man in his fifties who certainly looked more than a little out of shape. It started to budge. It was much harder to tell when you were pummelling it yourself, sweat dripping into your eyes, desperately trying to give it your all while not dropping where you stood.

He hadn't been trying for long when the torch fizzled out. The lord commander took over, blindly kicking in the dark with only the gentle rattle of dust to hint at their progress.

It was Garrad's turn again. They didn't make him work as long this time. They took over and kept rotating through in blind hope it would eventually give way. There was nothing else they could do.

He'd ceased wondering why Aran hadn't come, even though Tom and Mark seemed convinced he would. He'd stopped caring why someone had bothered to build such a solid door but hadn't bothered to guard it. Why the sound of the kicking hadn't drawn attention. He kept going, doing the lion's share of the work as the youngest, fittest, and the idiot responsible for the princess's capture.

He was dripping in sweat and aching all over when at last the thing gave way; the door slipped free, fixings scraping down the walls. One or two more kicks and it dropped to the ground. The flow of fresh air hit them with a blast; greyish gloom peeked out ahead. They scrambled over the door and out into the unknown, Garrad leading, the first to emerge into the blazing sunshine of another world.

24. It Could Be Worse

Tom squinted as he stumbled into the daylight. 'Where the hell are we?' He was looking straight ahead, and almost fell headfirst into a pool – his foot splashed into the water.

'Careful, mate!' Mark grabbed a handful of his shirt and hauled him back just in time. Mark clambered down and joined him in the pool and they both stood and stared like meerkats in a puddle at the strange new world they'd entered. They were in a narrow valley with steep rock walls. Crooked, stunted trees, lanky bushes, and drooping grasses filled the bottom of the valley.

'This ain't Kenya,' Mark muttered, a hand shading his gawping eyes.

'You think?' Tom sniped as his eyes roved around the smooth red cliffs framing their view.

Tom suddenly remembered Garrad. He turned to regard the young sergeant; they'd overtaken him at the tunnel mouth. The strange new land mystified Tom, but he'd travelled between planets before and was getting over it already. Garrad's stretched-out jaw painted a picture of awe on a whole other level. His hands were grasping the tunnel sides, fingernails pressed rigidly into the rock. His face was drained and pasty white. A corner of Tom's mouth squeezed upwards. He couldn't resist. He gently reached forwards and closed Garrad's mouth. The sergeant jolted back into focus.

'You alright, lad?' said Tom.

'Yessir,' Garrad snapped, hands slipping from the rock.

'Tom. It's Tom, remember?'

'Um, yes… Tom. I'm in my third land in three days… I'd never even left Vorn before the portal.'

'Welcome to Earth!' Tom patted him on the shoulder.

'There's no welcoming committee,' Mark observed.

'No, something's up.' Tom scratched his head. 'I don't think we should hang around to find out what.'

'Aye, I'm with you there.' Mark was already splashing his way around the pool edge and towards the trees. Tom and Garrad followed.

They wound their way down the gulley and past the trees and were soon out in the open. The gulley ended suddenly. The rock split to the left and right, walls of red stone towering into the distance on either side. Before them, the land was flat for as far as they could see. Flat, red, dusty. Scattered trees, brown grass. The occasional bird.

Tom spotted movement in the distance. He tried to make it out, but it was a long way off. It bounced and Tom's suspicions were confirmed.

He turned back to Mark. 'Australia,' he said confidently.

'Australia? How can you be sure?'

Tom pointed to the distant bouncing animal. 'Kangaroo.'

'Kangaroo? Where?'

'There, right there, between those trees.'

Mark strained his eyes. 'Oh yeah!'

'And if I were to guess, I'd say the rock behind us is Ayers Rock.'

'Pushing it, don't you think?'

'Know of any other giant red rock features in Australia?'

'No, but I ain't exactly studied a map of the place – have you?'

'What's a kangaroo?' Garrad asked.

They spun in unison to face him.

'It's an animal – erm, like a big rabbit, more like a big hare. They only live in one part of Earth. That's how we know where we are,' Tom said.

'Oh. You're certain we're on Earth?'

Tom would have found the slightly nervous quiver in Garrad's voice every time he spoke amusing if he wasn't still angry with the lad.

'I knew as soon as my magic ran out,' he replied dryly. 'Still no sign of Aran. Odd, don't you think?' Tom said to Mark.

A sigh hissed from Tom, and he shook his head as he watched Mark begin his fives and twenties. It was an old army drill: check the foreground, check the mid-ground, look for anomalies. The blatant flick of his eyes from one spot to the next gave away his friend's never faltering commitment to his old training. Tom just had a good look round.

218

'Yeah,' Mark concluded at last. 'Let's not look a gift horse in the mouth though. We need to get out of here. Can't imagine Aran's forgotten about us.'

'Good point.' Tom spotted something quivering in the distant sky. 'Is that a plume of smoke over there?' He pointed.

Mark followed his gaze. 'A faint one.'

'Do we head towards it, or away from it?'

Mark breathed out heavily and rubbed his chin. 'We're in a desert, right?'

'Yeah.'

'We can't go any further than our water supplies allow. We'll die of dehydration pretty soon otherwise.'

'We can fill up from that pool.'

'Great, we'll start with full water skins, but how long do you think it will last?'

'Good point.'

'We need to find civilisation and some way of getting out of here, or at least a way of calling for help. Smoke means people, people means civilisation. I certainly don't fancy hanging round that pool waiting for Aran.'

'Good logic. But if we are at Ayers Rock, it's a tourist hotspot, so surely there should be loads of sightseers knocking about?'

'Probably. Then maybe we're not at Ayers Rock.'

Tom raised an eyebrow. 'We'll see.' He pulled out his waterskin and finished its contents. 'Let's refill from the pool and head off, shall we?'

They were soon walking through the empty desert, winding between the scattered trees, slowly getting closer to the smoke. It was further than Tom first thought; the plume was bigger than it looked. As they approached, the smell of charred timber wafted through the trees and the smouldering remains of a building emerged.

'Shit!' Mark shaded his eyes with a hand as he surveyed the devastation.

'Shit indeed. Someone's had a bad day.'

The smoking remains of the building was the headline of the show, but the burnt-out trucks and bodies spread on the ground definitely made a good supporting act. They cautiously edged forwards. It was quiet – just the wind, a few birds, and the odd buzzing insect added to the sound of

219

their marching footsteps. They passed a body splayed on the ground, a bullet hole in the top of his head.

'How the hell was he shot from above?' Tom was baffled.

'Maybe there's been an ariel assault, gunners in choppers, perhaps? Look at that guy.' Mark pointed at another corpse. 'Bullet hole in the top of his shoulder – he looks to have been shot from above too.'

A few more bodies were scattered about. Some looked to have been killed after emerging from the visitor centre, with more bullet holes that looked like they'd come from above. The two trucks had been hit by missiles or mortars. One was wrapped around a tree. Their drivers and passengers were blackened corpses inside.

'Uluru Cultural Centre!' Tom exclaimed, as he pointed to a sign on a post that had avoided the blaze.

'Uluru? What the fuck is that?' Mark asked, frowning.

'It's Ayers Rock, numbnuts – it's what the Aboriginals call it.'

'A likely story,' Mark jested, 'but I don't suppose it matters, does it? Whatever the rock's real name is, you can't deny there's been carnage here. Something's not right with this place. Shit's gone on since we left.'

Tom turned to check on Garrad. He trailed behind, his face aghast. 'Seen much death before, kid?'

Garrad shook his head slowly.

'Suppose there's not been any wars for a while so not a surprise really. You get used to it, trust me.' Tom let him catch up and slapped him on the back.

Garrad clenched his jaw in an apparent attempt to take control of his face. 'What's that?' He was pointing to the mangled truck.

'Oh, it's a car – actually, a pickup truck,' Tom began. Garrad stared blankly. 'It's a vehicle. It carries people around without the need for horses.'

'How does it do that?' Garrad asked, a scratching finger teasing his dusty scalp.

'It has something called an engine. It uses fuel, a liquid that burns, and the engine uses it to drive pistons, which in turn make the wheels spin. It—'

'Tom, we can give Garrad all the lessons he likes on the internal combustion engine later,' said Mark. 'But right now we need to think about getting out of here. We're gonna have to head down the road and try to find someone and hope it's not Aran.'

'Great plan,' Tom replied.

'You got a better one?'

'Er...'

'Thought not. We should take what we can from here – some clothes off the corpses. Make ourselves look more local.'

'You want me to stick on some sweaty dead man's clothes?' Tom said with a frown.

'Nah, stay as you are. You can tell anyone we meet you were on a stag do and got lost.'

'Ha, ha. Fine.' Tom sighed. 'I hope these guys showered this morning.'

Tom looked for the cleanest man who was about the right size to have clothes that fit him. His T-shirt wasn't too bad, but the jeans stank of piss and made him gag. Most people seemed to forget that folk pissed, and quite often shitted themselves, when they died. But this guy must have had empty bowels when he went.

It certainly felt odd to put on trousers with a zipped crotch and a steel button after all these years, but he couldn't deny it was nice to put on such simple clothes. He hoped they stank less when the piss dried out.

'You call these boots? They don't look like any boots I've ever seen,' said Garrad.

Garrad was on his arse, attempting to pull on a pair of high desert combat boots.

'They are proper boots,' Mark retorted. 'Boots you can actually walk in for more than five minutes without your feet falling to bits.'

'I've never had such a problem with footwear before,' said Garrad.

'Lucky you, twinkle toes. Get the things on and let's get moving.'

'They're on.'

'They aren't laced up.'

'Laced up?' Garrad tilted his head.

'For fuck's sake.' Mark sauntered over to where Garrad sat on the ground. 'I never thought I'd have to teach a twenty-year-old how to tie his shoes.' He crouched and began to pull on the laces. A snigger escaped from Tom.

'I'm twenty-two.'

'Whatever.'

As Tom finished lacing his own boots and scrambled to his feet, something caught his eye. A plume of dust was spraying into the air and getting bigger and closer. 'Someone's coming!' It was vehicles.

'Are they friendly?' Mark called over.

'How the hell should I know?'

'We better hide until we can figure it out.'

They crouched in a seared but still standing outbuilding, peeking out at the vehicles headed their way. There were four of them in the convoy, two Jeeps and a couple of pickup trucks. Three of them headed straight past where the men hid, the last drove straight towards them.

They kept still and silent as the vehicle stopped and two men climbed out, both big, one tubby and the other brawny. Both had AK47s, one slung over his back, the other clutched his rifle in one hand.

'They don't look too friendly,' Mark whispered as the men began to inspect the corpses. The brawny man rolled over a corpse and took a long look at his face. The pair of them continued to nosy around the area, inspecting as they went.

'Bazza, this one's been stripped!' Tubby called to the other.

'You what?' Brawny strolled over to a corpse lying face down on the ground. 'Fuck me, who'd do that?'

'Someone who wants a change of clothes?' Tubby picked up a dusty shirt he'd found on the ground nearby with the muzzle of the rifle.

Tom peered through a gap in the charred timbers, Mark tugged at his sleeve. He was indicating to make a move. The two new arrivals now had their backs to them, it was now or never.

'Drop the gun.' Mark pressed his sword into Tubby's neck.

Brawny looked up. 'What the...'

'You too.' Tom was behind Brawny, his blade similarly placed.

Brawny looked at Tubby and nodded ever so slightly.

'Tom, look out!' Mark had caught the glance, but the warning came a moment too late.

An elbow sank into Tom's stomach, he gasped. Tubby started to squirm, but Mark held him from behind firmly, his sword still on his throat. Brawny managed to wriggle free. The AK was still in Brawny's hand; he raised it to shoot.

Tom swiped with his sword. Brawny leapt back. The gun fired and rounds leapt into the air, far from their mark. Brawny made ready to aim again. Tom prepared to strike, sword raised, shoulders tensed, but the rifle slipped from Brawny's fingers and dropped to the ground. He sagged forward and stared with disbelieving eyes at a blade that was protruding from his stomach, he'd been stabbed from behind. A second later it was ripped out, and drops of blood sprayed from its tip as it went. Brawny's neck was sliced clean through. His wide eyes were fixed in eternal shock as the head somersaulted through the air and tumbled to the ground. The lifeless body sank at the knees, arteries spewing their final gushes as the dying heart thumped its final beats.

Behind Brawny was Garrad, bloody sword in hand, knuckles white, shock plastered across his face. The lad looked down at the corpse and trembled as he tried to re-sheath his sword.

Tom felt as shaken as Garrad looked; it had been a long time since he'd seen any action.

'You'll want to give that a clean before you put it away,' Mark suggested, a smirk creeping up his cheek as he held Tubby firm. The captive man was frozen in terror.

Tom's eyebrows furrowed. 'Good work, lad,' he managed to spout, sucking in a deep breath and getting a grip, hopefully before Mark noticed he'd been flustered. He made his face relax and shrugged before turning back to his old friend. 'What do you reckon? Guns, car, fuck off?'

'Sounds like a plan. Those shots probably attracted attention.'

Tom swept up Brawny's rifle and the other one Tubby had dropped by his feet. He slung one over his back and pointed the other at Tubby. Mark kept his sword on the man's throat.

'Answer my questions and answer them quickly, and you'll live,' Tom growled.

Tubby nodded.

'Who do you work for?'

'Aran,' he squeaked.

'Did he send you here?'

'Yes.'

'What for?'

'To pick up two guys who were supposed to be trapped in the tunnel.' He swallowed hard.

'Right. Where can I find Aran?'

Tubby's eyes darted from Tom to Garrad questioningly. 'Don't you know?'

'Would I be asking if I did?' Tom snarled. Mark pressed his blade against Tubby's rolls of fat.

'He lives in Alice Springs – that's his HQ!' he blurted as the steel dug into his neck.

'His HQ? His HQ of what?'

'Have you guys been on another planet for the last ten years? How could you not know this?'

'You could say we have,' Tom said, with a grin. 'Answer my fucking question.'

'The HQ of his drugs empire. He owns the whole of the Northern Territory and Queensland.'

'Shit.' Tom narrowed his eyes. The sound of vehicles approaching drew his attention. He edged out of cover to take a look.

'Think they heard the gunshots?' Mark said to Tom.

'Probably. Definitely looks like we're gonna have company,' Tom warned. 'Fuck.'

'Keys for the car?' Mark demanded.

Tubby fished in his pocket and dropped them into Mark's waiting hand.

'Thanks, now run, fat boy, run over there,' Mark said, pointing into the distance and dropping his sword from his throat. 'Don't look back and live to see another day.'

Tubby nodded and set off as fast as his flabby legs would let him.

'Let's go,' said Tom.

Tom set off at a sprint, glancing over his shoulder to check Mark and Garrad were following. They were right behind him as he hurtled towards the Jeep. He threw himself into the passenger seat as Mark ran for the driver's side. Garrad was stumped as to how to get in.

'Grab the door handle!' Tom wound down his window and pointed. 'Yeah, that one, grab it and pull.'

Garrad nodded and managed to get it open.

'Close it, there's a good lad.'

The engine roared into life. The Jeep shot forwards; a whimpered yelp escaped from the young man from another world, who was sitting behind Tom. Despite the rapidly approaching pursuers, despite the sudden mortal danger they were in, a smirk escaped onto Tom's face at the blatant terror they'd unleashed on the sergeant who'd let Aran take their daughters.

'Like riding a bike!' said Mark, who clearly hadn't heard Garrad yelp; he was too busy enjoying himself. He was grinning from ear to ear as he drove for the first time in twenty years.

'Jesus, mate, if you rode a bike like this, you'd get hit by a lorry. Shit!' Tom instinctively ducked as a tree branch smashed over the windscreen. 'Are you watching where you're going?'

'Course!' Mark glanced into the rear-view mirror. 'The fuckers are gaining on us, and a straight line's the quickest.'

Tom spun in his seat and looked out the back. 'Crap. Faster!' A man was leaning out of the passenger window behind and was aiming his rifle. 'Garrad, get your head down!' As a well-trained soldier, Garrad didn't ask why. Tom ducked as a round smashed through the rear windscreen. 'Faster!'

'What do you think I'm doing!'

The Jeep bounded along over the tufts and the rocks, bouncing as it went. They hit a road; the Jeep sped up.

'Get some fucking rounds down, you stupid Sapper!' Mark screamed at Tom.

Tom ignored the insult as he dived into the back seat, dragging a rifle as he went, and began to shoot straight through the rear window. It cracked and warped but held in place.

'Garrad, smash out the glass!' Tom's vision was becoming obscured by the sea of cracks.

Garrad started to pound at the rear windshield with his boot, doing some impressive contortions from the backseat as he kicked. The rear window was mangled, and it didn't take much persuasion to come free. It flew back and smashed into the windscreen of the truck behind. The vehicle swerved and slowed. Tom's view had cleared – he took a carefully aimed shot at where the driver should be. The truck veered violently to the side before screeching to a halt.

Another truck overtook it and began to gain on them. Another gunman was leaning out of the passenger window, shooting at them. Only a couple of rounds hit the Jeep and they missed the men inside. Tom returned fire, his arms steadied on the back of the rear seats; he was in a better position than his pursuers to take aimed shots. He kept firing single rounds, conscious of the amount of ammo in his magazine. He tried to make every one count. He hit the windscreen once again. He must have missed the driver. A third time. The truck veered sharply off road and smashed into a tree.

Another drove round it but kept its distance, following, out of range. It kept on their tail, seemingly content to follow as they continued driving into the west.

25. Curiosity And Conspiracy

'Fuck!' Stark exclaimed as Jon hit the brakes. 'Fucking fuckers!'

'It's the border, Stark. We can't go any further or we will be asking for trouble.' Jon was pissed, as pissed as Stark — he was just better at hiding it. He gritted his teeth and stared at the road ahead as the truck disappeared into the distance.

'God damn Fucking Fuckers of Arseland will have 'em soon. How the hell do we get them back?' Stark pounded the dashboard with his fist.

'From the FFA? We don't.'

'What do we tell Aran? Fucker will have our nipples for this, probably our balls too!'

'You're being melodramatic, Stark. Sarah will protect us, she always does. Anyhow, this is Sniper's task, not ours. He's the one with his arse on the line.'

'He's probably dead. He was in the truck that got wrapped around a tree!'

'He wasn't driving — if he buckled up, he might be OK. We should go check.' Jon sighed as he spun the steering wheel and pressed the accelerator, turning the truck back into their territory.

They trundled down the empty road to find the vehicles that had been taken out, shot at by their own rifles from their own vehicle. It didn't look good whichever way you looked at it. Aran would definitely be unhappy.

Jon and Stark weren't in charge of this job. Aran had given it to Sniper. The man was the flavour of the month, Aran's latest pet. A nasty sadistic bastard like their boss. Jon hadn't been keen on getting too nasty. He'd beat a man where needed, and a bullet in the leg was fine if you needed to teach someone a lesson, but he drew the line at women and kids. Well, women who were bystanders like the girlfriends and wives of men who'd crossed Aran. The ones in the business were fair game as far as he was concerned.

There were some jobs Jon wouldn't do, and Stark worked with Jon. If Jon said no, Stark said no. So they were cut out of the big stuff. They didn't work for Aran, not really. Aran might think they did, but their real boss was Sarah. She looked out for them; she made sure Jon wasn't forced to torture kids to make their parents behave.

The truck that had hit the tree was shagged. Another vehicle gone on top of the four that were lost a couple of days back, plus the one the men Aran was after had nicked. Things were not looking good for the townsfolk of Alice Springs. Jon sensed a vehicle requisition task coming up.

Sniper didn't look hurt – at least there was a clear target for Aran's rage when they got back. He was already out of his truck and was busy yelling at Ford, the driver of the last vehicle in their convoy, when Jon and Stark climbed out of their truck.

'…and what do you think Aran will do when he learns his targets escaped!' Sniper roared. 'It's not your fucking arse on the line here, is it? It's mine! If you'd have kept up…' Sniper suddenly realised Ford and the others in his truck were looking past him. He spun. 'What the fuck are you arseholes doing here!'

'Checking on your sorry arse, dickshit,' Jon growled.

'Why the fuck are you not still chasing our men?' Sniper's face turned so red it looked like he had a bad case of sunburn.

'We hit the border. I'm not committing suicide by throwing myself at the FFA. You think I'm stupid?' Jon shrugged; his calmness seemed to infuriate Sniper even more.

'And when I tell Aran, it will be your neck on the line too!'

Jon shrugged again. 'We'll see about that.'

Stark stood next to Jon, arms folded, leaning against the truck, a self-satisfied smirk on his face to match Jon's. 'Oh yeah, you're Sarah's bitches, aren't you? That's fucking awesome for you, and—'

'Whatever, Sniper,' Jon snapped, cutting him off. 'We stopped to check you're OK. Looks like you are. Gaz is dead, I assume?'

Sniper glared in response.

'Thought so. Ford, did you see how Nidge was?' Jon wondered about the driver of the lead truck.

'Shot in the shoulder,' said Ford. 'I've got him in the back, should live I reckon.'

Jon strode over to Ford's Jeep and opened the back door. Nidge's white T-shirt had turned red, his face white. But his eyes were open, and his shoulder was bandaged. 'You alright, mate?'

Nidge was one of the decent ones. Jon always had time for the man, past his prime, slower than some of the others, but he did what he had to do to survive, like Jon. The man had morals; not so many as Jon, but a few.

'I'll live. I can't say the same for Sniper though,' he said with a crooked smile.

'Yeah, fucker knows he's screwed. It's why he's pissed.'

'Aye. I'd keep out of the way of Aran for a while, until he's taken his anger out on Sniper.'

'Don't need to tell me, mate. Got a few bits of business to attend to before I head back,' Jon said with a wink. He slapped the top of the truck. 'Gonna shoot—'

Sniper started yelling again, this time at Stark. He was a man of few words, that one. Sniper might try to get a response, but Stark would glare at him until he got bored and shot Sniper in the face.

'I need to rescue Sniper – can't deprive Aran of his fun later.'

Nidge shook his head and blew a stray hair out of his eye. 'Can't say I envy Sniper, I wouldn't fancy being on the wrong side of Aran.'

The tell-tale signs of Stark reaching the end of his tether were there. He was licking his lips, tapping his fingers on his pistol holster. Jon could almost hear the voices in the man's head counting down to the draw of his gun.

Jon jumped into the driver's seat. Stark took the hint, he slapped his pistol, and inclined his head towards Sniper as he opened the passenger door.

Stark took a seat, Jon turned the key in the ignition and the truck rumbled down the road, Stark glanced at Sniper in the wing mirror. 'Lucky bastard,' he said, grinning to himself.

'How long did he have?' Jon asked.

'Another ten seconds,' he replied dryly.

'That long, eh? You're getting soft.' Jon glanced at his passenger, a smirk creeping up his face.

'So what's the plan?'

229

'Dunno. Need to keep out of Aran's hair till things die down. I had a thought. I was wondering...' Jon trailed off as he stared at the distant mound of Ayers Rock.

'That's dangerous, mate, be careful.'

'The tunnel Aran dug – where does it go?'

'Don't know, don't care. If you have any sense, you'll leave that one alone.'

'He wanted to capture those blokes he sent us to get,' said Jon. 'He set his trap up so they'd come in from the other side. Where the hell would they have come from? The tunnel doesn't exactly pop out of the north end of Ayers Rock.'

'No, it don't. That nutter Aran has something mystical about him, summat not right. I can tell you what's in the tunnel. Trouble. Nothing else.'

'He was goddamned keen on telling us not to go in. Told us we'd be dead if we did. What's he hiding?'

'I don't like where this is going...'

Jon continued as if he hadn't heard. 'He told me to do the electrics so he could trap someone coming in from the back. I did the sensors and the cameras. They've been trashed; nothing I put in there is still up and running. Aran is blind to that tunnel now and the door has been knocked down... If we went in, he wouldn't have any idea.'

'There's still another gate in there, remember?'

Jon's eyebrow popped up as he regarded Stark. 'I did the electrics. You think I can't get the thing open? I can get it closed too. Aran wouldn't have a clue if we went for a look.'

'We? Who said anything about we?'

'Just me then. I'll take a look. You can watch the truck.'

'And when you don't come back and the gate's still open – who do you think will get the blame?'

'I can shut it behind me if you like?' Jon suggested.

'When you don't come back and I need to come and find your sorry ass, how do I do that?' Stark was still, hands on thighs, his face as emotionless as ever.

'Aww, you're starting to sound like you care about me, mate,' Jon mocked.

'Don't be fucking stupid. I don't fancy finding another partner. The rest of Aran's men are dicks.'

'You'll come?'

Stark sighed in resignation. 'Fine.'

***

Jon was an electrician before the war, before Australia was almost wiped off the face of the planet. He was from Sydney but had been hunting in the outback when the bombs landed. He'd made a good living as an electrician, and being self-employed meant he could take as much leave as he liked. The outback became his second home.

The nukes killed his missus. She'd been pregnant. He was taking some time to himself before the baby came and he was needed at home. She'd been killed along with his whole family, his friends, and a part of his soul. A small part of Jon that made him soft died that day.

He'd lived in the bush, surviving on game for months, unable to face the world. Eventually, he went to Alice Springs – he needed supplies. He found Stark trying to rape Sarah in an alley. He'd tried to save her. She kicked both their arses, and somehow, they found friendship, or at least comradeship. Being alone in this place was a sure way to die quickly. Everyone needed someone to watch their backs and two was better than one.

Jon did jobs like this for Aran, electric gigs that needed doing. Aran seemed to trust Jon, and trust him he could. He could trust him not to tell anyone about what was in the tunnel... except Sarah and Stark.

***

Location: Zargon observation ship, 400 km above Earth (Planet B13536)

Beep, beep, beep. The alarm was accompanied by a vibration on her wrist monitor, and Lukin was rattled awake. She quickly silenced the device and jolted it to eye level to check if it was alerting her to what she expected. She read the Zargon symbols. She was right, someone had gone through the wormhole.

She rolled herself out of bed and groggily sauntered to the desk in her small quarters. With a tap on the glass panel, her personal computing device rolled out onto the surface. The control pad appeared in the middle of the desktop, a holographic screen projected above it.

231

She tapped a few buttons, still too sleepy to feel ready for voice commands yet. The screen changed from black to bright; the image of the entrance to the tunnel leading to the wormhole was on the screen. There was nothing to see there. She wanted desperately to spin it, to turn it, to scan the area behind, but she couldn't. The bug she'd placed in the monitoring drone allowed her to see what the rest of her crew could. They were probably looking at this exact same drone on screen, and they'd know if she messed with it.

She turned the volume up on her control room bug. She heard her colleagues chatting. She pulled up their rotas to double check who was due on duty. Her recollections were proved correct. Cork was due on shift, but she wasn't due to be on shift with the captain too. Cork had clearly called Garkan to the control room but had left her out, as usual. Her jaw clenched.

She heard the chime of an incoming call through her bug. 'It's Darkle!' She heard Garkan announce the presence of the captain of M69245's observation vessel with a degree of excitement.

'Garkan, Cork, good to see you both,' Captain Darkle replied. Lukin was listening in to the conversation with interest.

'And you too. Did you get our message? Do you have them?' She heard Garkan ask giddily.

'Yes, they popped through. One moment, I'll share my visuals…' Darkle replied.

There was a pause in the audio as the other captain sorted out the screen. Lukin suddenly regretted not taking the risk of setting up a camera in the control room. A camera would have been much easier to detect, but probably still too much of a challenge for her luddite colleagues to spot.

'Can you see them?' Darkle asked.

'Yep, got them,' Garkan confirmed.

There was a pause and Lukin assumed her crew mates were studying the view. She could see them herself on her screen; the specimens were in view of the monitoring drone she'd tapped into.

'Do you have these two down as Specimens of Interest, Garkan?' Darkle enquired.

'No, not these two,' said Garkan, 'but they work for H108 and our most recently allocated SOI, specimen H118, is the partner of H108.

She seems to be the real brains behind his empire. We thought it was worth keeping tabs on her.'

'Interesting, and worrying,' Darkle replied.

Lukin was getting bored of listening already. They were going to prattle on about how this transfer of species from one place to another was such an issue, that the future of the precious M-Class planet was at risk again, blah, blah, blah. The details she needed would be in the drone logs. She had set up a live feed of data, so she'd still have a record of anything that was deleted.

She decided to call Jink – she was curious as to what her colleague on the M69245 ship made of this. The musical ringing sound abruptly ended and a darkened image of a half-asleep Zargon blurred on the screen.

'Lukin?' Jink murmured. The image wobbled; the visual was coming from the camera in her wrist monitor.

'Jink, sorry to wake you. There's stuff going on in our control rooms. I thought you might want to know.'

Jink nodded. She commanded the lights to come on and sat up slowly, blinking a few times, clearing her eyes, making them sparkle like they ought to.

'What's going on, Lukin?' Jink asked, her image quivering.

'Two of our specimens have turned up on your planet. Non-designated specimens, but they work for H118.'

Jink's eyes widened. She stood up and walked across her quarters. 'H118, you say? You had high hopes for that one – is she aware?'

'No idea. I've not checked the logs yet. I imagine she will be once these two get back. Can you get them on your screen? I can't get into the drone at your end.'

'One moment… I'm going to cut you off and dial you back in on the desktop.'

'No problem.' The screen went black. 'Ship, carrowcel.' She placed an order for a drink with the AI system, and a droid trundled to where she was sitting just as the screen came back to life.

'Got them. I've shared my visuals, can you see?'

Lukin took a sip of her carrowcel as she studied the image of the tunnel entrance on the faraway M-Class planet. Two humans stood talking; there was no audio though. They pointed at this and that, picked up a few plant samples, and headed back into the tunnel.

'Got there just in time! I'll have them back before long,' Lukin observed.

'Yeah, it was good to get confirmation. It will be interesting to see how long it is before our crew mates tell us about this.'

'It will. Any delay can go in the log. I'm building up quite a collection of their misdemeanours.'

Jink smiled mischievously at her colleague. 'Me too. It will take more than the odd bit of info delay to get them out though – we must bide our time—'

Lukin cut her off, rolling her eyes as she did: 'Yeah, yeah, you keep saying. But does this not present another opportunity? These specimens will probably tell H118, but it's her we need to get through the wormhole. If we can get her established at your side somehow… If you want a disrupting force, she certainly has potential. Much more than the halfwit she keeps as her frontman.'

Jink folded her arms, the grey rims of her mouth pursed, apparently disgruntled at Lukin's dismissive tone.

'Sorry Jink, I didn't mean to—'

Jink cut her off, returning the favour: 'Yes, no need to apologise. I'm used to your impatience.' Jink sighed. 'You're right though. To get H118 onto my planet could be very interesting, especially if she's worked out how to get off the island the tunnel leads to, and if she can work out how to use magic. But it's more of a challenge than you might think.'

Lukin nodded thoughtfully. 'I guess. We will need to put thought into this, if you agree it's something we want to achieve.'

'I do indeed concur, but thought and patience are needed here. If we rush in, we may end up being clumsy and our shipmates may notice,' Jink warned.

'Yep, I get it. I'll give it some thought.'

234

26. History Lesson

'**W**e've lost our tail.' Tom clambered back into the front seat. The adrenaline was fading, and his body was certainly not keeping it a secret. It creaked, it whined. It was shouting at him that he was not as young as it used to be. He couldn't bend like that without expecting punishment. He ignored the aches in his torso as he settled back into his seat.

'You sure?' Mark's eyes flashed to the rear-view mirror. 'Hell, the buggers *are* turning back. Should we be worried?'

'I'm not sure...' Tom dared to twist his body to look, nice and slowly this time.

The vehicle that had chased them for miles was growing smaller and smaller on the long, straight road, the dark outline of the rumbling truck fading into a cloud of dust. Garrad was staring out the back too, watching their pursuers disappear. He must have felt Tom's eyes on him – he jolted round in a motion so rapid it made Tom cringe at the thought of it.

Tom winked and turned to face the front again. 'They are definitely sodding off... Question is, why?'

'I've figured it out.' Mark's gaze was fixed on some kind of structure in the distance, along with some vehicles parked nearby perhaps.

As they sped closer, he could see it was a small fortress built from lined gabion baskets. He knew it as Hesco Bastion, a kind of protective infrastructure solution that was used in war zones all over the world, yet the stuff was all made in a factory in Leeds. Tom had done the tour of the factory once, on a Segway for some reason. The baskets arrived flat-packed but could be filled with sand and rocks and stacked as a series of cubes to make a barricade; the perfect makeshift blast wall.

An iron bar cut across the road. As they grew closer it was more like a steel girder – a hefty bugger, solid, strong enough to stop a lorry at full pace. Either side of the road welded stars of iron bars were laid out in a winding barrier stretching far into the desert.

Men in uniform guarded the place. Men or women maybe; women in uniform didn't exactly look feminine from a distance. He wasn't sure if he recalled that style of camouflage – he assumed it was the Australian pattern, but whatever it was, there was no doubt these people were soldiers. Armed folk in uniform gathered round a roadblock; they were approaching a checkpoint.

'We're going to drive right up to it?' Tom glanced across at the speedometer. Mark hadn't slowed.

'What other choice do we have?' said Mark. 'I'd rather take my chances with men in kit than Aran's cronies.'

'Fair point.'

The vehicle decelerated and stopped. A solider pointed a rifle straight at them. Mark wound down the side-door window.

'Show me your hands and get out of the car, nice and slow,' said the soldier.

Tom leaned over to get a look at the young man. He had a lance corporal's rank slide and was clean-shaven and in a crisp uniform – he looked half professional.

His eyes met Tom's; his rifle's barrel slid to him. 'You too – and him in the back.'

Tom thought it best not to argue. He lifted his hands.

'Put your hands in the air and get out of the car, Garrad,' Tom translated for their passenger.

Mark reached a hand through the window and pulled the door open from the outside to let the guards see what his hands were doing. Tom did likewise from the passenger side. Garrad managed to work out how to get out as he followed the lead of the others.

'Over there, no sudden moves,' said the soldier.

'You, hands up!' a private yelled at Garrad. Garrad stared back blankly; his hand went for his sword.

Tom noticed in time. 'Garrad, get your hands back in the air!' he translated again. Garrad's hands whipped up at the order. 'He doesn't speak English, I'm afraid,' Tom said to the lance corporal. 'If you give him orders, he won't have a clue.'

The lance corporal nodded. 'Tell him we're gonna take the sword belt off him, and if he makes any sudden movements, I'll plant a bullet between his eyes.'

'Roger,' Tom said calmly before translating. Garrad simply nodded. Mark and Tom hadn't been wearing their swords in the car. Garrad was inseparable from his.

The soldiers patted the three of them down to check for other weapons.

'I want that back!' Tom objected as his Leatherman combi tool was taken from his pocket.

The soldier who took it only shrugged. Tom had had the Leatherman a long time; he was rather attached to it. A female soldier had their swords. She'd grabbed Tom and Mark's from the car. They could keep the bloody swords, but his Leatherman... His eye twitched as it was pocketed by the grinning soldier.

After the frisking finished and they were left unarmed, the lance corporal seemed to relax.

'You three were in a hurry to get away from Aran's men. Why's he been chasing you?' His rifle was still pointed at Tom. Three other private soldiers stood nearby, two with guns on Mark and Garrad, one keeping his eyes on the road.

'I'll be dammed if I know,' said Tom. 'We were out doing a bit of sightseeing. Next thing I know some fuckers are shooting at us and chasing us down the road.'

'Tourists?'

'Yep.'

'In Australia?' A smirk crept up the corporal's face.

'Yep.'

The corporal laughed.

'What? Ayers Rock back there, right? Big tourist hub?' The conviction in Tom's voice was fading.

'Yeah, like ten years ago! Where have you guys been for the last decade?'

'Er—'

'Spin me another one. What are you really doing here, and why were you being chased?'

Tom looked at Mark. 'Any ideas?' he whispered.

'We um…' Mark began. He scratched his stubbly cheek as he bought time. 'We were due to do business with him, but um, things kinda went bad. He wants us dead.'

'You're drugs runners? Or what? Drugs barons? Traders? You guys are from the UK, right? You sound like it.'

'Yeah, we're Brits. I'm Mark, he's Tom. We're both English but him,' Mark pointed to Garrad, 'he's Welsh. Grew up in the valleys. Doesn't speak a word of English.'

'And you're here trying to cut a deal with Aran?' the lance corporal said slowly, hands still set on his rifle, finger stroking the trigger.

'Yeah. That's it. Trying to do honest trade,' Mark replied.

'Honest trade in drugs?'

'What's wrong with that? We gotta make a living, right?' Tom said, his eye's wide.

'I guess so,' the soldier replied with a shrug. 'It's the only trade going in these parts, and we all got to eat!' He seemed to be buying it, Tom was holding his breath. 'Where you heading?'

'West.'

'You got extra gas in your trunk? Hopkins, check it out,' the corporal ordered one of the privates.

'No, just what's in our tank,' Tom replied.

'You're not going to make it to the west coast then. You think there are gas stations on the way?'

Tom fidgeted in the face of the interrogation. Mark stood there, cool as anything. Something in the chilled-out stance of his old friend brought a smile to Tom's face, a smile he worked bloody hard to suppress. Mark had spent his youth lying his way out of shit to the police.

Mark shrugged. 'We'd work something out.'

Tom was almost convinced himself.

The corporal looked Mark up and down. 'Not often we come across foreigners in Australia these days. I should say it's not our business to stop ordinary folks going about their lives, even if they are doing deals with Aran. Almost everyone on this screwed-up continent has a finger in the drugs pie, but you guys are Brits, and that's not normal. No one with a foreign passport from a half-decent country lives here out of choice. I'm afraid I'm going to have to take you in. The colonel will want a chat, I suspect… Private Brown!'

'Yes, Corporal?'

'You got those PlastiCuffs handy?'

***

Garrad's hands were bound, secured one over the other with strange, thin material. He had no idea what it was. It was flexible – thin but strong as hell. Garrad certainly couldn't snap his hands out of these things no matter how flimsy they looked. Once the deep red lines he'd cut into his wrists looked about ready to leak blood, he gave up trying. He walked compliantly towards the peculiar fortress ahead. He'd never seen anything like it – baskets made of grids of iron, lined with sack cloth and filled with something lumpy, formed its walls. There were no turrets on the top, and it didn't look like anyone patrolled the walls. A couple of watchtowers were poking out at the corners – there were soldiers in there, staring out over the walls, long-barrelled guns held ready.

The heavy iron gates swung open, and he was led inside by a small, slight soldier. The two who led the prince and the lord commander were taller and heavyset, like he'd expect a soldier to be. The small one who led him had long hair tied in a ponytail and effeminate features. Could it be a woman? The face was feminine, but they wore the same clothes as the men, carried the same weapons, did the same job. They said something to him in a language he didn't understand. The voice was definitely female; far too high-pitched to be a man. A female soldier.

'She says keep up, lad,' the prince translated, 'and while you're at it, close your gob and remember to blink. We can't have you with knackered eyes.'

Garrad snapped his jaw shut; he hadn't even realised he'd dropped it. He gave his head a quick shake and made himself focus. He'd said "she". It was a woman.

They were taken into an olive-green canvas tent, a large one built of heavy fabric and with steel poles. Inside were a couple of cages – iron bars formed a secure cube. The female solider pushed the cage door open and ushered them inside then sliced a knife through his wrist ties with ease. She left them unbound as the door clicked shut. An exchange between the soldiers and the prince in his native language followed, and they were left alone.

Garrad stood in the middle of the cage, not knowing what to do with himself. In one corner was a stack of blankets, pillows and strange looking thick green sheets bound up in a roll. The prince and lord commander seemed to know what they were, they grabbed one each and unrolled them, threw them on the ground and collapsed onto them.

'Sit down, lad, you're making the place untidy,' the prince instructed.

'Sure.' Garrad slumped down against the bars.

'Here,' Tom threw him a green roll, 'sit on this, you'll get a numb arse otherwise.'

Garrad took it and regarded it with confusion.

'It's a roll mat, you sleep on it.'

Garrad nodded and did as instructed, unfastening the ties and lying the thing on the ground as he'd watched the others do. Another odd material. He didn't know what this was made of either, but it was certainly very light and definitely took the edge off the hard ground. He reached for a pillow and tucked it behind his back, then quietly studied the place. A stack of boxes of bottles of water were in another corner, and there was a bucket that looked like a latrine. There were dark green walls of fabric on all sides, and the tent doors were closed – not much light. Hot, sweaty, still. The prince began to chat with the lord commander, thankfully in Garrad's own native tongue this time. Perhaps he'd have a chance to work out what the hell was going on.

'What the fuck has happened since we left, Mark?' The prince shuffled on his roll mat, lifting his knees, trying to get comfy.

'I haven't got a clue, mate.' The lord commander was on his back, hands behind his head, remarkably unruffled.

A pause. Silence, no answers. For Garrad, it was a chance to breathe after the last few mental hours. From being shot by some mad sorcerer to being healed by the queen's own sister. Dragged through a tunnel into another world. Another fucking world! He'd had no idea there were even other planets with life on them this morning. Now he'd been through a magic tunnel to a place where the prince and the lord commander didn't have magic, where they weren't even the prince and lord commander, where they'd told him to call them Tom and Mark.

He still wasn't comfortable doing that. Hell, he was struggling to open his gob and ask a few simple questions. *Breathe, they're just people.* They looked a lot more chilled. Earlier, they'd looked like they might be about to kill him when they'd learned about their daughters.

Garrad was riddled with curiosity. He forced himself to grow a pair. He took a sip of water from a bottle the lord commander threw at him. Took one last breath and spoke.

'Um, is this not how you expected things to be here? Have things changed since you left?' His voice quivered, and he grew angry with himself. *Get a grip!*

The prince had been lying back, comfortable, but he sat up and smiled at Garrad. Shit – could he see how uncomfortable Garrad felt? Was he trying to put him at ease?

'Not quite,' the prince replied, after a pregnant pause. 'I can't say I'd been to Australia before we went to Gemini, but I'm pretty darn certain it wasn't like this when we left. There were no armed soldiers running roadblocks, no shootouts at Ayers Rock, and I'd always thought they made most of their cash round here from mining, not drugs.'

'Something's kicked off here, mate,' the lord commander said. 'No idea what. Something big. World War Three, you reckon?' Mark stretched out his legs as if he were struggling to find a comfy way to lie on the hard floor.

'Not a clue. It's possible,' the prince said.

World War Three? There were two before? Garrad's eyebrows furrowed as he looked from man to man.

'I'm not cut out for this shit anymore,' Mark complained. 'I've spent too long on feather mattresses and silk cushions.'

'You've changed,' the prince said, a hint of mockery in his voice.

The lord commander laughed.

'Do you think the princesses are OK?' Garrad dared to ask. The thought of them pressed on his mind like a lead weight.

Mark's grin vanished.

Thankfully, Tom answered before his old friend got a chance. 'It's possible. Something's wrong here. If everything was going to plan, we wouldn't have been able to break out. And if something's gone awry, maybe that's good news. Maybe the girls escaped, maybe Aran was busy chasing them. It's the only thing I can think of to explain why there was no one there to meet us, why we managed to escape. Aran's an arse but he wouldn't make it that easy for us, not through choice.'

'You think kicking that door down was easy?' Garrad asked incredulously.

'Yeah. No magic needed, no tools used. A lot of kicking and out we got, to find no one guarding the place, a still-smouldering building, and a load of dead guys. Something's not gone to plan somewhere.'

'You're right, Tom. We should try to find out.' The lord commander climbed to his feet and shouted through the bars. 'Private! You out there!'

A soldier poked his head into the shadow of the tent. 'What do you want?'

'Who's in charge here?'

'Captain Miller runs the base. Sergeant Bennet tends to lead on the checkpoint.'

'Can we speak to Captain Miller?'

'She's out on patrol.'

'When she gets back?'

'I imagine she'll want to talk to you anyway – it's her call what happens to you guys.'

'Any idea how long she'll be?'

'Not long, I imagine. She's been out a while. Is that all?' The private appeared to be growing bored of the questions already.

'You got any food?'

***

Garrad tossed and turned. He lay on his back, his side. It was no use, he couldn't sleep. It had been one of those nights, where you kind of sleep, drift in and out of an almost-there snooze, where the time passes but you feel like you never actually nodded off. He'd had enough of trying. He sat up. He shuffled back on his roll mat, pulling his blanket with him to protect against the night-time chill. He propped his pillow against the bars and stared into the darkness.

A dark shape in the middle of the cell stirred too. The prince's eyes caught a stray beam of light from the FOB outside; they glistened and met Garrad's.

'You too?' the prince said and yawned.

'Huh?'

'Can't sleep?'

'No,' he whispered.

'No need to whisper, lad, Mark won't wake. I've never known anyone who can sleep like him. During basic training, we'd be bouncing across the Barossa training area in the back of a Bedford, rifles between our legs, and there he'd be, helmet resting on his SUSAT, dozing. Somehow not bouncing his eye into the muzzle of his gat.'

Garrad couldn't help but snigger. 'I have no idea what you just said.'

The prince smiled. His teeth flashed white as the tent flaps billowed in the night-time breeze and a beam of light flicked across his face. 'Don't worry, most of the civvies on this planet wouldn't have a clue either! You get my point though; Mark won't be woken by chatter.'

'That's normally me. I can't recall struggling to sleep before, not recently anyway.'

'Alcohol can help with that,' Tom said dryly.

Garrad shot him a look, but it was perhaps too dark to see – he hoped. It appeared not.

'Sorry, lad, I didn't mean to have a dig. I know you've been off the stuff for a while. Or so I heard. Can't say I checked up on you. Always so much to do.'

'I've mostly done OK.' The words stuck in Garrad's throat, and he tensed. He'd had a drink problem; he'd been a disgrace. It took the Prince of the Realm to drag him from despair. The shame was hard to overcome.

He dug deep, found some balls, and swallowed the lump in his throat. 'You know... Tom.' It still felt strange using the prince's first name. 'I never said thank you. Thank you for dragging me out of the gutter. I wanted to say it, in case we don't get out of this. I wanted to tell you I'm grateful. If I die now, I die as a soldier, not as a nobody.'

Tom shuffled back on his roll mat and wriggled until he leant against the bars opposite. A long sigh slid from his mouth. 'I didn't do it for you, I did it for your father. He wouldn't have wanted to see you like that.' Tom took another couple of deep breaths. 'When I first met you, you said you were ashamed to have his blood. You didn't want to be his bastard. I kind of get it, you'd been told the man you thought was your father wasn't who you'd thought he was.

'But you shouldn't think of it like that. You should be doubly proud. Proud that another man loved you and your mother enough to raise you as his own, and proud to learn your blood comes from such a

243

good man. You should be honoured to have the chance to continue his legacy. When you killed that man, I got a glimpse of the man I used to know. Garrad Gragor wouldn't have hesitated, and you didn't. He would have seen an ally in trouble and acted, without thought. Duty always came first for him.'

'It was just my training.'

'Have you killed before, Garrad? Or was it your first?'

'I, er...' A wave of embarrassment swept through him.

'Thought so. I knew the answer. I've seen your record, remember? I've killed more than I care to count. Most fade into a memory of nothing, of numbness. But I remember the first one. I remember being in Afghanistan when our base was under attack. I remember aiming my rifle at the man running towards me. I can still see his face – deep brown skin, black eyes, black hair, a long black beard. I remember the scratty shirt he wore and the sandals on his feet. I remember the look he gave me before he died, the shock on his face as the bullet pierced his chest. The thud as he hit the ground.

'I remember how my heart was pounding. I remember how his face was stuck in my mind for months – even after I'd killed more, I always remembered the first one. I was in charge that day. I was the troop commander, but my mind went blank regardless as I stared at the death I'd created. The training kicked in and I pulled myself together. I cracked on, I shouted orders, I kept my guys going.'

The Prince of Vorn. Garrad had never thought of him as a soldier. Whenever he saw him, he was dressed as a courtier, in a prince's finery. Except the first time he met him – that was different.

'You were in the Army? Here on Earth?' Garrad pieced bits together from what he'd said, but he was still unsure.

'Did I not say?' Tom scratched his head in the gloom.

'You've said bits. I'm not sure you fully explained.' Garrad's curiosity was overcoming his discomfort of prying, and the darkness certainly helped. It was easier to forget you were talking to a prince when the light was low.

'Yes, I was in the Army. I was a Sapper, an Engineer. When I first tried to explain that to your father, he took the piss. He didn't get what an engineer was for in the Army – he kept calling me a builder. The Army on Earth is different to the one on Gemini, but I couldn't tell him that.'

'And you were an officer?'

244

'Yep. I was a captain when I left, and Mark was a major. He was in the infantry though, not the Engineers. Higher rank and trained as a foot soldier, not a glorified builder like me, he's better at war stuff than I am. Don't tell him I admitted that!'

Garrad smiled. Hearing Tom talk casually about himself – the man he had revered as much as the lord commander – helped humanise them. They were people. Fathers who'd lost their daughters. Not royalty, not lords, just men like his own father, or adoptive father, he corrected. No, Davod would always be his father, even if Garrad Gragor was his blood.

He lost himself in his thoughts for a while. Tom remained silent, apparently lost in thoughts of his own. As the first hints of dawn began to seep into the tent, Garrad found the courage to speak again.

'It felt strange, as he collapsed to the ground,' he began. 'He was there one minute, but not the next. The sword thrust felt like nothing, like I'd hit a training dummy, but when the head fell, and the blood splattered... I've tried not to think about it. But after, I didn't have to think, did I? I had to do what I was told. You told me to get in the truck and I did. And that was it, no thinking required. I'm no officer, I'm a sergeant. We follow, we don't lead.'

Tom leaned forward. 'For fuck's, sake don't let Mark hear you say that!' Tom chuckled quietly.

'Why not?' Garrad said seriously.

'Mark is in charge of the Armed Forces, remember? He's been shaping it for years. Who do you think invented the sergeant's cadre?'

'Er...'

'Mark, you muppet! And if you think sergeants aren't trained to lead, I'm not sure if you get what sergeants are supposed to do.'

Garrad stared at the sliver of light creeping thorough the gaps round the window flaps. He turned back to Tom. 'I guess you're right. We were told we'd have to lead if our platoon commander got hit.'

'At last! There are some brain cells in that noggin of yours! Your father wasn't stupid, but I was starting to wonder if you'd inherited his brawn and not his brains.'

'Garrad Gragor...' Garrad let the name of his father hover in the darkness like an echo of a memory. 'You told me he was your friend. You said he was a general in the Walrian Army. How did the Prince of Vorn meet a general from another land?'

'Flipping heck, Garrad, that's a tale.'

'We have time.'

'We do. I'm glad you asked. I've told you before he was a good man. You should know more about the man whose blood you carry.'

'I didn't want to know at first—'

'Really?' Tom cut him off with a snigger.

Garrad tried hard to hide his own smirk. 'It's taken time to get used to things, but I'm ready to hear more about him.'

Tom took a deep breath. 'You know I came to Gemini twenty-four years back, right?'

'I recall you saying.'

'I was twenty-nine at the time. I'd married the queen. She was Emma back then. Neither of us had any idea who she really was – her memory had been wiped. God, Emma's story is a whole other thing. But I'm going to focus on Garrad. We came to Gemini. The idea was, I could learn to use magic and help Emma get her throne back. I couldn't do it at first, the magic wouldn't work for me. You know Arndal?'

'I've heard of him – he's a palace sorcerer, isn't he?'

'Yes, just about, although I keep trying to get him to retire. Anyway, Arndal was living on an island in the Inland Sea, off the coast of Walrie, and he was trying to release my power. He couldn't figure it out. In the end, he decided we'd have to go to Vallume, to the woodland elves, and hope they could help.'

'Sounds simple enough.'

'You might think. And I thought so at too the time. Arndal knew better – he thought help from a local guide, someone who knew how to use a sword, might help us get to our destination alive. He called on his old friend Garrad Gragor, who he'd known since he was a boy when they both lived in the palace of Vorn – before Queen Lila turned them both into outcasts.

'He introduced us to Garrad. Retired general, aged thirty, after working his way up from nothing. A general in the Walrian Army who still hung onto his devotion to his home country of Vorn. Where his father served as Master of Sword, where he'd lived in the palace and known Queen Emma as a child. He couldn't give up his allegiance to the queen. He agreed to help us get to Vallume.'

Nostalgia was plastered across Tom's face as he stared off to one side.

'And did he? Help you I mean?' said Garrad.

Tom snapped back into the present. 'Oh, hell yes!' A grin spread across Tom's face. 'The first time we met, he saved my life, and Emma's too. I was a bit of a dick back then. I wasn't grateful, I resented needing his help. We got off to a bad start. He thought I was useless, not good enough for his queen. I couldn't ride a horse. I could barely wield a sword...'

'You couldn't ride a horse? At twenty-nine?' Garrad said incredulously.

'Have you seen any horses round here since you arrived?'

'I guess not.'

'Course you haven't. We have cars, we don't need horses. Only little girls ride horses on Earth.'

'Just little girls?'

'I'm probably being unfair – little girls and toffs, and jockeys and women in their forties who like to pretend they're still girls and—'

'This place sounds odd.'

'You could say that. To clarify, go back a couple hundred years and everyone did use horses. Then we developed cars, and horses ended up just being for fun.'

'Right...' Garrad said, still confused.

'Anyway, despite Garrad not liking me too much, and me not liking him, Emma forced us to work together. She made him teach me how to use a sword properly and to ride a horse, and that came in handy as we went north. In Noelind, the goblins came. Emma got captured and Garrad saved my life again. This time he got injured for his trouble.

'The guy nearly died. We were trying to find Emma. He didn't complain about the fact that he was pissing blood out of his side. He pretended he was OK and kept going. It was only when he fell off his horse that I knew something was up. I had no choice but to keep him alive.

'I'm not sure if it was because I'd finally figured out I needed him, or because of my officer training, or sheer belligerence, but I sat by him and kept what blood he had left in his body, until Eskalith came, with my wife.'

'Who's Eskalith?'

'He's an elven sorcerer. Another great guy. He's the chap who eventually taught me to use magic. When he turned up that day, he saved Garrad. He healed him, and he lived to fight another day. After that your father decided he liked me. To this day, I don't know if I deserved it – I said I probably saved him out of belligerence. He thought otherwise. I thought *what the hell?* Emma needed us to get along and we did. And after that, we were mates.'

'He saved your life twice?'

'Three times, if you take into account the time in the woods. After Eskalith healed Garrad, we went north, trying to get to Vallume. We were being chased, first by Noelindians, then by goblins. Eskalith did some magical shit to me, and I blasted a load of the goblins, and I was out cold after that. The goblins kept coming and Garrad fought on until the elves came and saved us.'

Garrad fingered the edge of his sleeping roll. Thought battled thought in his head as he tried to absorb what he was being told.

Tom continued. 'We spent the winter in Vallume. Garrad helped where he could with the elves' sword skills. It came in handy when Queen Lila attacked in the spring. He fought with the elves, and between us, we beat her off. The following autumn, we went to Thost, where we spent the winter, where Garrad met your mother.'

Garrad waited for Tom to finish the tale.

'Lilian worked in a pub. She and Garrad hit it off straight away. He'd been married before, in his early twenties I recall, but his wife died in childbirth. He'd stayed single ever since, or so he said, until he met Lilian, and they hit it off.

'On the day Queen Lila attacked, I was defending the city using magic. Garrad stayed with Emma. When my magical shield fell and I was captured, they knew the city would fall. Garrad had to get her out, but not without Lilian. Together they fled through the dwarven city to find Lilian and her parents. They ran towards a hidden tunnel to take them to safety. The dwarves turned hostile; they attacked any human they found. Emma was shooting arrows, and your grandfather tried his best to help. But Garrad took the brunt of the attack, and he became the target of a crossbow bolt fired from a window above, unseen. He was unable to defend himself. He fell, but not before the dwarves who had attacked with crossbows had fallen too. Emma put an arrow in them both.

'Emma, Lilian, and her parents – your grandparents – were saved that day because of Garrad. And you were an unknown seed in Lilian's belly. She didn't even know she was with child.'

Garrad could see the sadness in Tom's eyes. The piercing blue eyes of the prince bored into his soul. He looked away, images of a memory he'd never had flashing through his mind. His mother, the queen, a man without a face fighting to save those he loved. Tom was unspeaking, a hand touched his eyes, wiping tears maybe? I was too dark to tell. The man appeared lost in his own thoughts, reminiscing about the friend he'd lost perhaps.

'He sounds like a good man,' Garrad said at last.

'He was. And if you had any sense, you would acknowledge him as a father. A great man like that deserves a great son to carry on his legacy.'

'I can't. It's not right. Davod Bramston raised me; he is my father. I am the son of a merchant, not a general. Surely by working my way up, by staying the son of a nobody, I am embracing Gragor's memory. You said he worked his way up from nothing. I plan to do the same.'

'Look, kid!' Mark's sudden words came from nowhere. He wriggled up on his roll mat as he continued. 'I've been listening to Tom's nostalgic shit for a while. I've heard most of it before. Tom has prattled on about how much he was in love with your daddy till the crows come home.'

'Oi!' Tom objected. 'I wasn't in love with him, fuckwit!'

'Whatever. Anyway, what I heard as I was trying to get some sleep, and failing due to noise pollution, was the back end of a story about some amazing dead guy, and his brat wittering about wanting to *work his way up*. Right, I'm going to ask for hands in the air here, who in this room earned the position they are in today?'

Mark made a show of swinging his head from right to left, glaring at them both in turn as he did. 'No one, eh? Good, right answer. Let's be clear here, no fucker in this world wins by playing fair. Winners take the gifts they are given and make them work. Let's look at me, shall we? Do I deserve to be commander of the queen's Armed Forces? Do I fuck. I got the gig because I'm mates with him.' He pointed to Tom. 'And because I was crazy enough to follow him through a tunnel, I didn't get it through merit. I became a major through merit. I've said before I was a bastard. *I'm* the son of a nobody – compared to you, lad, I'm scum. Half my family are crooks. I've got half-brothers in and out of prison, not to mention my dad. But I joined the army and because I scraped a few grades at school, I blagged my way into Officer School, where I met this idiot. Now look at me, married to a goddamned princess!

'And him?' Mark nodded towards Tom. 'His parents might have been all well to do. Dad an accountant? Mum in HR as I recall?'

'Yep,' Tom confirmed.

'What's an accountant?' Garrad asked.

'A dick who sorts other dick's taxes. It's irrelevant. Yeah, Officer School was practically gift-wrapped for this idiot.'

'Hey!' Tom objected.

'Oh, dry your eyes, princess, you know I'm right. But becoming a prince? A jump. No one, not even Earthlings from nice families, normally crack that one, but he happened to fall for the right girl. A girl who, it turns out, was the heir to the throne of Vorn. Bloody lucky, basically.

'It turns out you have stumbled on some luck too, Garrad. Your daddy is someone fucking awesome, someone whose memory got you dragged out of the gutter by a prince. If you've any sense, you'll make the most of that. When you get back… actually, let's go with *if* you get back, because mark my words, if one hair has been put out of place on my little girl's head, your head will be detached from your shoulders before you can blink. But let's assume for the moment she's OK, and we get out of this. If you don't change your name to Gragor and go for officer, I'll… I'll laugh. And decide you are a fucking idiot.'

27. An Unexpected Offer

Location: FFA HQ, Australia, Earth (B13536)

Eliza watched as Alora edged into the cell. The door slammed shut behind her — *clunk, click.* The bolt shot into the lock. Her cousin stopped in the middle of the room and sighed, looking unsure of what to do with herself. Eliza turned her gaze on the ceiling, lost in her own daydream. She was lying on her steel-framed bed, hands behind her head. Alora sighed again, louder this time.

'What's wrong, Alora?' Eliza twisted her neck to the side.

'It's not right, Eliza, I can't get used to it.'

'Used to what?'

'Wearing breeches or *trousers*, as they call them. I have to unbutton and unzip every time I go to the lavatory. It's unladylike.'

Eliza smiled. 'If that's the most that's bothering you, we can't be doing too badly.'

'I must admit, I like that they have running hot water, the flushes on the lavatories certainly work better than the ones we have at home, and the showers? I was never sure about the ones Uncle Tom cobbled together in the palace, but the showers here, they are lovely, and the shampoo they have? My hair has never felt so soft.'

'It's the conditioner you are talking about.'

'Oh yes, the conditioner. We need to get some at home.'

Eliza couldn't help but be bemused by how her cousin switched from complaint to compliment in so little time. She was such a fickle character at times. Eliza liked the shower and conditioner too, but it was no compensation for their forced incarceration.

'We're still prisoners,' she grumbled.

Alora collapsed onto the end of Eliza's bed. 'I know, but as far as prisons go, I couldn't imagine a better one... Actually, I could — one where they give you dresses to wear would be far better.'

Eliza giggled and shook her head. 'Are you not bored? I'm bored out of my tree! It's been two full days since we were brought here, and we have nothing to do!'

'What about those books they gave you? Can you not read them?'

'I can speak English. But my reading is just about passable at best. It's hard work reading the books they brought us, and I did find the topics bizarre. One started with some woman on something called a train. It didn't explain what the train was! She was on this train thing every day and met some man and was imagining all kinds of strange things. I couldn't make head nor tail of it.'

'At least you have something. I've had nothing but my own thoughts to keep me busy.'

'I suppose. It could be worse, a lot worse. They have treated us OK, and kept us fed, even if some of the food is strange,' Eliza conceded.

'Those orange fish sticks were very odd. But when I tried them, they were actually not too bad.'

'Fish fingers, they called them.'

'Mm,' Alora replied as she sagged back against the wall. She folded her arms and stared at the blank white wall in front of her.

Eliza resumed staring at the ceiling, trying to think of home, of what else she might be doing if she wasn't held captive on another planet. Something meaningless, no doubt. Chatting to the other ladies, going for a ride, or maybe embroidery. Her thoughts didn't stay there for long. They kept drifting back to concerns for her future – trapped in this strange land where the women dressed like the men and the magic she knew meant nothing. But here, there was a different kind of magic: the magic of machinery, of technology, tools and equipment that meant women could be soldiers and the equals of men. The kind of world she never imagined possible. Part of her was terrified by whatever future awaited them, but as the hours turned into days, fascination had begun to take over, curiosity gripped her, and excitement began to bubble.

'What do you think the soldiers will do with us?' said Alora.

Eliza sat up, she swung her legs off her bed and shuffled up to Alora's side, joining her in staring at the white wall. 'I don't know.'

'Do you think they will hurt us? Like Aran was going to?'

'No, I doubt it. They have been OK with us so far; you don't treat people well if you plan to hurt them.' Just saying the words out loud somehow helped Eliza believe them.

'What if they want to make us feel safe? What if they are trying to trick us?'

'I don't think that's what they have planned. Didn't Lieutenant Joe say he was fighting to get rid of people like Aran?'

'He did, but his men killed those others. I saw some of them fall. These men are murderers, Eliza.'

Eliza turned to study her cousin's face. She smiled. 'All it takes for evil to prosper is for good men to do nothing.'

'What are you on about?'

'It's a quote father told me about – he said someone from Earth said it once. What it means is that good people have to do bad things sometimes to stop the bad people doing bad things.'

Alora raised an eyebrow.

'I mean they had to kill Aran's men. What do you think they would have done to Lieutenant Joe's men if they hadn't done what they did? You have to be ruthless in war. And don't forget, if they hadn't, we would still be in Aran's hands, and so far, the FFA have treated us infinitely better than he did.'

'I guess,' Alora conceded.

'Oh, and don't forget, Lieutenant Joe doesn't just command men, he has female soldiers too.'

'But they aren't like proper women, are they?'

'How do you mean?'

'I mean they were dressed like the men. They fought alongside them; they did what the men did. But it's like they'd forgotten they were women.'

'So? Do you not think women can do what men do if they want to? I don't think that makes them any less of a woman.'

'I – erm, I suppose.' Alora thought for a moment. 'If your society thinks that kind of thing is OK, and if you have guns and not swords, maybe you don't need to be quite as strong.'

'Father told me it was normal for women to be in the Army on Earth. He said he worked with some when he went to war. Did you know even my mother did a bit of military training?'

'She did?' Alora gasped.

'Yeah, when she was on Earth, and young. About our age.'

'I honestly didn't know... She's so ladylike!' From the look on Alora's face, it appeared her world was suddenly turning on its head.

'She can turn it on and off. I've seen her on the hunt, although not for a while. She wears breeches and shoots a bow with incredible accuracy.'

'How did I not know this?'

'Because I never told you, and my mother doesn't like to advertise the fact. It's not normal for women to do that back home.'

'I know!'

'But here?' said Eliza. 'It's like men and women are equal. They can do whatever the other does. The colonel Lieutenant Joe mentioned is female. He referred to her as "she".'

'If she is a woman, it will be interesting to meet her, but I'm still not comfortable with the concept of women and men being the same.'

'There's no helping you, is there, Alora?' Eliza chuckled.

'What?'

Eliza shook her head. 'It doesn't matter.'

The hard wall Eliza leant against was making her back ache. She grabbed her pillow and stuffed it behind her back. She smiled to herself as she thought about how Alora saw the world. Through her mother's eyes, she presumed – her entire life had been spent on Gemini, a world where women had their place.

Already, Earth was opening up new possibilities for Eliza. She was seeing things with her own eyes that she'd only ever been told about by her parents. Her head was spinning. Thoughts rattled around, but somehow her mind settled on her father, and thoughts she'd been trying to avoid. A lump sank into her stomach.

'Do you think Father and Uncle Mark have got through yet?' Eliza was grave. 'Do you think Aran has them?' she said quietly.

'I've been trying not to think about that.'

'Me too, sorry.' Eliza started picking at her fingernails.

'Our fathers aren't stupid,' Alora said at last. 'They wouldn't run straight into a trap. They'll find a way to escape him, they'll find us.'

'Are you sure?'

Alora bit her lip and pulled one of Eliza's fidgeting hands from her lap. 'I…'

The door lock clunked, and the door opened. It was Lieutenant Joe Morris. 'Good afternoon, ladies, are you well?'

'We're fine, thank you,' Eliza replied, forcing a smile.

'Have you had everything you need here? They been treating you OK?'

'Very well, thanks... for prisoners.'

'I'm sorry we locked you up, it's protocol. When we find unknowns like yourself, we have to detain them until the colonel has interviewed them, and she's very busy. I'm sorry it's taken this long.'

'Is she ready?'

'That's what she said. She sent me to fetch you. Are you good to move?'

'I guess.'

'What did he say?' Alora asked Eliza anxiously, as soon as the conversation paused.

'We're going to see the colonel,' she confirmed, and reached for the strange, laced slippers they'd given her to wear. She'd learnt they were called trainers and they were in fact very comfortable. She actually liked the clothes they'd given her. Their own dresses were sweaty, filthy, and torn from running in the heat and scrambling under the bush. The soldiers kindly found them something clean to put on. The Earth clothes were stretchy and easy to get on and off on your own without maids. The trousers were practical, with no skirts to trip over or get caught in anything. She'd suddenly developed an envious disposition towards men's clothing.

They both stood and followed Joe out of the room they shared and down the corridor of the makeshift detention facility. The building was one of several in a small village that had been taken over by the FFA and turned into their headquarters.

He led them out into the sunshine. The wave of heat hit them like a blast from an oven. They'd barely realised how well cooled their building had been until now.

'How is it so cold in there?' Eliza asked Joe.

He stopped and turned to her, his face quizzical. 'You've never come across air conditioning before?'

'Air conditioning?' she said slowly.

'Yeah, it works like a fridge, cools the air down, makes it feel comfortable.'

'What's a fridge?'

Joe stopped and stared at her. Eliza thought he was trying to work out if she was being genuine. She looked straight back, her face full of innocence.

'Where the hell did you grow up?' he said.

She stayed silent.

'Ah, I remember, you ain't talking about that one. But I suggest you tell the colonel. If you don't tell her what she asks, you might end up stuck in that room for ever.'

Eliza couldn't work out if he was being serious or not. He had a twinkle in his eye, and he was smiling crookedly. He had blue eyes, like her father's and hers. They were rare in Vorn. She might have thought him handsome if he didn't remind her of her father, the man who she'd led into a trap, putting his life at risk.

As the thoughts rushed through her head, her jaw dropped.

Joe cocked his head to one side. 'Are you alright?'

Eliza was conscious of how she looked; she snapped herself out of it. Thoughts like that wouldn't help anyone. 'Yes. Sorry. I just remembered something.'

'I imagine you two have been through a lot, eh? If you don't even know what a fridge is...' He paused and opened his mouth as if to speak, then closed it, as if he'd decided better of it. 'Let's go and see the colonel, shall we?'

Joe set off walking again. Eliza managed to focus. She desperately tried to think of a cover story to explain where they'd come from and how they'd got here. She should have done it earlier. *Why didn't I do this while we were stuck in the room?* She brushed the thought aside and tried to think.

The buildings in the village were surrounded by a wall of bulging wire baskets lined with sack cloth. Eliza glanced over them without giving them much consideration as her mind swam. Ordinarily, she'd have been looking around with interest, trying to work out what everything was for, but she barely took in the vehicles, the tall masts and curved dishes. She kept her eyes forward.

Joe led them into another building. As the wall off coolness hit her, she thought she had something. Her father had taught her enough about Earth for her to make something up. She prayed it was plausible.

Joe popped his head into the open door of an office. Eliza tried to read the sign.

'Ad-ju-tant,' she read aloud. *What's that mean?* She thought. She didn't think about it for long. Joe reappeared with another young man with floppy hair and a big grin, who bounced towards the office next door. He knocked.

'Come in!' a woman's voice called from within. The floppy-haired man spoke briefly with the colonel before directing them inside.

Joe guided the two women into the office. Eliza regarded the colonel. Her sun-kissed skin tone looked strange against her yellow hair. Weathered skin gave her the look of an older woman, but her bright blue eyes were clever, and looked young. She could be younger than Eliza's mother, perhaps by as much as ten years. It was difficult to tell.

'Take as seat, please.' The colonel rested her hands on the desk in front of her, her hands clasped, her thumbs fidgeting as she smiled warmly at the two young women.

There was a knock on the door.

'Come in.'

The door swung open, and the floppy haired man reappeared, smiling in the doorway. 'Sorry, Colonel, I should have asked – can I get you a drink? And one for your guests?'

'We have some water here, we'll be fine. Thanks, Sam.'

The door closed.

'Would you like a drink?' She gestured towards the jug on her desk.

Eliza translated for Alora; she shook her head.

'No, we're fine, thank you,' said Eliza.

The colonel nodded lightly. 'That's an interesting accent you have, not one I'm familiar with. Where abouts is it you ladies are from?'

'Russia. We're from Russia.' Eliza felt Joe's eyes on her. She'd been evasive with him, yet she answered the colonel's question quickly.

'Russia, you say?'

Eliza nodded.

'Mm. Joe tells me you didn't tell him where you were from when he found you – why did you keep that a secret?'

'We were scared. We didn't know who he was. We didn't know if we could trust him.'

Joe's eyebrow rose.

'Russia? And your friend, she speaks Russian? Any English?' The colonel asked.

'We speak Russian. Alora doesn't speak English.'

'I can't say I have much of an ear for accents, but I can't say Russian would be the first accent that came to mind.' Her head twisted slightly.

'We're from a remote part of Russia, right in the middle. We have a slightly different dialect, and a completely different accent.' Eliza remembered seeing how big the country was on the map her father sketched. She remembered him saying how most of it was scarcely populated. She desperately hoped what she said made some kind of sense.

'I see.'

Eliza realised she'd been holding her breath. The colonel seemed to be accepting her story; Eliza let herself breathe.

'How have two Russians ended up in Australia? Wearing fine dresses from another era and running from Aran and his men?'

'Our fathers sold us to him. They owed him money; they couldn't pay. We were given to Aran as payment.'

'Uh-huh.' The colonel paused. Eliza thought she could hear the wheels turning in the woman's head as she took in what she'd been told. At last, she turned to Joe. 'Does this story sound plausible to you, Joe?'

Joe glanced towards the women and appeared shocked to have been asked. He covered it up quickly. 'Ma'am, since I picked the two of them up, I've been desperately trying to guess at their story, but I've been stumped. I don't know one way or the other if they are telling the truth. What I can say is that no one runs across the field of fire like that unless they are desperate to get away. I am pretty certain they are no friends of Aran's. It's plausible he took them from a rival or some of his men he wanted to get back at, but I don't think so.

'They were terrified when we took them. They've been baffled by everything modern in this place – hell, they didn't even know how to open a car door or what a fridge was. Wherever they grew up, it was some crazy backwater is my guess. If it was Russia? I'm no expert but I know it's a big old place, and well away from Moscow there are some backwater parts of it. Maybe they did grow up there? Do we have any Russians in the regiment, ma'am?'

'Not that I know of.' She fell silent and slumped her chin onto her waiting palm.

Eliza quickly whispered a translation to Alora. The colonel seemed content to let Eliza finish before she continued.

'I'm going to be honest, ladies. I'm not sure about you. I spoke to Corporal Gregory earlier, the lady who runs the detention wing, and she said what Joe did about you two being... how should I put this? She said it was like you'd grown up on another planet. She said you were either scared of or fascinated by everything, even the shower! If you acted all that – hell, you deserve to be let go for putting on such a good act. Personally, I think it's genuine. And if it is? God, you have had a troubled life.

'We aren't exactly in the business of running a prison here. When we capture folk, we talk to them nicely, or sometimes not, depending on the character. We either kill them or let them go. We can't afford to do anything else. I'm not about you kill you two ladies. You haven't done anything to warrant that. I'm going to let you go free.'

Eliza stared at the colonel.

'What did she say?' Alora whispered in her ear.

'She said we are free to go.'

'Go? Where to?' Alora asked.

Eliza's jaw fell open; she wasn't sure what to say. At last, she turned back to the colonel. 'If we're free to go, can you take us back to where you found us?'

'Ayers Rock?' said the colonel. 'Sorry, not a chance.'

'Why not? We have to get there. We have family trapped there, we have to find them,' Eliza blurted, barely considering her words.

'Family at Ayers Rock?'

'Yes, um – our uncles,' she improvised. 'Our uncles were going to come for us, they knew to find us there.'

The colonel's eyes narrowed. 'The plot thickens,' she said with a smile. 'Anything else you want to tell me about what you were doing in Aran's company in the middle of the desert?'

'Er, no. It's just ... Our fathers were happy to give us up, but our uncles on our mother's side, they wanted us back. And they knew we'd be at Ayers Rock. That's where they'd look for us. They'd never know where to find us anywhere else.'

'An interesting tale, but whether I was minded to have you taken back there or not, it's impossible. We have intelligence telling us Aran has built up his numbers there; he has men teeming all over the place. They look to be building some fortifications and are starting to bed in. I don't think it's a place you want to be.'

The blood drained from Eliza's face.

'Something tells me that's not the news you were after.'

Eliza shook her head and swallowed a hard lump of nothing.

'Look,' the colonel said with a sigh, 'do you two have any place to go if we let you go? We could get you to the south in a week or two, or maybe the west. We are keeping those parts pretty secure. Things are starting to come back to life. You could find work, I imagine.'

'No, we can't. We can't go any further away – we have to get back to Ayers Rock.'

'You are a strange pair.' The colonel let out a heavy breath. 'I hope I'm not going to regret this... The thing is, it's no secret we want to drive Aran out. We want Australia back from the drugs lords; we want to take it back for the Australians. Sooner or later, we'll take his patch and his fortifications with it, and if you want to be around when we do, there's one option I can offer you.'

'What's that?'

'Join us.'

'Join you?' Eliza barely managed to find the words.

'Yes. We are always trying to find new recruits. We know little about the background of most we sign up and we don't care to ask. Everyone round here has some skeleton or other in their closet. We need as many men and women as we can find to push this fight forward. I've worked for years to turn us into a credible, respectable force, and at last I've managed to persuade New Zealand. They are equipping us. We're starting to get to a point where we can out-gun the drugs lords. It's soldiers we need, and if you have no place else to go... How about it?'

28. Old Habits Die Hard

Location: Central Australia, Earth (B13536)

Summer in the desert was bloody hot. Aran was sick of being hot. He'd been away from air conditioning since yesterday; he'd had to sleep without it. Air-con was one of the few things that made life on Earth worth it. He could cope with not having much magic and with not being the king. Being a drugs baron in a place without rules was almost as good. He could do what he wanted, kill who he liked, dip his cock in anything he fancied. It was like being king, but here he had air conditioning, flushing toilets, the internet, and guns.

Or at least, his men had guns. It made control of the plebs much easier. He was still amazed at how few of the ordinary folk carried them. But he didn't need guns, he had magic. In a world where he was the only one to have such a gift, a little was enough to tip the balance of power in his favour, enough to make him seem like a king. The king of a patch much bigger geographically than piddly Vorn; he ran about half a continent.

The truck rumbled along, windows open, hot air blasting his face like a fan oven. He stuck his head out of the window and took one last look at the part-built mini fortress before it shrank from view. Sarah had done a good job; the defences were coming along nicely. They couldn't get gas for the air-con in the truck, but Hesco was easy to come by, or some kind of Chinese rip-off that looked like Hesco but did the job just as well.

The excavators were working night and day under Sarah's watch, filling the gabion baskets, building the blast walls, creating the rectangular protection for his tunnel – the route back to Gemini, the route he'd secured. If Mark and Thomas and their little girls wanted to get home, they would have to get through Sarah and her fortress. Assuming they escaped his clutches again.

The truck rumbled on towards the west and the checkpoint where his target waited for him. His men had turned back when they'd been chasing Mark and Thomas, but they'd sent out drones. He knew where the men he sought were. The fucking FFA – they'd interfered again. First with the girls, now with the men.

He'd been idle. Complacent. He'd let the Freedom Fighters have the south and the west; he'd assumed they weren't a threat, and he was right. But those fucking foreigners got involved. New Zealand started kitting them out. The tables started to turn. He was about to turn them back. China was more than happy to sell him what he needed at a good price. They didn't want to see their lesson to the world turn back to civilisation after a mere six years.

Aran rode in an ordinary truck. He had magic, he didn't need armour, but his men did. He had armoured vehicles – freshly imported Chinese-built CSKs, a kind of armoured Humvee with machine guns and grenade launchers. He had rocket launchers, more machine guns than he needed, war drones, rockets, recce drones, armour piercers. The arms race had begun, and Aran would win. Money talked, and he had shedloads of it.

***

Wheee, boom! The blast took the FFA unawares. It landed on the hardened shelter. The reinforced concrete roof was designed to take the hit – it was the one part of the FOB where a grenade could do the least damage. It was the spot where Captain Rachael Miller was, the spot she'd rushed back to after her patrol. She'd got eyes on the brand-new FOB, the forward operating base Aran was building, right at the side of Ayers Rock. He looked to be pushing south, towards the FFA's territory, which was concerning enough, but not as worrying as the fact that their drones hadn't spotted the brand-new structure. It had taken a ground patrol with real human eyes to see it. It meant Aran had some decent kit, kit from overseas that kept their spy drones away – kit he didn't have before.

She hit the deck. Instinct took over when the airwaves pounded into her eardrums. Fragments of concrete rattled off the roof; dust swept over the IT kit. The ceiling held.

The siren rang. Someone had had the good sense to hit the alarm. Rachael peeled herself off the ground and grabbed her headset.

'All units, battle stations, we are under attack. Platoon commanders, get eyes on targets and report when ready.' She felt stupid for saying *we are under attack* already. Fuck, she could feel her sergeant major's eyes rolling as the words spewed out of her mouth. Never mind, the message was out. Her guys and gals were well-drilled. The response would be quick, and the sergeant major would have the counter drones in the air in seconds.

'Ma'am, we have drones in the air.' The reassuring, if at times patronising, drone of her senior warrant officer rang into her earpiece.

Boom. But no rattle. An air blast this time. The countermeasures were already working. She grabbed her body armour, helmet, and rifle and rushed outside. She needed to get a grip of the situation before the sergeant major took over. She knew he would, given half the chance. She was just the acting officer commanding, and new in the post besides. Her OC had got cancer – cancer! How could a thirty-five-year-old get that?

They were short of majors. Good senior officers were hard to come by, and she was left in charge, for now.

***

Garrad sat on his roll mat, back against the bars of the cage, arms hugging his knees as the blasts rattled around them.

'It's got to be Aran,' Tom concluded.

'Yep, he's found us,' Mark agreed.

'What kind of magic is this?' Garrad asked. They'd told him there was no magic here, but there was no other explanation for the roar of explosions detonating all around him.

'Not magic, tech. War tech. Rockets, at a guess. Although a lot are being air-triggered by the sound of it. That's the kind of tech they didn't have much of in my day. We mostly had to hide in the shelters.'

Garrad barely had a clue what Mark had just said; he still wasn't convinced it wasn't magic.

'God, Mark, have you any idea how old you sound?' Tom taunted.

'I am old! I'm in my fifties, for fuck's sake. I'm not in denial.'

'Good to hear it.'

A blast erupted above. Shrapnel hit the tent roof like a rainstorm, and holes burnt through as fragments rained down.

'Shit!' Tom screamed as he took cover under his blankets.

'Argh!' Garrad yelled as a scorching bit of metal hit his leg.

'Fuck me, we ain't safe in here,' Mark declared. 'Private!' He climbed to his feet and yelled. 'Private!' Mark screamed again, louder this time.

The tent flap peeled back; a shell-shocked young man faced them.

'Private, you need to get us out of here. We have no body armour, no overhead protection – we're sitting ducks!'

'I'm sorry, I don't have the authority to make that call.'

'Find someone with the authority, dickshit!'

'Oh, er, sure.' The private vanished.

'Who are these bloody FFA morons?' Mark asked no one in particular.

Something hit the ground outside. A blast wave shot into the tent, sending Mark flying. He landed on Garrad, who somehow managed to catch him.

'Erm, cheers mate,' Mark murmured as he peeled himself free.

They sheltered in their cage under roll mats and blankets until a lance corporal burst into their tent, flanked by a large private with his rifle pointed firmly at the prisoners. The corporal's face was ashen as she dashed towards the bars.

'Captain Miller says to let you out. I'm to take you to the ops room, it's a hardened shelter.' The keys rattled in her hands; her fingers shook as she tried to find the right key.

'Great, nice to see the Geneva Convention at work,' Mark jested.

The lance corporal's look was so scalding that Mark flinched. She cuffed them and led them at a jog across the FOB towards its centre, where the shelter stood. She used another set of PlastiCuffs to tie them to an exposed bit of re-bar before running back to her duties.

The sound of machine guns, rockets, and rifles rattled across the base, adding to the orchestra of confusion that already clattered about the HQ.

Garrad stood nervously by the wall while he took in the mayhem which was unfolding around him. The place was filled with a small collection of men and women sitting at desks with a collection of odd-looking equipment in front of them. They all wore strange devices on their heads. They had pads which covered both ears and were connected by a curved strip.

264

A woman with long blonde hair seemed to be in charge. She was barking out orders to the soldiers who were furiously tapping at their equipment or apparently chatting to no one in particular.

Garrad was trying hard not to show his fear. The cracks and booms, the dust that kept sprinkling with every explosion, the thuds of the guns, the chatter of voices talking all at once – it was alien to him. It was not warfare as he knew it. This was outlandish, strange, different. Something hit the roof. The whole place rattled. More debris rained down on the chattering soldiers, who barely noticed; they dusted the bits of concrete off their equipment and carried on. Garrad started to tremble. He tensed, trying desperately to hide it. *Get a grip*, he told himself. *You're the only one who's terrified here.*

***

Tom leant casually against the wall as he watched the commotion of the operations room unfold around him. He was finding the experience both fascinating and nostalgic in equal measures. It was like a blast from the past, from his days back in Afghanistan when he'd been working out in a remote base when they came under attack. It seemed that military doctrine hadn't changed much. Some of the kit and equipment looked a bit more fancy, but the basic principles of command looked the same.

He tried to tune into the hubbub of conversations that were being relayed over the radio net between blasts and the crack of rounds outside. He could hear talk of drones, vehicles, weapons. He heard Aran mentioned more than once. He heard reports of casualties, the descriptions sounded like fatalities to him. Fascination suddenly became sorrow; nostalgia became flashbacks of the bits of his operational tour he'd rather forget. With a shake of his head he quelled his emotions and forced himself back into soldier mode. Sentiment could wait.

The day drew on. The attacks came and went in waves. Eventually, someone brought them water, and in one of the lulls they were allowed to use the latrines. As dusk fell, they were even fed. The three of them sat on ridged aluminium floor sheets with numb arses and ate from their cold boil-in-the-bag rations. It was the first time they'd eaten all day. It was the same for the soldiers, so Tom didn't feel badly treated.

As the wave of violence died down, those in the ops room were knocked off by Captain Miller, one by one. The duty watchkeeper stayed up. The sergeant sat at the other end of the shelter, staring at his screens, oblivious of the captain, who was collapsed on a folding chair.

Tom and Mark had tried their best to stay out of her way. They knew the crack – they had to let the ops room function without them worrying about the irritating prisoners in the corner. Garrad had followed their lead. The poor kid had looked terrified at first, but after the first couple of hours in the midst of the attack, Garrad eventually appeared to have calmed himself down. Tom didn't blame him for being scared; anyone who experienced this stuff for the first time would have been. He knew Garrad wouldn't even understand what the blasts were, how explosives worked, how they were propelled, or what countermeasures did, and it was too noisy to do anything other than just give a basic explanation.

It was getting late now. Garrad and Mark had drifted off, backs propped against the wall, heads flopping forwards, but Tom wasn't sleepy. He had no idea why. It was late, so he should be, but he wasn't. His eyes settled on the exhausted-looking captain. She should be in bed. His fatherly instincts took over and he felt compelled to speak, breaking the near silence of the deserted ops room.

'You should get some sleep.'

Tom's words made her jump out of her skin. She looked at him like she'd forgotten the prisoners were there, in the corner, moved in to be safe from overhead missiles.

'Hi. Yeah, I guess.'

Tom recognised that look. It was the face of someone who had stayed awake too long and developed a misguided devotion to being the one person in charge.

'You have a second in command, right?' said Tom.

'Yeah, the sergeant major.'

'And where is he?'

'Getting some rest.'

'How long has he had?'

'A few hours?'

'Great, give him one or two more, then get him up. You're no use to anyone if you're shattered.'

She studied him, trying to work him out. He remembered what it was like to be a not-so-senior officer in charge of men and women, their lives in his hands, the pressure of duty pressing down on him like an anvil on his head. He could see that feeling in her eyes. She was young, late twenties perhaps. Inexperienced, out of her depth. He smiled — the fatherly smile he'd perfected over twenty odd years and practiced on three kids. This woman could be his daughter. Older than Hellenia, his eldest, but still young enough for it to be possible.

She nodded slowly. 'I guess.' She sat up in her chair. Something sparked in her eyes, perhaps telling her to wake the fuck up, she had work to do, always. 'Lance Corporal Dowson tells me you guys are drugs runners. British drugs runners, is that right?'

'No.' Tom glanced at Mark. He knew the sleeping man wouldn't like what he was about to say, but the situation had changed.

'What are you, then? Why are three Brits here? Running from Aran?'

'He has our daughters, his and mine.' He indicated towards Mark. 'We came to get them back. He wants us even more than he wants them. He is attacking your base to get to us. He won't stop until he has us.'

'Why are you telling me this? Do you want me to hand you over?' Confusion spread across her face.

'No. I don't. I've been Aran's prisoner before, and let's say it wasn't pleasant.' He rubbed his disfigured knuckles, a legacy from his torture as Aran's captive, many years ago.

'I've heard the tales of the shit that sadistic bastard does to folk who cross him.'

'Which is why I don't think you'll had us over.'

'You sure?'

Tom swayed his head from side to side and smiled. 'Fifty-fifty.'

She smiled back.

'How long have you been in charge here?'

'In charge? Six weeks. Our OC was taken sick.'

'Got it. I don't for a minute want to try to suggest you aren't up for command here. I've watched you today. You did good, you kept on top of stuff. You kept your men and women alive, but I know you have casualties. Your comms are cut off. If you stay here, you'll die, and we'll end up as Aran's prisoners.'

'Not if I hand you over.'

'You think that will stop him?'

She shrugged.

'You hand us over and you think he'll just take his prize and leave? It will only take a few of his men to keep us secure, that leaves a lot of his guys at a loose end. I know this arsehole. I've fought him before. He's ambitious, he's angry, but most of all he never lets a slight against him go unpunished. You've sheltered his prisoners; you've made his life difficult. He'll wipe you out whether we are here or not.'

'We might be cut off, but we have protocols!' She countered. 'When we don't send regular sit-reps it automatically triggers a drone recce and—'

Tom cut her off. 'How long will that take?'

'A drone recce? Not long. Once it's launched it will be here in an hour, maybe.'

'And what if Aran shoots it down?'

'They'll send another.'

'He'll shoot that one too.'

'They'll send out a road patrol.'

'Big enough to take on Aran? And after how long?'

'I don't know exactly – what's you point?'

'You'll be dead before help arrives.'

Her eyes narrowed. 'Who are you?'

'My name is Thomas Taylor.'

'Great, and I'm Rachael Miller, but that means fuck all, does it?' She tilted her head and squinted in thought. 'You're no drugs runner, you're something else. UK Special Forces?'

Tom couldn't help but laugh.

'Washed-up old mercs? A lot of mercenaries came from overseas in the early days – did you get stuck here?'

'Less of the old, thanks!'

'You are a mercenary?'

'No. I'm something else. I can't tell you what exactly. But I can tell you this. Twenty-four years ago, I was a captain, like you. In the British Army. I didn't see a *lot* of action. I saw a bit in Afghanistan. But since then? Not quite military service, but I've certainly been in the thick of a few battles. Although I should say, the last time was a few years back.'

'You're a mysterious man, Captain Taylor.'

Tom grinned. He hadn't been called that in a while. He couldn't deny it felt good. 'I am. On a serious note, I was a captain in the Engineers, but the sleeping oaf there,' he prodded Mark with his toe, 'he was a major in the Rifles, and a bloody good one to boot. If you want a way out of this alive, I suggest you ask him. He's got out of some shit in his time. He'll help you find a way out of this.'

Tom could see the wheels in her head whirring as she took in what he'd said. She nodded, eyebrows furrowed, forehead creased.

'You give that sergeant major a nudge and get yourself some sleep. When you've had a rest, give him a kick.' He pointed to Mark. 'He'll sleep forever if you let him. Kick him awake and then rack his brains — if anyone can find a way out of this, it's Major Mark Harrison.'

29. There's No Magic On Earth

Tom's chat with Captain Miller had worked. She'd had a nap, woken up, and spoken to Mark. Tom had been sitting next to him as they talked, listening, chipping in where needed, but as he'd expected, Mark had taken the lead. He'd somehow talked his way out of being a prisoner as he started to rabbit on like he knew what he was talking about. He'd come up with a plan that might work – to bug out before they were slaughtered where they sat.

The firefight continued throughout the day, Aran's forces making attempts on the gate. Half-arsed attempts in Tom's opinion, but enough to make the FFA worried. Like a castle under siege, all Aran's forces had to do was keep the FFA firing their rounds until they ran out, then everything else would be easy. The soldiers would be slaughtered, and Tom and Mark would be captured.

Aran was backing them into a corner. They'd have to make a break for it, and that was exactly what they were making ready to do, but not in the way Aran might have been expecting.

Tom climbed into the back of the Bushmaster: an Australian-built armoured vehicle sent over from New Zealand, he'd been told. Tiny windows, bulletproof glass – a hell of a lot safer than the truck they'd driven here in. He had his rifle slung over his shoulder and his sword at his hip. He'd nearly tripped over the bloody thing as he clambered around the other soldiers from the FFA to get to his seat.

Mark had ordered Tom to get inside the armoured vehicle. He'd obeyed, without question. It was not his own blind obedience that surprised him, it was the fact that Mark was now in charge. This morning he'd been a prisoner, cuffed and without weapons – and now he was sitting with a loaded rifle and a sword in the back of a military vehicle. Why the fuck was he wearing a sword? The weapon had been returned to him along with the AK47 and a couple of boxes of rounds. He'd strapped it on; what else was he going to do with it?

The clatter of Garrad's sword on the vehicle steps as he tried to get in rattled loudly. Everything was always louder in the night. On this occasion, it wasn't a big deal; they were not making a secret of the fact that they were about to bug out.

Garrad had a rifle too – he carried it by its sling like a handbag. Tom had given him a lesson in how to use it earlier while Mark was in full command mode, strutting around the FOB, bellowing orders, getting everything how he wanted it in preparation for the move.

Tom took his sword belt off and rested the thing on the floor. You could keep it on when you rode a horse, but they weren't exactly designed for wearing while sitting in armoured vehicles.

He sat and waited for the next phase of Mark's plan to kick off. A twenty-something soldier was sitting opposite, staring blankly into the nothingness behind Tom, rubbing his calloused hands. Tom glanced down to his own and tentatively prodded at his blisters. He'd been digging. He'd dug until his shoulders ached and his fingers bled. He'd dug until he was close to collapse, until Garrad had practically forced him to sit. Tom had tried to keep up with him – he'd tried to match the young man's pace – but Tom wasn't in his twenties anymore, and he wasn't used to hard work.

It had all been part of Mark's strategy. To dig their way to freedom. He'd come up with a deception plan, something Aran wouldn't expect. They'd positioned the vehicles to make out like they were preparing to bug out though the front gates but instead, they were going to make a run for it thought a gap they'd cut into the back wall.

Everyone in the FOB who could be spared had been digging, ten tons of Hesco fill would not shift itself. Under the cover of darkness, with thermal blankets providing cover from the infrared sensors on Aran's observation drones, they'd dug through their own defences. Just a set of wire cutters was all that was needed to get out, and the clipping was about to begin.

Duh, duh, duh, duh, duh. AKs set to automatic began to fire. The machine guns had been packed away. *Duh, duh, duh. Clip, clip, clip.* The gunshots hid the sound of wire being cut. *Woosh.* A flare went up, lighting the sky above. The glare blazed through the Bushmaster window.

Grumble, rumble. The engines started, the doors slammed shut – it was time to move.

Tom didn't have a headset. He was deaf to the commands that rattled into the ears of every solder around him. He was a passenger, an observer, a bod. He was doing what he was told this time. This was Mark's show; there wasn't room for another officer to interfere.

Wheels squealed. They found traction. The rear vehicle shot off in reverse. *Slam, scratch, screech.* A gabion basket wall was breached, paintwork shagged on stray wires, and a one-eighty turn was handled expertly.

A second vehicle followed, then Tom's. A jolt backwards; he was off. His heart raced. It had been a while, decades even, since he had seen any real action. Back then he'd been in charge. He'd been too preoccupied with achieving his mission, with keeping his men and women alive, with keeping himself alive – he'd never had much time to think. That was what he told himself as he internally screamed at his pounding heart to calm the fuck down.

The Bushmasters shot off through the rear of the FOB. The convoy headed south, towards their HQ. It was the nearest base big enough and well defended enough to see off their pursuers.

A flash of light caught Tom's eye a fraction of a second before the blast of sound found his ears and the vehicle surged forwards. The colossal boom marked the point of no return, as trucks and kit and anything remotely useful to Aran's forces was blown to bits. A worthy application for the last of their plastic explosives.

The Bushmaster bounced over the tufts of grass, small shrubs, and rocks. It pounded over the rough terrain, weaving between the scattered trees. The feint had worked; they'd escaped the ring of defence waiting outside the FOB entrance. They'd avoided the grenade launchers trained on the road and the attack drones poised to fire as soon as the FFA came forward out of their base.

They'd exploited surprise and gained a lead. Aran's forces were on the back foot and some way behind. The FFA's weapons were already set to defend. Roof-mounted guns were manned, drones were already covering their tail, and what was left of their rockets were ready to launch.

***

Garrad gripped the hilt of his sword. He wasn't even sure why. Habit? Comfort? Reassurance? All of these, probably. He loosened his grip, realised how pointless it was. He regarded the soldier sitting opposite – a sturdy man with dark skin. Curiosity took his mind of the mayhem for a moment. Dark-skinned people were rare in Vorn. They mostly lived in the south, in Allantra, his mother's homeland. Her mother had been dark-skinned too. He'd inherited a rich tone to his own skin and her black hair, but he'd never met his kin from the North Allantran Plains.

The machine gun on the roof of the vehicle thudded again; his wandering mind was ripped back into the fucked-up reality he found himself in. Something went *boom*. The vehicle swerved; the muzzle of his rifle bit into his ribs. He suddenly remembered the gun. It was an AK47, he'd been told. It dangled from its sling, leaning against his side. Prince Tom had taught him to fire it. He'd been shown the intricate mechanisms inside, been told it was powered by some kind of explosive powder in every bullet that was lined up in the magazine. It sounded nuts to him, like some kind of Earth magic. He knew he could pull the trigger and it would go bang, it would recoil, and a hole would appear in the target ahead. He wouldn't see anything come out of the end. He'd been told there was no magic on Earth, but he didn't believe it. The AK47 seemed magic, as did the vehicle he was sitting in. As it rumbled across the desert at some crazy speed without a horse in sight, he couldn't figure out what was making it go, other than magic.

More machine gun thuds; more things going *boom*. He leaned over to look through the thick glass window. Other vehicles were chasing them. They'd been on their tail since they'd left the fortress and they were outnumbered.

He instinctively ducked as an enemy vehicle that had pulled alongside them exploded. More Earth magic. He gathered his wits and looked back out of the window; the vehicle had vanished. He could see precious little through the dirty pane of glass, but he sure as hell had seen the blaze and he'd felt the vehicle swerve away from the blast wave.

Garrad at last let go of his sword. He'd pulled his rifle round and held it between his legs like the other soldiers in the Bushmaster, gripping the barrel with the same white knuckles that had held onto his sword earlier.

Tom caught Garrad's eye and winked. The poor lad looked half-terrified, half-baffled. Not a surprise. Yesterday morning he didn't even know Earth existed. Now he was on another planet and in the middle of a rather kinetic dash across a desert, surrounded by tech that Gemini likely wouldn't come up with for another thousand years. It was a lot to take in.

Tom twisted and looked out of the window behind him. Rockets found trucks, drones battled drones, and Aran kept coming. He mostly had jeeps and pickups, but he also had a few bits of armour of his own: Chinese-built assault vehicles, by the looks of them. They were keeping pace, but they didn't have the power to gain on the armoured Bushmaster vehicles of the fleeing FFA.

Missile after missile was thrown at their pursuers. Blazing streaks zoomed through the dim light of the breaking dawn, and he noticed something strange. One armoured vehicle seemed to be going faster than the others. It soon became the target of choice for the FFA. A rocket was launched, a guided missile he presumed. It looked to be bang on target, but it missed. It swerved to the side at the last moment and exploded on the ground.

The pursuing vehicle edged closer, its own gunner firing on the soldiers, machine gun in range. Rounds rattled off the armour of the Bushmaster. Through the racket of the engine, the thuds of bullets on armour, and their own gun returning fire, someone yelled out.

A hit? Someone had been shot.

Tom spun. The gunner was already being helped down by another soldier. Blood oozed from under his body armour, turning his camouflage shirt deep red. Tom wasted no time. He wasn't thinking, he just acted. He clambered towards the top hatch, stepping between the seats to give the wounded soldier space as he climbed round him. He swiped a helmet from a private's head. His chin strap hadn't been fastened; he deserved to lose it.

He gingerly edged up, clearing the Bushmaster's roof as he got sight of the approaching vehicle. Tom had a feeling he knew who was inside. The Bushmaster windows were dirty. Tom wanted a clear view.

The vehicle wasn't close, but Tom could see the cropped black hair and caramel skin thought the windshield. He knew who it was, and he knew they were using magic. It was Aran, he'd found a way. He was making his vehicle go faster, he was keeping the missiles away, and he was about to turn the FFA's own weapons on itself.

Tom felt something – a wave of power approaching from behind his right shoulder. He spun; a rocket was heading straight for him. Instinct took over, self-preservation. He raised a hand and did what came naturally. He dug inside and reached for his magic without thinking. He gathered it, he launched it. The rocket changed course, it smashed into the desert floor, and detonated on impact. The blast was so close his vehicle was thrust sideways.

Tom had found magic – here, on Earth. He had no idea how. He tried to gather it again, to use it to attack. He was struggling to grasp it, but it was there. He suddenly realised waves of the stuff existed around him. But its signature was almost too faint to feel.

Tom tuned in to a stream of something. It pricked his skin like a chill causing goosebumps. It made him turn to the vehicle ahead of their own, at the gunner who suddenly looked panicked, unable to control his weapon as it turned on its own to point towards Tom.

It was Aran again; Tom sensed it. The chill grew colder. An internal tingling bubbled. Magic. The force of self-preservation was not about to let Tom die this day. He reached forwards, his palm facing ahead. He convulsed, he shook. Power amassed as if from nowhere and shot from his hand. As the terrified gunner was about to pull the trigger against his will, the barrel spun sideways. The rounds flew, but into the desert, harmlessly.

Tom spun back to face Aran's vehicle; something caught his eye behind it. Trucks were flaming and stationary in the distance. An armoured vehicle was hit by a rocket and all of a sudden, the FFA's weapons were finding their marks. Yet the hit rate had been inexplicably poor before. Tom assumed it was poor training and poor kit. Perhaps not. Perhaps it was Aran, using magic.

Something rushed towards his head from the sky above. The drone-launched grenade was on course for a direct hit. Tom tried to find his magic again; he was already becoming drained. He felt the missile – he slowed it, tried to divert it.

At the last moment, training and survival instinct took over. He grabbed the roof hatch and slammed it down as he ducked back into the cabin. The grenade glanced, it detonated, but off the side. The blast threw the Bushmaster to the side, tipping onto two wheels, but not enough to throw it over. It dropped back to the ground with a heavy thud.

Tom was thrown towards the injured soldier who lay on the floor between the opposing lines of seats. Garrad grabbed him in time.

'Shit, that was close!' Tom blinked hard, clearing the dust from his eyes.

'Are you alright, mate?' a private asked.

'Yeah.' Tom reached up for a handle on the ceiling, hauled himself to his feet, and plopped himself back in his chair as his head spun.

'What happened?' Garrad asked, his voice barely audible above the roar of the engine.

'Aran.' Keeping his eyes open was suddenly a challenge.

'He's here?' Garrad's fingernails dug into his knees.

'I'm certain, and he has magic.' A wave of weariness swept over Tom. He swayed and reached up for the ceiling handle again.

'That lead vehicle, it's starting to drop back!' a private at the back of the cabin called out.

'Aran's tiring,' Tom said sleepily.

'He's here for you, isn't he?' Garrad said solemnly.

Tom nodded.

'And the lord commander.'

'Of course he is. But he's Mark here, remember?' Tom slurred.

'No one can understand me,' said Garrad. Tom caught sight of Garrad leaning towards him though his now-flickering eyes. 'Are you OK?'

Tom flopped over sideways and fell asleep, his head resting peacefully on the soldier to his side.

30. Jailed Again

Jink thumped the control panel with her fist. Lukin's report hadn't been the one she'd been hoping for. When she'd learned H108 was attacking the base where her two specimens were, she'd hoped he'd have got them. Lukin said the odds were stacked against them. She'd said it was only a matter of time before those who protected specimens H694 and H110 ran out of ammunition. She'd even been managing to help. She'd been on shift alone. It hadn't been difficult to make any communications drone that escaped their base mysteriously crash. It took barely any effort and was easy to cover up.

Jink was thinking about how much easier it would make things back on her planet if those two never came back. The only two pure-bred Earthlings who still resided on M69245. The two most powerful sorcerers on the planet. They'd got away, and specimen H694 had managed to use magic; that's what Lukin said. How irritating.

It wasn't over yet. H108 and his partner, H118, had built a base to protect the wormhole that joined the two planets. There was no easy way for her specimens to return. And now H118 had now been to her planet, she knew the wormhole existed. It would surely make her as keen to keep H694 and H110 from returning home as her partner.

She'd been surprised when her captain told her that detail, but she presumed they'd decided to open up about everything; she knew too much for them to try to pull the wool over her eyes any longer.

'Ship, check rest status of my shipmates,' she ordered the AI system.

'Both Captain Darkle and First Mate Zark are resting in their sleeping pods. The progress of their cycles indicates they will remain asleep for six storns and two storns respectively.'

Good, she thought. *I have time.*

277

'Ship, call Associate Anark.' She waited nervously while the chime jingled. Calling associates on her native planet was always risky. As a second mate, all her calls to anywhere other than her fellow ships were supposed to be cleared with the captain. If anyone caught her... The screen in front of her lit up.

The smiling face of Anark greeted her. 'Jink, what a pleasant surprise.'

'Anark, it's good to see you too. Are you alone?'

'Do you think I would have answered if I wasn't?'

Jink let out a deep breath. 'I shouldn't have doubted you.'

'No, you shouldn't.' Anark folded her arms. 'To what do I owe the honour of your call?'

'Things have been happening on my planet – interesting things.'

'And could you not have put them into your reports?'

'Of course. Um...' She hesitated. Was this call really necessary? It didn't matter, she concluded. She was committed. 'I'm not sure what to do next. I could do with advice. I know you said we could interfere, nudge things now and then, but I don't know how far to go.'

'Mmm.' Anark's arms dropped as she gently swung from side to side in her chair. 'Tell me the latest. What has happened recently that you have not yet reported on?'

'Specimen H118 has been to my planet.'

'Remind me who that is?'

'She is one of Lukin's specimens. She's from B13536—'

'I worked that out.' Anark rolled her large black eyes.

'She's the partner of H108,' Jink continued, 'the specimen who originated on M69245, my planet – the human male who was close to causing the anarchy we hoped for before several other Specimens of Interest interfered. But I'm more interested in H118 at the moment.'

'Ah yes, H118. I recall Lukin had high expectations of that one.'

'She did. The specimen's a nasty piece of work and the brains behind H108's empire, but if she gets to my planet and learns to use magic...'

'It could prove interesting.' Anark finished Jink's sentence. 'You said she had already been?'

'Yes, she has. Two of her minions went first, though. I believe they persuaded her to enter too. She went, but she came back.' Jink paused. She fidgeted, picking at the fingernails on one hand with the other. 'The

278

thing is, the wormhole brings her to an uninhabited island. There is no way off. And even if she did get off, she doesn't speak the language. I can't see how she'd manage easily, or indeed even want to go there. There are things I can do to help her along—'

'You want to know how much you can do to assist, don't you?'

'Yes.'

'My answer is simple. The Cooperative is clear in its aims. It is content for you to do whatever is necessary as long as it does not cause direct harm to any specimen, and cannot be detected by your crew mates, or leave a record in any logs.'

Jink stared at Anark for a moment. She found her long fingers drawn to her bald head and she scratched, even though she didn't have an itch. 'Are you sure?'

'Quite.' Anark leaned forwards in her chair. 'You must understand though, if you are caught, no members of the Cooperative will help you, no matter how high their standing in government.'

'I wouldn't expect anything else.'

'Good.' Anark leaned back and folded her arms. 'You are doing well, Jink. The Cooperative is impressed, especially with the evidence being collected in respect of the misdemeanours of your shipmates. You will have enough to remove them before long. Perhaps you could ensure any trails you leave in your actions lead directly to them? You could be the one to finally cause their demise?'

Jink let a nasty smile spread across her face. 'Trust me, Anark, that thought had most certainly already occurred to me.'

***

Location: Central Australia, Earth (Planet B13536)

Sarah sat, waiting for Aran to wake. She knew he'd want her there when he did. He would want the bad news right away, and she wanted to get his tantrum over and done with. She lost herself in thoughts; thoughts of the strange land at the end of the tunnel Jon had finally persuaded her to visit. The place she'd avoided because Aran told her to. She rolled her eyes at her own pathetic weakness. When had she ever not done something just because Aran said no?

The tunnel was a mystical path into the unknown, the route to the answers to Aran's mysterious power. At first, like a kid who never wants to find out Santa Claus isn't real, she hadn't wanted to go, in case it was a dead end, in case it led to nothing, and it proved Aran was a fraud and his driver had been right all along. But Jon and Stark had been through the tunnel, and they talked about a jungle at the other end. Eventually she'd grown bored of them going on about it and decided to go through. She'd been trusted with a key to the door that they'd built over the tunnel entrance, and she'd been trusted not to use it. Unless she had to. And as far as she was concerned, shutting Jon and Stark up was a good enough reason for her.

Magic was real, she was now certain. There was no other logical explanation she could think of for a jungle a couple of hundred meters down a tunnel from a desert. She'd been pretty sure before; Aran had told her he could use it and she'd seen him do shit that looked pretty darn magical to her.

Aran had been brought back by Fred not long ago. He was asleep when he'd dumped him into her care, and he still dozed. She knew he was always knackered after he'd done his magical stuff, and from what his driver had said, she'd figured that this time he'd used it to exhaustion. And now she was sitting like a pitiful, doting wife, waiting for him to wake.

She regarded the sleeping form of the man who had given her status, the man who'd dragged her up from being some nobody talent scout for a junior league drugs baron to second in command of a patch covering half of Australia. And all she'd had to do was suck his cock every now and again. Men were easy to manipulate.

He stirred; he'd be awake soon. She pulled a lipstick and a compact mirror out of her pocket, applied a fresh coat, and whipped out a small bottle of perfume for a fresh spray. Her scent would be the first thing he smelt when he woke. It would help soften the blow.

His eyes blinked open. He breathed in deeply. *Success!* she thought, and smiled. He smiled back.

'The sight of you makes waking up worth doing,' he said.

She leaned forward and kissed his forehead, her cleavage angled perfectly for the best view. 'I'm glad to hear it,' she purred.

For a moment, his face was content, almost deliriously so, but the cloud of anger descended. It didn't take long, but it never did.

'What are you doing here? Where am I?' He began to pull himself up onto his elbows.

'We're at Ayers Rock, safe in my newly built base.'

Aran gritted his teeth and hissed air through the gaps as he swung his legs round onto the ground. 'Ayers fucking Rock? What the hell am I doing here?'

She shrugged. 'Fred dropped you off.'

'The mission...' His voice faded away as he turned to the side in thought. 'I conked out, didn't I?'

Sarah bit her lower lip; her silence was enough.

'I ran out of magic! Which means,' he took a deep breath, 'Mark and Thomas got away!'

'I'm afraid I didn't see any prisoners brought in when you came back,' she dared to report.

Aran clambered to his feet. He swiped at his camp-cot, flipping it on its side. 'They escaped me. AGAIN!'

He was panting with fury. Sarah rose to her feet and walked towards him, thrusting her chest forwards as she did. She gently stroked his arm. 'They will not escape a third time. They will have to come through me next. I will not let them pass. I have built this fort. Not even the entire FFA can get through this one. I have air defence and missiles, grenade launchers, and the latest war drones. Fuck all the kit the New Zealanders are giving them; I have taken delivery of a plane-load of kit from the Chinese. The latest and the best money can buy.'

'A plane got in?' Aran seemed incredulous, and she didn't blame him. The UN had maintained a no-fly zone across the whole continent for six years.

'The Chinese are getting very good at building stealth jets. And they'd hate to see the FFA win. Stability is the last thing they want – hence I got a very good price.' Her hand stroked his arm and she pressed herself against him; his mood was visibly softening as his cock grew hard.

Without warning, she whipped a leg around his and pushed him to the floor. He fell down hard. She launched herself on top of him and began to nibble at his neck. He groaned in pleasure. Men were so easy to manipulate.

***

Tom's eyes flickered open. Whiteness filled his blurry vision. He blinked hard a few times to clear his sight and realised he was staring at a ceiling – a smooth white one. He'd not seen one of those in a while; the ceilings in the palace tended to be panelled wood.

Something soft was under his back. A sticky, damp bed. No, wait, that was just him. He was drenched in sweat. He turned his head to one side. A white wall. To the other side, another bed, an empty one. He sat up. The sticky, olive-green plastic-covered mattress squeaked as he rose. His bed wobbled.

Another mattress squeaked, and Mark's head popped up from beneath him, just his head and shoulders visible.

Tom shook his head and looked again. Ah, he was on a bunkbed. That made more sense.

'Morning, sleepyhead,' Mark greeted him, with a grin. 'Or should I say evening? You've been asleep most of the day.'

Another mattress creaked, and the bed opposite wobbled. Garrad emerged from the bottom bunk of the other bunk bed and appeared next to Tom, the same inane grin as Mark's plastered on his face.

'You're awake!' he said. 'Gods, I was starting to think you'd be out for days. I've never known anyone to sleep so deeply. Over those bumps – and the bangs. You even fell off your seat in the car-thing and stayed asleep!'

'Magic has that effect on people,' Tom said groggily.

'You used magic?' Mark looked stunned.

'I think so. So did Aran, somehow.' Tom wiped his sweaty forehead.

'Shit, that's how he did it...'

'Shall I tell him, Mark?' Garrad squawked like an excited schoolboy.

'No!' Mark snapped, with a forced frown.

'Tell me what?' Tom looked from one man to the other.

Mark's frown vanished. He grinned. 'Do you want the good news, or the bad news?'

'Go on, hit me with the bad, get it out of the way.'

'The bad news is we're locked up – again. The FFA thinks we are evil people traffickers who sold our daughters into sex slavery.'

'What the fuck?' Tom scratched his head.

'Yeah, funny story! Anyway, the good news is our girls are safe. I'll have to kill them myself when I get my hands on them though.'

'Hang on a minute,' Tom's fingernails dug deeper into his scalp, 'the girls were sold into sex slavery?'

'No, I didn't say that. I said that's what the FFA thinks.'

'And why would they think that?'

'Because our lovely daughters told them that, that's why.'

'Why the bloody hell would they say that?'

'Probably because Eliza got her bluffing skills from you!'

Tom stared at Mark. his head wasn't quite up to full speed again after having just woken up, it was taking him a little while to take in what he was being told. But as he figured it out, he began to smile. 'Oh,' he said at last, then suddenly noticed the bars on the window. 'That's why we're in prison! Thanks, Eliza.' He couldn't help but laugh.

'I suppose we can't just credit your daughter. Alora is with her too.'

'Yeah, but Alora doesn't speak English, does she?'

Mark laughed. 'Good point. I should have known it was just your crazy genes that were behind this.'

Tom leant forward, resting his face in his hands. His cloudy mind was still making sense of things. 'Where are they? And where the hell are we?'

'Ah-ha! This is the best bit. You'll like this.' Mark chuckled.

Tom wiped more sweat from his face and turned to Mark, his eyebrows raised. 'Go on.'

'They're in basic training.'

Tom's jaw dropped. 'They're in what?'

'Basic training. They joined the FFA.'

'OK. I'm going to need to lie down.' He lowered himself back onto the bed.

'He took that well,' Mark said to Garrad, a smirk creeping up his cheeks.

Tom shot up and swung his legs off the bed, nearly kicking Garrad in the face. 'The second and...' He counted on his fingers for a second. '...fifth in line to the throne of Vorn are learning drill and how to shoot a rifle?'

'Err, I guess,' Mark replied.

'Emma's going to kill me.'

'You've got it easy, mate. Emma might kill you, but Kia will slice my balls off and make me eat them when she learns her little girl has been wearing trousers.'

'Fuck, we have to get them back!' Tom exclaimed.

'We can't. We're stuck here. For a few weeks.'

'Why? Surely they need to talk to the girls again, check they told the truth!'

'You might think, might you? But they're not prepared to do that.'

'Why the hell not!'

'From what they told me – and frankly it wasn't a lot after some jumped-up lieutenant started getting arsey with me – like in junior term in Sandhurst, they like to keep their new recruits cut off from the world. They don't let them have phones. No outside contact, no nothing until the first six weeks are up. Then they get a couple of days off. That's issue one. The second issue is they won't ask 'em. That jumped-up two-pip wonder isn't willing to, and he's in charge around here at the moment.'

'You still haven't said where we are,' Tom reminded him.

'Oh yeah, we're at the FFA HQ, about two hours south of Ayers Rock.'

'And there's a lieutenant in charge?' Tom asked, confused.

'Yeah, I thought that odd too. It turns out this is some kind of temporary HQ. They move 'em around a lot and they aren't very big. And also, the colonel who is normally in charge is off on some mission or other. The lieutenant didn't give me the details; he wasn't very friendly.'

'After you saved the arses of those idiots in the FOB? We get rewarded with jail?'

'Pretty much sums things up.'

'Did Captain Wet Behind the Ears not stick up for you?'

'Oh, she tried. But when Lieutenant Fucknut told her we were runaway sex traffickers, she suddenly became a lot less friendly.'

'Great.' Tom sighed. 'I suppose I've been in worse prisons though. Certainly beats Aran's torture chamber.'

'Oh, there you go, whinging about that again. You only did two weeks; I did three fucking months in his dungeon!'

Tom raised his hand and imitated someone talking with his fingers. *'My time was worse than your time, Tom,'* he mocked.

'How the fuck do you compare two weeks to three months!'

'More intensive.'

284

'You had magic to hide in! I grizzed it out!'

'There you go, whining again.'

'You two were both Aran's prisoners?' Garrad butted in, interrupting their exchange of banter.

They both turned to where he was sitting on his lower bunk.

'What do you think happened to my hand, kid?' Tom raised his deformed left hand, with its bulbous knuckles.

'Oh, we're playing that game, are we?' Mark pulled up his shirt. 'Do you think I have these scars for decoration?'

Garrad's jaw dropped.

'Close your mouth, lad, it was a few years ago,' Mark told him, a sad smile of remembrance replacing his earlier cheeky grin. 'Remember, Aran's a sadistic arsehole. Don't give him any chances, not ever. I did when I left the fucker alive twenty years back, and that's what's got us into this shit.'

'Why didn't you kill him?' Garrad asked.

'Because I thought for him to live on Earth without magic would be worse than death for him, and I wanted him to suffer.'

'And now he's a drugs lord,' Tom said, with a sigh.

'Indeed.' Mark turned to Tom. 'Fine, I admit, it was my fuck-up that got us into this, but we'll sort it. I should say, though, the only reason he's come to anything is because he's found a way to use magic, and it sounds like you have too. If he has, and you have, that means I can. If we can use our stretch in this cell to learn how to use it when we want to, it might give us half a chance of killing Aran properly this time round.'

31. The Way Out

'**M**a'am, what's your decision?' Colonel Marie York heard Major Wallace's words through her earpiece. They rattled round her head for a few seconds before her brain got itself in gear and the decision jolted into place.

'We withdraw. Send out the order,' she said into her microphone.

'Corporal?' She turned to the driver by her side.

'Yes, ma'am?' he replied.

'Let's go.' He started the engine and hit the accelerator, spinning the Bushmaster in a rapid one-eighty turn and leading the way out of Alice Springs.

Marie took a deep breath. She tried to steady her pounding heart while her vehicle thundered out of town. The sound of gunfire followed her for a while; the top gunners kept firing as her unit covered their retreat. The booms of the rockets and missiles from the drones kept going a while longer before they faded into the distance.

When the houses had disappeared and scattered trees on dusty ground filled her windows, her heart finally stopped pounding. They were clear of the town. The situation reports, or sit-reps as they were known in the military, still echoed into her ears. One dead, eight injured – two seriously. Five war drones down, plus one recce drone. Ammo state low, but vehicles still on the road. Good. Vehicles were the hardest thing to replace round here. Getting the shipments in from New Zealand was a challenge while the entire south and most of the east coast remained contaminated with nuclear waste, and the ports of the north were controlled by the drugs lords. The west coast was the only way in by sea for the FFA, and that was a long way from New Zealand.

With the initial verbal reports in, and the company commanders busily compiling their written reports, it was quiet now, except for the steady grumble of the engine. She switched her headset to a private chat with her second in command.

'Paul, you there?'

'Yes, ma'am.'

'How'd you think we did? Honestly?'

'Honestly? We didn't achieve our aim, but out aim was unachievable. You knew that, right?'

'Yeah.' She sighed deeply. 'I knew. But I couldn't say so to the guys.'

'What? You couldn't tell them we were just going to give Aran a bloody nose and not kick his ass?' Major Paul Wallace chuckled down the net. 'Not sure it would have sounded too good in a mission statement.'

'I thought maybe we could have done it, finished the arsehole off this time.'

'We were never going to achieve that, not with the kit and numbers we have. We are in this for the war, not just the battle. And spat by spat, skirmish by skirmish, we are wearing him down.'

'I suppose,' Marie droned into her microphone.

'Jesus, ma'am, what's come over you? Alice Springs is a big town; it needs a battle group to take the place as it stands. We are little more than a battalion. Our main effort was to destroy the drugs crops, remember? Hell, I remember your orders even if you don't!'

Marie suddenly had a sharp hit of reality. What the hell was she doing? Wallowing in self-pity with her second in command over the net, her driver sitting listening by her side? She straightened herself in her seat and had a quiet word with herself.

'Yes, Paul, I remember, and you're right,' she conceded. 'We trashed his poppy fields and bombed his meth labs. He's only got the cocaine and cannabis farms in the northeast now, and whatever else we don't know about. The snake's head might not have been cut off yet, but we've certainly reduced its food source.'

'Yes, ma'am. And that fucker is going to be pissed, very pissed. But we need to be careful; we're starting to turn him into a cornered rat.'

'If we give him little to lose, who knows what he'll do?'

'Something we don't expect, if his track record's anything to go off.'

'We need to expect it.' Marie stared out of the window in thought as she considered her own words. 'Let's war game this, shall we? We've assaulted Aran's town, his HQ. We've blown his labs to shit, wrecked his crops. What's he gonna do?'

'Get his labs back up and running ASAP, I imagine.'

'And the fields?'

'Re-grow? Maybe with better defences? You heard in the reports about the Chinese kit he has, didn't you?'

'Yes, a worrying development.' A bird of prey of some kind was hovering over its victim in the distance.

'You think they could be kitting him out?'

'It's possible. But how does he get stuff in? We've not tracked any big convoys heading south recently.' The bird dropped like a stone as it went in for the kill.

'Maybe they slipped under the radar. The New Zealand spy satellites aren't the best in the world. If we could get the US on board...'

'Those arrogant arseholes don't give a fuck about us; they've proved that time and time again,' Marie spat.

'You're right,' he conceded. 'They don't give a fuck about anyone but themselves and their own interests, but I'm not sure they'd want China to win a proxy war down here.'

'Possibly. But first things first, we need to get a foothold and make a name for ourselves. We've convinced New Zealand. If we keep making progress, a few more countries may follow.'

'And China's support for Aran and his cronies will keep growing. This will only get bloodier,' Major Wallace warned.

'Perhaps. That's not a concern for just now.'

The vehicles rumbled along the Stuart Highway, the 2,700-kilometre road joining the north of Australia to the south. They were making good progress. A few more hours and they'd be back at base. They were already into their own territory and Colonel York had received confirmation that no enemy forces were in pursuit.

They'd be back at the HQ after dark, still early enough to get a decent night's sleep before dawn. As the Bushmaster broke track and headed cross-country for the last part of their journey, Marie felt herself drifting off, despite the jolting of the vehicle over the rough terrain.

She dialled back in to talk to her second in command to help keep herself awake. 'Paul, you still there?' Her driver was fine for exchanging pleasantries with; but he was not the easiest person to chat to.

'Yes, ma'am.' Major Wallace's voice slurred over the airwaves.

'Did I wake you?'

'No, ma'am.' He yawned before hastily turning his microphone off temporarily.

'Yeah, right!' She sniggered.

'It's been a long day,' he said.

'I know, I'm struggling myself. I was thinking about our hit rate.'

'What about it? It was generally good. Our drones got all the meth labs our intelligence knew about...'

'Yeah, I know. But the rockets we fired at the headquarters, at Aran's house – I can't recall hearing one report of a direct hit.' She tapped a fingernail on her teeth.

'Unlucky,' he replied.

'We were firing for days; we can't be that unlucky.'

'I don't know what to make of that. I'd have to look at the hit reports when we get back.'

'Aran, he's a slippery fellow,' said Marie. 'Every time we get close to him, he manages to give us the slip. A few weeks back, when Lieutenant Morris came across him, he said their rockets shot away from his vehicle at the last minute.'

'Defective rockets?'

'They are heat-seeking!'

'The ground gets awfully hot in summer.'

'What if he has some secret tech from China to divert missiles away from him?'

'It's possible.'

'Paul, I want you to look into this. Talk to everyone who has been in contact with him directly over the past few years. Find out what they know, see if there are any pattens.'

'Yes, ma'am.'

***

Tom watched Mark finish his ten star jumps then start on his burpees. Push-ups were next, then jogging on the spot with high knees.

'Why, Mark?' Tom groaned from his bunk. 'It's still early. Enjoy not having to get up while you can!' Tom was out of shape. Seeing other people do exercise only made him feel worse.

'It's cooler first thing,' Mark panted.

'They won't let us out for showers for ages, and I'm going to have to smell you all that time!'

'Suck it up, Princess. How 'bout you join me? You look like you need it.' Mark bounced back into star jumps.

Tom grabbed a handful of flesh from his own belly. 'Just skin there, mate, you cheeky bugger.'

Garrad started sniggering to himself.

'Watch it, Junior!' Tom reprimanded the young sergeant. 'Don't forget I'm the prince again when we get back.'

Maybe he had put on a few pounds, Tom concluded, but he was losing a bit. They were being fed crap rations, boil in the bag. It was easy not to eat as much when you didn't have royal chefs cooking you fine dining at every mealtime.

'Mind if I join in?' Garrad asked.

Great, two of the buggers making him feel bad! Tom was getting tempted to join in, but he knew he couldn't now, not after his jibes, he had to hold his ground.

'Fill your boots. There's enough space if I shuffle forward,' Mark said between breaths as he moved back onto burpees.

'Great. I'm living with two fitness nuts,' Tom muttered. 'No point sucking up to him, lad, it won't get you promoted any quicker!' he called out, louder, to Garrad.

'He doesn't need to suck up,' Mark took a few more breaths, 'he needs to acknowledge his dad for a hasty commission.'

'He'd have to get through selection first!' Tom protested.

'Fuck me,' Mark panted, 'I've seen idiots with half his brains and ability pass though.'

'I guess we're fishing from a small pond,' Tom conceded. Selection for officers in the Army of Vorn was only open to young men from high-born families. 'Despite your best efforts to change things.'

'Burpees next, lad,' Mark puffed at Garrad as he began his high-knees jogging again. Garrad stared back blankly. 'Do you even know what a burpee is?'

'Er...' said Garrad.

'I was just doing the blasted things! It's one of these.' Mark put his hands on the floor and kicked his legs back, then forward, and jumped.

'Oh, yep, got it.' Garrad continued to repeat the movement.

Mark looked like he'd had enough. He'd probably been at it for a while before Tom even woke up. Mark grabbed yesterday's T-shirt, wiped his forehead, and flopped his arms onto Tom's top bunk.

'Get your sweaty mitts of my bed!' Tom protested.

'Why? They're here now, what difference does it make if I lift them off?'

'Dick.'

Mark grinned. 'What was it you were on about? Officer selection?'

'Yeah, it would be nice if we could select from everyone.'

'It would be nice if we could make everyone go to school and introduce a welfare state too, but that ain't going to happen either. Can't change a society in a few decades, especially when it's a hereditary system. How 'bout you think about kicking your wife off the throne and introducing democracy instead?'

Garrad paused his burpees as he looked on in confusion at Mark's comment.

'Who said you could stop? High knees next!' Mark ordered.

Garrad snapped to it at once.

'Ha ha,' Tom said sarcastically, in response to Mark's suggestion.

'Exactly. That would work no more than trying to convince the nobles that ordinary kids can actually make good officers. Democracy has to grow over time as attitudes change if anyone's going to accept that leaders should be chosen on merit, not bloodlines. Unless you're French. Didn't they kill off their aristocracy?'

'I think so. But I'm no historian. Good reason not to piss the peasants off too much, though!'

'You're no historian? You did War Studies at uni! That's basically history!'

'Only a bit of it, but that was just about war shit,' said Tom, 'and anyway, I never said I liked it. You did history at school, right? Does that make *you* a historian?'

'Pah. I got a D in that GCSE.' Mark chuckled to himself. Something appeared to catch his eye, he headed over towards the bars on the window. 'Something's going on outside, mate – loads of people milling about. About twenty or more Bushmasters look to have rocked up at some point in the night. Looks like the colonel's back.'

Tom crawled to the end of his bed to look himself.

'Who said you could stop!' Mark turned to Garrad, who seemed to be showing interest too. 'Get on with your push-ups!'

A grin spread across Tom's face. He caught Mark's eye and shook his head.

'What? Phys is good for the lad!' Mark protested.

***

Tom lay on his bed, staring at nothing, Mark and Garrad were doing the same. It was too hot to do much. It was too hot to talk, even, assuming they had anything left to talk about. They'd been locked up for four weeks with nothing to do. They were only allowed out to shower once a day. They weren't even allowed out to go to the loo – a plastic porta-potty in the corner was emptied daily and despite the chemicals, it still stank in the heat.

The air-con in their cell didn't work. There was a unit on the wall, but it wouldn't come on. Mark said he was convinced the FFA disabled it on purpose. Ever the cynic, he suspected their guards held them in particular disregard owing to the crimes they were accused of.

They'd had virtually no news since they arrived and were told about their daughters. They'd been locked up ever since. The guards who brought them food or escorted them to the showers wouldn't talk. All they'd been told was that it would be a maximum of six weeks until the girls would be questioned, after which they'd either be let go or face punishment.

Tom had already clocked that they were not in a proper jail, just some makeshift facility for temporary prisoners. From what he'd heard of the FFA, they were in no position to run proper jails. They'd be freed or killed.

It was five days since the colonel returned, or that was what they'd surmised by gauging the activity outside. Other than talking, watching the soldiers go about their business outside was the only entertainment they had. Tom had been trying with limited success to teach English to Garrad. That wasn't exactly fun.

They'd also been trying to practice magic. It took so much of their strength, the entertainment value evaporated pretty quickly. Once they'd managed to become tuned in to the faint veins of power and learnt to recognise the signature, which was weak compared to what they were used to, they found harnessing it was not too difficult. But it took huge amounts of energy to do anything significant. They spent most of their time practising the basics and working out how to translate such little background magic into a usable resource, which wasn't exciting.

Footsteps in the corridor outside. Nothing new there; guards wandered up and down fairly regularly. A jangle of keys – a little more odd at this time in the afternoon, but there were other prisoners in the block with business of their own. The turning of a key in a lock.

They sat up in unison to see who was making such an unusual visit.

The door flew open. A lieutenant flanked by two armed soldiers greeted them with a look of disgust.

'Ah, Lieutenant Fucknut!' Mark beamed at the young officer.

'Might I remind you my name is Lieutenant Morris? But you can call me sir.'

'You could remind me, if you'd introduced yourself. Sorry for the unpleasant nickname, but I had to call you something and it was just the first name that came to mind. It seemed to suit you.'

'Sir will do.'

'Uh-huh.' Mark grinned and shook his head. 'You should call me sir. I'm a major, *Lieutenant*. The day I call a subbie *sir* is the day I watch hell freeze over.'

Lieutenant Morris glared at Mark, clenching his jaw and his fists. 'The colonel will see you now,' he spat, before turning and marching down the corridor.

'Out you come,' one of the private soldiers ordered, barely able to control his own smirk.

They set off down the corridor at gunpoint.

'What was that about?' Tom muttered to Mark.

'The little shit was an arse when we got here, he pissed me off. I reckon he broke our air-con.'

'I've been sweating my balls off for four weeks because you wound up a subbie?'

'Who said *I* wound *him* up when I met him?'

Tom raised an eyebrow. 'How long have I known you?'

'Fair point,' Mark said, with a chuckle.

They were taken out into the sunshine, their first time outside since they were incarcerated. They headed across an open space between buildings. A space that had once been gardens perhaps, with a street where kids might have played. The village was tiny and the location so remote there would have been no fear of traffic here.

A couple of lamp posts remained, sad relics of a time when the grid worked. The hum of generators was the ever-present reminder that the grid had long since failed; the workers of the power stations that weren't destroyed were killed by the nuclear fallout. Generators and solar panels were the only way to make electricity now.

They walked along an old garden path, with brown strands of grass poking out between the dusty flagstones, they were heading towards a building that looked like a house. They had left something that might have been a school once, or maybe a health centre or some other public building. Certainly not a house.

The lieutenant opened the door. Mark, Tom, and Garrad followed him up the steps and inside, into a wall of cool. Working air conditioning.

'That's it, I'm never going back to my cell,' Tom declared.

The lieutenant stopped and turned to face him. A sneer spread across his face. 'We can arrange a lovely hole in the ground for you instead.'

'Calm down, Junior, you never heard of innocent until proven guilty?' Tom sniped. He was starting to figure out why Mark and the junior officer got off on the wrong foot.

'Wait here.' Lieutenant Morris left them in the hallway with the guards as he set off down a corridor to one side. Some muffled voices echoed back to where they stood. His footsteps announced his return. 'The colonel will see you now.'

'Shit, should we salute?' Tom asked Mark, tongue-in-cheek. He gave a crooked smile.

'Ha, ha. How about we get Garrad to?' Mark whispered to Tom. He cast a glance towards Garrad who had his jaw open as he surveyed the strange architecture of the grand old house.

The lieutenant led them to an office and entered first. 'Ma'am,' he threw up a salute, 'I have the prisoners.'

'Thank you, Joe.' She cast an eye towards the three men. 'Take a seat, please, all of you.'

The lieutenant seemed horrified at the suggestion they should sit, but he obeyed regardless, pulling seats into a line facing the colonel's desk. Tom, Mark and Garrad took a seat, and the armed soldiers followed them in and took up position in the two back corners of the large office. One closed the door.

'G'day gentlemen, my name is Colonel Marie York,' she began, 'It's nice to meet you at last, I've heard so much about you.' She paused; blank face unreadable as she regarded them. She leant forward, resting her chin on her hand, her elbow propped on her desk as she regarded the prisoners.

Tom suddenly felt like a naughty subaltern dragged into the commanding officer's office for some mischief or other he'd got into. A bit of light-hearted thievery from another mess perhaps – he'd done that. His trusty Leatherman was good at unscrewing a souvenir or two. Perhaps he'd been caught doing naked bar after it was specifically forbidden, he'd done that too. He'd never got caught for real though, he was generally good at hiding his tracks.

The colonel had that way of looking at you that commanded respect, that told you she knew her shit, a way of holding herself that said she'd earned her rank the hard way. Like a late-entry officer, someone who'd worked their way up from private, ticking off every rank as they went to get all the way to colonel. A bloody hard gig, that one. But she was in her forties. She wasn't old enough to have gotten her rank that way – not in the Army Tom remembered.

At last, when she was starting to make him twitch like a nervous schoolboy, she spoke. 'It's been a few weeks since I met the two young ladies who told me their fathers had sold them into slavery, and I have to say, I do see a family resemblance. You see, I'm good with faces. They tend to stick in my mind. But you,' she regarded Garrad, 'I'm not sure you are related to these two, even though you look about the right age to be their son.'

Garrad stared back incomprehensively.

'He doesn't speak English,' Tom advised her.

She raised an eyebrow. 'You do, clearly. Please tell me, where are you from?'

'England, Surrey to be more precise. Mark here is from England too, Manchester, if you know it. And him,' he indicated Garrad, 'the lad's Welsh. Grew up in the valleys, doesn't speak any English.'

'He's Welsh?'

'Yeah.'

'How is it you have a young lad from Wales with you who speaks no English?'

Tom gulped. What was it about her that made him think she saw straight through his lies? 'He's my nephew, step-nephew actually. My brother raised him like a son even though he wasn't his own. He met his mother when the kid was a baby, the father wasn't on the scene.' Tom chirped off his made-up story as convincingly as he could. He suddenly regretted not letting Mark do the talking; he was much better at this than him. He could feel his friend's disapproval radiating outwards, but he did his best to hold his nerve.

'I see.' She took out her phone from her pocket and used it for few seconds. 'Ask him to tell me the name of the town or village he's from.'

Tom had a nasty feeling his lie was about to unravel. He did as was asked, speaking to Garrad in Geminian. Garrad replied that he was from Tannel in Vorn in a tongue incomprehensible to anyone but Tom and Mark.

'Thank you,' the colonel said. 'Modern translation software is fairly good. Voice recognition works on pretty much any major language, and Welsh counts as major, believe it or not. Unfortunately, on this occasion, I can confirm that whatever language you spoke, it isn't one that's recognised by Google Translate.'

Tom shuffled in his wooden chair as she continued.

'When Captain Miller found you, she said you were running from Aran's men. I've spoken to her at length since I came back. She tells me you three helped her escape from a siege on her FOB. She speaks very highly of you. Major Harrison, in particular.'

Mark looked taken aback by the use of his name and rank.

'Yes, she told me you claimed to be ex-British Army too.' She took a deep breath and sat back in her chair before continuing. 'She told me you were looking for your daughters and that Aran had them. You already know we found some young women who matched the descriptions you gave of them. Lieutenant Morris here was the one who found them, his patrol came across Aran's men next to Ayers Rock. There was a firefight. Most of Aran's men were killed but Aran got away, as did the young ladies – by running across the line of fire, one with her hands still tied.'

Tom's mouth dropped.

'Why didn't we teach them about guns!' Mark whispered.

'They didn't get hit, right?' Tom asked the colonel.

'By the mercy of God, no. They were fine. Joe found them hiding under a bush and brought them back here.'

Mark turned to the lieutenant. 'Oh, er, cheers, mate.'

Lieutenant Morris glared at him.

'Here's the strange thing. One of the ladies spoke English, the other didn't. They told me they were from Russia. I didn't question it at first. When Captain Miller told me you guys were British, I thought, *something doesn't stack up here.* I asked for a recording of their native language to be sent over so we could check it out. Google Translate didn't like that either. Whatever language they were speaking, it wasn't Russian. I'm going to play that recording to you. I was wondering if you would be so kind as to translate it for me?'

'We're backed into a corner here, mate,' Tom whispered to Mark in Geminian. 'What we gonna do?'

'Come clean?' Mark shrugged.

Tom blinked at his friend — was that the best he could do? The man who spent his youth lying his way out of trouble? Who'd even fooled Aran's magic, he did it so well?

'They'll think we're nuts!' he whispered incredulously.

'What choice do we have? She'll see through our bullshit. There's a time to bluff and a time to come clean.'

'Erm, you sure?' Tom asked.

'We need to prove we are telling the truth. What's the worst that can happen? She decides we're nuts magicians and kills us? She'll kill us anyway if we can't convince her we aren't evil sex traffickers, and our tangle of lies ain't working too well on that front. *Your* tangle of lies. You should have let me do the talking.'

Tom took a deep breath.

'You two finished your chat there?' the colonel asked.

They both nodded.

'You were whispering. I heard a hint of what you like to call *Welsh* in there.'

Tom shrugged.

She shook her head dismissively. 'Right, I have the recording. It was taken when the women weren't aware, so it is probably chatter.' She hit play on her phone.

Mark and Tom listened to the voices of their daughters, alive and safe. Tom hadn't been prepared for the sound of his daughter's voice. It hit him like a blast of cold air on a hot day. His little girl, alive and well and talking about guns? He cocked his head to the side. As he listened to them chat, the wave of relief that engulfed him quickly transformed into humour. He couldn't help but chuckle to himself.

'Kia is not going to chop my balls off. She'll take my dick too, and make me barbeque it,' Mark muttered to Tom.

Tom laughed.

'What's so funny?' the colonel queried.

Tom worked to straighten his face. 'The topic of their chat – it's not what we are used to hearing our girls talk about.'

The colonel raised her eyebrows expectantly.

'They were talking first about how to fire a rifle. Eliza was explaining a few bits to Alora, as Alora never learned English. That makes sense. They were talking about the best places to aim to kill someone, and the best body position to take a shot from. They were talking about lying in the dust and controlling their breathing.' Tom couldn't stop himself laughing again.

'Why is that funny?'

'Ah, you'd have to know more about those two for the answer to that question to make sense,' Tom said.

'I'm listening.'

Tom inhaled deeply. 'They aren't from Russia, but you figured that out already. You don't know where they are from, or where he's from,' he nodded towards Garrad, 'or how it is we speak a language not even Google knows. It's a long story. How open is your mind, Colonel?'

Her eyes narrowed. 'I'm open to believing anything there's evidence for.'

'And yet you referred to God earlier. Are you religious?'

'Not really, but I believe in God, yes.'

'I'm not asking for faith here. Everything I can tell you is based on fact and science. Thing is, I don't have all the evidence to hand. I have some of it. I can tell you our story, but only if you are willing to give it due consideration, however nuts it may sound.'

She looked at the three prisoners, two clearly battle-hardened, one who looked like he'd never seen anything beyond a training exercise. Tom was being judged again, assessed, as she made up her mind. She'd seen a fair bit of action herself, Tom surmised. You could tell. Even if the physical scars weren't visible, the eyes always told the truth. People who'd seen action knew crazy shit could happen. In most cases, it was the only way they could work out why they were still alive and their mates weren't.

'Fine, I'll listen,' she said at last.

'Good. But our tale is for you, and you alone. There is some sensitive stuff I want to say. You can decide for yourself after if you want to tell everyone. I suggest you don't.'

'I get that. Lieutenant, Smith, Harker, leave us. I'll call if I need you.'

'Ma'am, is it safe to be alone with them?' Lieutenant Morris appeared genuinely concerned.

'I'll be fine. I'm pretty certain my demise isn't what these guys are after.'

The lieutenant lurched to his feet and saluted. 'Ma'am!'

'Keep the cameras on. I'll mute the microphone for now.'

'Yes, ma'am.'

Privates Smith and Harker were followed out by Lieutenant Joe, who pulled the door closed behind him. Tom, Mark, and Garrad were left alone with the commander of the Freedom Fighters of Australia.

***

'That's one hell of a tale, I have to say.' Colonel York dropped her chin into her waiting palms, her elbows resting on the desk. She took a few deep breaths, rocked back in her chair, and put her hands behind her head.

Tom regarded her nervously, not sure if she thought them complete nutters or just eccentric. He'd been listening to himself as he spoke. The world he'd lived in for twenty odd years was normal. He was a sorcerer and a prince. That was normal too – or it was, until he came back to Earth. Now it sounded fucking ridiculous. He barely believed it himself.

'I don't know what to make of that. Either you tell one hell of a story, or this world got an awful lot more crazy,' the Colonel said.

'You know,' Mark began, 'when Tom first told me that shit, I thought he was taking the piss. I followed the fucker to Kenya to watch his mad story fall to bits. Do you know what happened?'

Colonel York shook her head.

'I went through a wormhole to Gemini and got captured.'

'You got away, I assume? Why didn't you come back when you could?' She was smiling. Tom got the feeling she was humouring them.

'I fell in love... with his sister-in-law. Been stuck there ever since.'

The colonel shrugged. 'I can't just believe you. Much as I'd like to believe Aran is some sorcerer from another world who is using magic to keep him safe, I can't. You're talking hocus pocus there, I'm afraid.'

Mark nodded. 'What if we gave you a demonstration?'

'Of what, magic?' she said with a smirk.

'Yeah. We were sorcerers in Gemini, and we've found we can do a bit of magic here too. We've not had quite as long as Aran to master it on Earth, but when you're locked up, you can spend a lot of time figuring stuff like that out,' Mark replied.

Colonel York smiled, disbelieving. She shook her head. 'Sure, why not?'

Mark nodded towards Tom, indicating he should go first. Tom raised his right hand, his palm facing forwards. He took a few deep breaths. He reached for the magic, what little there was, and he latched onto the faint signature, hidden amongst the background energies of Earth. He drew it into himself. He gathered it in his core and when he was ready – he released. He sent his power forwards; he lifted the desk tidy off the colonel's desk. It floated through the air. He turned it upside-down. Pens, pencils, rubbers, and pencil sharpeners rattled onto the desk.

Tom spun the desk tidy in circles, round and round. He lowered it back down, picked up the items he'd spilled with his power, and replaced them back in the tidy.

Colonel York's hand slapped over her gasping mouth. Tom sat back down and folded his arms and gave Mark a smug nod.

'My turn,' Mark said with a grin.

Like Tom had, he held out his hand. He muttered a few words in imperceptible ancient Geminian and a small ball of fire appeared above his palm. He sent if forwards slowly, towards the colonel, close enough for her to feel its heat. He brought it back to the centre of the room and with his other hand, he drew a crumpled bit of paper from the wastepaper bin. He brought it towards the fireball and let it burn.

The smoke alarm beeped. Mark waved his hand and extinguished fireball and paper with a blast of freezing wind. Tom hopped onto his chair and pressed the button to silence the alarm.

Lieutenant Morris burst into the room. 'Is everything OK, ma'am?'

'Yes, fine, thank you,' she said, as if in a trance. 'Joe?'

'Yes, ma'am?'

'Who is monitoring the camera?'

'I believe Lance Corporal Fergus is in the security cell. I'm not sure if she's alone.'

'Tell her the contents of the video of my office are confidential. Have her download the footage of the last five minutes and send it to me and delete any other records.'

'Yes, ma'am. Is that all?'

'Yes, thank you, Joe.'

His face betrayed his confusion as he obediently left the room.

'Can you guys do that in battle?' she asked, leaning forwards, wide-eyed and open mouthed.

32. Strange Shit Can Happen

Colonel Marie York had got the report back from her second in command. She'd read it over and over. The pattern she'd expected was there. Not a single direct hit on Aran – not his vehicle, not his house, not anywhere he was confirmed to be. His men were hit, he'd lost vehicles aplenty, and he'd lost buildings and kit, but despite rockets and bullets and missiles being thrown at him, nothing had found their target. Some of the missiles were heat-seeking, some guided. The guided ones shouldn't have missed. Every time, they did. Whoever filed the report had come up with some theory as to why. None of it made sense. The only thing that added up was what her strange British prisoners had told her.

She'd interrogated Tom and Mark again later, after she'd gathered her thoughts. She asked for more demonstrations, made sure they weren't using some kind of trick, and eventually she was convinced they could use magic. As they'd suggested, she kept it to herself. That kind of info could be dangerous. It would make her subordinates think she was nuts if she started talking about magic, and there was little to be gained from convincing them of the strange abilities of the prisoners.

It was clear Tom and Mark could escape from their cell at any time using their power. Marie saw no point in keeping them detained any longer. She had given them some freedoms and ordered them to be moved to an unlocked cell with working air-con while she did more digging.

She managed to get to some background on Captain Thomas Taylor and Major Mark Harrison via the New Zealand government. It was confirmed Tom had gone absent without leave, or AWOL as it was commonly known, in 2016. He reappeared in Kenya the next year, and was court-martialled and deported to the UK before being tracked back to Kenya while on bail on a stolen passport along with Mark, who'd gone AWOL himself soon after. Neither had been seen since.

She had their pictures; the facial recognition software confirmed a match. They were telling the truth about their military backgrounds.

There was no record of their daughters or Garrad. Not anywhere. Overseas nationals were normally traceable from somewhere. They usually popped up on someone's immigration system at some point. Anyone who'd ever boarded an aeroplane was logged on a system. But the geeks in the NZ government found no trace.

She'd done a DNA profile check on the women – it confirmed paternity of the men. She'd had them interviewed by their company commander; they'd been told their fathers were here. They changed their stories. With a nudge and some gentle persuasion, they started to talk about their homeland on a video call with the colonel.

Their fathers had had no access to any phones or means of contact since they got here, and the women were banned from having comms while in training. It was impossible they could have been in touch to corroborate their stories.

Marie was convinced the men could use magic. She was pretty sure the rest of their story was true too. It was crazy, but sometimes crazy shit did happen.

Seven years ago, she'd a baby, a husband, a nice house, and a promising career in the Army. If anyone suggested the Chinese would nuke Australia, that almost everyone she knew would be killed, and her baby would die of a simple infection because there were no proper hospitals and no decent drugs available, she wouldn't have believed that, either.

She wouldn't have believed the world would do nothing, that Australia would be left to rot, and she would end up leading the fight back. But here she was. Strange shit could happen; stuff you would never have believed possible.

It was time to have another chat with her prisoners.

***

'I trust you've been enjoying more space?' Marie queried.

'Yes, thank you, Colonel, and the air-con? I haven't slept so well in weeks,' Tom replied.

'Good. I have some news for you.' She waited while Mark told Garrad what she had said. It was such a strange language, unfamiliar, like nothing she'd heard before. 'I've been doing some digging,' she announced when Mark finished. 'Your story checks out, as far as I can tell.'

'Great. Can we get our daughters back now?' Tom asked.

There was no hint of surprise in his face, nor in Mark's. She'd questioned a lot of people in her time. If they were in any way shocked by her answer, they'd have given her a clue.

'You will be reunited shortly.'

'Why the delay?'

'They want to finish their training. Basic, at least,' Marie confirmed.

'You're kidding me?' Mark grinned. Fatherly pride, she assumed.

'No. To be honest, I'm as surprised as you. I'm not sure I've ever come across two women as unworldly as your daughters. I only offered them a place in our forces as they had nowhere else to go. I was shocked when they accepted, and even more shocked to find out they had adapted quickly and were doing well. Recruit Harrison, in particular, shows exceptional skill with a rifle – she has the best grouping on her course – and Recruit Taylor proved very adept at driver training, being the first non-driver to have passed her assessment.'

Mark's jaw practically fell into his lap.

Tom scratched his head. 'It took me four attempts to pass my driving test. No idea where she gets that from,' Tom noted, puzzled but clearly impressed.

Mark's jaw snapped back into place. 'You drive like a pansy! She must get it from Emma,' Mark said. 'Alora's shooting skills, all me. I could get a twenty-pence piece grouping at a hundred meters, back in the day.'

'Fifty-pence piece, at best!' Tom insisted.

'Sod off,' Mark rebutted, scowling at his friend. Tom smirked back.

'Sorry, Colonel, back to the question – how long before we can see them?' Tom asked.

Marie shook her head gently; she barely hid her own smile at the way they spoke to each other. Banter, light-hearted mocking of one another – the Brits were good at it. She'd worked with them in the past, been deployed in joint headquarters and met plenty of them before Australia got nuked. A nostalgic sense of what was, what could have been, began to chip into her consciousness. She forced it to sod off back to the mental vault where it belonged.

'They'll be done with phase one in a little over a week. After, they get a weekend off, and I can arrange for them to be transported here. It's up to them if they want to go with you. They are grown women, and I can't allow you to force them to do anything against their will.'

'Yeah,' Tom began. He paused, as if he was suddenly contemplating a completely different future for his daughter than the one he'd imagined. 'We'll talk to them.'

***

Garrad swung his sword. Mark ducked at the last minute, unable to get his own steel up to parry in time. He skidded, but found his footing. He whipped his arm up and tried to get a hit. Garrad parried. The lord commander was quick, Garrad conceded, but not quick enough.

The blades clashed, and Mark leapt back, gaining distance to reset his footing. Garrad wouldn't let him rest. He lunged forwards, swinging his sword across Mark's belly. It might have actually sliced him if Mark hadn't stepped back, sucking his stomach in as he went.

Lord Mark danced to the side. He pirouetted with an agility Garrad found himself admiring in a man of his age. He swung his sword as he went, he built momentum, and his face hardened. Garrad caught a determined look in the man's eyes, accompanied by a grin, like he thought he had him this time.

Garrad saw him coming a mile off. When the blade came, he was ready. Momentum like that could be turned against you, and he didn't miss his chance. He whipped his sword up as fast as lightening, let it clash against the lord commander's, and he twisted as it hit. He wrenched his sword as steel met steel. With a yank in the right direction, he was able to rip Mark's sword from his grip, launching it into the air and nearly hitting an onlooker.

In a flash, he had his blade at Mark's throat, its tip gently prodding his skin while his face erupted into a wide, toothy grin. A cheer rang out from the crowd of FFA soldiers who were gathered to watch. Garrad spotted Tom in the audience, his arms folded, sniggering to himself.

'Three out of three, Mark? Had enough?' Garrad sniped.

'Fine,' Mark conceded with a sigh. 'Let's put it down to age, shall we, kid?' He shook his head in defeat and went to retrieve his sword.

Tom took a step forwards and slapped Garrad on the shoulder. 'Good work, lad, your father would be proud to see you wielding a sword like that.'

Garrad nodded in acknowledgment. Tom turned towards Mark.

'You actually thought you could have him, didn't you?' Tom said, shaking his head, eyebrows raised.

Garrad's grin widened.

'I've been training with a blade since that sprite was a baby!' Mark protested.

'Maybe, but he has the genes for it,' Tom said. 'How was your dad at sword fighting?'

'Ha, ha!'

'He still can't beat your rifle grouping though, take consolation from that… if you're obsessed with doing better at him at everything!'

Give it time, Garrad thought. He'd get good at that too, given the chance.

'The little shit is actually a good shot too!' Mark sniped. 'And he's only been training for a few days. No more range time for him. I need to keep hold of something.'

Maybe I should smuggle a gun back to Gemini, Garrad thought, grinning to himself.

'I'm going to get a brew, fancy one?' Tom suggested.

'Sure,' Mark replied.

'Garrad, coming for a drink?' said Tom.

***

In the days since they'd been acquitted of their alleged crimes, Garrad was almost starting to enjoy his time on Earth. He was nearly at the point where he saw the prince and lord commander as ordinary humans, he was beginning to get used to all the weird technology that was all over the place, and he'd even started to get the hang of a bit of the local language.

They'd been given free rein in the FFA HQ. The place consisted a of a small, remote village in the northern reaches of South Australia. Another settlement abandoned by its occupants as many of the county's residents fled overseas. The FFA had taken it over, built a wall of Hesco round it, fortified it, and turned it into their HQ. It was sited in the north of their territory, aspiringly close to their next target.

After Colonel York concluded Tom and Mark could use magic at will if they wanted, she told them she saw little point in keeping their weapons from them any longer, and allowed them to take them back. Sword practice was always a good way to keep fit, and as Mark, Garrad and Tom drilled away, the soldiers of the FFA started to enjoy the entertainment.

Alora and Eliza were due back later that day. The men had made no plans for their time after that; it hinged on what the women had to say.

It was midmorning. The cookhouse was not serving food, but it was always open to allow soldiers to get a drink. Garrad was sitting drinking tea with Tom and Mark when he heard the high-pitched call of the princesses in unison.

'Father!'

His heart skipped a beat. A sense of relief descended through his being, sucking the air from his chest. The steel legs of Tom and Mark's chairs scraped across the tiled floor, and there was a thud of boots on the ground. Garrad took a deep breath, rose to his feet, and turned to see the two young women wrapped in their fathers' arms.

He'd been told they were safe, and they'd be brought here once they'd finished basic training. Somehow, he couldn't bring himself to fully believe it until he saw it with his own eyes. There they were, alive. His failure of duty had come to nothing, he thought for a fleeting moment, then he had another good look at them. They wore no jewels; their hair was tied back. They sported the green, beige, and brown camouflage uniform of the Australian Army. They wore shirts, trousers, and the sand-coloured boots he'd seen the soldiers of the FFA wear. The princesses were in trousers; they were wearing men's clothing. He'd seen other female soldiers, but that certainly hadn't prepared him for the sight of two senior, female members of the Vorn royal family dressed as men from another planet.

No, he thought to himself. His failure hadn't come to nothing. He'd allowed the princesses' world to be turned upside down. He silently prayed that after all this was over, their lives would be changed for the better.

After a time, they both stepped back from the embrace of their fathers. Alora was engaged in quiet conversation with Mark, while Eliza turned to Garrad, her red-rimmed eyes regarded him. She smiled, and his trance was broken. He couldn't help but smile back.

'Here, you're dribbling snot.' Tom passed her a napkin from the table. She widened her smile and bit her lower lip as she wiped her face.

'I'm sorry, Father,' she muttered. 'Sorry I got you locked up again.' Fresh tears started to flow; Tom pulled her back to his chest.

'It's OK, Eliza, trust me. As prisons go… it could have been a lot worse.' He squeezed her reassuringly, gently moved his hands to her shoulders, and pushed her back to look at her face. She dropped her head as she flicked away another tear. He placed a hand on her chin and gently lifted her head. 'I'm glad you're safe. Seeing you alive? God, there's nothing I've wanted more since that muppet told me what happened.'

Tom turned to him. Garrad was still frozen to the spot, hands clenched, feeling more than a little uncomfortable with the emotional exchange before him.

'It wasn't his fault!' Eliza exclaimed. 'We used magic on him, we got away from him on purpose. We—'

Tom cut her off. 'He told us. But just so you know, Mark would have had his balls if we hadn't got you back.'

'Father!'

Garrad couldn't help but smirk as Eliza chastised the Prince of Vorn.

'Six weeks with squaddies and you are still offended by improper language?' Tom said.

'You're a prince, you should have higher standards!' Eliza said.

Tom laughed. 'It's good to have you back, Eliza. You should be aware though, when we get back, you're grounded for a year.'

'A year!'

'Your mother will ground me for a month. She'll blame this on me. It's only fair.'

Eliza chuckled. 'You can't be grounded!'

'Trust me, I can.'

'If I'm grounded for a year, I'm not going back. I'm going to complete my training here and fight for the FFA.'

'No, you're not' her father replied.

'Yes, I am. Colonel York told me I could. She said you're not in charge of me here.'

Garrad's eyebrows sank as he listened to the princess talk, his head cocked to one side.

'Fine, stay,' Tom said.

'You sure?' Eliza said.

'Oh yeah, you stay here, on Earth. No magic, no jewels, no servants, crap food, no horses... You stay, you live in the dust, and fight for the FFA. Be my guest.'

Is the prince being serious? Garrad continued to watch the exchange.

'You don't mean that?'

'Oh, I do. You'd be an idiot, and I'd have to stay too because if I go back without you, your mother will skin me alive, but if you want to stay, stay.'

'You'd stay here with me? Would you join the FFA as a captain?' Eliza asked.

'Er, why not?' Tom shrugged.

Garrad was baffled. Why was the princess suggesting such a thing? A flurry of explanations flashed through his mind. None stayed around long enough to grip, to stop his jaw from flapping, to keep the words in his mouth.

'You dishonour your father, Your Highness,' Garrad said.

They turned to him in a flash – the prince, the lord commander, the two princesses. He'd spoken louder than he'd planned. He started shaking, but he had to say his piece; he couldn't let whatever game the prince was playing blow up in his face like this.

'You disobey your parents, you run off to another world, you put yourself and others in mortal danger, and you suggest you will not return home?' Garrad took a few steps forwards; his heart pounded in his chest. 'I care not for my own safety; I would follow my duty to the ends of the world. But I will not see Vorn deprived of its prince and princess because you wish to put your own desires above that of your duty. My father died for duty; he would be ashamed to hear the daughter of his queen dismiss her own lightly.'

They stayed quiet. Princess Eliza looked aghast. Prince Tom seemed to be struggling to keep a straight face; he must have been bluffing. From the look on Eliza's face, she hadn't realised. The water boiler hissed to itself in the corner while they waited for someone to break the silence. Tom shrugged and at last took a couple of paces forwards and slapped Garrad on the shoulder.

'Well said, lad,' he said.

Eliza shook her head and looked mortified. 'Your father's dead?' Garrad suddenly realised she didn't know who his father really was. 'Sergeant Bramston, I'm sorry, when did that happen?

'Before he was born,' Mark answered for him. 'That's a long story, for another time. Alora, like Eliza, you need to decide what you want to do next. Will you come back with us?'

'We were told Ayers Rock is defended by Aran. The colonel said there was no way to get there. We discussed this, Eliza and I. We said we'd fight with the FFA until a way home can be found.'

'That's not quite what you were saying, Eliza,' Tom said to his daughter.

'Um, I didn't mean it,' she said, without much conviction. 'As Sergeant Bramston said, we have duty to consider. We should get home if we can. Right now, we can't though, can we?'

The corner of Garrad's mouth twitched into a smile. He wasn't sure what had just happened, but he had a suspicion he might have just persuaded the princesses not to stay on Earth.

***

The ground-penetrating radar provided by the New Zealand satellites had found the tunnel where Tom and Mark said it was. It looked man-made in parts, but natural in others. From its entrance in a gulley at the side of Ayre's rock, the tunnel went more or less straight for a couple of hundred meters, like it had been bored out by machinery. The piles of spoil near the entrance that were visible from the satellite imagery bore this theory out. But after the straight section, it began to weave like it was following something natural. A watercourse was detected at the base of this section and the radar showed it was big enough to walk through. The natural part wound on for perhaps a few hundred meters more, then it just stopped, like someone had sliced its end off. More and more of what the Brits had said was being borne out with evidence.

Marie sat in her office, reviewing her documents – file upon file of data she'd collected since she'd first been told about a wormhole connecting Earth to another planet. A planet hundreds of thousands of light years away, where magic was real, or so they said.

She read another contact report involving Aran. Yet another account of rockets and missiles strangely going astray, not hitting Aran, not even coming close. There was a report of a rocket doubling back, doing a one-eighty in mid-air and hitting the vehicle that fired it. Another report of freak weather events, odd gusts of wind taking men off their feet, strange bouts of fog, even a bolt of lightning.

She went back years. She dug into the records passed to her from some of the militias that were the FFA's predecessors. They'd been fighting Aran long before she united them and turned them into the FFA.

She was in no doubt Aran was using magic, and to defeat it you needed some of your own. There were only two men besides Aran she knew of who had any idea how to use it.

Colonel Marie York had got to where she was by exploiting opportunities. Right now, she had one, but she didn't know for how long. The time to act was now.

33. Last Chance, Only Chance

Tom had studied the radar images; he'd noticed they showed more than a cave with an abrupt end. He'd identified a weakness in the defences of Aran's newly built base. Ayers Rock was riddled with natural caves, the water that flowed from Gemini to Earth tracked along just one.

There was another cave that started at the far side; it wove through the rock and joined the one Aran guarded. It intersected at a section that had been bypassed by his dug-out stretch. It looked like a widening of the narrowest part was all that was needed to get through, then there would be a clear route to Gemini or the inside of the FOB, depending on which way you turned.

Tom and Mark had worked with the Colonel and her team to form a strategy to defeat Aran once and for all. Its first phase involved a hair-brained plan to break into Aran's FOB from behind, to take him by surprise. They just needed a few of the Colonel's soldiers to make it work. And Lieutenant Joe Morris had volunteered his platoon. Better the devil you know, Tom thought, when the lad volunteered.

Phase one of the plan was underway. Tom, Mark and Joe's platoon were now working their way through the cave Tom had spotted at the far side of Ayres Rock. One of Joe's platoon, a corporal called Benson, said he'd been a builder before Australia got nuked. It was agreed he was probably the most qualified to operate the pneumatic drill, followed by Tom. As an ex-officer in the Corps of Royal Engineers, there was no way he'd have it any other way when anything remotely resembling construction was involved.

Tom followed Corporal Benson through the cave. Mark was behind him, the rest of the platoon trailed behind. They could walk in the tunnel at first, then they had to stoop, then crawl. The cave floor was smooth and dry. The waterway that had formed it had long since diverted down another route.

With his head down, and eyes checking for pebbles that he'd rather not crawl onto, he didn't notice when the corporal ahead stopped.

'Ow!' Benson exclaimed as Tom headbutted him in the buttocks.

'Sorry.' He backed up and felt his foot collide with Mark's arm.

'Watch it!' his old friend growled.

'I'm gonna have to start digging now, it's too shallow ahead,' Corporal Benson announced. He was armed with a pneumatic drill and a head torch. He could hardly be considered a poster boy for *Health and Safety Magazine* as he lay on his belly and chipped at the rock above him, but as the fragments tumbled into the passage, it quickly became evident their plan might work.

The shallow section was a few meters long. Corporal Benson only had to break away a bit of the rock to make it deep enough to wriggle through. With Tom and Mark behind, clearing rubble as needed, it took him little over an hour to make a passage. Then they were through. They splashed into the section of tunnel that Aran had bypassed then crawled until they could stand, and before they knew it, they were at a T-junction. Turn left along the natural cave towards Gemini, turn right down Aran's man-made tunnel towards the FOB. To turn left wasn't an option. Life with a memory of cowardice and without their daughters by their side was no life. They went right without hesitation.

The steel bars that had prevented their retreat to their adopted home all those weeks ago were the first obstacle. But they'd come prepared, with a laser steel cutter. The tool made short work of the bars. Aran had replaced the door they'd kicked down; this gate was heavier, sturdier. This time they had the right kit. A few cuts around the locking bolts was all it took, and the door swung open.

Tom probed ahead with magic. Back at HQ, he'd found he had the power to sense life a little distance away. In Gemini, he could search across continents. Here, close to the link to the magical planet, he was able to do better than expected. He felt the presence of every soldier in the base. He focussed on his power; it crackled over him. It suddenly clicked. He was soaking from the stream they'd crawled through; Geminian water touched almost every part of his clothed skin.

'Mark, the water,' he whispered. 'The magic is in the water; I can feel it.'

Mark closed his eyes and concentrated for a few seconds. 'Shit, yeah, you're right! Do you think Aran knows?'

'Probably. If he's been making use of it, it might be why he held out so long when he attacked the FOB. And now we know, it might give us the boost we need to take him down. Anyway, there's a sentry at the tunnel entrance, a guard outside. And I can sense another barrier at the end of this tunnel.'

'Think you can blast it?' Mark asked.

'We'll have to look at it, find out what it's made of.'

Mark turned to Lieutenant Morris who'd followed on behind Mark, with the rest of his platoon behind him. 'Right, Joe,' Mark whispered. 'You got comms?'

'Yes, *sir*.' A hint of resentment at having to use Mark's rank was evident in his voice.

'Are we good to go?'

***

Garrad was sitting in the back of the Bushmaster with Eliza and Alora. He'd been relegated to babysitting duty again. The main assault was underway. The missiles were flying, the drone strikes had begun, and the blast waves shook the vehicle. He was probably the best swordsman in the Army of Vorn. Here, he was a rookie. Tom had taught him to shoot straight. He could manage a rifle, but they were out of range.

The battle was being fought with unmanned aerial vehicles, or UAVs as he'd been told they were called. The drones flew through the air and launched rockets and missiles. He'd been told there was no magic on Earth, which was bullshit. There was magic here – a different type. The kind that could make the drones fly, create light with the flick of a switch, or make vehicles go three times the speed of a horse at full gallop without needing to rest for hours. It was a magic that could make stuff explode, and bits of metal fly through the air so fast and with so much accuracy you could kill a man at five hundred paces with ease, then the next man, and the next, without even needing to reload.

Garrad couldn't do magic in Gemini, and on Earth, he hadn't a clue how it worked either. He was no more use here than he would have been back home in the midst of a battle of sorcerers. He was sitting with the princesses, waiting for their fathers to destroy Aran, being useless while the battle raged around him, and he was being babysat in turn.

314

There was a soldier from the FFA with them. He wore the uniform and the rank slide of a corporal, but he didn't look like he could do much fighting. He had an electronic device in his lap. It had buttons and a screen. The corporal was typing on it furiously, monitoring the screen, directing weapons. His headset chirped; the corporal spoke intermittently. Garrad didn't have a clue what he was uttering. He'd barely learnt the basics of English, despite Prince Tom's best efforts to teach him.

'What's he saying, Your Highness?' he said to Eliza.

'You can call me Eliza while we're here. Father said so.'

'We'll be back before long, and I don't want to break that habit. Familiarity isn't good in a master–servant relationship.'

'You're not our servant, Garrad!'

'What am I, then?'

'You're our – our, erm, bodyguard.'

'Yeah, a kind of servant. And a pretty crap one. Don't worry, I'm going to ask to be reassigned when we get back.'

Eliza's face fell. 'You can't do that!'

'Why not? You two don't want me around, you made that clear. And to be honest, my talents can be better used elsewhere.'

'I'll tell Father not to let you go.'

'It's up to Lord Harrison, I believe.'

'I'll tell my father not to let you go,' Alora interjected.

Garrad rolled his eyes. 'I'm going, whether you like it or not. If I have to go for a commission to do it, maybe I will.' *Did he mean it? Shit, he hadn't given it consideration until he said it.*

'How can you do that? You need noble blood to go straight to officer without working your way up.' Eliza managed to do a very good job of sounding like a snobby noble. Garrad couldn't work out if she meant to or not.

'You remember what your father said about my father being dead?' he said. *Fuck.* The cat was escaping from the bag. No going back.

'Oh.' She paused. 'I remember, but your father was a merchant in Tannel. I read your file...'

'He's not my real father.' Saying the words felt hard, bloody hard, but somehow it was a relief to hear the words come out of his mouth.

'Oh. I – um...'

A large explosion boomed nearby. The vehicle rocked sideways, its two wheels coming off the ground; it landed back down with a thud.

'What was that!' Alora exclaimed.

'Not sure.' Garrad climbed up and lifted the top hatch.

The corporal yelled something at Garrad.

Garrad couldn't understand him. Eliza took hold of Garrad's hand and tugged. 'Garrad!' she called up. 'He says to get down, it's not safe!'

He reluctantly obeyed, shutting the hatch as he dropped back into his seat.

'It's not looking good over there,' he said. 'I saw something like magic spray out of the base, and lots of debris flying everywhere. There's gunfire aplenty up ahead but it's inside the base. Why are we not moving forwards to help?'

'I'll ask for you,' Eliza said to Garrad, before repeating the question to the corporal. He didn't seem to hear. She reached over and pulled an earphone from one of his ears and asked again. He scowled at her irritably.

He snapped something at her before snatching his earphone back and continuing to type.

'He says it's not secure yet. We need to stay out of range until their main weapons are neutralised and the gate has been opened.'

'This battle has been going on for ages. Do you think our fathers are OK?' Alora asked, her voice betraying the hint of a quiver.

***

Lieutenant Morris was proving his worth. Tom was impressed; he even caught Mark giving him the odd look of approval as he ordered his platoon during the attack. They'd made a good entrance, caught Aran's men by surprise, and had them on the back foot. Joe had quickly made good use of the ground and got his men and women into secure positions as the firefight began in earnest.

Meanwhile Tom had found Aran, skulking in a hardened shelter at the far side of the base, diverting missiles, sending some back. After his weeks of practicing, Tom had trained himself to be tuned in to the weak fields of power. He felt Aran's manipulation nearby.

But right now they were pinned down with the rest of Joe's platoon. Mark and Tom could use their magic here on Earth, but they'd

316

been practicing for just a few weeks. Aran had been at it for years. What little they could use sapped their energy at a rate of knots, and the boost from the stream water was wearing off; they were drying out quickly in the relentless sun.

Getting a foothold was easy. At first, they had surprise. Joe's men had pushed forwards and got the platoon into a secure position. Aran's men soon got their shit in order; they returned fire and held them in place. They got their drones in the air and started firing. Mark and Tom were able to use their magic to keep the drones away, but they were draining fast.

The signal had been sent, the attack from the FFA outside had begun, the drones were pulled away. The firefight continued.

Something whizzed above them. A rocket, one of their own most likely. It jolted in mid-air and diverted straight into the rockface. *Boom, crack, rumble.* A chunk of the cliff behind them collapsed into a heap on the ground, filling the gully leading to the tunnel. The buzz of magic rippled through the air; Aran had started to play.

Tom felt his presence, his power, as he moved towards them, radiating as he cast a spell. He felt the tingling as one of Joe's soldiers was lifted into the air. A round found the poor man's face and he dropped before Tom even managed to counter. Another one began to rise, desperately flailing as he went. Tom was ready this time. He shoved against Aran's power, he strained. Mark helped; the soldier dropped. Aran tried to lift another, another. Sometimes they could be saved, other times Aran yanked them up too quickly. A morbid scene of whack-a-mole was being played out in front of them, interrupted only when Aran had to divert an incoming rocket his own countermeasures missed. The platoon was getting wiped out. Tom had to act.

'Mark, stay here. Keep trying to save the guys. I'm going after Aran.'

Mark didn't have time to argue. Tom shot off across the base. The soldiers of the FFA desperately tried to react, putting down covering fire to protect his run. With luck and the help of magic, Tom managed to avoid being shot. He sprinted past the line of attackers and continued towards the shelter where Aran lurked.

Rifle in hand, Tom wasted no time unloading a shot into the guard outside. He dropped before he'd even fully clocked Tom running towards him. Tom shot the door lock with his rifle. He kicked it – it flew open. He was blasted backwards as Aran threw his power at him.

Tom found himself on his back. Aran was approaching. He anticipated the attack and threw a shield up. It was enough to hold back the wave of energy that would have torn him to bits.

He climbed to his feet and scrambled back. Aran launched another attack. Tom dived to the side. The blast hit a wooden shower block; timber shards scattered everywhere. Tom gathered his magic and tried to fire a blast back. With a wave of his hand, Aran deflected it easily. Tom tried to strike again, but his attack didn't even get close. Aran halted the wave of magic and pushed it back, throwing Tom from his feet.

A missile exploded in mid-air above them. It wasn't Aran this time. It was some kind of countermeasure, but the shockwave threw him back to the ground he was desperately trying to rise from.

Aran advanced. He sent a jet of energy towards Tom. Tom had nowhere to hide. He tried a shield. He'd drained his energy quicker than he'd anticipated. The shield was weak. He watched with wide, helpless eyes as the magic came at him, quick as a flash, yet somehow the world decelerated into slow-motion. The blue steaks of power washed over his shield, and it began to crumple under the strain, tendrils of energy sweeping towards his body. Hundreds of jets of magic filtered through his failing shield like water through a colander, hot pokers stabbing his flesh, slicing and searing his skin. A multitude of tiny fingers pushed him back, taking his balance, throwing him to the ground. Limp body falling, arms flailing, head flopping, ground colliding – *thud*.

Day turned to night.

***

As the blood splattered from of his unconscious adversary, a wide grin spread across Aran's face. It was a grin tinged with regret that it was about to end quickly. Thomas deserved a much slower and far more painful demise. Aran was in no position to take any more chances by letting the bastard live. He advanced, he summoned his power – but his senses twinged. He felt the prickle of a rocket heading straight for him; another one his Chinese defence systems had clearly missed.

There was a moment of indecision as he stared at his prey. The instinct of survival took over. He spun and sent his power towards the

318

rocket, diverting it, doing enough to keep it from killing him, saving his power for other things, better things. With a flick of his wrists, he sent it hurling into the side of Ayers Rock. Another crater blasted into its side, another shower of shards of rock to hopefully hit those loathsome Freedom Fighters who dared to infiltrate his base.

With the satisfying sound of screaming men rattling into his ears, he spun back towards his target, and readied his magic. He didn't strike soon enough. Something went *boom*. A rocket hit a vehicle in the base. The fuel exploded, and Aran was hurled from his feet in the blast wave.

His ears rang as he edged onto an elbow. He nearly sank again. The fall had grazed his skin; his elbow stung like hell. He pushed through the pain and sat up. The ringing in his ears gave way to a different king of hum, the tingle of magic. Someone else was using it in his base. It could only be Mark.

Thomas would have to wait. Aran couldn't waste the last of his power on him when Mark, the arsehole who'd tricked him out of his kingdom, was still alive. He forced himself to his feet and staggered around a tent. He wound his way round the debris and past a generator, peering around the side.

His men were being held off. Not advancing, but not retreating either. The FFA were clearing rubble from the gulley he'd blocked. The first few started to climb over. He spotted Mark; he couldn't let him escape. He launched his magic. Mark seemed to feel it approach – he dodged just in time. He threw himself to the ground, rifle in hand, butt at his shoulder and rounds cracking out of the muzzle as soon as he hit the deck.

Aran threw up a shield. The bullets almost found his chest. He forced them to the ground as he dodged back behind the generator. The rounds kept flying, keeping his own men down as Mark covered the retreat of the FFA. He sat with his back to the generator as he caught his breath, assessed how much magic he had, tried to work out what to do next.

Another rocket flew over the walls. He grabbed it with his power and threw it towards the gulley entrance, but Mark had seen it too. He used his own power to pull it to one side, far enough away that it hit the cliff side instead, leaving the route towards the tunnel open.

***

'What's going on, Your Highness? Can you find out, please?' Garrad asked, fidgeting in his seat. The battle had been going on a while, and the corporal had stopped tapping away on his equipment. He was packing it up and preparing to go somewhere. He got out a smaller, handheld device and chatted away on his headset, like he was preparing to move.

Garrad was getting nervous. The distant booms had quietened down while more and more were sounding nearby. He didn't know what to make of them. Were the vehicles getting hit or were the blasts being deflected? He'd popped his head up through the top hatch long enough to see a missile meet one of the FFA's and explode in mid-air. They had some other kind of magical defensive system, he presumed.

The princesses both looked similarly nervous, like they sensed something was coming. Eliza seemed to have had enough of waiting, she didn't even wait for a polite break in the Corporal's conversation. She jumped from her seat and pulled off the corporal's headset.

'What's going on!' she demanded.

The corporal reached for the headset. She pulled it out of his reach. 'Give that back.'

'Only when you tell me what's happening. Are we about to move forward?'

The corporal clenched his fist and grimaced. 'We are about to pull back. Give me the headset if you want half a chance of getting out of here alive.'

'We can't leave. Our fathers are in there!'

'We can. That's the order. The platoon inside has failed to take the base.'

'No. There's still fighting in there, I can hear gunfire. We have to help them!' she yelled desperately.

'That's not my call!'

She quickly translated to Garrad. His heart dropped into his stomach. They couldn't leave, they had a mission to accomplish! And Prince Tom and Lord Mark were still in there. He couldn't go and let this bunch of cowards abandon them. He had to do something. He rapidly formed a plan.

It started with a punch to the face of the corporal. The startled soldier collapsed into unconsciousness. Eliza opened the back doors. Garrad and Alora pulled the corporal out the back of the Bushmaster and left him on the ground. They ran to the front. Garrad opened the door and drew his sword; he held a point to the throat of the driver.

Eliza ordered him to do something in English – probably to get out.

The driver's hand slipped towards his pistol. The point of Garrad's sword pressed against his neck. He raised his hands and complied. As he stepped down, Eliza swiped his pistol.

Someone shouted from nearby. The three of them ignored whoever it was. Alora was already climbing through the passenger door. Garrad sprinted to the other side and got in after her, while Eliza climbed into the driver's seat.

A soldier came into view, he was yelling at them as he pulled the butt of his rifle into his shoulder and aimed it at them. Eliza slammed the door shut. Rounds hit the door. The glass was marked, but didn't crack. The armour was doing its job. She turned the ignition, put her foot down, and the Bushmaster shot forwards.

***

Colonel York stared in disbelief as a Bushman shot forwards. It was the one that the two young women and the mysterious young man from another world had been assigned to.

'What the hell are they doing!' Colonel York yelled over the net. No one answered. It had been a difficult call to order the retreat. The women shouldn't have been told, having the women know that their fathers were going to be left to their fate was unlikely to go down well. Someone clearly told them. The airway was quiet; no one knew what to say.

'Shit!' she said to herself.

What now? Her choice between retreating and advancing had been almost fifty-fifty. But she'd erred on the side of caution. If she retreated, she'd have to accept the losses of some of her guys and two men no one would miss. However she'd get to keep her kit, keep her vehicles and no one else would die. Now one of her Bushmasters was rushing forwards and would be lost if she did nothing. She knew the occupants wouldn't be missed, but to leave them? It wouldn't look good. It would be bad for morale. Her heart pounded. Quick decision time; she had to make a call. Was this the excuse she needed to order the advance? To have done so earlier would have been reckless. To call the retreat was the right decision. Joe's platoon hadn't secured the gate; they must have lost the element of surprise. He knew that if that happened, he'd have to pull out, but the situation had changed.

'Shit.' She turned on her mic. 'Covering fire. Move forwards, cover the vehicle.'

Sometimes you had to take risks. All or nothing, and it could be all. If that happened, she could try to claim it was part of her plan.

The line of FFA vehicles got close enough to be within range of the machine guns. Only one sanger was manned, and no new gunners arrived. So far so good. Their gunners opened fire; one sanger was easy to suppress. No grenades came, no rockets were fired, and the battle still raged inside, somehow. Lieutenant Morris had just radioed in to say his guys were out, but he'd said nothing about the Brits. The two crazy magicians must still be inside, keeping up the fight on their own, keeping Aran's men busy.

She ordered an increase on the assault rate. They were running low on rockets, but she'd committed. She watched as the rockets flew. No mysterious diversions this time. Their countermeasures couldn't handle so many at once, and loads started to get through. Rifles still cracked somewhere out of sight. It wasn't over yet.

The lead vehicle taken by the three young people from another world continued to rush forwards. It was being fired upon. A rocket was on target. It nearly hit, but one of her own countermeasures took it out. It kept going at speed and veered around the entry chicane.

More men started to appear in the sangers. They were shooting at the Bushmaster. A grenade was thrown. Another one of her drones shot it down before it landed. She couldn't quite see what was going on through the Hesco chicane, but she did spot the head of a man as he leapt on top of his vehicle. He was high enough for her to see his shoulders and the sword he carried in his hand. He launched himself from the top of the vehicle, grabbed the top of the gate and somehow vaulted over. Her jaw dropped. She blinked and her brain tied itself in knots as she tried to work out what the fuck she'd just seen.

**

322

Mark and Joe were working together to keep Aran suppressed. Aran's men had rushed off to the wall. The FFA had advanced at last, drawing their fire.

They ran, they fired. Aran ducked. He hurled an oil drum at them. Mark deflected it with his power. Aran blasted the vehicle they sheltered behind. The fuel tank caught. Mark managed to shield him and Joe from the worst of the blast.

Mark lay on the ground. Something caught his eye near the gate. Someone vaulted over the top. A nutter with a sword — it could only be Garrad. He landed in the middle of a cluster of men, wielding his sword with fury. Three were cut down where they stood before they got their rifles to bear. Another was beheaded as he got ready to aim.

Another aimed at him from the sanger; he was about to get shot. But the man was hit. Someone was standing on top of something behind the gate with a rifle in hand, someone with a ponytail. A woman. It was Alora. Mark looked on in horror as he saw her exposed. He whipped his own rifle round and started shooting at the men in the sanger. Alora was taking shots at anyone who popped their heads up. The gate began to open.

Garrad had got to the gate bolts; he'd got the gate open a crack. He backed off. A vehicle advanced — a Bushmaster came through and whacked them open, thrusting corpses out of the way as the gates swept apart.

Aran ran to face the vehicle. Mark jumped to his feet, Joe rushed to his side. Joe fired, but his shots couldn't find their mark. Aran shot his magic at Alora, who was still propped inside the top hatch. Mark hurled everything he had left at the blast, deflecting its power. Joe took another shot. This time it hit, but only just. A glancing blow across the shoulder blades. Aran staggered, drained and injured. He wobbled across the base. Joe shot again. Aran was hit, this time in the leg. He fell. Joe was about to give chase, Mark stopped him, grabbed him and threw him to the ground. A band of Aran's men regrouped at the far side of the base and were about to open fire.

Mark and Joe took cover and began to return the shots. The Bushmaster kept coming; another followed it in. Its rear doors opened, and soldiers of the FFA flooded out. More came running through the gates on foot.

Another foe down, a second for Garrad to catch his breath. The soldiers in front of him were running. They were under fire. He spun. They were being shot at from the tower. Princess Alora had somehow got into the sangar and was using their own machine guns against them.

Eliza had bashed the FOB gates open with her vehicle. Another from the FFA trailed behind. The FFA had joined them! Relief flooded Garrad. Courage followed, more of it.

He scanned the scene. None of the enemies were in sight. He set off at a run towards where he'd last seen them. Gunshots, but this time in front. He sped towards the sound, wound round a tent, and his targets came into view.

To this side, towards the rock, were Lieutenant Joe's men. They'd come from nowhere, but they were advancing, shooting and running and shooting some more. Aran's men were so transfixed by this latest threat that they didn't see Garrad coming from behind them like a wind of fury. He slashed at one, two, a third, before a fourth even realised he was there.

A fifth had seen him, he turned and aimed at Garrad. Garrad raised his sword, a flash of panic gripped him as he realised he was powerless to defend himself. But the man suddenly dropped like a stone. A shot had been fired from behind where Garrad stood, he spun. Uniformed men were approaching, shooting at whoever was left. Aran's last few remaining cronies were outnumbered and trapped. No time to run, no time to surrender, seconds to live.

Garrad let the soldiers of the FFA run past him. He listened to the last few shots and the last few screams. He took a moment to breathe, his back against a wall of Hesco. He wiped his bloody sword on the shirt of a corpse. As the air filled his lungs, the metallic fumes of spilt death seemed to cling to his throat. Blood. It was everywhere. It pooled under the corpses; it was splattered on his skin. It was smeared on the ground and dripped off his fingers. He lifted his hand. Blood trickled down it. He tracked the stream up his arm, saw the source. A gash on his tricep. A bullet must have nicked him; he'd not even noticed. He couldn't help but grin as the wound started to throb. A scratch. A scar in time, a memento of his time in this fucked-up world.

It was quiet, then the men and women started to yell in a language he didn't understand. Orders were being given. Soldiers rushed about the place. The base was being secured. A couple of shots were fired – a dying man being put out of his misery, he assumed. He sheathed his blade.

A passing female corporal said something to him in the language of Earth and patted him on the back. He smiled in response and went to find the princesses.

They weren't where he'd left them. Princess Alora's sanger was unmanned, and Princess Eliza's vehicle was empty. He searched for them. Dread gripped him, and he started to jog, this way and that, zigzagging more and more wildly, when at last he spotted them. Difficult to see in their uniforms, hard to make out in the group of soldiers who swarmed around someone who was lying bloodied on the floor, but it was them.

He edged forwards as Princess Alora sank to her knees, appearing to be trying to help the person on the ground. Princess Eliza turned away, sobbing. He rushed to her; he held her.

'What is it, Your Highness?'

'It's Father! I think he's dead!'

34. Afterwards

Tom opened his eyes; a green, canvas ceiling was overhead. He blinked as his fuzzy mind began to comprehend... He was in a tent. He tried to clear his head, trying to work out where this tent was and why he was in one. A young woman's smiling face appeared above him, ponytail dangling over one shoulder, sparkling blue eyes piercing his own.

'Eliza!'

'Father!' She leaned over and hugged him.

'Ow.'

'Oh, sorry.' She released him suddenly. 'How are you feeling? Would you like a drink?' She grabbed a water bottle from a table by the bed and offered it to him.

He nodded and tried to rise, his face betraying the pain as he moved.

'I really don't think you should be getting up,' Eliza said, as she gently rested a hand on his shoulder.

'I'm fine,' Tom insisted, trying to persuade his face to lie as well as his voice. He shuffled up onto his bottom and took the bottle. 'Thanks.' He downed the contents. 'What happened? Where am I?'

'Oh, we won. Everyone got killed. Aran's men, I mean. Killed or captured.' She spoke in such a matter-of-fact tone he wasn't sure if it was actually his daughter speaking. 'We're in his base. The FFA plan to make it their own.' She looked at him with concern as he lifted his shirt and inspected his bandages, grimacing as he did. He let it fall and started to twist his legs onto the floor. 'Father!' she yelled. 'You can't get up! You lost a lot of blood. Alora said you should rest for a couple of days.'

'Did they do a blood transfusion?'

'A what?'

'Did you see them rig up a pouch of dark red liquid and attach it to me with a tube?' he clarified.

'I, um, I think so.'

'How long ago?'

'Yesterday, not long after you were injured.'

Tom peeled back a bandage and inspected a wound. 'They've used recovery enhancer, too.'

'What's that?'

'Something pretty awesome I learned had been invented since I left Earth – it makes you heal up a lot quicker. Not as quickly as you would with magic, mind, but certainly quicker than you would on your own and with a hell of a lot less scarring.'

'Oh.'

'I reckon,' he battled to hide the pain from his face as he put weight on his legs, 'I should be OK to walk.'

Eliza took his arm; he let her wrap it over her shoulder as he began to rise. He turned to look at her. She regarded him with his own blue eyes, but the delicate features of her mother. A smile engulfed his cheeks. He didn't need to fight to hide the pain anymore. The sight of her face was enough to bury any discomfort, any agony, any memory of the struggles of the last few weeks.

'If you insist on getting up, let me help you,' she protested as he tried to pull away and take his first few steps on his own.

He immediately abandoned any thoughts of arguing. He paused for a moment as his creaking wounds pulsed with pain. He took a few deep breaths. 'Is everyone else OK? Where's Mark?'

'Mark and the others are probably in the HQ. But I don't think you should be walking.'

Tom's smile re-emerged. 'Trust me, I'm OK. I'm mostly knackered from too much magic. My wounds might look dramatic, but I don't think they're very deep.' His face was dotted with plasters; the rest of him was bandaged like a mummy. Blobs of red seeped over his front, making him look most ridiculous. Eliza laughed; it couldn't be that bad, he presumed.

He let Eliza lead him to where she thought Mark might be, across a patch of bare ground marked with bloodstains, around a burnt-out Jeep, and into a hardened shelter. As his eyes adjusted to the dim light in the gloomy building, he clocked Mark, Garrad, and Lieutenant Joe sitting round, looking like they were enjoying a natter. A glance at the rest of the room showed him the smashed IT equipment in the corner, a broken table leaning against the wall, and a few crates full of kit waiting to be set up. It was a HQ in name only at present, but it provided a nice quiet spot for the three of them to sit in the shade on folding chairs, having a chat.

'Ah, he lives!' Mark mocked as Tom hobbled in. 'Nice that you could join us. Did you enjoy your rest?'

Garrad stood to offer him a seat. Tom plonked his arse down without argument.

'Ha, ha, arsehole,' he said. 'Go on, fill me in. What did I miss?'

'Not much. Jut me and Joe single-handedly suppressing the enemy in the FOB, before Lieutenant Nutjob here launched himself over the gate and kicked the shit out of everyone.' Mark indicated towards Garrad.

'Huh?' Tom squinted at the young man, who was turning a deep shade of crimson.

'I gave him a field commission. Decided he deserved one, not just because he did a ridiculous act of heroism, but because it turns out the rest of the FFA were about to leave us to rot before he and our girls nicked a Bushmaster and drove hell for leather towards the gate. Without this lunatic, we'd be dead, and this base would still be in Aran's hands.'

Garrad was trying to sink into the corner to hide his blushes.

Tom couldn't help his mouth creeping into a big grin. He shook his head in disbelief. But he'd known the man's father; lunacy for the sake of honour was in his genes. 'Good job, lad,' he said, knowing it would be enough. The kid looked embarrassed enough as it was. 'Changed your name too, have you?'

'Told him he had to; he was adamant he wouldn't at first. But he seems to be coming round to the idea,' Mark added.

Tom wasn't personally fussed either way. But the lad had to show his noble blood if he had any chance of being accepted by the rest of the army in his new rank, that chat could come later.

'Right.' Tom forced himself to his feet, ignoring his oozing wounds, and held out his hand to Garrad to offer a shake. 'I know I'm not the queen, but will you accept the prince as a second best to commend your commission?'

Garrad stepped forwards and took it with a firm grip. 'I'd be honoured, Lord Prince.'

'What have you been talking about?' Joe asked from across the room. They'd been speaking in Geminian.

'I got an update on a few things and said thanks for helping us out, that's all you need to know.' Tom looked from Joe to Mark and back. 'You two getting along? You said you held the FOB together?'

'He grew on me, once it turned out he was actually not that shit,' Mark said.

'He has such a way with words.' Joe sniggered.

'The lad sent his guys back through the tunnel and stayed behind with my sorry arse, pretty much a death sentence after he told HQ his men and women were out. That's when the FFA decided to bug out. We'd made more progress in here than they thought, and with you keeping Aran busy, it provided a window so Garrad could do his hero impression.'

'Here, I have something for you,' Joe said. He fished something out of his pocket and offered it to Tom.

'My Leatherman!' Tom said, with undisguised delight at seeing his old combi tool again. He took it gratefully and started doing a check to make sure the blades and tools were still working.

'A private passed it to me earlier today, said it was yours and asked me to give it back.'

'Thanks, mate.' He grinned at Joe. 'He's starting to grow on me too,' he said to Mark as he safely tucked his tool in his pocket.

'You and the bloody Leatherman.' Mark shook his head despairingly.

'Me and that tool have been through a lot together.' Tom was trying his best to sound serious. Tom looked around the room. 'Where's Alora?'

'She's playing nurse. Can't help herself, even when she doesn't have magic to help. It was her who bandaged you up. She said you're peppered in flesh wounds. Not much to worry about though, just a few more scars for your collection.'

'Okay, Alora's playing nurse, everyone else is here... Now what?'

'We're good to go. We were waiting for you to wake up.'

'Right, and Aran? Is he dead?'

'Um, inconclusive.'

'He's either dead, or he isn't.'

'Let's go with isn't. We don't have a body. We checked everyone in the base. He wasn't with them. Probably got out.'

'Or went back to Gemini!' Tom said, horrified.

329

'We don't think so,' Mark said.

'How the hell would you know?'

'Because Joe's men didn't all go all the way through the tunnel when he told them to. A few stayed inside, a little way up, just in case. Turns out they were right to do so. When things kicked off again, they came back out and stopped Aran's men escaping while a couple kept guarding the tunnel.'

'Oh, alright. He's probably still here, cloaked. Either that or he managed an illusion and got taken out with the corpses. I hope you shot them in the head before you buried them.'

'We weren't exactly expecting a rise of the undead here.'

'Right, I guess not.' Tom sighed. 'Not much for it. We'll find the colonel, tip our hats, and go home.'

'Yep, home to be castrated. I'm looking forward to it.'

Tom shook his head. His growing grin burst into a laugh. 'Kia will be happy just to have you both back safe and well.'

Mark raised an eyebrow. 'You have met my wife, right?'

***

Location: Varden, Gemini (Planet B69245)

Garrad was in Varden alone. Prince Tom, Lord Mark, and their daughters had headed back through a portal to Vorn without him. He couldn't get through the portal himself; he didn't have any magic. Only those who had magic could get through. He still didn't quite understand how Aran had brought him through, when he'd drawn him and the princesses to this place, all those weeks ago when this crazy adventure had begun.

Prince Tom had told him to wait here. He'd said Princess Kia had been investigating how to get him through while they'd been away. He was sitting on his own in a humid forest, praying someone would come to get him before he was eaten by wild animals.

He was sitting on the ground, back against a tree, trying not to fall asleep. He was knackered. Yesterday was manic and he'd barely slept last night. It took forever for the excitement of the day to eventually leave him. Now the hot, sticky air smothered him like a blanket. The babbling stream was like a lullaby; his eyes drooped.

Something crackled. His head shot up. A swirling ring of flickering light appeared nearby, and he scrambled to his feet. The centre of the ring cleared. He could see the walls of a room in a building. Princess Kia emerged. She elegantly vaulted onto the ground and smiled at him warmly.

'Good news, Lieutenant. I can get you back through the portal.'

He sighed a deep sigh. 'Thank you, Your Highness.' The prospect of weeks or even months in this place while a boat got here, then weeks more at sea as he travelled home, did not exactly seem like an attractive prospect.

He walked over to her, his face questioning.

'Take my hand. I have to do magic. You might feel a tingling sensation but otherwise, step through as I do.'

He nodded and did as instructed. As he approached the swirl, he couldn't help but close his eyes, and he blindly lifted a foot. A chill flooded through his body. He lowered his boot on the other side. It hit something hard. He opened his eyes and found himself in the grand surroundings of the palace.

Densely woven fabrics were hanging at the windows. Intricately carved wood panelling, velvet cushions on the soft furnishings. The prince, lord commander and the two princesses were sitting on sofas around a coffee table, teacups in hand, heads twisting to look at him, every one of them smiling.

He froze. His reality shifted again. *Shit.* The setting changed everything. Tom and Mark had gone. The prince of Vorn and the lord commander were back. The princesses had stopped being soldiers, even though they were still in uniform. Here, they were royalty again, and he was the soldier who'd been tasked to keep them out of mischief. No, he was a lieutenant now; he was an officer. But he was still a hell of a lot of ranks below every one of those who looked at him.

'Take a seat, lad, you're making the place look untidy,' Mark chided.

Garrad jolted, and he obeyed. Orders felt good; he was used to orders. He found a space on a couch and sat down, rigidly, hands gripping his knees.

Princess Kia walked round to his side. She stood with her arms folded, staring at them all sternly. None of them had changed their clothes yet. All of them were still in their dusty attire from Earth. They'd changed into clean kit since the battle, but being in Gemini in the uniform of the Australian Army, they looked ridiculous. Ridiculous and scruffy. They'd left Garrad in Varden a couple of hours back, by his reckoning. He assumed the pleasantries with Princess Kia had already been exchanged; perhaps now it was time for a different kind of chat.

***

Everyone was back safe, back in her home, back where she wanted them. Now the reality of what had been returned to her was starting to sink in. Kia studied them in turn; her gaze settled on her daughter, Alora, dressed like a man. She'd tried hard to raise her to be ladylike and graceful. Taught her what was appropriate and what wasn't. As she stared at the filthy urchin who had once been her daughter, her mouth opened and closed as she tried desperately to work out what to say.

As she stood in silence, her audience waiting nervously for her to speak, a memory flashed into her mind. She remembered the time long ago when she'd freed Tom from Aran's clutches. She remembered how her dress was trashed as she tried to climb up a gulley as they fled, and how Tom had lent her a long shirt to wear instead of her dress. She recalled how they'd hidden for days in a cave while they tried to work out how to portal, and she had nothing else to wear. She must have looked far worse than her daughter when she finally got back to civilisation. It was a long time ago. She'd almost forgotten that. Twenty years of living in high luxury since had changed her, but not completely.

She smiled at the memory. Her anger evaporated. She rushed to where her husband and daughter were sitting side by side and embraced them both in a hug, squeezing them and weeping, like she had when they'd first appeared a couple of hours back. The medley of emotions since then had upended her, but she didn't care about anything except that they were all back safely.

***

Tom shook his head and smiled. 'It took six weeks away, but they've finally broken her,' he whispered to his daughter. 'Let's hope your mother's cracked too.'

As if on cue, the door was flung open, and Emma came rushing in. Eliza jumped to her feet. Tom's body groaned as he rose to his; he'd not yet bothered to ask Kia to heal him.

The queen was oblivious to his injuries. She rushed over to her husband and daughter and engulfed them both in an embrace, kissing them in turn. 'I'm sorry I couldn't be here at once. I was in council, and Kia's maid struggled to get the word to me.'

'It's fine. Don't worry,' Tom replied, kissing his wife on the lips.

***

Eliza managed to escape; her parents' display of affection was starting to make her feel ill. She edged away to another part of the room and noticed Garrad sitting rigid and alone, still looking incredibly uncomfortable. A smile crept up her cheeks, and her head cocked. He was four years her senior, but his boyish charm had never been so blatant. His nervousness made him vulnerable, and she felt herself drawn towards him.

As she padded over to him, she found herself looking at him in a way she hadn't before. She'd never noticed his chiselled jawline or his powerful shoulders. Before, he was a clean-shaven and well-built sergeant, but now... The image of him leaping over the gate, sword in hand, fearlessly diving into the unknown to save her father, flashed through her mind. She shook her head to clear the vision. His dark-brown puppy-dog eyes were warm and yet terrified.

She took a seat by his side, close enough for her thigh to touch his. He noticed her at last. He flinched at her touch, pulled away. She shuffled closer. He twisted, his mouth slightly open.

'Sure you don't want to be our guardian anymore?' she said softly, in a tone she barely recognised. Where had that come from? She pouted and her eyelashes fluttered. She had no idea what she was doing but whatever it was, it was making her heart pound.

'I... I can give it some thought,' he stuttered. His mouth closed at last; his Adam's apple bobbed as he swallowed. 'I mean, er, if Lord Harrison doesn't have any other plans for me.'

'Oh, um, please do... give it some thought.' She turned and looked at the floor for a moment. She turned back, placed a trembling hand gently on his thigh. He flinched again, and she pressed softly with her fingertips. 'I didn't say thank you, for coming up with that plan, for getting into the base and saving my father.'

'There's no need. I was doing my...'

Her pulse pounded in her ears. 'Thank you,' she whispered.

Carnal instinct took control of her senses. His thigh was tense under her hand, his torso rigid as she leant forwards, and her lips found his. The gentle touch of his warm flesh on hers sent a tingle through her body like nothing she'd ever known, but it didn't last long. She was in a room filled with her family, after all. A sturdy hand landed on her shoulder.

***

'That's enough of that, Eliza,' Tom said firmly to his daughter.

'What?' she replied innocently. She trembled under his touch.

Emma was biting her lip, apparently battling a smirk as she walked over to them.

'Eliza.' She held out her hand for her daughter. 'What on earth are you doing in men's army clothing?'

Tom eyeballed Garrad, who still hadn't moved an inch. He gripped both his thighs with his hands and stared straight ahead, looking even more terrified than when he'd first come through the portal.

'Erm, it's a long story,' Eliza said.

Tom shook his head and sighed as he disregarded the young lieutenant's discomfort and returned his attention to his family.

'I've cancelled my engagements for this afternoon. We have time,' his wife replied.

'Mother?'

'Yes, Eliza?'

'Do you think you could change the law here so women can join the army?'

Tom couldn't help but chuckle to himself.

35. That Will Have To Do

The following evening, healed by Kia with just a few more scars for his collection, and refreshed after a good night's sleep, Tom set out alone into the mountains. He had a mission to do, one he had to complete alone. He arrived near the secluded spot by a pond he'd had in mind, in a dip, out of sight.

He dismounted and tied his horse a goodly way from the pond, in a peaceful spot with a good crop of grass. He strolled down to the pond and watched as it glistened in the moonlight, glass-smooth top rippling as a fish broke the surface.

'Sorry, fish,' he muttered, as he started to use his power. He placed a hand in the water and heated it. It was soon too hot to touch. Dead fish rose to the surface. He hovered his hand above the water and kept heating it until it boiled. The pond life simmered to the surface like veg in a giant pan of soup. Steam gushed away from the surface. Tom used his power to collect it, to stop it rising. He gathered it in the bowl-like valley and let it surround him.

As a vector of magic, water vapour was the perfect device to carry out his task. Water held magic. He'd be able to sense every droplet, feel every part of the cloud of his making, and spot any gaps where the magic wasn't present. He closed his eyes and concentrated. He searched through the cloud for the gap he sought. He couldn't find it. He kept the pond boiling and filled more of the dip in the landscape with the steam.

The cloud top rose. He searched through the vapour, checking every part of the cloud, slowly, methodically, and at last he spotted it. The disc-shaped hole he was looking for. He waited until the cloud was higher. He wanted to be sure the disc was surrounded, that his magical net could be closed for certain. And when he was, he sprung the trap.

With a flash, he sent a blast of energy through the mist. The vector of water made it spread so quickly the disc had no chance of escaping. He caught it and held it. It pulled against him, but his magic was too strong. He drew it towards him, hauling it in with his power until he was able to take it in his hands.

He could feel something with his fingers, and see the gap in the magical mist, but he couldn't see the invisible object creating the gap.

He let the mist clear, The moonlight shone down, yet his eyes still saw nothing between his hands.

'Bring me in,' he said to the invisible object. 'I need to talk to you.'

Nothing happened.

'I know you are watching. I have your drone. We have to talk. You can't let this new wormhole remain; we need to get rid of it!'

The invisible object remained still and unseen in his hands.

'Last chance. Bring me in or I'll go back through the wormhole and start telling everyone on Earth about you and your spying missions. I'll tell them about the wormhole. I'll take them this drone that I have in my hands. I'll show them the wormhole. I'll let them enjoy interstellar travel from Earth to Gemini. I'll let them——'

Tom's hands began to fade.

***

He awoke with a jolt, dazzled by the brightness of the ship; he sat up on the inspection table.

'Greetings, Thomas,' an alien said, smiling with her tiny mouth. Her hands were together, and she was bowing her head as she spoke. 'It is good to see you again.'

He tried to clear the mental fuzz of transportation from his mind, as he stared at the blurry form of what he would have described as a little grey man in front of him. Then he recalled that they weren't men at all, they were hermaphrodites if he remembered correctly. His lips stretched into a crooked smile.

'Hi,' he began as he screwed up his eyes in an attempt to clear his vision. 'Which one are you? Zark or Darkle?'

The alien looked hurt.

'I'm sorry, you look similar.'

'It is no matter,' Zark said with a sigh. 'It has been a long time, by human reckoning. I am Zark.'

'It's good to see you again, too, Zark.'

Shhwup. The sound of the door into the control room zipping upwards caught Tom's attention.

'Greetings, Thomas.' Another alien entered the room.

'Darkle?' Tom hoped he'd guessed correctly.

'Yes, it is I, the captain of this ship. Are you well?'

'Yeah, I'm good, thanks.' He jumped off the inspection table and offered his hand for the Zargon to shake. Zark regarded the hand with confusion. Darkle stepped forward and shook it.

'It's an Earth custom,' she said to her first mate.

'Ah!' Zark copied her captain and shook Tom's hand.

'Would you like to take a seat?' Darkle gestured towards the three chairs near the control panel.

Tom nodded and made himself comfortable; the Zargons took a seat themselves.

'Ship, carrowcel for three,' Darkle ordered.

Tom couldn't help but be in awe as a small door in the wall opened and a little droid floated out. A glass dome sat on a circular panel on its top, with three cups of carrowcel. The dome slid back, and the droid went to each in turn and offered them a cup. Tom took his and sipped cautiously. He swished the drink in his mouth, nodded in satisfaction, and took a longer drink.

'You wanted to speak to us?' Darkle said, cutting to the chase about the reason for their gathering.

Tom placed his cup in the holder built into the arm of his chair. 'Yes.'

'How can we help?'

'There's another wormhole linking Earth to Gemini.'

'We are aware of this.'

'How long have you known?'

'It became apparent when specimen... sorry, Aran,' Darkle corrected herself, 'appeared back on Gemini.'

'He's been there?'

'He has. He was not there for long.'

'Is he there now?'

'No.'

'Is he alive?'

'We would have to consult our colleagues who look after Earth for that information.'

'Oh.' Tom took another sip of his drink. 'Can you ask them, please?'

'I'm afraid I'm unwilling to do that. You see, as I explained the first time we met, Zargons have a policy of no interference. Any information I give you is a form of interference, and it would not do to have other ships being made aware that we are having this conversation.'

'Are we supposed to be having this conversation?' Tom cocked his head to one side.

'No. It is unauthorised. We are taking considerable risks with our own careers to speak to you.'

'Why did you bring me up?'

'We thought it in the best interests of the planet we seek to preserve, and of Earth.'

'I see.'

'You made a number of threats when you were on the surface and you made it clear you wanted to get rid of the wormhole,' Darkle said. 'I'd firstly like to point out that we did not believe your threats. We have profiled your personality and we think it improbable that you would risk either Earth or Gemini in the manner you suggested. And secondly, I'm sorry to inform you we are unable to destroy the wormhole.'

'Hang on, one thing at a time here. You said you didn't believe my threats? Why did you bring me in then?'

'Abduction is a high-risk affair,' Darkle replied. 'The biggest risk is the abduction being noticed by the specimen, or specimens nearby. It is imperative that our presence is not revealed. In your case, however, you were already aware of our presence, so the first point is moot. And in the case of the second, you appear to have deliberately chosen a secluded location to try to get in touch. So the second point is moot too.

'With the normal risks mitigated in this case, we considered it of little consequence if we did abduct you. We were concerned for your subsequent actions should we continue to avoid contact. Not necessarily in terms of the threats you mentioned, but in terms of the unknown consequences. Humans can be very unpredictable.'

'I see,' Tom said, with a slight shake of his head.

'Furthermore,' Darkle continued, 'as the preservation of Gemini is our primary concern, we thought it might be useful to give you some information to help the continuing security of the planet.'

'Hang on a minute. Are you about to interfere?' Tom raised one of his eyebrows.

Darkle blinked, a significant affair owing to the size of the alien's large black eyes and heavy-set eyelids. 'Yes.'

'Will this not get you into trouble?'

'If we are discovered, yes.'

'Right...' Tom scratched his head. 'You said you couldn't destroy the wormhole. You did destroy the one Queen Lila came through, the one Mark and I used in the past. Mark saw you do it. Is that not interfering? The thing you are not supposed to do?'

Darkle's face was still unreadable. 'Our ability to destroy wormholes was removed as a result of that incident.'

'You weren't supposed to do that, were you?' A grin escaped onto Tom's face as he regarded the sheepish Zargons.

'Zark did it!' Darkle spluttered.

Zark's face broke into a smile.

'Did you get into trouble?' he said, still grinning.

Darkle turned to her first mate and let her answer.

'Um, we were suspended for a while,' said Zark. 'After the investigation, it was concluded that on balance, the wormhole's destruction was in the best interests of the connected planets, and although our action was unauthorised, if the IDI had been consulted, they would have agreed to its destruction.'

'What's the IDI?' Tom queried.

'It is the Intergalactic Discovery Institute. It's who we work for' Zark replied.

'Oh, so would they not authorise the destruction of this wormhole?'

'No,' Darkle answered.

'Why not?'

'The IDI no longer has the autonomy it once did, they would be unable to authorise the wormhole's destruction without government authority.'

'Oh. Would they not be able to ask for permission?'

'I suspect the IDI would be reluctant to do this,' Darkle replied. 'I'm not sure the chair would want to bring the presence of another wormhole to the government's attention, especially when I think it unlikely that they would authorise its destruction, anyway.'

'Why not?'

'There are some in power who are very keen to interfere with our planets, especially ones of significant interest, like Gemini. To put it bluntly, they want catastrophe, they want war, they want cultural destruction. They want any excuse possible to stick their oar in and start meddling. It will be done in the name of *preservation* at first. They will say it's in the best interest of the planet. Over time, their true intent will become clear as preservation becomes experimentation. There are some who would fight against any proposal to destroy something that might help them achieve this aim.'

Tom's jaw dropped. 'They want to experiment on us?'

'Some Zargons do, yes. We are trying to avoid such an eventuality.'

'Shit.' Tom inhaled deeply.

'That is why we brought you in, or one of the reasons. There is a new threat to Gemini, one which we suspect may be as a result of covert interference from government agents. We thought it would be sensible to warn you.'

Tom felt his eyes widen. 'What is it?'

'More Earthlings have come to Gemini – three of them. They were met by an elven sorcerer who, mysteriously, seemed to expect them, and he managed to persuade them to travel with him to sector five.'

'Where the hell is that?'

'Sorry, I should have said - South Allantra.'

'And which elf? How did they know to go to Varden? Most people don't even know the place exists!'

'The elf in question is a renegade from the elven realm of Ballachdor,' Darkle confirmed. 'Your log indicates you have not had previous contact with him. We are uncertain what made the elf go to Varden, we are still investigating that one.'

'I have a log?'

'All our Specimens of Interest have logs.'

'I'm nothing but a lab rat to you, am I?' Somehow, Tom found himself laughing as he enjoyed the confused glances between the two Zargons. 'Never mind,' he said at last. 'Anyway, there are three Earthlings on Gemini – can you tell me who they are?'

Darkle nodded and offered a reply: 'They were employees of Aran.'

'Fuck!' Tom said with a sigh. 'Three drug-toting nutters are on Gemini with some renegade elf. That's gonna turn out well.' He forced a smile. The Zargons stared at him, apparently confused. 'It's sarcasm,' Tom advised. 'There are three humans with the potential to be mega sorcerers like me. Evil bastards too, if they worked for Aran. But unless their magic is triggered, they are no threat, right?'

'Their magic has already been triggered,' Darkle informed him gravely.

'Fuck!' Tom rubbed his face with his hands. 'How did that happen?'

'Aran did it a number of years back. He used his magic on them on Earth. It is unclear if they are aware that their magical potential has been unleashed.'

Tom dropped his hands into his lap. 'And you expect me to fix this?'

'We hope you will try. The results otherwise could be catastrophic, especially if the wormhole remains accessible. We can't destroy it; however, we can tell you of a way to make entry very difficult,' Darkle replied.

'It's already being plugged with concrete and guarded from the other side. That's what the FFA said they'd do,' Tom advised. 'But of course a man-made plug can always be dug out, that's why I wanted the wormhole destroyed.'

'We are aware of the concrete plug and have been notified that the commencement of construction appears imminent. However, even once the plug has been built, it will still be possible for a little magic to seep through, and as you point out, concrete can be dug out.'

'So what do you suggest? Should I use magic to blow up the rock on this side, too?' Tom asked.

'I'm afraid that you would be unable to explode the rock which hides the wormhole on Gemini, and even if you could, simply blasting

341

the rock would not prevent the flow of magic to Earth, there would be gaps in the rubble and magic can flow easily through air gaps,' Darkle said.

'What's so special about the rock that means I can't blast it?' Tom asked.

'We have been unable to detect the presence of the wormholes on Earth and Gemini because they have been set into geological features riddled with a mineral known as anthrophcite. It is not yet known to humans on Earth or Gemini, but it is there, in amongst the rock particles. Anthrophcite is an interesting mineral as it not only cloaks wormholes, it also creates a barrier for magic and is very difficult to shatter with magical power alone. If you tried to blast the rock in Varden with your power, you would make very little headway. You will need to try something else.'

'Right, so what can I do?'

Zark interjected. 'You must melt it. Once anthrophcite is melted and set, it condenses and becomes very hard to break apart without further heat. Solid anthrophcite is also impenetrable to magic, so it will stop the flow of magic to Earth. You must create enough heat to reduce the rock to liquid. Allow it to melt, sink then solidify so it plugs the tunnel. It will prove a very difficult barrier indeed to break through. Should the escaped humans try to return, they would be unlikely to break through if they did not work out that they needed to melt it. Only mechanical tools would do the job otherwise, and with the equipment available on Gemini, that would take years, I imagine.'

'Right, thanks, that's good to know.' He slid his hands onto his thighs and tapped them gently, perplexed by the Zargon's willingness to give him such detail.

'I suggest you act on this information quickly, in case any more humans try to come through, or our latest visitors try to return to their home planet. It would be unwise to let these specimens return, their knowledge of Gemini poses a significant risk, should they choose to share it with others on Earth,' said Zark.

'Noted. I'll get on it,' Tom replied.

'One more thing, Thomas, before you go,' Darkle added.

'What?'

'Whatever you do, try to make it look like you found out any information we have given you yourself. You are not the only ones being watched.'

Tom nodded slowly. 'I get it. I'll figure it out.'

'Great. We must hurry and get you back to the surface. Our colleague can only be kept asleep for so long against her will before she becomes suspicious.'

'You have another crew member?'

'Yes. More government interference, I'm afraid. If you'd be so kind as to return to the inspection table.'

***

Zark and Darkle were sitting in their chairs by the control panel, watching the floating screens in front of them. Tom was lying on the ground near the evaporated pond and was starting to stir. Dawn was breaking and the daylight seemed to disrupt his sleep.

'That's him up and about,' Darkle said. 'Good. I'll head off. I don't want to be here when Jink comes on shift, she'll get suspicious.'

'He's waving, right at our drone... How does he know where it is?' Zark wondered.

Darkle smiled. 'We still have a lot to learn about magic.'

*Read on for a preview of The Queen's Daughter,
book 2 in The Offspring Trilogy*

THE QUEEN'S DAUGHTER

The Offspring Trilogy
Book 2

1. Lost Threat Found

Tom's eyes fluttered open, through the gloom a collection of flickering beams of light danced on the wall. The familiar crackling of magic spluttered into his ear and his sleepy brain fog began to clear. He lurched from his side to his back and stared up at the swirling source of the flicker; a whirling ring of radiance spun above his bed. Through the dark of the night and glare of the hovering halo, the blurry face of an elf stared down at him. He rose onto his elbows and squinted, the image clearing just enough for recognition to seep into his eyes. 'Eskalith?' he whispered.

The grey-haired elf nodded patiently. 'Yes, Thomas, can we talk?' His reply was equally muted.

A yawn gripped Tom's mouth. 'Sure.' He shook his head trying to clear the haze from his mind, 'two mins.' He glanced to his left, his wife was still contentedly snoozing, the gentle whistle of her breathing glided through the night air. She looked so peaceful when she slept, the rippling light hid the years, she looked as young and beautiful as she had the day Tom met her, a day so long back it seemed like a lifetime ago.

He stroked her dark chestnut silky hair, its growing collection of greys muted by the gloom. He kissed her softly on the cheek before raising his chest, swinging his stiff legs carefully out of the bed, and searching with his toes for his soft sheepskin slippers.

He groaned onto his feet, his creaking body reminding him of his encroaching years as he staggered towards where his nightgown hung on a hook on the wall. Shivering as he wrapped himself in the woollen robe, he tied the cord snugly then crept out of the bedchamber and into the private sitting room next door.

The swirling magical circle followed him as he went, Tom knew it would, Eskalith was well practiced at portal control. He could hear the reassuring crackle just over his shoulder as he closed his bedchamber door as quietly as he could. With a wave of his hand he lit every oil lamp with magic, flooding the room with light. He collapsed on the sofa and squinted towards the clock on the wall. 'It's the middle of the bloody night, Eskalith!' he exclaimed, at last allowing his voice to carry.

The portal floated along until it hovered just in front of where Tom sat. The ever-solemn face of the old sorcerer now looking him straight in the eye, 'not quite, its early morning by my clock.'

'You know you're in a different time zone to me, right?' Tom sighed. He knew his chastisement would have no effect on his old teacher.

'I am aware that for me the morning comes sooner than for you,' he replied with infuriating patience.

'But it's still dark where you are!'

'It is winter, and I have my drapes closed.'

Tom rolled his eyes. 'To what do I owe the pleasure, Eskalith?' Despite the early hour, it was still good to see his old friend.

'I need to talk to you.'

'Well that's bloody obvious!'

'Alone.'

'Well you have me alone, is that why you called at such a ridiculous hour?'

'It is indeed. You spend much of your day in the company of others.'

'How do you know? Do you spy on me Eskalith?' An eyebrow flicked with grey climbed towards his receding hairline.

'I observe, on occasion, just to see how you are,' Eskalith replied dryly. His face unreadable, it was always so hard to work out what the bloody elf was thinking.

Tom shook his head in despair, but somehow the corner of his mouth twitched up into a half-smile. 'Not fair, Eskalith, I can't get to you inside your little Ballachdor bubble. One way spying? It's just not cricket.' Tom felt the other corner of his mouth rise, his upper lip

2

followed to reveal a toothy grin as he watched a twinge of perplexity seep onto the elf's face. 'It's an Earth term,' he confessed at last.

The baffled expression vanished. Back to plain unreadability. 'I see.' The old elf's hand began to stroke his beard as he regarded Tom, Tom could have sworn he spotted a hint of disapproval flash across the old sorcerer's deep green eyes, but he was too tired and groggy to care.

'Come on then Eskalith, tell me what you need to say then let me go back to sleep, please?' Tom pleaded.

Eskalith nodded once.

'We have heard reports of a trio of human sorcerers in the free city of Anvol.'

'That's it? You dragged me out of bed for that?' Tom reached into the air to stretch; his back clicked satisfactorily as he elongated his spine.

'They are not ordinary sorcerers; I suspect they are from Earth.'

Tom rubbed his eyes, 'Earth?'

'Yes, your homeland.'

'I know where bloody Earth is,' he snapped, a little more sharply than he intended, 'why do you think they are from Earth?' he continued with a sigh.

'They have incredible power and have begun to use it. Anvol has already fallen to their leader; a woman by the name of Sarah.'

Tom's eyes widened, 'Fuck.' He collapsed forwards, elbows digging into his knees, face buried in his hands.

'The name means something to you?'

Tom rolled his eyes upwards to look at Eskalith though his fingers. 'Uhuh,' he replied simply.

'You knew her from you time on Earth?'

'Yep.'

'That was so long ago, how can you be sure?'

'Ah, not quite as long ago as you think.' He dropped his hands and met Eskalith's gaze as the elf patiently waited for Tom to continue. 'I went back there, the year before last I think it was…' He stared without focus into the corner of the room as he tried to recall when he'd returned from Australia. 'Er, almost two years ago I think.'

'And you didn't think to tell me?' Eskalith's chastising tone caught Tom off guard, he found himself jolt up straight as a sudden feeling of sheepishness washed over him. It was normally only his wife that could

3

have this effect on the Prince of Vorn, he'd almost forgotten how his old teacher could do it just as well.

'Um...I,' his eyebrows furrowed as he regained his composure, 'hang on a minute, how was I supposed to tell you? I can't call you, remember? Not without penetrating Ballachdor's defences and upsetting all your elders at least.'

'We have spoken since you say your returned, have we not?'

Tom scratched his head as he tried to remember the last time Eskalith called. 'No!' He snapped at last.

'Hmm,' the elf leant back in his chair and resumed stroking his beard in thought.

'Oh,' Tom nodded to himself smugly, 'got you there, haven't I?' He said with a smirk.

'It is of no consequence when we last spoke, we must discuss the issue at hand, the issue of the Earthling sorcerers.'

Tom considered pursuing his point but decided to let it drop. With age, a certain degree of pragmatism had evolved from his younger belligerent self. 'Ok, so there's Sarah and two others... do you know their names?'

'I have heard they are referred to as Jon and Stark.'

Tom wracked his brains as he tried to think if those names meant anything, but at last he conceded they didn't. They were certainly Earth like names, Jon definitely; Stark could be a nick name or a surname perhaps. But either way it had an Earth-like ring to it. 'Sounds like they could certainly be Earthlings,' he said with a sigh. 'So what's the problem with them? Why did you feel the need to call at stupid o'clock in the morning to tell me?'

'Our reports tell us the humans have taken control of Anvol and are building their strength, and perhaps more importantly, their wealth. Power alone can achieve much, but without wealth it is difficult to achieve one's ambitions.'

'Ohhh, fuck.' Tom's face collapsed into his hands again as a hint of a memory was reawakened.

'Indeed, the situation does not sound good but at this stage...'

Tom lifted his head and interjected, 'I was warned about them, Eskalith. I know who they are.'

'You do?' The smooth grey eyebrows of the old elf drew together amidst a sea of wrinkled skin.

'Yup, the Zargons told me.'

'The extra-terrestrials who brought you here?'

'The very same.'

'And you did not think to act on this warning?' A hint of a growl was betrayed in the sorcerer's normally controlled words.

'I did!' Tom protested. 'I tried to find them, they told me they were in East Allantra, I went there, I searched. I scanned for magic, but I couldn't find anything. I'd never met Sarah on Earth, I just heard about her, she's a nasty piece of work by all accounts, magic in her hands was never going to work out well, but I couldn't find her. I kept looking, I still search periodically for strong magical signatures, but I've never found anything! I'd pretty much assumed they'd died or maybe not worked out how to use their magic or something. But they haven't gone back; I know that much. I check on the wormhole entrance every day to make sure it's still secure. No signs of tampering there.'

'You said the wormhole had been destroyed, has it reappeared?' Eskalith asked, a baffled look sweeping across his weathered face.

'Um, no. Sorry Eskalith, I guess that's something else I haven't told you. There's another wormhole in Varden. It's how I got back to Earth, and how these three came here, I presume. But we blocked it, its sealed from both sides. And as I said, there's no sign anyone else has come through since I returned a couple years back. If more have come through, they arrived before I sealed the entrance.'

Eskalith simply shook his head as he stared at Tom with a disappointed glower. He leant back, he folded his arms and stayed silent.

Tom was growing impatient. 'Well? Do you not have anything to say?'

Eskalith raised his eyebrows and tilted his head slightly in an almost perfected teacher-like look of condescension. 'You still have much to learn about patience.'

'Good God Eskalith, I'm fifty-four years old, I've probably learned as much patience as I'm going to, and compared to the twenty-nine-year-old sprog you first met, I've probably become so laid back I'm almost horizontal!'

'One should never give up in their pursuit to improve oneself.'

'Whatever,' Tom sighed. 'So, you've told me the three Earthlings are in Anvol and that they are happily building power and wealth and stuff – what's it got to do with me? Or you for that matter?'

'We are concerned because of the vicinity to our border, as I'm sure you are aware, Anvol is the closest free city to Ballachdor. To have such an extraordinary build-up of magic near to us is a threat we cannot ignore. Should they choose to, the three of them would have the strength to penetrate our defences, we would be largely powerless against them in a coordinated attack.

'When Aran attacked, he was just one sorcerer and without your help he would have devastated our land. But if three attacked? There is nothing we could do in defence of that amount of power. We are gravely concerned about the threat these humans may pose should they develop an interest in our land.'

Tom sat back on his sofa and folded his arms, 'I don't get it Eskalith, if there are three powerful sorcerers in East Allantra, why can't I sense them?'

'They are cloaked, they have amberallions, they were given to them by one of my kin.'

'One of your own is helping them?'

'His name is Thorallan, he is a sorcerer who was banished from our lands, he somehow found the Earthlings and it appears he has been training them to use their magic. It was our interest in him that led us to discover this new threat to Gemini.'

Tom sagged further into his sofa, 'And today was going to be such a nice day, just a few duties to sort in the morning, but the light kind, you know? The bits of your job you actually like? Then the afternoon off with Olli... And then you drop this bloody bombshell on me. So much for going back to sleep.' He glanced again at the clock. 'Barely worth it now, anyway.'

'You do not need to let it ruin your day, I tell you this as a warning, that's all. I thought it important that you should be aware of this potential threat. You do not need to do anything.'

'Really? Are you not telling me so I can be on standby in case you guys get attacked again? Or do you want me to go and try and kick their ass or something before they get more power?'

'We expect nothing, but I'm sure you appreciate that a threat to Ballachdor could later become a threat to Vorn, or indeed the rest of Gemini. I felt it important to make you aware.'

Tom puffed out a long breath through his teeth, 'yeah, I get that. 'I suppose it's worth knowing this stuff, so thank you for telling me. I'd rather have known than not,' he conceded resignedly.

A hint of a satisfied smile brushed across Eskalith's face. 'You are welcome. I give you this knowledge in private so you can do with it as you wish. Ballachdor has no expectations of help, but we would always receive it gratefully should it be offered, and we of course remain in debt to you for your assistance last time. Our intelligence indicates that at this stage Sarah is yet to show interest in expanding her reach, but our assessment suggests it is quite possible that this indifference will not last. If she does become ambitious, it is likely she will start with the other free cities, then perhaps look south towards Jendo and Daro, their defences are far inferior to Ballachdor's.

'However, despite there being perhaps no imminent threat to my realm, three sorcerers, each with a power to rival your own, is a grave threat to Gemini, if left to grow unchecked.'

Tom forced an ironic smile and regarded his old friend through the still swirling ring of sparkling magic. 'I'm getting too old for this shit, Eskalith. Why can't we just be left to live in peace?'

'Peace only survives as long as good men prepare to fight evil.'

'And women,' Tom added.

Eskalith grinned, 'Indeed, your wife is testament to that.'

'And daughters and sister-in-law…' Tom grinned back. 'But anyway, your point is valid. Peace is something you have to work to maintain. There's always going to be arseholes in this world who want to screw you over, I guess you just have to make sure they never get the chance.' Tom sighed. 'Thanks for the intelligence, Eskalith, I'll need to chat to Emma and work out what we need to do. I know I can't call you, but how about you call me back in say a week? Let's go with noon next time, if I know to expect you, I'll make sure I'm alone, or maybe with Emma or people I trust when you call. Please don't wake me at sparrow's fart again, I'm getting too old to tolerate broken sleep.'

Another rare smile crept between the elf's beard and moustache, 'I will call you in a week at noon.'

Also by Charlotte Goodwin

The General's Son is the first book in The Offspring Trilogy, which is a standalone trilogy in the Gallantrian Legacy series.

THE OFFSPRING TRILOGY

The General's Son, March 2023

The Queen's Daughter, April 2023

The Prince's Nephew, May 2023

The Homecoming Trilogy is a prequel to the Offspring Trilogy, and will be released in 2023

THE HOMECOMING TRILOGY

The Queen of Vorn

The Prince of Vorn

The King of Vorn

To find out more visit

www.charlottegoodwin.co.uk

Acknowledgements

The original idea for The Gallantrian Legacy series first manifested in my mind over a decade ago. It survived two prior attempts to drag it from my head and onto paper before I finally managed to get going properly in the Autumn of 2021. And once I started, I couldn't stop.

The last 18 months have been a journey (apologies for the cliché). Not just for my characters, but for me too. In that time I've moved from one job, to another, to none – or at least, no full-time employment. I'm still an Army Reservist and will be until they kick me out at age 60 (probably). I've spent my life not really knowing what I wanted to do. But I think I know now, I'm pretty sure I want to be a professional author.

That's why I took the plunge late last year and decided to devote my working day to writing; which brings me to my first acknowledgment. I'd like to thank my husband, Andy Goodwin for his support. For making sure we can still afford a roof over our heads while I embark on my latest career, and of course, for believing in my work as an author.

I'd like to thank my readers. I enlisted a group of victims to read my raw manuscript that was so full of typos and badly-worded sentences that I'm still surprised they stuck with it! But they did, and without fail they loved my story. They also gave me feedback which was invaluable. So many thanks to William Hearnshaw, Stephanie Gee, Jules Ward, Jamie Scott and of course my mum, Sue Metcalf.

Sue gets a special mention because not only has she read everything I have ever written, she's read some books more than once. She also put her English degree to good use by conducting a final proof read of this book.

My last two acknowledgments go to my editor, Rachel Rowlands who took my mangled sentences and made them make sense, and my cover designer, Ryan Schwarz, who has patiently put up with my endless requests for tweaks to create a cover I think is truly special.

Printed in Great Britain
by Amazon

23529013R00209